SPIRIT OF  TIMES

Spirit of *Modern* Times

JAMES PARKE

Illustrations by

MADELYN LEHDE

PALMETTO
PUBLISHING
Charleston, SC
www.PalmettoPublishing.com

Spirit of Modern Times
Copyright © 2024 by James Parke

First Edition

Hardback ISBN: 979-8-8229-3348-4
Paperback ISBN: 979-8-8229-3349-1

Cover design by James Parke: images of people and scenes in Pontiac, Michigan, 1860's era, courtesy of Oakland County Pioneer and Historical Society; also Lee M. Withey, and Parke family archives.

To Lana

PREFACE

IN THE story that follows, the reader will be immersed in an American community that existed 160 years ago, a thriving town poised to grow steadily in an era of new industries, new livelihoods, and new social possibilities. For one full day as an out-of-town visitor, the reader will meet several friends and acquaintances before attending a large, outdoor reception scheduled at one of the local homes. There is much news to learn, and gossip to keep up with, as it turns out that this year promises to bring on the long-awaited, mighty events that are bound to change the character of the town forever.

It is the spring of 1861 and the nation has just begun forging its way into the reality of a War Between the States. A month has passed since the southerners have bombarded Fort Sumter, and now everywhere there are volunteer armies assembling for the campaign to come. People are thrilled and obsessed with the prospects for war news, dramatic reports, and gallant action. A person's future success is at stake here and now; in fact it may be decided this very day.

Meanwhile community life goes on in its customary form with day-to-day work, social engagements, and civic planning. The town continues to expand. It won't be easy to see how this war episode is going to work out for everyone, and nobody knows how long the boys will be away in the army. Such is the topsy-turvy nature of modern times that people have come to accept.

—

This is a work of historical fiction wherein all of the named characters are, that is they were, real people. Their depictions and the words they speak are presumptive, based on genealogical data and chronicles published about their town and the surrounding county, and from newspaper articles written during their era. Personalities, relationships, and opinions have all been contrived from this research and they are offered here, with the best of intentions, to enable the modern reader to peer into a community that vanished long ago.

In writing this story, the conjecture is serious, the narrative at times whimsical, and the research never final. Further biographical details may someday be discovered, but as a friend once wryly noted, historical accuracy is "definitely a moving target." So it is, that in this spirit, in the pages of this book the reader will find sketches of the characters drawn by a modern-day artist. Her sketches are based on original photographic images but have adapted to enliven the faces and recast their ages to conform to the same day in 1861. True images of most of the characters, posing stiffly before 19th century cameras, do exist for those readers who are more keenly interested in historical records. These will be presented at the back of the book.

CONTENTS

CHARACTER GUIDES

Character Guide, page c-1

*Notes: Characters' **ages** are shown as of May 23, 1861, the day of the McConnells' reception.
Names of deceased persons are ghosted; minor characters are shown in parentheses.*

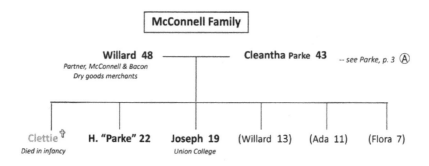

McConnell Family

Willard 48 ———————— **Cleantha** Parke **43**   *-- see Parke, p. 3* Ⓐ
Partner, McConnell & Bacon
Dry goods merchants

Clettie †   **H. "Parke" 22**   **Joseph 19**   (Willard 13)   (Ada 11)   (Flora 7)
Died in infancy   *Union College*

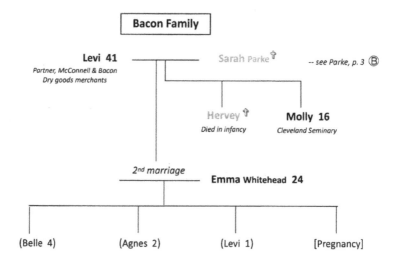

Bacon Family

Levi 41 ———————— Sarah Parke †   *-- see Parke, p. 3* Ⓑ
Partner, McConnell & Bacon
Dry goods merchants

Hervey †   **Molly 16**
Died in infancy   *Cleveland Seminary*

2nd marriage ———————— **Emma** Whitehead **24**

(Belle 4)   (Agnes 2)   (Levi 1)   [Pregnancy]

Character Guide, page c-2

*Notes: Characters' **ages** are shown as of May 23, 1861, the day of the McConnells' reception. Names of deceased persons are ghosted; minor characters are shown in parentheses.*

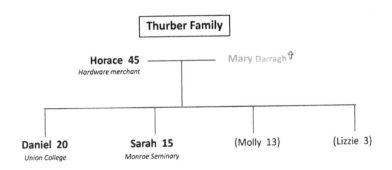

Thurber Family

Horace 45 ——————— Mary Darragh ✝
Hardware merchant

Daniel 20   **Sarah 15**   (Molly 13)   (Lizzie 3)
Union College   *Monroe Seminary*

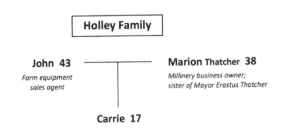

Holley Family

John 43 ——————— **Marion Thatcher 38**
Farm equipment   *Millinery business owner;*
sales agent   *sister of Mayor Erastus Thatcher*

Carrie 17

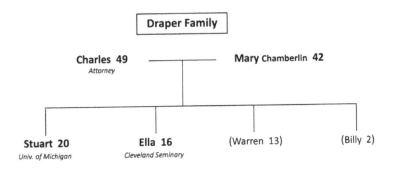

Draper Family

Charles 49 ——————— **Mary Chamberlin 42**
Attorney

Stuart 20   **Ella 16**   (Warren 13)   (Billy 2)
Univ. of Michigan   *Cleveland Seminary*

Character Guide, page c-3

*Notes: Characters' **ages** are shown as of May 23, 1861, the day of the McConnells' reception.
Names of deceased persons are ghosted; minor characters are shown in parentheses.*

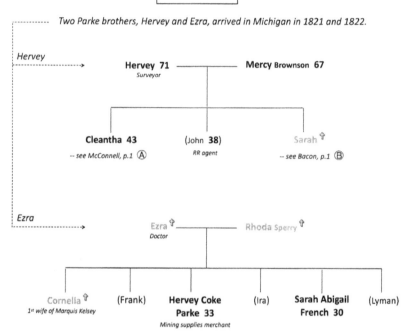

Parke Families

Two Parke brothers, Hervey and Ezra, arrived in Michigan in 1821 and 1822.

Hervey

Hervey 71
Surveyor

Mercy Brownson **67**

Cleantha 43
-- see McConnell, p.1 Ⓐ

(John **38**)
RR agent

Sarah ✝
-- see Bacon, p.1 Ⓑ

Ezra

Ezra ✝
Doctor

Rhoda Sperry ✝

Cornelia ✝
1st wife of Marquis Kelsey

(Frank)

**Hervey Coke
Parke 33**
Mining supplies merchant

(Ira)

**Sarah Abigail
French 30**

(Lyman)

Character Guide, page c-4

*Notes: Characters' **ages** are shown as of May 23, 1861, the day of the McConnells' reception.*
Names of deceased persons are ghosted; minor characters are shown in parentheses.

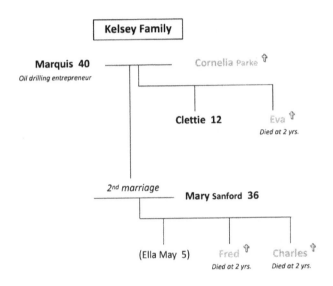

| Kelsey Family |

Marquis **40** — Cornelia Parke ✝
Oil drilling entrepreneur

Clettie **12** — Eva ✝
Died at 2 yrs.

2nd marriage — Mary Sanford **36**

(Ella May **5**) — Fred ✝ — Charles ✝
Died at 2 yrs. — *Died at 2 yrs.*

Pontiac Families

Surname	Husband		Wife	Son *	Daughter *
Bacon	Levi	Dry goods merchant	Emma Whitehead		Molly
Baldwin	Augustus	Editor of "Jacksonian"; attorney; militia commander	Isabella Churchill		
Comstock	Elkanah	Banker; head of school brd.	Eliza Holden		Nieces: Julia, Emma
Crofoot	Michael	Judge	Annie Fitch		
Darrow	Frank	Justice of the Peace	Augusta LeRoy		Emily
Drake	Morgan	Attorney	Sarah Stannard	Lewis	
Draper	Charles, Sr.	Attorney	Mary Chamberlin	Stuart	Ella
Holley	John	Farm machinery sales agent	Marion Thatcher		Carrie
Kelsey	Marquis	Oil investor / prospector	Mary Ann Sanford		Clettie
Mathews	Abram	Mill owner	Harriet Hatch	George	Fannie
McConnell	Dr. Abiram	Doctor	Helen Stewart		
McConnell	Willard	Dry goods merchant	Cleantha Parke	Parke; Joseph; Will	Ada; Flora
Parke	"Cap't" Hervey	Retired surveyor	Mercy Brownson	John	Cleantha
Parke	Hervey	Mining supplies merchant	Fannie Hunt		
Taylor	Eber	Farmer	Charlotte Jennings		Malvina
Thatcher	Erastus	Mayor of Pontiac	Fannie Richardson		
Thurber	Horace	Hardware merchant		Daniel	Sarah

* -- list includes only the sons and
daughters who are active in the story.

Other Characters

French, Sarah Parke, Housewife; younger sister of Hervey Coke Parke

Green, Reverend Augustus, Minister in the African Methodist Episcopal Church

Howell, Myron "M.E.N.", Editor of the Pontiac Gazette

Jackson, David, Stablehand and groundskeeper for the McConnell family

Richardson, Israel, Colonel, 2nd Michigan Volunteer Infantry

Wisner, Moses, Attorney; former Governor of Michigan

Character Groups

Republican party members
Willard McConnell
Levi Bacon
Moses Wisner
Israel Richardson
Morgan Drake
Charles Draper
Myron Howell

Democratic party members
Horace Thurber
Frank Darrow
Erastus Thatcher
Augustus Baldwin

Founders of Pontiac Gas Co.
Willard McConnell
Levi Bacon
Horace Thurber
Michael Crofoot

Univ. of Michigan - classmates   (ΔΦ = Delta Phi fraternity.)
Joseph McConnell (before transferring to Union College) ; ΔΦ
Daniel Thurber (before transferring to Union College) ; ΔΦ
Stuart Draper ΔΦ
Lewis Drake ΔΦ
George Mathews
Charlie Palmer, Jr.
Charlie Taylor (from Waterford; sister: Malvina)

Cleveland Female Seminary - classmates
Molly Bacon
Julia Comstock and younger sister Emma
Ella Draper
Larissa Lockwood
Fannie Mathews
Malvina Taylor and younger sister Libbie

Union public school - classmates
Carrie Holley
Fannie Pittman
Emma Adams

Monroe Female Seminary
Sarah Thurber

MAPS

ALL MAPS in this book have been created by the author to depict a street map of Pontiac, Michigan, in 1861. The author's plans are a composite based on two historical maps of the city: the 1857 "Hess" map and the 1872 "Ward map". These maps are available for reference at the Oakland County Pioneer & Historical Society (OCPHS) office in Pontiac.

- Outline of State of Michigan
- Map 1: City of Pontiac in 1861
- Map 2: Detail of downtown area, Saginaw Street – North portion, from Huron to Pike
- Map 3: Detail of downtown area, Saginaw Street – South portion, from Pike to Andrew
- Map 4: Plan of McConnell House on Church Street

Map of the State of Michigan
Upper and Lower Peninsulas

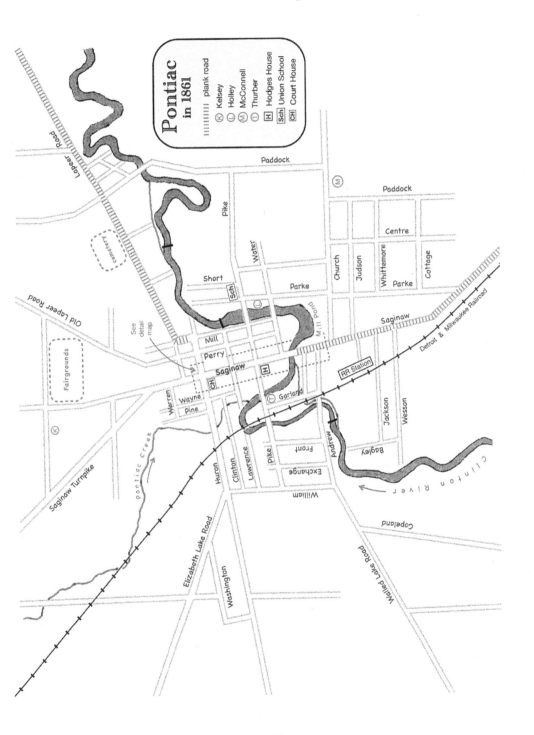

Pontiac
in 1861

▥▥▥▥▥▥ plank road
Ⓚ Kelsey
Ⓛ Holley
Ⓜ McConnell
Ⓣ Thurber
H Hodges House
Sch Union School
CH Court House

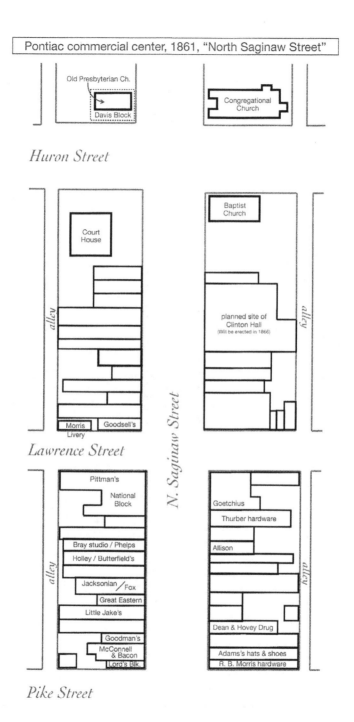

Pontiac commercial center, 1861, "North Saginaw Street"

Old Presbyterian Ch.

Davis Block

Congregational Church

Huron Street

Court House

Baptist Church

planned site of Clinton Hall
(Will be erected in 1866)

alley

alley

Morris Livery

Goodsell's

Lawrence Street

N. Saginaw Street

Pittman's

National Block

Bray studio / Phelps

Holley / Butterfield's

Jacksonian / Fox

Great Eastern

Little Jake's

Goodman's

McConnell & Bacon

Lord's Blk.

Goetchius

Thurber hardware

Allison

Dean & Hovey Drug

Adams's hats & shoes

R. B. Morris hardware

alley

alley

Pike Street

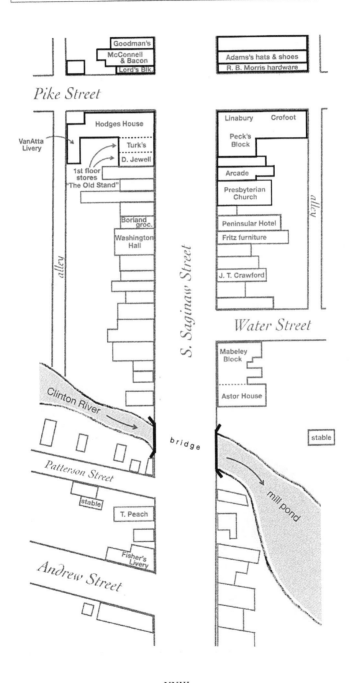

Pontiac commercial center, 1861, "South Saginaw Street"

Goodman's
McConnell & Bacon
Lord's Blk.

Adams's hats & shoes
R. B. Morris hardware

Pike Street

Hodges House

VanAtta Livery

Turk's

D. Jewell

1st floor stores "The Old Stand"

Borland groc.

Washington Hall

alley

S. Saginaw Street

Linabury   Crofoot

Peck's Block

Arcade

Presbyterian Church

Peninsular Hotel

Fritz furniture

J. T. Crawford

alley

Water Street

Mabeley Block

Astor House

Clinton River

bridge

stable

Patterson Street

stable

T. Peach

Fisher's Livery

mill pond

Andrew Street

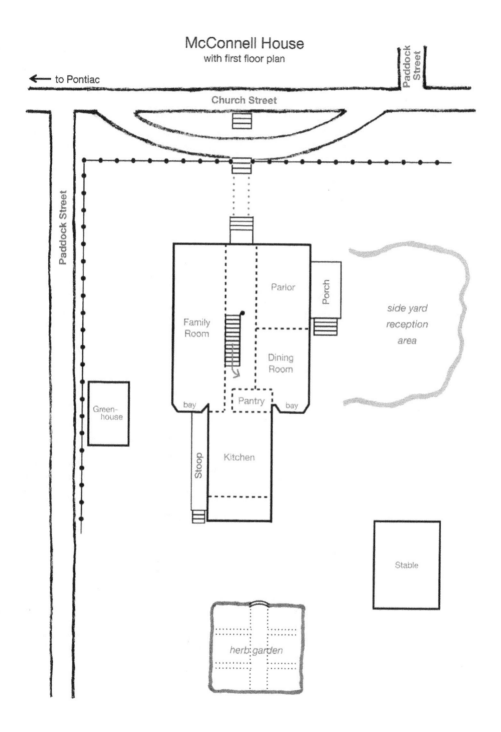

McConnell House
with first floor plan

OAK HILL CEMETERY, PONTIAC, MICHIGAN

"Who were they?"

"McConnell."

"Good-sized family plot. Must have been important folks."

"They were. Big money, for a town that size back then. The father ran his own business."

"Hmm."

"Big house, big family. You know—society types. But they're all gone now. There aren't any descendants around here, as far as I know."

"So there you are . . . another prominent family fades into history. I wonder what they were like."

"Busy, very involved in their community. No doubt highly respected. Proud folks in their day. Probably couldn't imagine their entire world distilled down to a clump of stone monuments."

"Makes me think of the old Ozymandias sonnet. Do you think they might have known that one?"

"Ozymandias? No, I doubt it. I think that's a modern poem."

PONTIAC TALES:
A LETTER

PONTIAC, MICHIGAN
APRIL 15, 1900

To my honorable friend,
Please accept this letter as my personal assurance of how thoroughly I enjoyed our conversation at Clinton Hall last month and yes, I agree, we are both to be congratulated on our safe arrival in this new century, never mind the precarious vagaries of our respective advanced ages. Alas, our prime years have long since elapsed, though my health has remained stubbornly robust, somehow. I trust your fettle is likewise finely sustained. Now that the world is spinning faster and faster, I find our acquaintance serves us well to withstand the pace of reforms and folly ever around us, such is the life in our vaunted Progressive Era. Rest assured: your opinion of my lucidity of mind is, and will always be, an assessment that I value foremost.

Tommyrot, you say, and enough of all that. The point herewith is your interest in history, and the questions you have posed about earlier times in Pontiac when the great "pioneer families" were still running the show. You were accurate on two of your inquiries: first, that it is difficult to create a picture of the town in the years before the War Between the States; and second, that I was resident during that time and might help you to recreate the picture.

As I understand it, these two truths are pertinent to your interest in old Pontiac. If you wish to dramatize the past or revive the particulars of what people were doing here fifty years ago, then I am only too ready to toss what I have into the pot. I have little experience in formal historical research, though I have seen numerous published chronicles about Pontiac the town and histories of Oakland County. But that is not your pursuit, I think! What you pursue is the creation of a *narrative*, a story that can span over many facts and records and convert everything into one memorable reading. If you will abide my opinion, I would commend just such a narrative, with an aim to lay out something more enjoyable for other historians to read and research.

Since our meeting I have been thinking back on the "ante bellum" days at length. There is much to say about it, and I am not a man of few words as you well know. Yet, I am sensitive to the foible of unfocused oratory and the risk of losing my audience. How best, then, to take you back with me to the streets of old Pontiac—hah!—and lead you about from scene to scene as would Mr. Dickens' ghost of Christmas Past?

Read on, my friend, to see the approach I shall take. There is some context to it.

I would start with the words "dreams of long ago". It is an expression that I have used blithely in conversations about times past or personal memories, where the talk has digressed too far into timeworn stories or trivial nostalgia, and it's time to move on. In due course an opportune moment will arrive to wrap things up on the subject, and that is when you can say "Ah well, dreams of long ago." You won't sound dismissive—it's just that you are more interested in restoring the conversation to more current matters. Your listeners are assured that you are attuned and disciplined, that you won't bore everyone by going on about The Old Days.

A colleague of mine would resort to this phrase now and then, particularly when he wanted to check himself from burdening listeners with long stories about his experiences as a younger man. But he had good stories to tell, all about events that happened years ago when he had occasions to travel to Pontiac. It was before the war, and at that time Pontiac was still a small city in Michigan. His visits there on business had made quite an impression on him, apparently, as he got to know many of the more notable inhabitants and he saw first-hand the progress of the town through the war and afterward. So it was that he still enjoyed reminiscing on those days, even decades later at various social gatherings. We all grew accustomed to this recurring topic in our friend's discourse; no one really paid much attention or grew impatient with it. Yes, we all thought, here you go again with another rendition of your visits to that old town. What have you got for us this time—more about the posh hotel you stayed in? Or the rich family, or that grumpy widower? How about the young love-struck couple—any progress there?

So there we were, obligingly quiet in amused expectation as our friend would proceed with yet another of his yarns about Pontiac. These would go on for only a few minutes or so. Whether oddly humorous or sometimes tiresome, the stories were reliably *non sequitur*, pulling us away from whatever we had just been discussing. And a well-delivered yarn is usually welcome in any social evening that's grown dull with routine small talk and tasteless jokes. When the drinks are served and the chatter is idle, that's when people are most receptive for any diversion more focused and entertaining.

But something more subtle was also happening with all this storytelling. As time went on and my friend related more and more pieces about Pontiac, I began to perceive how each piece would build on the ones we had heard before. Indeed each anecdote, each vignette, was only providing another installment within a larger, more dramatic tale. Moreover, these "dreams of long ago" were weaving a collection of parallel stories covering the same a group of people—a cast of characters, so to speak. These were normal, everyday people, each of them finding their way through that tumultuous era leading up to the war. Some were thriving, others discouraged, but whatever their circumstances, I could visualize them back in their day. I began to appreciate their point of view about "modern times." For them, then and there, their community was a vibrant place, colorful and busy. Never mind the discomforts and risks, normal fare in any era, as these were balanced with new inventions and conveniences that were becoming just as normal. It's the novelties that keep life interesting, not the age-old complaints.

This is why I believe my friend's whimsical portrayals of these ordinary people might deserve a closer look. He was describing not only what happened in their lives but also how they felt about it—an insight worth telling, in my opinion. I find that for us today it is easy to overlook the larger stories in the lives of our ancestors and their contemporaries, stories hidden behind all the records and dates and impassive daguerreotype images. Stories requiring our imagination and inference.

Lest I neglect to mention it, the man is also a first-rate raconteur, ever entertaining with his breezy manner of describing people and places. Like any good chapter book, the more details you hear about his friends and acquaintances, the more curious you become, wanting to know what will happen to them. They were, after all, real people. You probably have known people just like them in your own life. That's the key, as I think on it, why his yarns leave you wanting to hear more.

Why not have these stories written down? *Rara avis* it is, this sort of depiction of day-to-day life back then and what it was like to be there. There was deeper value in this, and I meant to sit down with him sometime to encourage him to set these "Pontiac tales" on paper. Collectively they would make a fine record, even if the events were somewhat mundane and the characters not famous (although one would become quite well-known), with plenty of material to engage the modern reader. Here we can meet a variety of people in a time very different from ours, facing new realities and a war impending but still something far away. Especially the young people: we can observe how they assess their parents and families as they come of age in a town that is itself coming of age, just as they are. All these personal stories, told separately and seemingly off-hand with no connections—they could be linked into one long narrative, presenting a much broader picture of the town. You might begin to feel as though you were a visitor there yourself, walking down the main street and calling upon old friends.

Of course, my friend would never take it upon himself to write it all down. Writing requires discipline, which is not one of his known talents. His skill is in the creative narration of his a story, in accents clear, before a group of bemused cronies with drinks in their hands. But writing a coherent monograph to put it all together? No—I will have to do that part myself, as best I can with whatever cooperation I might conjure from the story-teller, our chief witness. It should be an interesting project, and I suppose helpful for posterity, in the style of a first-hand account.

There's the gambit, then. I shall write his book.

That's what this story could do: take you there for a day, just for one day, and let you see for yourself whether all the reminiscences are true. You should meet the characters *in situ*, as they were on that day, your impressions of them simple and unaffected by knowing their futures. Our perception of the nature of people in times past gets distorted, unavoidably, if we know what will happen to them, who will go to war and survive, who will marry, who will stay in Pontiac and who will leave, who will have children, who will die young and who will live to old age. So here, for this narration, let us give everyone a fresh start. What was on their minds—what were their desires and worries, their daydreams—on that one particular day?

We should also be mindful of the conditions of life in my characters' world, in contrast to the world we know today. Singularities and nuances of life in the old days can be difficult to portray to everyone's satisfaction, inevitably, so I will color my renditions of events with a few hints in that regard. Perhaps the best tact would be this: to mix my friend's recollections with a few suggestions of my own—and I'll put you directly into the story yourself. That might help. You should experience "in situ" what might happen if you were to visit the town for a day and encounter all these characters on your own accord.

Enjoy your stay. The train ride is not difficult, the hotel is surprisingly plush, and most everyone will be glad to see you. If the weather is nice, don't hesitate to go for a walk through the center of town. You should allow yourself a sense of familiarity in the surroundings, as if you have visited the place before. Perhaps someone will ask whether you have already met on one of those occasions.

Upon your return I shall presume our next meeting with great expectation, ready to hear you out on all your impressions and observations from the journey. Then might we consider, *en tout cas*, whether a story can become a dream.

With sincere regard,

Spirit of Modern Times

PART I:
THE OLD DAYS

AN ALMOND CAKE

CLEANTHA MCCONNELL was standing by a side table in her kitchen where she could look through a window into the east yard. She had been working over a large stoneware mixing bowl, beating sugar and lard together with a steady rhythm, but had just now paused. At age 43 she knew better than to strain her wrist too far in such an effort, and had stopped, using a minute to rest and take in the view of trees and blue sky on a fine spring morning. It was enjoyable once again to take in the sight of green grass spreading around and below the witch-hazel and rhododendrons. The forsythia were largely green now, with just a few stretches of yellow still lingering among the

Cleantha Parke McConnell

strands. Off towards the edge of the yard she could see the rhubarb plot was still marked with a few surviving plants, though most had been picked for making a large batch of rhubarb shrub drink for the party. Most of her store of sugar had likewise disappeared into mixing the shrub, and Cleantha was gratified to find enough sugar in a canister this morning for baking. One less problem to worry about – especially this morning, already 9:30, with so much to accomplish before 4:00 when the guests would start appearing.

Guests, indeed many callers, a houseful, were expected this afternoon. Cleantha had much on her mind getting the house ready, although she also liked to picture the arrival of each of her friends coming through the front door, one after another. She and her husband Willard were about to host a reception, a large one for some forty people, planned as a two-hour party in the late afternoon, outdoors in the east yard. There would be hors-d'oeuvres and light beverages served, and accommodations made across the road for the guests' carriages. In the current social season the McConnell's event was one of the first on the calendar, having been scheduled hastily, on a Thursday no less. But just about everyone was coming. The guest list included close friends, and key acquaintances—social and business—as well as the usual extended family list. And this time Cleantha had broadened her invitations to cover not only the older set of her circle of friends, but also to accommodate the younger set, the friends of her own grown children. This brought about some complexity, or rather strategizing, as to how to use the rooms on the first floor of her house while the party was underway in the yard.

Where to greet arriving guests—indoors or outdoors? Cleantha had resolved to have people come first into the house, and to use the formal parlor for receiving. The advantage of the parlor was its two window doors that provided access to the east porch, so that guests might proceed directly from the receiving out onto the porch and down to the yard. This was most sensible, although it meant opening up the household's "sanctum sanctorum" room for all society to troop through. That was, perhaps, a bit unconventional. Willard had at first objected but he agreed that it would work best for Cleantha's aging parents, given the access to the porch—and besides, the porch was always useful in case anyone might be planning on making a speech to a crowd in the yard. It was mildly amusing to Cleantha, knowing that her husband would of course acquiesce to the unusual format; Willard's interests would always lean towards popularity over convention. He was a merchant, first and foremost.

There was another part to this plan. Cleantha had further resolved to provide a venue for younger folks to gather separately on their own for an hour or so before coming out to the yard. By using the parlor for receiving, she could reserve the rear half of big family room across the hall for this purpose. This would be sufficiently isolated, where her son and all his friends—boys and girls—could meet in something like a salon setting, providing a short recess away from parents and meddlesome relatives. *Boys and girls?* —Cleantha caught herself thinking. *I suppose it's high time we see fully grown men and women.* Even if such a "get-away" might seem a tad indecorous, it was surely harmless and Cleantha knew it would earn high praise among the escapees. And especially now in springtime it was vital for the young men returning home from college to be mixing with the girls just coming of age after high school, in any social opportunity.

So the plan was set: entertainment for everyone, old and young, outdoors and indoors. This was going to be a lively affair by any measure.

But not *too lively*. It wouldn't do for afternoon entertainment to be serving wines or ales to her guests, no, not in the afternoon, and outdoors in warm sunshine. There would be a punch, however, prepared with a little "spirit" as everyone would expect. The punch should suffice. In any event the punch was sure to draw compliments just by presentation—served from the McConnell's new sterling silver punch bowl that Willard had just purchased from the Gorham Company in Rhode Island. The bowl would be set out on the refreshment table in the yard, with its tray and ladle (but without the cups), making its debut ingenuously even as it gleamed in the sunlight. Cleantha liked the

McConnell house, 1860

image of it. How sublime—and yet tactful. Her silver service had to be the only Gorham items in Pontiac, a coup of sorts, now that Gorham had just been selected by Mrs. Lincoln for her entertainments at the White House. Willard had picked up on the idea to opine about the "power of the tariff" serving Gorham's market interests most handsomely in this case, and the McConnell's interests as well.

By any measure, the McConnell house was certainly a desirable venue for a big social event. Willard had the place built ten years ago, after his dry goods business had flourished to become one the largest and best-known in town. One of the grander homes in the area, the house was a fine rendition of Italianate Villa style, with its four chimneys, its curvy "corbel" brackets under the eaves of the roof, and tall windows all surrounded by elaborate woodcut moldings. On the first floor outside the living room on the east side there was an expansive stoop which served more as a porch, upon which Willard had installed a wooden balustrade and a few slender pillars to support an awning. The rear wing, extending southward, provided for the kitchen on its first floor and servants' quarters on its second floor. Altogether it would be fair to describe the residence as stately, and tasteful, as one might expect from a successful merchant and leading citizen such as Willard McConnell. The property was framed by a wrought iron fence, its railings distinctive but not too tall, and the grounds inside contained a modest greenhouse for year-round plantings.

Not bad, not bad at all. Cleantha's home was a suitable venue where society might gather, for any occasion, any time of the year. Peacetime or wartime.

It was the war, in fact, that had brought on the reason for the McConnells' reception in the first place. Cleantha's second son, Joseph, had just enlisted in the army down in Detroit and was coming home on leave, just for a few days, before his military training began in earnest back at Fort Wayne. The whole family was very excited for him of course, along with everyone else in town, and so it was absolutely mandatory to host this gala in his honor before he left. Inwardly Cleantha fretted about her boy being exposed to weather and diseases and camp life, not to mention the inevitable immoral influences of unsavory types among the troops. *All mothers do*, she supposed. But she would avoid embarrassing Joseph, no matter what, especially in front of his friends or the army officers. Joseph was so careful and headstrong about his future. And he was hale and sturdy, like his grandfather Parke (Cleantha's father, "the Captain") who had survived so much hardship out in the wilderness territories during his years as a government surveyor. The Parke's and McConnell's were a hearty breed, after all.

The celebration was then duly planned, and the day was here, and Cleantha was ready. Earlier this morning, by the time her husband and her oldest son (Hervey Parke McConnell—everyone just called him "Parke") had left for work, the three

Horse-drawn surrey carriage

youngest children were already up and fed breakfast by Eliza the cook,

who was now seeing them all off to school. "The Captain" along with
the family's stablehand Jackson were now out in the east yard setting
up the tables and clearing the porch, which they should finish soon,
because the two of them were supposed to take the surrey over to the
depot to meet Joseph who was scheduled to arrive on the late morning
train. Then they could all have a lunch together, and Joseph would still
have plenty of time afterwards to rest before the reception. It should
all work out. Cleantha was mindful, however, that she ought to check
on her father soon, and ensure that he wasn't overexerting himself with
the tables. The elderly gentleman had been showing more fatigue, since
this past winter noticeably. Nowadays he frequently needed to "rest
his legs" and take a seat for a spell. But this morning he seemed to be
getting along fine and made himself particularly helpful in attending
to Grandmother Mercy while everyone else was busy.

Good, then. Ever the restless hostess, Cleantha was satisfied that
everything was in acceptable order, or well underway towards making
the house presentable in the time remaining. The porches outside were
already swept clear of whirligig seeds fallen from the maples, along
with any last traces of yellow pollen powder, so no worries there. The
lawn out in the east yard looked to be in proper condition—yesterday
evening Jackson and young Willy had clipped off any taller grass blades
and weeds that were still protruding, so by now the whole area had
become a smooth green expanse that the guests might appreciate in the
springtime weather. Cleantha smiled faintly with a slow shake of her
head as she thought back on how her two older sons were so keen on
obtaining one of those new "Silens messor" machines for cutting the
yard's grassy areas.[1] Her husband Willard finally called on John Holley, the
harvester machine agent in town, to place an order for one of these mowers

---

1   "Silens messor" was the trade name (Latin for "silent cutter") given to a push
     lawnmower patented in England by Thomas Green in 1859 with helical rotating blades,
     actually an improvement on the original 1830's mechanism, having a far more practical
     design and widespread commercial success.

but alas, none was available anywhere this far west in the country, apparently. Just as well—Cleantha deemed the machines as too new, too complicated, and too risky for a curious boy to fiddle with and end up cutting off a finger. The mower's fancy Latin name didn't impress her; to the contrary it just made her all the more suspicious. These days there were enough new dangerous implements around the house as it was.

I still have a few hours. What should I do with myself? Cleantha had spare time now, which was unexpected and therefore bothersome. She needed a task, to do something useful. She thought she might examine the floor bricks by the parlor fireplaces, in case Mary had not washed them sufficiently, but then changed her mind when the right idea suddenly took hold.

I should make my almond cake. There—resolved.

And so that is what brought her to this moment in the kitchen, with the batter started, and her wrist starting to tire, and the view of the back yard affording its calm repose. Yes, the cake was the right thing to do. The McConnells' young scullery maid, little Mary Plunket, was helping alongside Cleantha, and being especially attentive as was only proper with such a busy day ahead. For that matter, Mary was always eager to learn more about cooking and baking, and here was a chance to show her all the steps in making this recipe, with some extra practice in preparing the barm[2] and the egg whites. There was another advantage, too, in that Eliza the cook would be out for another half-hour or so with the children, so Cleantha and Mary would have the kitchen all to themselves. Mary would probably assist better without Eliza hovering about and making helpful suggestions.

In any event, the chief reason for spending time in the kitchen with Mary Plunkett, occupied as they were, was to plan and prepare not just the cake, but the party itself. Baking a cake was easy for Cleantha Mc-

---

2 Barm is a form of natural leaven, made by collecting froth from the top of a fermenting liquid such as beer wort and mixing it with flour and salt. As a liquid concentrate it can be used as a substitute for baking powder or yeast.

Connell, and it would keep her busy, help her frame her thoughts. In this way she would maintain her self-confidence while ruminating over all of the various social interactions that would soon unfold among her guests. Yes, these were considerations that a competent hostess should bear in mind.

This afternoon the world would once again show deference to Cleantha's status in Pontiac society, reliably a well-refined hostess for an elegant reception party, a social engagement not to be missed. She hailed from the Parke family—a founding pioneer name—and had always been well known as the respectable wife of a successful merchant, Willard McConnell. She was a Daughter of the American Revolution, a mother of five children, an esteemed matron in one of the finest homes. Even with a one-year-old baby at home, Cleantha continued to be very involved in her church and in supporting the local schools, along with her husband, and had served as secretary for the Ladies' Sewing Society. True to her humble beginnings in the early wilderness times, Cleantha was still eminently practical in all manner of managing a household, and an accomplished cook of course. No question, she knew how to bake an almond cake.

Inhaling a full breath at the window, she briefly stretched her shoulders up and then relaxed them down, and looking back into the bowl she resumed her mixing with the same heavy circular motion. A few more stirs and she would start to mix in the egg whites, but just now she turned her head towards Mary to tell her to check on the fire inside the stove. The lass stopped her barm preparation and snatched up a rag before squatting down before the stove, and deftly pulled open the iron door handle and peeked inside. Cleantha turned again to glance at the status of the kindling and the low flames, and with Mary the two of them silently exchanged a positive nod that all was well for now. Back to her stirring, Cleantha could hear the stove door behind her squeak and slam shut as Mary returned to her task at the barm mixture on the center table.

Cleantha poured in her egg whites and kept stirring, while Mary began to hum a tune, probably another of her Catholic hymns, which somehow made the time more pleasant. Cleantha was well satisfied with the lass's work, and with her enthusiasm to learn all the steps in preparing an almond cake. Mary had only arrived in town a few weeks ago, an Irish lass of seventeen—or younger than she says—whose family had settled in Detroit. She and some other girls had responded to employment offers in Pontiac and were now boarding in various homes, good proper girls, all working, the lot of them new obliging and faithful communicants at St. Vincent's on the north side[3]. No doubt Mary was happy with her live-in employment in such a large comfortable house as the McConnells' with its modern iron stove and a water pump in the kitchen, and a full array of tools and utensils. Cleantha watched for a few moments as the lass managed her tasks at the center table. Then facing back to her own work, with a resigned smile, she started to think, *This lassie could never understand how it was before, the pioneer life, in an earlier age before I married, in the little cabin where there was no stove, only the wide open hearth.* Back then, handling cookware over the fire wasn't easy, especially in winter. Cleantha remembered very cold days when she tended the pots, her face sweating by the heat of the fire, while the back of her skirt would be caked with small bits of ice and frost that formed where the steam had condensed. *Ah well, these lassies today don't want to hear about it. Could they even imagine stumbling over a corduroy road, or chasing a scruffy wolf out of a henhouse? No, they couldn't.*

The mixing bowl now needed the sweet milk, which Cleantha announced, and Mary responded on the spot by pulling the small ewer out of the cooler and bringing it to Cleantha's side, and as instructed,

3   St. Vincent's Catholic Church, in 1861 located on Saginaw Street at Lafayette Street.

carefully poured the milk over the batter while Cleantha continued her stirring. Cleantha watched, and she was thinking back on how the lass's friends pronounced her name as "Meery" and how annoying it was that here in the household everyone had taken to speaking her name likewise effecting an Irish lilt and by now it had become accepted as not even in jest anymore. Funny habits. Then again, Cleantha also enjoyed recognizing any amusing vestige of her husband's Scotch ancestry, even if the days of "ayes" and "naes" for the McConnell clan were long gone.

"Mary, is the barm measured and ready?"

"Yes, Ma'am, almost."

Most of the preparations for the party were well underway, with the rooms readied for a full capacity crowd. Mary had swept the floors and dusted the furniture, while Cleantha took care of dusting and re-arranging wall ornaments and the porcelain items, and placed all the flowers, and straightened the doilies. There was also the matter of bringing in potted plants from the greenhouse: two pots of beebrush to be placed in the family room, which would lend a fresh, lemony aroma, and a pot of lavender for the parlor. Cleantha had assigned this task to somebody but now she couldn't remember who it was.

Eliza had already set out the dining room table in preparation for the dainties (which should be ready for placement by 4:45); also there were two platters of oatmeal cookies freshly baked yesterday and ready in the pie safe in the pantry. Jackson was out in the yard helping the Captain put up the two outdoor tables and a few chairs—and preventing the old gentleman from overexertion, something Cleantha always worried about. Through the kitchen window she could keep an eye on her father, which was the careful thing to do, even if the man's physical condition was excellent, obviously.

This afternoon's occasion called for some speechmaking and a few extra refreshments outdoors, so the tables were to be positioned in such a way that all the guests might perceive that the side porch would serve as the dais for the speakers. In this regard Cleantha was also thinking that Joseph's friends might prepare their talks in the family room beforehand, and she visualized them proceeding through the parlor to assemble on the porch at the appointed time. Certainly Lewis Drake would come up with something to entertain the crowd. *They're all fine boys.* All in all, things should work out well. In the meantime, as long as the morning was this quiet, so far, why not show Mary how to throw together a simple cake?

"Yes, Mary, that's fine. We're ready for the flour and barm. Let's bring them over here, please."

The aromas of the various ingredients were more perceptible now. Cleantha felt more at ease, and she could indulge in visualizing a full panoply of friends and family in her home, in her yard. It was gratifying that a number of social notables were coming today, including former governor Wisner and the redoubtable Colonel Richardson. Wisner was a reliable socializer but the Colonel sometimes remained aloof, although he could spring to life at any moment. And Cleantha would have to show a special respect for Richardson—he was, after all, commanding the very regiment that her son Joseph had just joined—and here was the best opportunity to secure the Colonel's favorable affinity towards the McConnell name.

With two luminaries such as Wisner and Richardson the guest list could already lay claim to sufficient gravitas. Consequently there was reasonable space to invite a few lesser established townsfolk to the party such as Myron Howell, the handsome young editor of the Gazette newspaper. It never hurt to have a charming, witty bachelor on hand. And then there was that guest coming, a "familiar visitor" who was some out-of-town friend of Willard's. Cleantha vaguely remembered that friend as an agreeable sort if not somewhat nosy. Earnest, gregarious people—that was the key.

Mary was carefully shaking the flour into the bowl, while Cleantha started thinking again about Colonel Richardson. He would be dressed in full uniform, no doubt, a no-nonsense West Pointer now in his 40's and coming out of retirement to lead the new volunteer regiment. Cleantha smiled to herself: *Can you believe it? Imagine Richardson marrying that Fannie Travor next week—what a fitting match they make, the pair of them so compulsive and unpredictable.* A little tactful teasing there would help dispel any dark clouds brought over us by that pernicious Horace Thurber. Horace Thurber . . . *How strange that his son and my Joseph should become such fast friends. But I like that young Daniel—a little quiet, perhaps, but a sincere type. The daughters are nice. Interesting family.*

And Cleantha's friend Augusta Darrow was also coming, which was of course pleasing but, as always, a little bit exacting for her high standard of social graces. Of course Augusta and her husband would have to bring their daughter Emily, almost 30 and unmarried, perhaps somewhat eccentric, but intelligent nonetheless and occasionally amusing. Emily would likely spend most of her time with one of Cleantha's Parke cousins, "Cousin Sallie", a proven kindred spirit for Emily.

Frankly if there was anyone to worry about, it was Cousin Sallie, lively and fun although capable of becoming a bit too opinionated when in company. Sallie was also 30 years old, married now for almost a year but still living here in the house while her husband, a traveling book salesman, lived in Washington. The situation was unusual but not unheard of, and for now Sallie was content to be using one of the bedrooms in the rear wing in the servants' quarters. Moreover it was useful to have her looking after Cleantha's elderly parents, *and she has way of adding a measure of merry over the entire household, you have to admit.* Sallie ought to be counted upon for a lot more help around the house, but that was another story. And it was not altogether surprising when Sallie announced at breakfast that she had errands in town to take care of later this morning. She promised to return in time to help with the dainties, of course.[4]

How long Sallie's marital arrangement would continue like this was anyone's guess. Meantime, however, the fact that the husband would soon be arriving in Pontiac on his next sales trip did not seem to stir up much expectation or enthusiasm in the bride for their impending reunion. Nor in anyone else. Mr. French was not altogether likeable, a mercurial type really, or as Willard put it, "profoundly uncongenial." A proper social event like Cleantha's reception would always be better off without him.

"Mary, now bring the cream tartar. Here, I'll let you mix it in."

The lass took over handling the bowl while Cleantha stepped over to the stove and suspended a hand closely over the top, assessing the heat—yes, still good.

"Mary, wave your hand over the stove . . . there, feel that heat? That's what you want. Now stir the mix a little more."

Cleantha could take another moment here to contemplate another of her cousins to arrive, Hervey Coke Parke, Sallie's brother. Hervey was not at all like Sallie, with his reserved comportment, yes, very reserved, which Cleantha found somewhat tiresome. He was staying with other relatives in town and would probably walk over and immerse himself unobtrusively in the crowd. *I should make a point of talking to him,* Cleantha thought. These types of large gatherings always provided good opportunities to catch up on the cousins. Hervey was still working in the Upper Peninsula and was evidently back in Pontiac visiting his business suppliers. Cleantha and Willard suspected he had saved up a lot of money, surely after this many years, also having "married well" just last year, finally. So there were reasons to ferret out just what he's up to this time, hobnobbing with all the local merchants.

---

4   Dainties: hors d'oeuvres.

"Ma'am?" The lass had slowed her mixing and was looking at Cleantha as if ready for the next step, which she knew would call for adding bitter almonds into the batter.

Cleantha reached over to the small tin and pulled off the lid to look over the contents one more time—Mary had chopped and blanched the almonds yesterday, and when Cleantha with raised eyebrows uttered a simple comment, "good" it was a quiet moment of pride for her young helper. This was the last ingredient: taking a small spoon, Mary proceeded to scoop once into the tin and, with Cleantha nodding approval on the amount, she sprinkled the almonds into the bowl and stirred them in with a few final rounds.

"Very good. Now let's check whether the baking tin is well buttered. Yes, that's fine." The two cooks shared a glance at each other while Cleantha in a kindly tone of voice told Mary that she could pour the batter into the tin.

Mary went to work on this last step while Cleantha closed the lid on the spice tin and found its place to be put away in the cupboard. Then, keeping herself occupied, Cleantha gathered up a few spoons and a knife and took them over to the water table for washing, which she didn't mind doing herself. She was thinking about Cousin Hervey again, and whether he would bring little Clettie, his niece. In Hervey and Sarah's family there was another sister who had died after giving birth to Clettie, thirteen years ago already. Cleantha was always mindful about the girl growing up without a mother, and she enjoyed having Clettie over to play with her own younger children who were about the same age. It was somehow meaningful that Cleantha's own firstborn, a baby girl, had also been named Clet-

tie, but was lost after only 16 months. Sad times, very sad, long ago. But this afternoon the house will again resound with children's voices, and laughter, and mischief. *That almond cake might not even make it to the dining room table, if the little ones get to it first.* Musing about Clettie's visit now reminded Cleantha that she had bought a gift for her, the Hiawatha book, all about the Indian legends around Lake Superior. Clettie might favor reading some adventure stories about the frontier region where her mother and father used to live. Another item, then: *I'll have to find that gift and have it wrapped and ready, in the parlor, before the party.*

The cake tin was now filled, smoothed, and ready for baking. The two women bent down by the middle stove door, which Cleantha nimbly swung open and watched while Mary slid the tin inside. Door closed, temperature good. Cleantha had always been satisfied with her stove, which had come from Thurber's hardware store. It had turned out to be a reasonable purchase despite whatever doubts she had for Horace Thurber. His renown as a hard-nosed businessman wasn't necessarily a virtue.

"Thank you Mary. Now we should take the tablecloths upstairs, and some more cups. Please check on the cake after a half hour or so, would you?"

Oh, the cups, Cleantha thought, yes, she also meant to taste the switchel[5] again, worried that it may not have had enough honey, and there was so little sugar left if . . . ah well, too late for that now.

On the whole, her preparations were on schedule, her house was clean, and her family excited and all doing their parts. In good spirits Cleantha was circling through the family room on inspection, and here she recalled something that Willard had said last Sunday, an off-hand remark that she still found intriguing. It was last Sunday, at home after the Pentecost service at church. Willard was standing at the

---

5   Switchel is a beverage made of water and cider vinegar, seasoned with ginger, sweetened with honey or molasses or maple syrup.

family room fireplace winding the mantel clock, evidently in cheerful disposition as he hummed a melody from one of the morning hymns. He had turned to Cleantha with a satisfied grin and proceeded to describe how the Pentecost season always made him feel better about the future. The Holy Ghost was at hand, once again, to show how "good things were just getting started" for all the faithful and the fearful. *Isn't that right*, Cleantha thought then, and still this morning, of her husband's thoughtful asseveration.

And so the hostess felt a growing self-assurance that everything was coming into place, and her home would be ready, up to standard for a fine gathering of friends and family. Moreover this was something she could do very well, inviting people into her home, doing her part in upholding community, indeed civility, much needed during such times as these with everyone obsessed over declaring war.

Particularly for the younger people, surely they ought to understand how gatherings like this become the measure of a family, and how the family will be remembered, long after this war is all but forgotten. Cleantha was resolute about her responsibility to convey this wisdom to the younger ones who would soon be walking into her house, conversing with her friends, learning the ways of social discourse. A big party might have awkward moments for the young, but it has always been a tiresome process. Let them hear the same old stories about the early days, let them scoff and dismiss the old-fashioned behaviors, but the lessons of society will be imparted to them nonetheless. Eventually they, too, will understand the favor.

But despite all of these best of intentions, the one thing that Cleantha herself could not understand was this: that her children and their friends would never truly experience "the early days." For them, there were no early days. There was only the modern era, the very best times possible, the modern times that would never change or lose their momentum. In this reality, there were *advances*; advances in science, in conveniences, in foods and medicines, in ideas, in education. Things were always getting better and better.

Better and better for the McConnell children and their school friends, of course. These were the future inheritors most on Cleantha's mind, whenever she mused over the way things were going in the community. Given the times, perhaps, she felt no need to discuss "generational differences" with Mary Plunket, the Irish scullery maid working right beside her. All that mattered there was that the lass should happily complete all her daily tasks, with true respect and high regard for her employer, and keep her own assessments to herself. Imagine the Irish lilt in a tart retort such as *"Sure, as if the likes of her has ever watched a soul slowly perish in the famine, right in her own kitchen."* But if Cleantha and Mary ever openly shared a moment to commiserate over past hardships, what useful purpose would it serve? Mary was not schooled, yet she was an understanding sort, and both women understood very well in their own ways, deeply personal, how life was so much easier nowadays.

Spirit of Modern Times

PART II:
SAGINAW STREET

Joseph McConnell

I'm telling you--that bombardment of Fort Sumter turned out to be the last straw. What a godsend for us! Now we'll see some action, and it's about time. The politicians have been yammering about the South for so long now, on and on about their states' rights and their slaves and their precious cotton. It's all a matter of a few arrogant big shots down there who have no interest in progress or the realities of modern times, and now they're trying to expand their empire into the West, into Kansas, Mexico, as far as they can go. Buchanan was useless to stop it, but now at last we have a president who will. Just send the army down there and we'll set things right in no time. Once the flag and the steel show up might and main, you'll see very few southern boys jump to defend those plantation owners, I'll wager.

College studies will have to wait. You can't let a chance like this pass by, to join the army and make your mark. Do something useful, for once. Even if the campaign lasts only a few months, there's sure to be plenty more work for the army to do afterwards, and places to go. I'd like to see the frontier. Anyway I signed up for three years. I'll still be 22 when I get back, and meantimes my older brother will be at home to help Father run the business, so there you are.

You might say that I'm really following a McConnell tradition, of sorts: my grandfather a surveyor, my father removing here from New York, my uncle and my brother in the gold rush, my mother's cousins all over the country, they all understand my need to do this. My friend Danny? I think he's going to miss this boat, but his family situation is a little complicated these days. His mother passed away a couple months ago, and he has three younger sisters to worry about until things can get squared away, you see.

I sat on the train from Detroit, this time wearing the uniform, people looking at me with admiration – it would be nice to get a look like that from a girl like Danny's sister this time. So: we pull into Pontiac at the old depot, and I know I'll miss the place. It's a good life here, worth defending, and we'll all fight for it. Aye, I'll fight for the flag, and fight for my family. And for the young ladies, don't you know!

Saginaw Street, looking north from Andrew Street. The intersection with Huron Street is at the horizon, where the spire of the Congregational Church is on the right side and the large cupola of the Court House is poking over the flat roof line of the Hodges Hotel.

Saginaw Street, looking north from Andrew Street. Hodges House hotel is at top right in the photo.

A VISITOR'S STORY,
"Arrival"

"PONTIAC! PAAHHN-TEE-AAAC! Arriving Pontiac!"

The conductor passes your seat, heading rearward, announcing the train's arrival at the Pontiac depot within a minute or two. No surprise: the train had started to decelerate, the paired intermittent *clack-clack* sounds from the wheels gradually slowing, and you could feel the car jerk slightly to the right as train redirected onto the parallel track that was laid out for the depot. Several passengers had already stood up from their seats and were starting to gather up their belongings.

"PAAHHN-tee-aaac . . ." The exclamation trailed off one last time at the back of the car, followed by the slam of the rear door closing.

You get up, too, to fall in with several passengers who are standing in the aisle by the time the depot platform slowly creeps into view through the east side windows. The exit door is opened to admit more sounds, the creaking of metal and hissing of steam, the sounds of arrival. You also hear the clicks and thuds of a few windows slid open by other passengers who have remained in their seats, taking advantage of the stop to let in more fresh air while the engine smoke outside has dissipated. The car finally comes to a full stop, and as the people ahead of you file out through the aisle door onto the end platform, the interior behind you becomes quieter, so quiet that you can hear conversations from people outside on the depot landing. It's during these short periods of waiting that you're made aware once again of the smell of the varnished wood trim, with a slight tinge of mildew as one might expect in this sort of public accommodation.

Still waiting near the aisle door to the car's end-platform it's easy to overhear, in the stillness, the low voices of two gentlemen in top hats further behind you. Their comments are idle and impassive, as they fold up their newspapers.

"Did you read? North Carolina? —finally ratified secession."

"Indeed so. That makes ten. And Virginia meets today to ratify."

"Mmm, no surprise there."

"That will wrap it up, then. The dance is on."

No one around appears to pay any attention to their remarks.

Movement begins in the aisle out the door, and presently there you are, stepping down onto the station's wooden platform in the morning sunshine, in a small crowd that is rapidly dispersing to greet the friends or associates who have been waiting for them. It's always pleasant to see the smiles and the waving hands, to hear the subdued laughter and the small talk of folks reunited. There's a banjo playing, from somewhere, with a sprightly rhythm that lends a jolly mood to all the commotion on the platform. The music may be faint but it lifts your spirit, even if there is no one there to meet you. It doesn't matter—this is a solo jaunt, and you'll be seeing old friends very soon anyway, in town, once you get squared away with the reservation at your hotel. Moreover it's quite exhilarating just to be back in Pontiac, in good springtime weather, with plenty of time to take in what has changed and what is still familiar.

The train remains in place behind you, motionless alongside the dock, the engine up ahead emitting a blast of hissing steam now and then. A few more passengers are stepping down from the car doors, and there's a man stacking five or six small crates on the dock, each crate stenciled with "West & Wilson" and below it, "Sewing Machine" —it's hard, swift work just to gather his inventory off the train. He must be the local sales agent. You take a last look around at the car, catching the eye of the conductor. He's standing close to the side of your car where the large letters "D&M" remind everyone that this is the Detroit & Milwaukee Railroad line, and the cap of his hunter green uniform also has a tiny rendition of the same logo on the front crown. The two of you exchange respectful nods, the conductor tacking on a casual salute. So, then, now to make your way into town for the Hodges House hotel. Should you walk? It's only a few blocks away, up Saginaw Street, and you're carrying only one valise. Ah, but why not hire a ride, and let a horse-drawn carriage take you slowly down the center of Saginaw Street so you can look upon the sights and people on either side. You cross the dock and begin descending the stairs to street level, and at this point you're reminded of another fact of life in these times—the unfortunate odor of sulfur or lime or whatever it is that's emanating from the coal gas plant, just south of the depot, that feeds the town's illumination gas mains. There's only a brief whiff or two that reaches your nose, but it's enough to justify moving on from the area.

At the bottom of the short staircase you can now free yourself from the procession of people making their way out onto the lane. While you look around to see the available choices for a carriage ride, a thought crosses your mind about the good-and-bad aspects of the general situation you're in just now: that is, on the one hand you have to put up with smelling the obnoxious factory odors; on the other hand, you're hearing some enjoyable banjo music, right here in the lane, where you discover the source of the music. There are two men seated on stools, one plucking a 5-string banjo while his colleague rests idly with a fiddle in his lap. The banjoist wears a bowler hat, but the fiddler is bare-headed; oh, of course, there's his felt top hat upside down on the ground in front, ready to accept any monetary contributions from the admiring public. And there you are, admiring the banjoist's rendition of "Shove that Pig's Foot Further in the Fire," so it's altogether fitting that you pull out a half-dime coin from your pocket and toss it down into the hat. This brings a respectful nod from the fiddler. Good, then. Now let's find a ride into town.

There are two carriages parked below the depot building on the little connector lane that leads to Saginaw, both of them one-horse hitches. Their drivers stand nearby in attentive postures, glancing over the arriving crowd and conveying an appearance of available-for-hire. No takers for now so it seems, aside from the numerous flies buzzing about the horses. You can take a moment, therefore, to make your choice. The first carriage is a fairly good-sized vehicle, sort of a converted wagon with double seats in front and a flatbed behind for luggage. For your purposes it's really too large a rig and probably a bit bumpy. The second one appears more appropriate, a smart-looking cabriolet[6], two-wheeler, with a single padded seat for driver and one passenger sitting side by side, and a narrow bin behind to hold your valise. On the front of the dashboard the words "Livery" and "J. H. Morris" are painted in large, gold letters. You'll take this one. The driver is a young man, ginger-haired and freckle-faced, happy to transact a short ride to the Hodges House, and the fare is reasonable. The two of you climb up to the seat from both sides while you tell him that you're not in a hurry and would appreciate a leisurely pace along the way. He nods and settles in, and with a flick of the reins his horse begins its well-familiar re-

---

6   Cabriolet, or "cab," for hire in this situation.

turn trip to the center of town. Soon the cabriolet is proceeding down the connector lane, at first barely outpacing the several pedestrians who also heading towards Saginaw Street or to one of the several family carriages that are parked along the lane, awaiting an arriving traveler.

It's only a short ride down the lane to Saginaw, perhaps a minute or so, and as you sit side-by-side with the driver you can hear the bustling and voices at the station diminishing behind you, and watching the horse in front you imagine its relief in getting away from the flies, most anyway, except for a few of the more energetic ones still tagging along. Clip clop clip clop. It's good to be moving away from the coal gas plant and its intrusive odors, although now you're discovering that your driver's shirt is definitely overdue for a good washing. Ah well, these are the types of smells that you will just have to get used to during a two-day stay in town. Clip clop. When the cab has safely separated away from the crowd the driver offers up a question to see whether there's any interest in small talk.

"Fair ride in from Detroit, sir?"

"Yes, thank you, very pleasant. Less than an hour, even with the stops in Royal Oak and Birmingham."

"Not much of a journey nowadays," he agrees.

True. The train ride was comfortable, uneventful really. The coach car was clean, with upholstered seats and a modern ventilator system; moreover, outside conditions were right for opening windows without worry about the exhaust smoke billowing in, which helps. Your car was about half full. A few of the passengers were soldiers in blue army uniforms, as one might expect these days with the war getting underway; and other young men, new recruits you're guessing, on leave and going home to Pontiac to see their families one last time before mustering in. Observing their expressions and quiet demeanor it was clear, to you at least, that they were feeling confident and important, and perhaps for the first time in their young lives, very grown up.

Here, now, your buggy is pulling into the intersection with Saginaw Street and the driver steers the horse left to head north into town. It's the main street of Pontiac, and impressively wide here, this close to town, in contrast to the narrower country road that it is trailing off to the south towards Detroit. Looking back in that direction you can see that it's a "plank road" covered with narrow logs and roughly sawn lumber boards laid closely side by side across the width of the road, which, as a form of pavement, over time becomes firmly settled under the wheels of so many wagons rolling across the top. This serves well to support the heavy traffic, especially on bad weather days, though it makes for a fairly bumpy surface. But from this point northward into town the planking becomes gradually sparser, with a few short stretches where it has been completely removed and loose gravel spread out in its place—apparently the authorities are trying out a more permanent improvement to this important thoroughfare.

It's surprising how many wagons are moving along Saginaw. You wouldn't think there would so much activity this far from Detroit. Everyone is staying off of the central strip of bumpy planking, and it's interesting how the strip seems to serve as a median such that there is a flow of traffic heading north on the far side, and a southward flow, less busy, on the near side. Accordingly, your driver steers your cab across the planking to reach the far side where he has to spur on the horse for a few moments in order to fall in ahead of a large, two-horse buckboard in the northbound flow.

Up ahead now is Pontiac, and you can see how Saginaw descends slightly for a few hundred yards until it crosses the Clinton River, and then rises again as it runs through the main commercial area off to the horizon. You'll get a better view soon enough, but for now your attention is drawn to neighborhood on your right, with its tall chestnut trees and small, tidy homes. The immediate attraction is the sight of a large construction project, just off the road, for what will evidently become a very large building—a church probably?

"That's the new Methodist Episcopal going up," the driver explains, nodding and just as impressed as you are. "They say it's going to be just as big as any of the churches in town, maybe even taller."

Well, that's something. Looking upon the dozen or so workmen, and the scaffolding, and the piles of lumber and bricks, it makes you wonder whether the town's commercial area will also be expanding this way south. The view to your left side is not as encouraging, however, leading back to the railroad depot, an area that is mostly storehouses and supply yards. Maybe these properties will be supplanted with newer houses and storefronts, some day. There's one advantage, at least, in that the offensive odor of the coal gas plant is not as detectable at this distance.

"What was that side street back there by the church? Was it Judson?" You think you remember, but you ask the driver anyway. There are no street signs.

"Yes, Judson Street."

A minute later the cab is approaching the next street corner on your right, which you know is Church Street, where you will be heading later today to attend a reception at the home of the McConnell family. It's supposed to be one of the more notable houses in Pontiac, you understand, but you can't see it from here—it must be almost a half mile away, down Church.

The bridge over the Clinton should be discernible by now—and it is, but just barely, blending in with the look of the street as it does. In fact the bridge is as wide as Saginaw itself, and its top surface is practically flush with the street, since enough dirt has accumulated on the bridge over the years to hide its original structure. Saginaw, at this point, no longer has any planking and is now entirely packed earth, so this dirt surface just continues uninterrupted across the bridge and on into town. When the cab actually reaches the bridge the only indication you have that you're crossing a bridge is the pedestrian railing on either side. But you do notice it—if anything, how the river crossing presents the lowest point of elevation before making your approach into central Pontiac, like some historical marker to remind you that this was, and still is, a mill town. Now the cab is on a gradual upslope as you head towards the larger buildings ahead.

Welcome, traveler, indeed. The town is obviously growing and has no trouble accommodating all this traffic passing through on its main avenue. Saginaw must be at least thirty yards wide, running between the raised wooden pedestrian boardwalks on either side. There's the big Hodges House hotel, up the street on the left side, perhaps a couple hundred yards away. While you're still passing mostly wooden buildings on either side you can see ahead that the "The Hodges" is where the main business district really begins and stretches beyond for a few more blocks. That's definitely the heart of Pontiac's commercial center, where the buildings become much more substantive, all of them corbelled brickware two and three stories high, crowded together along both sides of Saginaw all the way out to where the steeple of the Congregational Church pierces the sky at the horizon.

The grand view up the street encourages you all the more about making the trip, and so far it's been an enjoyable ride in the late morning air. The driver has been receptive to a few bits of conversation, tactfully so, just the usual pleasantries and some encouraging remarks about the Hodges House. He agrees with your remark about how Saginaw is a fairly busy road—but the boy's nonchalance is not helpful. There ought to be a lot more hubbub and excitement in the street, you would think, what with the war being declared and all the northern states raising armies to invade the South, and you've been anxious to return to this town to see how everyone is faring. But right here on

Saginaw Street the scene appears to be only normal, that is, busy as usual but mundane . . . Surely there must be more going on beneath the surface. Rallies, demonstrations, speeches, you'll just need to read the papers and ask around. Why aren't there more soldiers on the street, like the ones that just came in with you on the train?

"Rather quiet this morning," you observe aloud, "I mean, for a town in wartime."

At this the driver is eager to inform you otherwise: "Oh, but you should have come here last week. The 'Wide-Awakes' put on a swell affair.[7] A nighttime march, you see. Hundreds of folks—the whole town, all of us—parading up Saginaw, torches blazing a flags a-flying. So we all amassed at the end up at Huron, there by the courthouse and the steeple (he points towards Huron two blocks ahead) where the city swells made their grand orations. By ginger, it was a grand sight."

The cab continues along towards the Hodges House, passing a few wagons that are slower or even stopped in the middle of the street, and now it catches your notice that many of the wagons are empty, which you remark out loud to your driver.

Turning to look at you, he responds, "Farmers coming in to buy seed. Springtime, you see. Planting season."

"Ah, yes. Of course." You might have known as much, even for idle chatter.

Clip clop clip clop. You resume observing the street around you, and the boardwalks. As for pedestrians there really aren't that many, which is probably reasonable for mid-morning on this business day, just another Thursday, war or no war. Presently the driver has to rein in the horse to a full stop, and you both sit and wait while a pair of drovers leads a group of hogs in front of the cab, from right to left

---

7   Wide-Awakes: political activist clubs in the 1860's in northern states, sometimes paramilitary, supporting Abraham Lincoln and the abolitionist movement. They organized large, after-dark processions in city centers, torch-lit and characterized by loud fanfare and ending with rousing political speeches.

towards the west side of Saginaw, perhaps on their way to a livestock pen in the depot area. The hogs slowly waddle past, eight, nine . . . eleven of them. Twelve. You watch the scene, and during the pause it's amusing to count up the hogs as examples of wealth and prosperity in this growing town. Livestock, hardware, traffic: all of them measures of progress, of a sort, you suppose.

Truly, though, this region of America has continued to grow at a remarkable pace during the past 24 years from the time Michigan attained statehood in 1837. Back then Pontiac was only a small settlement in a forested, swampy wilderness, comprising only a few homes, mills, and taverns. But ever since, the population has swelled with newcomers from the eastern states pursuing better prospects for employment and farming. The westward movement has been greatly boosted by the Erie Canal, a viable and affordable means for entire families to move out of New England and New York and board the steamships on Lake Erie, bound for Sandusky, Toledo, and Detroit. Western territories in Ohio and Michigan still welcome the migration and actually compete to attract more settlers. Pioneers could turn south for Ohio's farmlands, or choose to head north into Michigan for its lumber industry. Michigan's interior offers vast forestlands, seemingly limitless, and plenty of rivers for watermills to power the manufacture of just about anything. Stay in Detroit if you want, but it is already crowded and expensive, and most folks landing there now prefer to keep moving deeper into the territory, and the next county northward, Oakland, already has 40,000 souls and is developing fast.

Amidst all this popular migration Pontiac is recognized as the established gateway, and has been since the settlement's earliest days. After the War of 1812, explorers and surveyors heading northwest from Detroit naturally started out on the "Saginaw Trail," the old Indian path through the forests and marshlands, which after a day's journey inland brings you to this good ground, "high" ground suitable for farming and construction, with easy access to two rivers, the Clinton and the Rouge, suitable for generating mill power. The reputation spread, the settlers followed, and in due course the mills went up, here and there: saw mills, plaster mills, grist mills, woolen mills—and the small villages that built up around them. The old Trail evolved into the modern toll road it is today, and a railroad line was soon laid out over the same route. So here, being the first major depot stop into the frontier, Pontiac's commerce serves not only as the hub for Oakland County but also as a springboard for the pioneers moving further into the woodlands, towards Flint, or Saginaw, and Shiawassee County. And, logically, in Pontiac a new local industry has emerged with rapid success, that of the manufacture of wagons, wagon wheels, and related items, to supply the needs of so many travelers.

A true boomtown it is, with all the character and action that comes with it. Here, then, is where the significance of Pontiac starts to become conspicuous. The Hodges House hotel is situated at a point where Saginaw's gradual upslope reaches its highest level, which accentuates the commanding presence of the 3-story hotel over the smaller wooden buildings nearby. It seems to anchor the southern end of the main commercial district where, beyond the Hodges, you can see how the buildings stand contiguously, all of them 2- and 3-story revival-style Romanesque facades with corbelled brickwork. Clearly, now—*that's* the real "downtown". Wide boardwalks on both sides, large storefront windows, awnings, gaslights, and pedestrians, wagons, herded livestock—it is, as they say, the largest "inland" city in Michigan. And that street up ahead could rival any scene in Detroit, if only for a few blocks and even if Saginaw Street is still unpaved.

Pontiac's own population has reached 2,500 and finally just this year, 1861, the village has become incorporated as a city. Now they have a mayor instead of a group of trustees to oversee all of the development. This new civic arrangement defines the city's executive authority more openly, albeit still reliant on a half dozen patricians, those merchants and lawyers who will surely make an appearance at the McConnell's this afternoon. The dry goods businesses in particular—like Willard McConnell's—have brought in a lot of money, supplying those lumber camps inland, and now there's more money being made by a number of wagon manufacturers. Throw in the city's status as the Oakland County seat and that means judges, attorneys, business contracts and investment. The money and the method are coming together right here, in those downtown buildings up ahead.

It should be an interesting day, exploring downtown and then going over to the McConnell house for the big reception. Meanwhile the cab rolls along again up Saginaw, no more hogs or other livestock to contend with. Now there is more evidence of enthusiasm for the war cause, judging from all the patriotic bunting strung up on gaslight poles and building fronts.

"Say, that cross street by the Hodges—that's Pike, isn't it?" you ask.

"Pike Street, yes sir. I can let you off at the corner."

"Fair enough. That's fine."

HODGES HOUSE BY MRS. M.A. HODGES,
Pontiac, Mich.

The driver steers the cab towards the left side of Saginaw, and past the main entrance to the Hodges House hotel by the corner with Pike. Just around the corner he pulls to a stop near the boardwalk on Pike, yanks back the brake lever with his left hand while still holding the reins with his right, and then turns to you as if to convey "here you are." But he sees that you are looking past him, towards the boardwalk along the side of the Hodges, and he turns likewise to see what it is that you're watching. Easy enough to guess—it's a gentleman, middle-aged, conspicuously sartorial in a fine broadcloth frock coat and high silk hat, striding resolutely up Pike Street and will soon pass by the parked cab.

Again the driver turns back to you, to offer some helpful explanation. "That there's Horace Thurber. On his way to work no doubt. He has a store on Saginaw, selling hardware, tools, metal goods. And stoves. Thurber is one of the big bosses around here. Made a fortune, believe it. One of the town's founding fathers, you might say."

"Hmm," you nod approvingly. No need to divulge that you're already acquainted with Horace Thurber. You make a quick decision not to call out to him, though, as there is another man with him, a younger associate, and the two of them appear to be engaged in some serious dialog. It wouldn't do, just now, to interrupt; perhaps you'll run into him at the McConnell's.

The men walk past, and with that, you're ready to leave the cab. Now as you prepare to get off, you've been wondering whether your young driver fully understands the larger picture of what is happening here in this town, historically, or is it just another work day for him.

HODGES HOUSE,

IRA G. HODGES, PROPRIETOR,

Corner of Saginaw and Pike Streets,

Pontiac, Mich.

BOARD ONE DOLLAR PER DAY.

Stages Leave this House Daily.

But, first things first: you pay him the fare, step down onto the street, and hoist your valise out of the rear bin. Very good, then, *arrived all well*, as they say.

"Have a good day, sir," he calls to you from up on his buckboard seat, and then hesitates, seeing that you may have one last question for him.

And you do: "Planning on enlisting, then, are you?"

"Oh yes! Me brother and me together. In the cavalry, as soon as the next call is posted—they'll see the pair of us know our way around horses. And I can't wait to get out of Pontiac. Hah! Too many *injun* names around here—like this one for our own town. They named this place after a savage, don't you know."

"So, yes, but Chief Pontiac was a great leader, actually, among the Indians."

The lad only grins, shrugging his shoulders. "Savages, anyway."

"And you know, back then after the war[8] they probably just wanted to name a town after something definitely American, just to stick it to the British."

He doesn't look as though he's interested in the history.

"Well good luck to you, son!" you rejoin, and you reach up so the two of you shake hands. "Your name, friend, might I ask?"

"O'Brien. Andrew O'Brien, at your service," he answers, doffing his wide-brimmed hat. Now you can see that he's a red-headed boy, and for the first time you can detect a hint of Irish accent in voice when he pronounced his name. It would seem Andrew meant to reveal his heritage, by dint of his hair and his accent, in one dramatic gesture.

"Good lad, then!" you say in closure, and Andrew flicks the reins and nods his head once in reassurance as the cab moves on.

So the livery boy wants to go forth and see the world. He's young and he's strong, and back at the depot he was clearly envious of the

---

8   War of 1812.

"fightin' men" stepping off the train in their blue uniforms. They all have their dreams. You can only shake your head and smile as you watch the cab roll away again, heading further up Saginaw and probably back to Morris Livery, you imagine. Let's hope the boy doesn't end up a mule driver in the army's supply corps. Well, still, he would get to see more of the country, and other places not named after Indians.

Now for your room. Walking now onto the boardwalk you stop for a moment at the Hodges' main entrance to appreciate the fine craftsmanship of the large, heavy door with its polished brass handle—it makes a good first impression. The lobby inside turns out to be somewhat modest in size but handsomely appointed in its décor, quite fancy, and it's a palpable change to be treading quietly over a soft rug as you approach the clerk behind the registration counter. Ah yes, he confirms, your room is ready for you. You've been looking forward to relaxing for an hour or so before lunch, and a chance to read the local papers. Maybe take a little stroll up and down Saginaw, later, since there'll be some time to spare. It must be a busy morning over at the McConnell's, you imagine, getting everything ready for this afternoon. Willard McConnell is a well-to-do merchant and you've been looking forward to seeing his house, one of the biggest and fanciest in town according to what you've heard.

WIDOWED, RECENTLY

HORACE THURBER stood alone out on Garfield Street in mid-morning, watching the front door of his house, his right hand in

Horace Thurber

his vest pocket ready to pull out his watch for another look. He was waiting for his son to emerge. No need for the watch —it had to be 9:45 because, behind Horace some 70 yards back, the D&M train to Lansing and Grand Haven was rattling northward with its usual trail of three passenger cars. The noise ebbed away and still no Daniel. What is keeping him now? Every morning they took their walk together, into town to start the workday at the family store on Saginaw

Street. Another minute passed. Horace began to feel irritated, but he became aware of it and made an effort to calm his feelings. It helped to hear the sound of a cicada bug, somewhere in the trees, start up a long, sustained buzzing trill, making time stand still while Horace gazed over the entirety of his house.

Well, Mary my dear, his thoughts turned to what he might say to his wife, *I reckon I really don't know what I should do.*

Or had he just said these words aloud to himself? It didn't matter. Horace had taken to using this phrase more and more often over the past few weeks. It was becoming a habit. The words were a comfort to him, something nobody else need hear.

Finally the front door opened and Daniel came striding out, down the porch stairs and towards the gate, cheerfully unaware of his father's resigned expression.

"Shall we?" Horace offered, and the two of them started off, up to the corner at Pike where they turned right, towards town. Horace maintained his attitude of forbearance, though he might emit a slight, sarcastic "hmff" and shake his head, assessing the younger generation's lack of regard for punctuality, lost while away at college presumably. But Horace enjoyed these daily walks with his son, and the private talks that sometimes came with them. He had a few more things he wanted to impart this morning. How best to broach these ideas and not sound too awkward? It was a three minute forty-five second walk to his store in the center of town, using Pike Street to walk up to Saginaw. Horace knew enough not to say anything while the two of them were just setting off. Let things wait until they turned the corner onto Pike and made it to the bridge over the creek.

His habit was to allow himself to dwell on a run of contentious thoughts, in a pattern that was consistent and somehow reassuring: business was up, yes, and the town had made remarkable progress over the past few years, especially with the new gas lights on the streets.

And the new woolen factory. All well and good. *So why, you fools, are you so hell-bent in destroying the country in this worthless war? Invade the south? Over what—states' rights? Abolition?* All this "call" for action, and nobody ever thinking about soldiers getting killed, homes and farms destroyed. Why can't everyone just wait for all their "causes" to be sorted out peaceably. Just politics, after all. But no, no, the people crave excitement: parades, uniforms, battles, heroes, medals, reputations, dispatches . . . it was all so damn idiotic. *You would have thought by now that we had transcended the need for this kind of conflict.* And now the boys' enlistment periods were for three years! *Oh, this has just gotten way out of control.*

And then the abyss. Just as the nation was succumbing to this monstrous folly, with Horace steadily becoming more cynical and resigned

Mary Thurber
Courtesy, Lee M Withey

about it all, he had suddenly lost the one person who had always been there to set him straight, to inspire him to keep his faith. Six weeks ago, actually six weeks and two days now, Horace lost his wife forever. Mary Darragh Thurber died on April 9, passing quietly in full faith and innocence. They had married 28 years ago, in Monroe, and she had borne their four children, all survived and hale. *Why snatch her away now?* It was hard to live through all of this. *O, for the wings of a dove, far away, far away would I rove.*[9] *It was hard to watch everything falling apart, not just his family but now the entire country. It was not right for him to end each day laying down in the very bed where she had slipped away.*

Same thoughts. Same passage. Horace grinned with sad eyes and looked away. They were already crossing the narrow bridge over the

9   Psalm 55.

Clinton, their shoes clomping on the wooden planks. The river still showed some lively current today, it being late Spring, as it flowed underneath to their right and on past the rear yard of the Thurber property with Dawson's Brewery building standing opposite on the left side. The brewery's chimney was already puffing out smoke to announce the new workday getting underway.

When Horace looked again upon Daniel, and saw his son's reassuring grin in return, he could feel his own composure returning. Today was different. Father and son were heading to work, for the first time not dressed in mourning attire but in daily business clothing. Later this afternoon they were both going to Willard McConnell's home for a reception, their first social appearance since Mary had died. So there it was. Whether or not things like this mattered any more, Horace would go anyway. He would stand among colleagues and friends, and their wives, all wishing him well, perhaps

Daniel Thurber

for once in true sincerity. He would play his part, if only to remind everyone that there were still cooler heads in charge. Much was at stake, after all, for a major business like his to continue to thrive, if only for the sake of his host of customers, and suppliers, and his employers. Horace was a father and he was a pillar of this society regardless, yes, regardless. *Daniel is worried about me. He'll be watching.* Horace's oldest daughter Sarah, too, would be at the party. *She strives so much to look all grown up.*

Horace and Daniel had walked side by side this far, without a word. And for his part, these were Daniel's thoughts: *Good so far, old*

Stone Face is holding his own. He'll make it to work; he'll make it to Mc-Connell's. The home was regaining a more normal kilter. One sign: his father had taken up again his rantings about the failings of former President Buchanan, and the disastrous consequences of the Supreme Court's Dred Scot decision ("Where, where was our Congress on that one? It's a legislative matter—they should never have handed it over to judicial! Worthless cowards!") In a way, the anger seemed to help his father, restoring his alertness and a desire to get things done.

Daniel's sister Sarah was excited about the party, as any girl almost 16 would be. Their younger sisters Mollie and Lizzie seemed less distraught, although it was hard to tell, one would suppose. The past weeks had been an ordeal nobody was ready for. Daniel was at college in Schenectady when the news came about his mother, and he had made the long train ride home alone, pondering his family's future, worrying about the unfinished term left behind, and finally when walking through the door he was not prepared for the profound anguish that awaited him in his father's greeting. And all their former lives had ended, so soundly, at their mother's funeral. After the gravesite service Daniel had taken to reciting, from time to time, the words from the old Psalm 39 lament—*"O spare me a little, that I may recover my strength, before I go hence and be no more seen."* He was finding a way to come to grips with this, to carry on and earn the respect of his friends and community.

But only a few days later in April the southerners bombarded Fort Sumter down in South Carolina, and outside the grieving Thurber home all of Pontiac rejoiced wildly in a new reality, the call to war, at last, the noble crusade of their times. In those days Daniel might gaze upon a parade or a crowd at a rally event, standing alone on a boardwalk just to watch, remote, taciturn. For the most part Horace and Daniel avoided the whirlwind; it was a week later, perhaps, when Horace started going back to work managing his business, Daniel going along to help with bookkeeping and writing collection notices. Gradually the new routine took hold, around the house and in town. Then Daniel's classmate and fraternity brother Joe McConnell also arrived home from Schenectady, all hot to enlist in the army and, strangely, no longer so moved to condolences for the stricken Thurber family as Daniel was counting on. Daniel wanted help in coping with the past, and Joseph could only offer excitement about the future.

Horace's grieving was still difficult to read. He had talked about consulting with a medium to try and communicate with his departed wife, and a business associate had given him an issue of the "Banner of Light" with its schedule of séance meetings and traveling spiritualists. But Horace didn't want to go through with it, probably apprehensive about how it might be perceived in society, or so Daniel surmised. There was another instance when Daniel came across a book in the library room, left alone on a side table, an edition of works by English poets. Noticing a bookmark clip visible on the edge of the page block, Daniel was curious to see what passages his father may have selected, and he picked up the book to open it to the clipped page. What he found was a sonnet by Percy Shelley, called "Ozymandias"[10] which Daniel was not familiar with, and he was struck by the doleful pessimism delivered within its few lines. The poem was using a heavily ironic tact to decry the vanity of a powerful man and his delusions of grandeur and lasting consequence—but in the end, just another a life rendered insignificant and forgotten in some long ago history. Ozymandias, was it? Daniel idly looked upon the strange-sounding name in the title. Was this the sort of text where his grieving father was finding a measure of solace? That was a bit troublesome. Only a deeply sorrowful man, a man losing interest in his own accomplishments and responsibilities, would mark a poem like this for future reading. *Vanity, all is vanity—that's what he's reading.* Strange, though. Daniel hadn't expected to encounter the

---

10 Percy Shelley, "Ozymandias" sonnet, 1818.

notion of vanity just then in his family's library. He murmured a short "hmm", closed the book and lightly placed it down on the table.

Then there came that singular moment in the middle of all this gloom—a quiet off-hand remark by Horace that caught Daniel completely by surprise. The two of them were alone in the parlor at home, one evening after dinner, a week or so after the funeral. Both sat in silence in their armchairs, Horace holding a folded newspaper in his lap that meant nothing to him, and Daniel leaning back with his eyes closed, resolving to wait for his father to go first in calling it a night. And presently Horace started to speak, to no one in particular, but eerily, as if talking in his sleep.

His tone was plaintive, soft. What he said was to recite a verse from Psalms:

"The sorrows of my heart are enlarged; O bring thou me out of my troubles."

Daniel remembered the psalm, too, and as if in answer to his father he spoke up to recite the next verse,

"Look upon my adversity, and forgive me all my sin."[11]

Then after a minute or so Horace spoke again, quietly: "You know, I just want to hear her breathing heavily, close to me, like when we were young."

That was all he said, and the room was again silent. Daniel did not move in his chair and he had not opened his eyes, but his brows furrowed, because inwardly he was completely jarred by these words coming out of a man as stoic as Horace Thurber. He would never have expected the saturnine, old man to express such intimate thoughts. Then he came to understand how sublime was this moment, and he realized he would never judge his father the same way again. The two men continued to sit, in tick-tock quiet, another rainy April evening spent doing nothing.

---

11   Psalm 25: 16-17, using the Book of Common Prayer 1789 version.

Now it was May, and here they were together again, walking to work in their morning coats and top hats, same route on Pike, same bridge now behind them, and up ahead the Hodges House hotel, grand and steadfast as on every morning. The normal racket of a business-day morning on Saginaw Street was becoming more audible, and now as they were crossing West Alley they could smell the horses in VanAtta's Livery where a few cabs were being readied just outside the large stable entrance. Daniel waited for his father to start the usual morning dialog, which would probably hit again on reasons for avoiding the military and returning to Union College in the fall. Or, maybe the time was right to think about selling the house and moving to one of the new neighborhoods further out, making a fresh start for all of us. *Or push me off on old Elkanah Comstock again to see about work at his bookkeeping and investments.*

And sure enough, on schedule as if mutually agreed, Horace began his remarks.

"You know, Daniel, if you really think it best to be in uniform these days, I could talk to Judge Baldwin about putting you into the home militia. I'm sure he could arrange for an officer appointment, and you could still..."

Daniel tactfully arrested this speech with a "No, Father, I really don't feel the call," and he went on to reassure Horace that the plan was to return to Union.

"Fine, then, I was just thinking how Joseph might be leaning on you about it. Willard and Joseph being so fired up to go save the world like they are..."

Daniel knew that his father was just taking his temperature, so to say, and this was all right with him. But Judge Baldwin? *No, Gus Baldwin needn't be bothered with such a favor, and the home guard surely would find enough staff officers of acceptable character.* Given that Horace and the

Judge were fellow Masons, Daniel could just picture them discussing his prospects at one of their Knights Templar meetings.

A few more paces, and Horace now brought up his next concern, all the young women who would doubtless be making an appearance at the reception. "So, you'll be meeting Julia Comstock at the McConnell's?"

Uh-oh, here we go: the matrimonial stakes. Daniel had learned the benefit of tact in these conversations. "I'm sure she'll be there, yes. All the seminary girls will have to make an appearance, I should think."

"Well, no doubt," Horace grinned in agreement, before making his point, "Julia's a fine girl, Daniel. Hard-working family, too. Julia graduates next year, doesn't she? Just so you know, Comstock and I would be gratified to see the two of you become, well, serious. After you finish Union."

Daniel smiled. "Oh, I know. Julia is truly something. We can all agree on that." Interesting. His father had said the same thing yesterday, almost word for word. And regardless of whether Daniel and any girl were becoming "serious" it was clear that his father only meant well. Especially now, a harmless topic, and why not.

But leave it there for now. Perhaps tonight, after the McConnell's reception, there might be time for a more thorough review of prospective daughters-in-law. Truth be told, Horace's occasional hints about society girls had succeeded in moderating the topic, and even though marriage was something still years away, Daniel could abide his father's passing interest in the matter. The issue was: Horace would only be perplexed to hear his son's views on what constituted a suitable match for a Thurber. Not Julia Comstock, and not necessarily the top family daughters—all those girls dispatched to the female seminaries in Cleveland or Monroe or wherever. More to the point, two girls that Daniel did find attractive came from less prominent families, take for example Emma Adams and Carrie Holley. What might Horace say about them? Daniel had spent much time talking with both of them last December at the Wisner's "Bell Party." Both of them were at the Union Public School and were working afternoons in town, Emma in her family's millinery (*"Finest hats and gloves in town!"*) and Carrie at Crawford's confectioneries. They were pretty, and they were enjoyable company. Emma was too young for him, being 16 he presumed, about the same age as his sister Sarah. Carrie could be 18 by now, graduating from the high school. *Carrie is also quite witty—it was flattering just to gain her attention. She certainly has changed while I've been away.* Daniel had still been distracted by the girls' faces, Carrie's mostly, afterwards when he was back in Schenectady. There was a second-floor classroom window that provided a view of the Adirondack Mountains far off on the western horizon that always seemed to awaken his memories of the Wisner party.

And Daniel had just seen Carrie again, last Friday outside the courthouse, when she and her mother had been speaking with Mr. Thatcher—Carrie's mother was also the mayor's sister—and Mr. Thatcher had beckoned to Daniel to join them and be introduced. The conversation had not lasted very long, and Daniel regretted not having more to say. But even if he couldn't remember the words Carrie Holley spoke he could recall absolutely the way she smiled and the sound of her voice, her laugh, her teasing expression. And perhaps every word, too, or whatever words that he dreamed she had said, whichever, it didn't matter. One memory about that meeting was very clear in his mind, however: as they were all walking along the crowded boardwalk there was a situation where Daniel and Carrie had separated for a moment to get around some other people coming the opposite way. Upon rejoining they had whimsically called out "Bread and Butter" at the same time[12], surprisingly, causing delight and embarrassment to them

---

12   "Bread and butter": a superstition that if a romantic couple are separated temporarily e.g. walking around an obstruction on opposite sides, that upon rejoining they should both say these words to avoid having an argument or quarrel soon afterwards.

both. Daniel hadn't meant to say anything so flirtatious by uttering the old saying, purely out of habit. But the girl had said it, too.

He started to ponder whether he might even broach the topic of Carrie with his father just now. Horace was already acquainted with her family, through the mayor and all, and probably wouldn't mind that they weren't old society, "Pioneer" families. Horace should appreciate how in these modern times a family's good works should earn as much respect as an old social standing. Even if old Stone Face wasn't impressed with Mr. Holley selling farm equipment, or Mrs. Holley separately running her own dressmaking shop, he could still commend Holley's industrious daughter. Couldn't he? Anyway, the "candy girl" was probably not on the guest list at McConnell's today. *Let's wait and see.* Daniel kept these thoughts to himself.

Horace had more to add. "So, you'll be taking Sarah with you. You'll remember to reserve a shay at the Ogle Livery – Sarah will be all dressed up. Good. Now, keep an eye on your sister at the party. We don't want Sarah cavorting about with those Cleveland girls. They're a little frivolous for my liking. Your sister is still only 15, not ready for that fancy crowd. I always thought she was too young for those 'bell parties' put on by Mrs. Wisner, but your mother insisted. Well there you are—the Governor's wife enjoys a sport of matchmaking, seeing the town's eligible daughters all gussied up, issuing invitations more like subpoenas . . . Now we've got Cleantha McConnell taking her turn at putting all the boys and girls together. I guess I'm, I'm . . . I just worry things moving along so fast this summer."

Daniel noted how that last sentence sounded almost like an apology. He waited for his father to talk his way out of these ideas and on to something else. Which Horace did, and continued, "Oh, and I suppose you'll be called upon to say a few words about Joseph. Have you prepared anything? There's going to be some important faces at this show. You'll want to make an impression."

"Thank you, yes, I'll have a few select stories sure to embarrass the honoree"—Daniel here made a slight reverential bow, catching his father's eye—"even as I honor The Cause."

Horace pushed out his lower lip in mock approval. "I know you will." And then with a wink, "Don't let your friend Louie Drake steal the show."

They had reached the corner of Pike and Saginaw, where they stopped near the main entrance of the Hodges House. Horace had just remembered that he meant to ask his son about his application for a clerk position at the courthouse, working for Mayor Thatcher during the summer months—was the appointment today?

"No, father, it's not today. Actually I'm prepared to talk with the Mayor about it this afternoon at the McConnell's.

"Mmm, yes, good."

"And by the way, I'll be joining Drake and George Mathews for lunch today, before we all go to pick up Joe at the depot. Does that work for you? I won't see you until the party, then."

"Yes, Daniel, that's fine." Now the two of them needed to cross over Saginaw and turn left to walk along its east side to Horace's hardware business half way up the block. They watched the traffic while deciding whether to cross here at the busy corner, or walk a bit further northward beforehand.

"Daniel, this morning start with a look at those plow bolts we took in yesterday."

"I will. Don't worry about Sarah."

Then while their wait was lasting a few more seconds, without looking at Horace directly Daniel threw in an extra compliment:

"You look good today, Father."

Levi Bacon , Jr.

Let me tell you, this town is a marvel. Business here keeps growing like it will never stop. And the prosperity is really starting to show. You can't lose. There's a never-ending file of settlers heading north, and everything they forgot to buy in Detroit, they pick up in Pontiac. Dry goods merchants like us, or Thurber, or Paddock . . . I reckon we set up shop in the right place at the right time, don't you know. And well-earned, I say. The early times around here were not so cozy, building a town surrounded by swamps and bugs. It took a lot of work, believe me. But it's paid off, for a lot of people.

Now you're seeing many of the first families starting to sell off some of the acreage that they bought up so cheap, before there was much of anything here – just take a look at all the chancery notices in the Gazette, every week. Keeps lawyers like Baldwin and Draper pretty busy. Our own Mayor Thatcher too, for that matter.

Willard McConnell and I go way back. We started this business some 20 years ago, in '42, when I had first moved here. We were young, but we knew our business. Pontiac was just getting started. You know, both of us married to Captain Parke's daughters: Willard with Cleantha, and me with Sarah. Sarah and I had a baby boy 10 years later. We named him Hervey, after the Captain. Ah but the birth was hard and we lost Sarah after it, and the boy too, after only a few months. Then a few years afterward I married again, with Emma, and started a new family. Kept going. Even served a stint in politics as a state rep.

So it's like this: Willard and I have always been good partners, but our family lives began drifting separately, you might say. He's been so deeply involved with that Methodist Episcopal Church of his, running the Sunday school, singing in the choir. He helped them get their first church built over on Pike, and now he's really in charge over there, putting up their big new place on south Saginaw, not far from his house. He and I have served on a number of committees together for planning schools and other investments – like the gaslights project. I can tell you, there's no finer man in Pontiac than Willard McConnell. Oh, he's what you call a builder.

Saginaw Street

Clinton River, east of town

A VISITOR'S STORY,
"Stroll on Saginaw"

THERE IS time to relax for a few more minutes in the hotel room, now that you're dressed and ready for the reception at the Willard Mc-Connell house later today. Glance at the calendar in your notebook: Thursday, May 23, 1861. The reception won't start until 4:00, and it's still only about 10:30 according to your pocket watch which lies open on the side table. Good thing you already finished most of your personal grooming early this morning before leaving Detroit, so there's some spare time now for Pontiac, and you have been looking forward to seeing a little more of the town before finding a place for lunch, yes, somewhere outside of the hotel. The day has turned out clear and sunny, a few clouds, some breeze, and you have decided that if it stays this nice through the afternoon then you might walk the half mile to the McConnell's party and enjoy the opportune weather. You should. Visiting this area has been a pleasant experience thus far, and quite comfortable. Your arrival at the Hodges House, the largest hotel in the center of town, has been an immersion into plush accommodation and fine service, which adds to your surprise overall at the improved quality of life around here. Your room is well appointed, right down to details like the bayberry candles and the candle snuffer with snuffbox attached—unnecessary but nicely ornamental. The staff are well-mannered, and the menu laid by for tonight's dinner looks promising. It's an impressive introduction to this thriving city, a wilderness landscape only a generation ago. Remarkable.

The room is on the north side of the hotel, third floor, with two windows looking out onto Pike Street. There's not much happening out there just now, but if you peer over to the right you can see where Pike intersects with the town's main thoroughfare, Saginaw Street. It offers a glimpse of a busier pace of pedestrians and wagons, if not fully audible through the glass then at least assuring that a typical day in town is well underway. Well and good. Having spent an hour or so catching up on correspondence you can now turn around to look back over the room, idly appreciating its furnishings, the bed, the armoire, the wall-hangings, and the small side table next to your chair where you had put down the newspaper, folded into quarters. It's the latest issue of one of the two weeklies in town, actually a few days old already, but still interesting for a traveler like yourself. Of course there are several articles about the country preparing for war, and the latest news from Washington, it being a month now since the southern states all seceded. It is equally impressive how much other news, local news, still occupies most of the paper's columns. There are commodity prices, business advertisements, chancery announcements, political letters, local gossip items, society reports. One fanciful story catches your attention: the balloonist Thaddeus Lowe had completed a 6-hour flight from Cincinnati, landing in Hamilton, Ontario. Apparently he was trying to sail his balloon *Enterprise* to the vicinity of Philadelphia but the winds took him way off course to the north. So now, according to the article, Lowe has been asked by the mayor of Hamilton to stay on for a few extra days and participate in the city's festivities honoring Queen Victoria's 42nd birthday! Of course! And why not? It brings a smile to read about yet another exploit of the daredevil Professor Lowe, aptly converting a navigation mishap into a chance to make some quick cash from all the Canadian revelers who'll gladly pay for a ride in the *Enterprise*. Balloonitics! My goodness – didn't Lowe just survive a close call on his last flight which landed him in the middle of South Carolina, with this war just getting started . . .

But there you have it. Whatever the news from faraway places, life in Pontiac goes on with the usual fare, and it will continue to do so, you suppose, until there is an actual battle somewhere. Anyway, now that you've read all the latest about the town, you're ready to walk about and see things first hand.

Let's attend to some final touches before you leave the room, starting with a quick rinse of hands and face at the basin on the side table by the door. The water is still fairly fresh, and the embroidered hand towel is well cleaned and bleached, deserving a careful refolding after you dabbed your face dry. Set the towel down on the table, and take out a copper nickel for the maid and leave it on the table. Now a look at the wall mirror for a final, gratuitous touch of the hair, it's all good. Keep the *Gazette* issue? No, no need. Let's be off, then. You reach up to turn down the gas valve on the wall pipe, diminishing the sconce light. Pick up your key off the table, and check to ensure you have your purse. Anything else? No—and so it's out the door.

The hall is quiet, carpeted, and spacious, another reminder that your stay is in a first-rate hotel. You lock your room door and walk towards the stairway, passing the common room where a maid is refilling her pails, pumping water up from the basement cistern—indoor plumbing on the second floor, very modern. Further on, a young attendant is arranging a bouquet in a tall hallway vase. He's putting the long-stemmed flowers in one-by-one, such that the end result is bound to be a bit spindly and sparse, but the red-orange petals are already very conspicuous in the empty expanse of the hall. Orchids?—no, too early for those, before June. A second look, then: wild columbines. The lad pauses in his work to wish you a good-morning, a friendly gesture all the more noticeable in the late-morning quiet. Good training, you note.

Down the main staircase, into the main lobby, and here at last are a few other gentlemen guests and staff of the hotel, and quiet conversations, and sounds of papers being shuffled, all the normal indications that you are rejoining the active world. There is an elderly woman sitting behind a small table evidently selling dried fruits, and there's also a stand for a shoe shine although currently not manned. On a side table there are small stacks of newspapers for sale: local papers such as the *Gazette* and the *Jacksonian,* and a few national papers -- older issues of *Frank Leslie's Illustrated* and *Harper's Weekly*. And of course, the latest issue of *Peterson's* magazine for the ladies. You step around to the front desk to leave your key with the clerk, a clean-shaven man about 30 with wire-rimmed glasses and looking quite very sure of himself in his matching coat and vest. He asks whether you will be having lunch in the hotel's own restaurant.

"I wasn't planning on it, but tell me, what hour are they serving?"

"Noon to one. Today's menu," he adds, his tone taking on more of a sales pitch, "includes a plate of oysters, canned oysters from Maryland, just delivered this morning."

You can see through the French doors to your left that the restaurant tables are just now being set for the lunch service. "Enticing . . . perhaps I'll be back in time, but I really shouldn't reserve a place for lunch. I do anticipate returning for dinner however."

"Very good, sir. Oh, dinner is served from five to seven—today they are offering veal blanquettes, German style. Of course, with a full menu of other plates."

"Done! I'll be there," you acquiesce politely, and follow up with a request to check for any messages for you arriving this morning; really your inquiry is only meant to help close the conversation. "None?— very good. See you this afternoon."

"Very good, sir," he replies.

You're about to turn away but you notice how he's still looking after you, good naturedly, as you're leaving, and so you pause, just for a second, and come back with one more question, probably the one question posed most frequently these days:

"I expect you'll be enlisting soon, yourself, then?"

The clerk's face changes at once to a more solemn look. "Not right away," he says. "The army wants a man for three years, and that's a long hike for a man like me with a wife and children to leave behind. I'll let the younger lads go first, and wait to see if they haven't won the war by next spring." His response is courteous, but definite, and probably repeated to many guests of the hotel.

"I see." What is there to do but nod back at him, respectfully. "You sound like a reasonable man."

"Very good, sir,"—the standard reply, once again.

Now you feel some embarrassment for having asked such a personal question. Your best tact at this point is a congenial "You will excuse me" along with a cordial nod and smile, and then make a tactful exit out of the lobby, through the front door and out onto the street. No harm done. Yes, let's get on with the business of seeing this town!

Stepping out onto the plank board sidewalk you can take in the scene here in the heart of town. It's worth a pause to look around. Saginaw Street is still lively with horses, carriages and wagons, and more people now, busy with errands and walking in all directions here in the downtown corridor. The sun is just about directly overhead—there are no trees to provide any shade, although shade is not really a priority hereabouts; moreover, your street views of the town are left fully unimpeded. Here where you are standing at Pike and Saginaw you have two impressive hotels, your own Hodges House and the smaller Peninsular Hotel nearby, and directly across from you is the Crofoot Building with its ground floor storefronts including Linabury's general store, a barber shop, and the American Express office. The real downtown district is clearly off to your left where the tall, brick buildings, "city buildings" replete with cornices and decorative parapets, continue almost a quarter mile up to the intersection of Saginaw with Huron, which you know is really the chief hub of the city. That intersection is the downtown's northern end, anchored by two of the city's most ascendant structures, the Congregational Church and the county Court House. That's the direction to go, if you mean to do some exploring.

There's a point to some of this exploration, of course, which is to check on the status of a set of three adjacent buildings which may soon be up for sale, if not already available. These stand on the east side of Saginaw, midway between Lawrence and Huron. They were still occupied, last time you saw them, but word was that the owners were entertaining ideas for improvements or outright sale. You've been meaning to take another cursory look, walking past them by chance, and if you like what you see you might inquire with a contact you have at the Court House about the situation, the owners and legitimate financiers. Overtures may be a bit premature; nevertheless the tact is to make your name and your interests known candidly.

So this will be your itinerary: a walk up to Huron, to take in more of the sights along Saginaw, and drop in at the new Court House before heading back this way for lunch. Perhaps you'll run into the mayor or some other acquaintance along the way, although no one is expecting a visit, but regardless of real estate conditions the real aim is to see what's going on these days, especially with the war becoming a reality. Moreover just now is a good time to take a little walk. It's nice to feel the morning breezes, which are not only refreshing but they also help to render unpleasant street odors less noticeable.

Begin your walk by crossing Pike to head north along Saginaw, timing your advance through the horse-drawn traffic and taking care to step over any "spots of unpleasantness." This is a moment to appreciate another civic improvement: at a main intersection like this one, the city has installed wooden crosswalks that connect to all four corners. The boards are set almost level with the street, and you can imagine how this would be a great help to maintain your footing especially in winter or on a rainy day. Thank you, city leaders.

At the far corner when another idea comes to mind: this would be an opportune time to drop in at the McConnell & Bacon dry goods store, which is just a few feet further up from the corner. Sure, given that the main event later today is the reception at the McConnell family home, why not drop in now at the family business and pay a call on Willard McConnell's partner Levi Bacon, a good acquaintance from your last visit to Pontiac. Indeed it's possible you won't catch him at the reception if he has to stay minding the store. Better not miss a chance to check in on Levi.

Here it is, McConnell & Bacon, and you turn into the door below a big, painted sign displaying the partners' names. Once inside you proceed a few steps into the front sales floor where there are several tables arrayed throughout the interior, mostly topped with folded woven items and bolts of clothing materials, curtains, area rugs, and so on. Other tables along the sides are displaying hardwares and household furnishings. The stock of clothing materials is impressive, including wools (probably from the Mathews mill in town) and new blends of wool with cotton or flax. There's also a selection of intricate Wamsutta floral prints from New York. Looking down the store's interior, which is narrow but extends deeply, you see a few women who are examining and picking through some of the bolts of pink-colored dress fabrics, and two young men in blue army uniforms, bargaining with a store clerk for a box of six mosquito bar sets. Ah, there – you spot him, Levi – in the far corner, in gartered shirt-sleeves, chatting amiably with another woman customer about to purchase a portable lantern. (You recall seeing a large advertisement for lanterns at McConnell and Bacon in yesterday's Pontiac Gazette.) What a friendly man, and what a charmer. Everybody knows Levi. Originally another "pioneer" from New York, he's a Pontiac man from way back, and now in his 40's a popular community figure.

And true to character, as he speaks to the woman over the counter you can easily overhear him tell her "Not to worry, Mrs. Foster, the constable's credit is never a problem at McConnell and Bacon." He beckons to a clerk to come assist with the packaging and jute twine, turns again to his customer with a smile to say "Johnny Hill will wrap it up for you," and the purchase of the lantern is concluded with a most deferential nod and thank you and come back soon. Now free to turn his full attention on you, he breaks into a cheerful greeting for all to hear, and you can't help but enjoy that irrepressible, avuncular spirit – right away you accede to it, nodding with a resigned smile. Your boisterous reunion gets underway as Levi runs through a number of catching-up questions. He wants to know: how is your family; have you been to Grosse Ile and are the Biddle's still there and is Lisette Forth still with them; how is Detroit and have they put up yet another big building along Griswold Avenue; are you going to the McConnell's gala; how is the room at the hotel and if you need anything, you see, old Ira Hodges is a good friend so just let me know; here, how about a jar of peaches—would that be of interest to you? "We had a bumper crop last year of late peaches," he adds. "Pontiac Seedlings—top quality fruit, it is."

MC CONNELL & BACON.

Daring Burglary.

On Monday evening last the Store of McConnell & Bacon was broken open and goods to the amount of $1,500, were stolen.— The Burglars entered from the back way by boring through the pannel of the door, below the latch and making a hole large enough to let a hand and arm through by which the bolt was withdrawn, and the door opened. Messrs McConnell & Bacon had probably the largest and richest stock of silk goods north of Detroit, every piece of which, was taken, besides other rich goods that could be easily carried off. The cash drawers were opened but the change was left apperantly untouched. One of the clerks slept up stairs, but heard nothing.

Eyes of suspicion are upon certain doubtful characters, one or two of whom had been in town but a short time. The guilty were doubtless aware that McC. & B. kept a very large stock of costly silk goods, and were acquainted with the premises, and with the manner in which the door was bolted. It is really to be hoped that the officers may get a " sure thing " on the miserable night-thieves.

Pontiac Gazette
August 31, 1860 p.3

Levi continues to converse on other topics but your attention is largely distracted by the glass jar holding the peach preserves. It's one of those new jars with a metal screw-top that you've heard about but haven't seen before.[13] The design is simple but clever, with the metal circular band snugly holding a separate disc-shaped glass lid to the threaded neck of a glass jar. No doubt it's all easily produced at the factory, and inexpensive to boot. Interesting—yet another little convenience for modern times. But now is not the time to be carrying a jar of preserves around town. You tell Levi you'll come back tomorrow morning to pick up a jar for your return home.

Levi breezily waves off your response as he goes on to say that he will try to make it to Willard's party, after he closes the store at 5:00. The reception is meant to be a salutation for young Joe McConnell's enlistment in the army; surely, much of Pontiac society will be on hand to wish him well. (Probably we'll see more parties like this soon enough.) It seems like he just got back from his year at Union College and now he's off again to march south with all the troops. "As you can imagine, in the swirl of all this war footing it's hard to keep up with people."

Speaking of which, Levi continues, there's also the story of the great "Pike's Peak expedition," or more to the point, the return of two of the McConnell clan to Pontiac after a summer out west prospecting for gold in the Rocky Mountains. Evidently Willard's younger brother Abiram, and Willard's oldest son Parke joined a group of "fifty-niners" looking to get rich quick. Turns out . . . too bad—they didn't. But they did bring back a wealth of tall tales about their adventures. Including one of Levi's brothers, Corbit, who had also set out in the fall of '58 and he's still out there, so he must have found something worthwhile.

---

13   The jar was designed and first produced two years before, in 1858, by John Mason, a tinsmith and inventor in New Jersey. His jar would become known as a "mason jar."

"Anyway, Abiram and Parke will be at the reception this afternoon, so be sure to ask them about it. Parke is now managing the store up-stairs—McConnell & Baines—another of Willard's commercial ventures."

"Yes, I saw the sign. What's the business upstairs?"

"Drugs, groceries. Doing well enough. Abiram being a doctor, you know, the venture made sense for both Willard and Abiram, although Abiram has become more of a customer than an investor. He also has his office up there." Levi shakes his head and smiles and then adds: "But can you imagine that fellow, a successful doctor, selling off his share of the business to Baines and then leaving behind a wife and three children to go panning for gold out there in the wilds? I'd say we're all lucky to have him back in one piece, practicing medicine in Pontiac where he belongs."

Levi pauses to nod goodbye to the soldiers who are walking out with their newly purchased mosquito bars ("I'm sure you'll be glad to have them in Virginia! Did you also see our gum blankets[14]? There're only a few left...") and you start out a new subject: So, how's business?

"Well, let's see ... we were robbed last August—in the middle of the night, someone drilled a hole in the back door and they let themselves in, and got away with all of silk stock."—Levi lowers his chin as he shakes his head—"But overall we're doing quite well. Actually very well, despite a whole new set of problems, what with Mr. Lincoln calling for his new army, which is buying up all the wagons and just about anything else produced around here that's made of wood or wool straight from the mills. But on the other hand, I have every mother in Pontiac coming in to buy socks and Bibles for their brave lads signing up for service. Soldiering means camping, and that means supplies, you know, personal things, whatever the army won't give you.

14 Gum blanket: made of vulcanized rubber, used for insulation under a bedroll or worn as a poncho.

So it's busy around here. And it didn't help me to lose another one of my clerks just last week, running down to those recruiters in Detroit."

More customers are coming into the store, and you should let Levi get back to work. While winding up the conversation you quickly ask about gloves, and does Levi have anything in stock?

"You can try next door at Goodman's—he carries a lot of gents' furnishings—or you might have better luck at Pittman Clothiers up the street at Lawrence."

"Oh, by the way," he calls after you, wanting to impart one last piece of news. "You know that a McConnell relative, Hervey Parke—a nephew, not the old Captain Hervey—will likely also be at the party. Keep an eye out for him. He used to work for us here at the store, years ago, until he left to seek fame and fortune in the copper business up in Hancock. He's in town now for a short visit, for the reception I suppose."

Could be interesting—a local boy returning home with stories about the U.P.[15] You've heard about Hancock, another of Michigan's boom towns. "Certainly. How will I know him?"

"Young 30's, very long beard. Well-mannered. Yesterday he dropped by just to say hello, but I think the main idea was to go upstairs and talk with Baines about supplies for his business in Hancock. Parke thinks he's also poking around for new business opportunities—for producing medicines." Levi leans closer to you over the counter to speak *sotto voce*: "I think he's built up some savings. You know he's been working up there for nine years now."

Well, no surprise there, but you nod as if to assure that the secret is safe with you, and reiterate how you'll keep an eye out for a U.P. man.

"Oh," Levi says, "one more suggestion: look for the mayor at the party. If a *Gazette* reporter is there, then Mayor Thatcher will be there, too."

---

15   U.P.— Upper Peninsula of Michigan. Copper mining with all of its supplier businesses was a thriving industry in the western region of the peninsula in the mid-19th century.

You again nod obligingly with a grin of acknowledgement. Ah, Levi. If anyone knows the comings and goings in Pontiac, it is he.

"So, then," you proffer in closing, "See you tonight—but if we become overwhelmed by the occasion, Levi, it's very good to see you again!"

"Indeed so—should the occasion overwhelm us," he replies, grinning broadly.

A quick wave, a respectful nod, and you make your way to the door. One last pause – you turn around and see that you still have Levi's notice, so you ask: "About the gloves, then. Best bet . . . ?"

"Pittman's," is the reply. Levi's lower lip is pursed outward, augmenting his positive nod.

You're out the door and you turn left on the boardwalk to resume your walk up to Huron. There's Goodman's store, right next door. You can see through the large storefront windows that many of the counters are empty or only sparsely stocked. Probably not worth going in to ask about gloves, and Pittman's is up ahead anyway at the corner of Lawrence, the next cross street. What a sure source of news is Levi Bacon. There's much to mull over, about war preparations, business ventures, gold rush expeditions. And another McConnell relative to look for at the party—Hervey Parke with a long beard. This day of exploration is underway.

Back on the boardwalk this section of town is becoming noticeably more crowded. It's getting close to lunch hour, after all. But moving among all people, close up like this, is by itself fascinating. Everyone around you is so focused on what they're doing, where they're going, it's as if you alone are able to observe and enjoy the liveliness and the sights. Along the edge of this commercial canyon the street-level storefronts are a continuum of businesses, all sorts of retail businesses, dry goods stores, offices, barbershops, apothecaries, a telegraph office, livery stables. There are signs up high showing the store names in large letters. There are large, glass storefront windows. There are gaslights on tall posts, and there are hitching posts placed in front of the boardwalks at regular intervals. You pass under storefront awnings, glance over the window displays, step around courtesy benches, nod and tip your hat as you exchange good-mornings with people making their way in the opposite direction. And meanwhile there is all that commotion still going on in the street, like an irregular parade of wagons and people and livestock. You may be declaring too much in it, but what you see does strike you as having a certain energy, a feel of progress. And once again, as in past visits, you're reminded of the colorfulness of your surroundings – the clothing patterns, the hats, the storefront signs and window displays. It's a far more vibrant world when experienced in person, compared to peering at it through static black-and-white images. In real life it's a marvelous assortment of colors. Even the brick exteriors of the buildings are sporting various hues like mustard yellow or cobalt blue. There is an exciting, modern look to it.

Some of the shop names are familiar, like Dean & Hovey Drugs and Groceries, and Judge Crofoot's law office, and Goodsell's dry goods store. You recall seeing these names in a published directory— names only, as there is no system of numeric addresses in a town this size. Some of the named buildings, the larger ones that rent out office spaces, are referred to as "blocks" in the directory, so the renters might indicate their location as being in the "Davis Block," or the "National Block," or "The Old Stand." Other listings just indicate which part of Saginaw Street where they may be found, for example, "Saginaw, bet. Pike and Lawrence." Apparently no one is worried about customers not finding them, and there are no maps to be had, anyway.

Further on, and here's another general store—Butterfield's. That must be Isaac and Fanny Butterfield's place. A woman is standing under their awning. Do you recognize her? It's not Fanny. Must be an employee, or some other shopkeeper, having a short break by the looks of it, just standing there with no hat, her arms hanging idly, her eyes closed as if resting for a few moments outdoors. Her serene, motionless posture amidst all the passersby draws your attention, and makes you wonder what could be on her mind. But you need to mind your own way on the boardwalk, stepping around people and avoiding various chairs and boxes. It's a two-block walk from Levi's to Huron Street, and you're approaching the end of the first block now, at Lawrence, and here is Pittman's at the corner. Pittman and Herrington Clothiers—seems to be a busy enough place. Let's take a look inside.

The layout is similar to Levi's shop with various tables arrayed under a white-wood ceiling, and a long counter running along the left side. A clerk approaches momentarily, and upon hearing your inquiry he is gratified to say that the store has just received a shipment of leather gloves (civilian gloves becoming a scarce commodity these days) delivered all the way from Saugatuck, made by the Wallin Leather Company. In fact you are familiar with Wallin products and their reputation for good quality, and as soon as a pair is found that fits just right, the sale is done. Simple enough. It's likely that this thick pair comes from leftover inventory meant for the winter season, but no matter, you only need them for handling your luggage or other dusty items, and the price is appropriately off-season. Your hands will be clean for company at the reception.

On Saginaw once again, you cross the Lawrence Street intersection, past Oliver Adams' hat store, and keep heading north, occasionally negotiating your way through an increasingly crowded boardwalk and avoiding a loose pig and the child

The Old Court House

running after it. Now on this last block getting closer to the Court-house you're seeing fewer stores and more offices for lawyers, insurance agents, notaries public . . . and, on the other side of Saginaw there they are, the buildings you've been meaning to evaluate in case they go on the market. There used to be three of them but now there are only two, with an empty lot now showing where the furthest north one used to stand. The remaining two appear to be still occupied, although clearly they are outmoded, one-story structures that might readily be razed and replaced. Should you walk over and take a peek inside now? Let's talk first with someone who should be more familiar with the conditions and current owners. Anyway for now you can't see any posters or notices pasted near the entrances.

Staying to the west side of Saginaw you keep walking until at last you're approaching the Court House on the big intersection of Saginaw and Huron. Looking at the Court House makes you slow down your pace as you take in the view—the large colonial revival-style building stands unique in the southwest corner, and the sight of it comes abruptly as there are no more storefronts to block your view. There is a cast-iron fence surrounding the grounds, enhancing the stateliness of the property from the ground up, and your eyes are drawn skyward, over the Italianate roofline, up to the enormous cupola which adds almost another two

Cong. Church w/
completed spire

stories in height. They say that Pontiac's Court House is even grander than the state capitol in Lansing, and now you believe it.

Across the intersection, cater-corner, stands the Congregational Church, its steeple still incomplete but already ascending as high as the Court House cupola. The pairing of these two landmarks is clearly the main focal point of the town's skyline, a special place, marking the chief crossroad of the town. On the northwest corner stands the big

Davis building "block,"[16] which keeps a commercial aspect on the crossroad, complementing the civic and religious structures, while the southeast corner . . . well, that's something a bit less grandiose: the old Baptist Church, a modest building compared to its Congregational Church neighbor. In a

Davis Block

way, though, it also contributes to the overall character of the intersection by providing extra open space around its street corner, something of a respite from all the commercial buildings packed together nearby.

This is as far as you meant to go, on this walk. It's enjoyable now just to take in the scene and the layout, with Saginaw running north-south and Huron running east-west, always crowded with vehicles and riders heading every which way, a kaleidoscope of throngs and racket now at full tempo. Huron Street runs westward off to your left, and leads to the Waterford area with its large farmsteads; eastward, off to your right, it will take you past the

Baptist Church

big mill businesses and become a plank road leading out of town towards Lapeer and other farming towns in rural Oakland County.

16　Davis Block: formerly a two-story building, the bottom floor being used as the first Presbyterian Church and the top floor used by a school academy; now undergoing a conversion for commercial use.

"Well call me Ishmael!"—a man's voice from behind interrupts your ruminating over the scene. A quick turnaround and here you are facing a man glaring back at you, severely, although within seconds you can sense that he is only teasing you with a deadpan expression which soon converts to a warm smile. Why, it's Mr. Elkanah Comstock, an old acquaintance, a fine gentleman about town, the kind who can lift your spirits just by recognizing you. He must have just come out of the Court House yard through the gate.

"Oho! Ishmael it is, then! Good morning to *you*, sir."

Your greetings and small talk follow happily, but cordial nonetheless, as you understand that Elkanah is busy with some paperwork errand, doubtless a contractual matter now filed inside the valise he is carrying. He looks quite fit for a man in his fifties, as one might expect for someone bearing as much social impact and authority—in addition to his banking business, Elkanah is also the director of the school board. You were hoping you find him in the civic neighborhood, and here he is.

"I'll bet you're here to scout around the Bagg and Flower blocks," he says. Wouldn't you know it, Elkanah artfully cuts to the chase for you, always a step ahead.

"Yes—Bagg and Parker Drugs, and Flower and Killam Hardware."

"Of course. Bagg and Parker will be moving out, doubtless, but probably not this summer. Theran Flower's farm machinery is doing well and he might stay on. Everyone wants to wait and see how long the war lasts and what it will do to the businesses around here. Especially the wagon makers."

He's right. Real estate values in a frontier town like this could react dramatically until the army completes a successful campaign. You echo Elkanah's opinion with your own "Of course," and then nod graciously to what he has to say next:

"I'll spread the word, though, that you may be an interested party."

That's what you wanted to hear. And from there, it comes out that you will both be at the McConnell's later today ("Oh, very good, we can catch up then!"), and he believes his two nieces, Julia and Emma, will be there, too, as they are home from the Cleveland Female Seminary. Can Elkanah join you for lunch? No, he has a lunch engagement with his former partner Kelsey, who wants to introduce yet another investor looking to invest in the drugs business. "But how about this new city of ours, then?" he asks, as if to affirm his own satisfaction. Before you can voice your agreement he has launched into enumerating the various civic improvements brought about by Pontiac's patricians and aldermen: they have unclogged and cleaned up the Clinton River; they installed gas mains and gaslights on the streets; improved the plank roads with spreads of gravel; laid in the walkboards at the street intersections; made some very visible aesthetic improvements on several of the prominent buildings in town including this Courthouse, and the Baptist Church, and Thurber's big general store.

Yes, yes, you're nodding responsively, the enhancements are clearly evident. And you point a finger back towards the Baptist Church across the street as you mention how it seems bigger, which allows him to confirm, "Yes—the entire front of the building has been extended by 22 feet."

"I think your father would be proud to look upon it today." You're paying respect to Elkanah's father, the Reverend Elkanah Comstock, who was the first Baptist minister to settle in Michigan permanently, a popular early pioneer and very successful in growing the Baptist church membership. Son Elkanah can now tell you, "Yes, a fitting legacy, don't you think? God rest his soul," but he deftly reverts the topic away from the flattery. He can't help but tout the lovely new homes that the local patricians have been building, which have dramatically enhanced various outlying properties around the city limits, especially around nearby Orchard Lake. "Or Willard McConnell's place, on the south end. Wait till you see that one. It really is quite something, for a little backwoods town like Pontiac."

But there is one headache in all the expansion, however, and that is the need for more school space. Yes, understandable, part and parcel. Elkanah's chief concern is the local public school which is no longer adequate for the city's growing population. The school really needs to be replaced altogether. Meanwhile there has been interest in starting a private academy, and the Ladies' Sewing Society had established a fund for founding a female seminary, like the one in Monroe, but it looks like that effort is dying out. We'll probably see a push to build a military academy, too, although it won't amount to much if this war turns out to be only a quick dalliance.

And just at that moment, right on cue with Elkanah alluding to a potentially inconsequential war effort, comes a timely *fermata*: from afar, a bugle call, or rather a number of bugles braying, from the fairgrounds training camp. Evidently the "Pontiac Volunteers" militia unit is holding some form of practice for beginners on these horns, and the resulting blasts are rather *unrefined*, almost comical honestly. It causes both you and Elkanah to pause for a few moments in shared amusement, and you can tell by that highbrow, caustic expression on his face that something witty is coming, and sure enough he finally delivers with "Well, apparently the players are not graduates of our school." Good point, yes, likely not.

"Nonetheless, I applaud the effort," you respond. Elkanah nods with facetiously solemn approval.

And with that it's a fitting point to break off for your respective affairs, Elkanah to his lunch and you to your sightseeing. The parting phrase "See you at McConnell's" is declared by both of you simultaneously, and the busy banker turns to head back south on Saginaw. You watch as he strides off, and you see him pulling a watch from a vest pocket for a quick glance at the time. Now it's time for you to start thinking about lunch. Something light, but not oysters, let's say. Where to? Earlier you had noticed the "Arcade" saloon across from the Hodges, hmm – they had a sign promoting an attached billiards room, but it shouldn't be yet a rowdy scene this time of day. Besides, you remember seeing a couple of army officers heading inside, a good indication of abstinence and suitable rectitude for the establishment and its clientele. And, you might catch some war news to boot if you're able to join a table.

You allow yourself one final viewing around the Saginaw-Huron arena, really to afford Elkanah a head start before you tactfully follow in the same direction, and then begin your return trip down Saginaw. Better move further away from Huron before crossing over to the other side of Saginaw, where it's relatively less crowded. Presently an opportune time comes to reach the east side boardwalk, and now you can take a closer look through the windows of the Bagg and Flower blocks—actually nothing much happening inside—and you continue strolling down the long, two blocks, south towards Lawrence and then Pike. Thinking back on Elkanah, you could say fairly that it was a lucky encounter. Interesting man. His life story makes for quite a narrative, as you remember it: married twice, he lost his first wife at the birth of their fourth child, and the baby, too. He remarried a year later, had two more children . . . and then up and took his entire family out to California for eight years during the gold rush! They all made it back to Pontiac, *Dei gratia*, whereupon Elkanah took up banking with Marcus Kelsey. With very good success, apparently. How's that for a resilient life? Hmm, if you see Elkanah again you should ask him about Marcus Kelsey, what he's up to, these days.

The boardwalk along here is less crowded and a bit more manageable, allowing for more leisure to look in through the store windows as you pass by. There certainly is plenty of diversity in the items for sale, and every store looks well stocked. It's good to experience the town this close up, in the midst of the boom times of 1861, in a land of plenty. It took a lot of work and risk to get this far. These people all around you on Saginaw Street – they're probably too busy working, moving about, too preoccupied to realize how they are living out the dreams of pioneers who came before them. This *is* that old dream, here and now, going on all around you. And that red-headed kid who drove your cab this morning can't wait to leave it all for the war. In the end it's all the same old spirit, the same hunt, now in a modern version.

You wonder whether that woman will still be there, lolling in front of Butterfield's, that you espied earlier. No . . . no, she must have gone back inside to her shop. Anyway, the Arcade is not far away, just across Pike. May as well go see what's on the menu.

SENIORS

THE THREE schoolgirls were in the far corner of the classroom where they were supposed to be busy putting away books, but their main effort at the moment was to stifle their laughter, even while ex-changing wide-eyed looks at each other which only made it harder. Carrie Holley had to cover her mouth with one hand, and used her other hand to wave at Fannie Pittman in a desperate appeal to keep quiet. The other girl, Emma Adams, had a tendency to snort in these comical situations, and sure enough, snort she did. This caused a brief sobering effect on all three, readying themselves for an inquiry surely to come

Carrie Holley

from Miss LeRoy, their teacher, who had been engaged in her own work in the front of the room, but facing away as she chalked words on the blackboard, preparing for the next class. The room was empty except for the four of them, so there was no other noise to obscure a stifled snort.

Happily, though, the remark from the girls' teacher was just the opposite:

"Thank you, ladies. Keep up your work—I have to step away for a few minutes. I have a meeting in the recitation room with Professor Corbin and Miss James."

Thereupon Miss LeRoy turned to her desk, picked up a few papers and briskly walked out of the room. The door behind her pulled shut, and now Carrie, Fannie, and Emma had the place to themselves.

A large place, and rarely this empty. This was the second floor of the two-story Union School, in a classroom spacious enough for some fifty or sixty desks, these days arranged into three groups, such that up to three separate classes might be conducted at one time. Right now the entire room was unoccupied for a lunch break, and Carrie, Fannie and Emma were working at the far right end, by the bookshelves along the side wall. They could hear the muffled sounds of teachers speaking loudly in the other classroom across the hall where lessons were still going on.

"Now can we *please* finish this task, without risking our reputations any further?" asked Carrie aloud, with feigned frustration that evoked only facetious laughter from the others. They were supposed to be serious about their work, helping Miss LeRoy prepare books and materials for her afternoon sessions. They were expected to behave like responsible girls in the senior class who had been requested especially for this task.

But it was late May, in the very last term of their high school career, and it was late morning, just a few minutes before lunch break. They had been working steadily along, in fact handling the job methodically and correctly, but they had been teasing and whispering to each other about the summer ahead, and, being close friends they also were whispering about boys and about suspected affections between others in the class. The badinage had reached a silly point when Fannie playfully pulled up the hem of her skirt a few inches from the ankle to expose some stocking above her shoe, her eyes half closed and her lips pouted. Carrie looked askance at her in mock indignation and whispered "Oh, you floozy!" which put Emma over the top and unable to contain her sudden outburst, that hallmark snort abruptly honking through her nose. After at a few seconds of suspenseful silence it was . . . no matter, anyway: evidently Miss LeRoy

Emma Adams

wasn't paying attention, or even if she had heard everything she didn't mind a little fun this time of year, with summer approaching.

The job at hand was to organize a pile of books and store them neatly on the long bookshelf, and there were three different groups of books to be sorted accordingly. One was the Spencer's Penmanship Compendium, another was the McGuffey Reader volume six ("Sixth Eclectic," for senior students), and the last was the McGuffey Spelling Book. Most of the spelling books were quite worn and had to be handled somewhat carefully; they were the oldest and would soon need to be replaced, and the girls knew how everyone managing the Union School wanted to preserve these as long as possible. Most of the older students respected the need to avoid the cost of providing new books.

Emma was working with the McGuffey "Spellers" and had stopped to open up one of the books to flip through the pages.

"What are you looking for?" asked Carrie.

"To see if it had the word 'telegraph'. It doesn't. But it does have the word 'semaphore'[17], wouldn't you know it."

"Well, maybe the next edition will. I'm sure the Webster's has it."

Not that it mattered how to spell telegraph, which was easy enough, like telescope, with its prefix "tele" someway meaning "long distances." But Emma was interested, as she was fascinated by the novelty of reading the telegraph messages that sometimes came to her household from faraway friends and relatives, and to imagine them preparing to send this information just minutes before. The world was becoming smaller, it seemed. Her parents had just received a telegram from her brother Anson informing them that he was about to board a train at Williams College in Massachusetts for his trip back to Pontiac for the summer.

Spencer's Penmanship Compendium

The girls had gathered all of the books from the desks in the classroom. After these were put away they would have to pull out a number of school slates and place them on the desks for the mathematics lessons after lunch. These smaller slates for individual use were now supplied by the school to all the students; in the old days which the girls remembered, each student had to bring their own slate that they owned, but now that the classrooms were equipped with a large blackboard on the front wall the small slates were used only occasionally for individual student activity. Miss LeRoy kept all the chalk sticks on her desk, handing them out only when needed.

17 Semaphore: a system of using flags or moveable mechanical arms for long-distance communication of messages.

There was also a pile of the students' practice papers, with each student's name written at the top, which needed to be reshuffled into alphabetical order before being placed in a stack on the shelf. This was the task that Carrie had taken, and she had to be careful to avoid smearing ink onto her fingers where there might be small amounts of excess ink in the writing, or in cases where she might apply a blotter.

Thus occupied with the books and papers, the girls were not in a hurry, as they wouldn't be able to go outside with their lunches for another several minutes anyway. And it was enjoyable to have a few minutes of privacy together and, with Miss LeRoy out of the room, talk to each other in normal voices. Fannie finished with her pile first and walked over to the large windows to look down over Parke Street and the Clinton River mill pond just beyond it. On the other side of the mill pond she could see the buildings of the mills where they were producing lumber, or flour, or what-have-you. Miss LeRoy had allowed the girls to open some window sections to let in the springtime air; not only was the air coming in but also the sounds of chirps and chortles of robins—or were they bluebirds—and the subdued, steady splashing of the huge mill wheels on the river, which was pleasant, and the more distant noise of the wood-cutters inside the mills, which was monotonous.

There was another sound, that of men shouting in the distance, which Fannie knew must be the militia soldiers training over at the fairgrounds, out of sight beyond the mills. This had been going on for a month or so, since the war was declared, and by now everyone was getting used to it. Sometimes after school let out, the girls with their classmates would walk over there to see if anything interesting was going on, and if the troops were formed for marching in dress parade, it was a spectacle worth waiting for. Watching from afar at the fence, the girls would try to pick out the boys that they knew. It was very strange to see so many young men behaving in such a disciplined manner, lining up, shifting their stance or their muskets immediately all together, and moving about in lockstep as if their formation had become a single ominous behemoth. The girls had never seen anything like it. The grown-ups who had also come to watch seemed to approve of these actions, admiring the boys' movements as if they knew that such capabilities were only natural and had always been there. There was some chiding about the boys' clothing, a hodge-podge of various militia uni-

forms and civilian attire; and about the absence of flags in the drills, and the fact that some of the recruits were still carrying wooden sticks instead of muskets. The girls nonetheless were still spell-bound by all the movement and pageantry, and the quickening sound of snare drums.

For those who were young it was a novel sight, unusual, and exciting. And it was a new experience to see teachers and parents looking on, so animated, argu-

Fannie Pittman

ing, wanting more news, talking about the country. All of this fuss and bother going on nowadays was on Fannie's mind, even as she watched the Clinton River continue to push the millwheels slowly around and around. In the schoolyard below there was a crabapple tree, its pink bloom now almost entirely turned to white, its flowers still fragrant, plainly. And so the scenery outside the window was just what one might expect, for the season, and too mundane for Fannie.

Emma joined Fannie at the window and the two girls stood pondering the tableau outside for a few moments.

"I love looking out windows," Fannie said. "It seems to stop everything in the world like a picture."

"Hmm," Emma agreed.

"But I suppose it's not true, is it?"

"No."

Carrie was smiling to herself with the idea that Fannie of course would appreciate an artistic view through a window. The Pittman's were all talented musicians and singers with a flair for the arts. And Fannie spent many working hours assisting Mr. Bray, her uncle, in his photography studio, which must be giving her an eye for the subjects' posture and attire. Fannie often wore gossamer shawls to school that were simply outrageous.

"What if we lose the war?" Fannie asked. "I mean, what if they let the Southerners start their own country, and they have their own capital, and their own flag? You think we'll have to change *our* flag again, and take some stars off of it?"

Carrie pondered the idea. The school had just amended all of it flags by adding another star to the middle row to stand for Kansas which had become a state last January. The flags all looked a bit off-kilter with the middle row of stars not centered and leaving a space for another star, for the next state, whatever that might be. But now, if the Confederate States separated from the United States, then *ten* stars would have to be taken *off* the United States flag.

"Perhaps you're right," Carrie answered. "Then we would have only fourteen states and fourteen stars. I suppose the blue corner of our flag could be replaced completely, showing just fourteen stars. They could put them in a circle like the old Revolutionary War flags."

A few more moments passed in quiet reflection before Fannie felt moved to speak her mind:

"I'll guess neither of you is going to the McConnell's this afternoon."

Emma shook her head and said "Not the Adams family," with a tone of ho-hum, almost cheerful acknowledgement.

"Nor the Holley's," rejoined Carrie. "My Uncle Erastus is probably going, if Mr. Wisner and Mr. Thurber will be there. But my father is calling on customers and won't be home until late, and I'm supposed to work at Crawford's today after school. You know, Mrs. McConnell only sent out invitations this week, because of her son coming home on leave, and she had to wait to be sure."

In fact none of the three girls would have expected their families to be invited, for that matter, since only top society would be going to an event like that. They had only heard about the reception themselves from talking with girlfriends who had just returned home from boarding school, girls who were the daughters of those top society families who *were* going. But even if the McConnells' reception was only an afternoon affair, in honor of Joe McConnell joining the army, as far as the girls were concerned the point was this: that many of the town's most eligible bachelors (or, at least, *future* eligible bachelors) would also be in attendance to help see him off.

The real reason, however, for Fannie's question was to probe whether Carrie might actually be going, since it was likely that a special someone would be there, one Mr. Daniel Thurber, recently home from college in

New York. This was a treasured secret shared only among close friends, how Carrie had so fallen for Danny Thurber. The romantic part of the story started with the Bell Party last Christmas, when Danny had first approached Carrie and the two of them spoke for a long time together, Danny clearly becoming more and more captivated by her. Normally he was a reserved young man, taciturn by nature and reputation, but there he was, in the midst of a crowded party, as expressive and animated as any schoolmate their own age while Carrie, usually chatty and engaging, for once behaved so out of character, suddenly becoming so refined and graceful.

Since that one occasion, the girls understood that whenever anyone spoke of Danny Thurber, it was a special subject for their friend Carrie, a place where her affections might be respected. And envied. The fact that Carrie rarely even mentioned Danny's name only made the idea of her relationship all the more compelling.

The situation was fully acceptable to them and made sense in terms of an overall social viewpoint. Carrie's uncle was the town mayor, Erastus Thatcher. And Mayor Thatcher was a close associate of rich, old Horace Thurber, a leading merchant and one of the town's renowned pioneers. And Mr. Thatcher had said he was going to hire Mr. Thurber's son Daniel to a position at the town hall during the summer while Daniel was home from college. So for the schoolgirls this was plenty of connection between the Thurber's and Thatcher's and Holley's. Fannie and Emma were mostly worried that Carrie might not pursue the attraction enough to keep Danny's interest, if she felt the match were beyond her reach socially. It would spoil all the romantic appeal of the story, indeed the enchantment, for everyone

Emma now voiced the unanimous opinion: "Carrie, there must be some way for you to turn out at the McConnell's. Couldn't you get away from Crawford's store for hour or so?"

The point was, Carrie's uncle would be there, and he would likely never report to Carrie's mother about Carrie attending the party. He was, after all, Danny's boss at the courthouse, and Danny would be there of course, being Joe McConnell's best friend and all. The girls knew well how Mayor Thatcher had a mischievous bent for this sort of subterfuge. Besides, wouldn't it be fun to run into Molly Bacon, and Ella Draper, and the other girls home from boarding school who would surely be there as well?

"I suppose I could get away, just for an hour. I'm not really dressed for a fancy tea, though, am I?"

"Oh I'm sure Danny wouldn't mind!" Fannie insisted. "There will be so many people there anyway."

Carrie went back to shelving books, but it was evident that she was thinking about how all this might succeed, without appearing too . . . designing.

Emma watched Carrie for a few thoughtful moments and then offered this encouragement: "You know, you will be the most interesting girl there."

". . . and-the-PRETTY-est," Fannie added, in a sing-song voice.

Carrie stopped her work, looked up at her friends with a knowing smile and said, "Well, I think you're wrong there, you two. But it is springtime, so I'm sure you both think you're right."

Emma and Fannie exchanged silent nods with raised eyebrows in an expression to mean *yes-we-ARE-right*, and that settled the matter for the next minute or so while the three girls completed their task. Then as they were gathering their own belongings to leave for their lunch recess, the classroom door opened and Miss LeRoy walked in. A brief glance towards the bookshelves assured her that all was in order there, deserving a quick word of thanks which the young teacher gave in a cheery tone as she sat down at her desk and cleared a small area to set down her oilcloth bundle with her lunch.

"A tidy job, girls. I trust the smell of the paint hasn't been too distracting?" By this she meant the school's exterior walls which had recently been re-painted, a project that had been approved by the school board last fall. The real question was whether or not the windows should be shut to close off the scent. But in truth the scent of new paint was not troublesome at all; to the contrary, it seemed to convey a novel sense of newness, even cleanliness, so all agreed to leave the windows open as they were.

"Well, even if this place is so over-crowded inside," Miss LeRoy admitted, "at least now it looks very presentable on the outside!"

"Yes, Miss LeRoy," the girls each replied. It was a little peculiar to hear their teacher intone a hint of sarcasm in describing the school's condition. Miss LeRoy's father, after all, was on the school board and a well-known civic leader in town. But it was a widely contentious issue, how the Union School after seven years could now barely accommodate its 275 students and staff, and the town was having difficulty finding the means to replace it with a larger building.

Carrie and Emma were moving towards the door, but Emma had paused in front of the large map of the United States that was mounted on the side wall.

"Miss LeRoy," she asked, "Is our army going to march all the way down to Fort Sumter in Charleston? It seems it would take a long time."

"No, I don't think that's what they are planning," Miss LeRoy replied, looking up at the map. "The first thing is to send troops to Washington to protect the capital, like they did with our first Michigan regiment. The confederated states will be making Richmond their capital, so that's where they are gathering *their* army. You can see how close Richmond is to Washington. So I think if these so-called Confederates are going to fight us, that's where it will be, at Richmond."

The girls all stood silently and gazed at the map, obediently following their teacher's geography lecture. "Is that where the McConnells' son is going, then?" asked Carrie. She was thinking about Danny Thurber's friend Joseph McConnell.

"He must be enlisting in our second regiment. I haven't heard where they'll be sent. Possibly some troops from our state will be sent to Ohio to help the Ohioans protect Cincinnati. It's also possible our boys won't go anywhere, if the Confederates back down once they're facing a big federal army in Washington. Then all those men in the fairgrounds over there (Miss LeRoy nodded her head towards the window) will have to stop their training and go home."

The teacher's last remark brought smiles to everyone, despite an understanding how disappointed most people would be, especially the boys, if the war campaign only lasted through the summer. It would be good to free the slaves, though, whatever happened. All of the senior class had read "Uncle Tom's Cabin" and there was unanimous consent in favor of the abolition movement. What they were hearing at home were the same sentiments. Most of their parents had been raised in New England or in the upstate region of New York, where anti-slavery politics were most prevalent.

It was now time for the lunch break, in particular Miss LeRoy's lunch at her desk, and the girls made their way toward the classroom door. As they were about to pass through, their teacher made one last observation:

"By the way, ladies, I don't think the boys should march off to war with the idea that all the girls back home are only silly, giggling 'floozies.'" The girls froze at the doorway, trading embarrassed glances. Miss LeRoy had said this while still looking down at her papers, but now she looked up at the girls and with a sly grin she added, "*N'est-ce pas?* In wartime you might be called to do some real work to help support the cause. Can the boys count on you?"

"Yes, Miss LeRoy," the girls answered in unison.

"Especially you, Miss Pittman, as a daughter of a school board member."

"No, Miss LeRoy," Fannie said alone. "I mean, yes ma'am."

"Good. You'll all do your part, I'm sure. Now off with you!"

As soon as they were in the hall and the classroom door had closed behind them, Fannie spoke first, glaring playfully at Carrie, and asked, "*Now* who's the floozy?" which succeeded in drawing sarcastic "uh-huh's" from her friends, putting an end to any more feelings of unease about their teacher's parting words. The mood returned to a happier state of readiness for whatever might come next on this afternoon in one of the final days of the school year. As Carrie walked along in the hall and down the staircase she was thinking back on how Fannie and Emma had once again declared her to be the prettiest girl, which evoked the same caveat that she always recited silently to herself: Vanity . . . careful, Carrie . . . vanity. And she was also weighing the chances of seeing Danny at the McConnell's, what her mother might think if Carrie just slipped into the reception on her own, whether it really mattered to anyone, anyway.

There was another complication in Carrie's schedule for the afternoon—she was also supposed to be joining her mother at Bray's studio and pose for a daguerreotype image in one of her mother's latest dress creations. Normally Carrie enjoyed these sessions, all the more so by helping to promote her mother's business, but oh—not today, of all days, if it meant missing the reception. Maybe she could work out a plan with Fannie, who would also be at the studio—Fannie had a job there after school similar to Carrie's arrangement at Crawford's candy shop. Fannie worked as an assistant to Mr. Bray, who was her uncle, preparing his camera equipment and helping customers to position themselves for poses, and carefully situating the studio's neck braces hidden behind them in each pose. If no other customers came after Carrie's session, then the two girls might succeed in finding a more appropriate dress for Carrie to borrow for the McConnells' party. A reasonable plan, at least. They could talk about it as they walked together from school to their jobs on Saginaw Street.

But whatever happened this afternoon there would surely be other occasions to see Danny during the summer, unless he too enlisted in the army. He and Joe McConnell were roommates at their college in New York, and doubtless both shared an interest in breaking away from their studies for a year to take part in the war campaign. Carrie's father had once joked about how all the college boys could now dream about becoming army officers. But Danny's situation was different. His mother had recently passed away, and his father was not a proponent of the war, at least from what Carrie could tell from her mother and her Uncle Erastus. There were reasons why Danny should stay with his family and continue his studies. Yes, Danny was too kind and thoughtful to become a soldier.

In a way, Carrie felt reassured by Miss LeRoy's idea that the war would not last long and everything would soon turn back to normal. There had always been so much talk about the war, when it would finally happen, and how despicable the southern people were. And there had been speeches and nighttime torch parades, and stories at home to remind her that her great-grandfather was a captain in George Washington's army, and other Thatcher ancestors who had fought in the War of 1812 and in the Mexican War. But now in Pontiac all of these rote notions had given way to the reality of blue uniforms being worn on the streets and shouts and gunfire emanating from the fairgrounds, and the McConnell's sending their son Joe off to Washington, and it was all becoming all too stark. Things ought not to be happening so fast, for everyone, not like this all at once. Carrie had never expected everyone's dreams to come true so quickly, so abruptly, just as the springtime was gently returning. Was she the only one among her friends to feel this way?

Her time as a schoolgirl would end in a few weeks. She and Emma and Fannie would become eligible single women, while all their parents looked at maps and talked about the war and the generals, and all the young men made plans to enlist. Carrie had no idea how all of this might play out—there was no telling. Not now. With the world turning so rapidly these days, one thing was certain to Carrie: she and her girlfriends had talked about how in modern times a girl should wait until age 18 before she married, or wait at least until she had finished all the high school studies that were available. In the olden days many girls would marry at age 16—strong and hale for having children, perhaps, but too young to understand all the new complicated sciences and businesses that were now required for a successful family life. Emma Adams, for example, still seemed childlike in many ways, despite a mature appearance which belied that fact that she was only 17, a year younger than Carrie and Fannie. But Emma was a true friend, and great fun, and always curious to know about things, so perhaps she could be an exception to the rule for allowable age for marriage.

Rules and exceptions might not matter much, anyway, not in wartime. Carrie was beginning to feel an uncertainty about the coming summer, as if it might prove to be a bleak, shadowy period, a summer lost, with so many boys gone away and all the town preoccupied with news about events in the south. The world cares only about the war and the army, so this might not be a good year for a girl to turn 18.

Vanity, Carrie, vanity, she thought, walking out onto the school's front walk. Nevertheless, as for today, her friends were right: she may as well go the McConnell house this afternoon. If Uncle Erastus were not there, then surely she would find a friend or a classmate to seal her attendance. And seeing Danny at the reception might turn out to be the most important thing for her to do.

Sarah Abigail Parke French

What do I think of Pontiac? It's interesting enough, for a small town. It can't compare to Detroit, for things to do, but it's coming along. The gaslights help. The Hodges Hotel is quite impressive, I have to say, and some of these big new homes are just beautiful, really striking. Well, Judge Baldwin's place is a bit ostentatious, could be said. Have you seen the Octagon House on Huron? Now there's some fun – very imaginative. And my cousin Cleantha's house where I'm staying this summer is fine trappings, too, of course. I've been telling Cleantha's husband Willard to do something with the façade, oh, something more decorative, more conspicuous, like a colonnade, say. Lord knows Willard's got the money. I know he's been in Detroit looking for an architect to design a third floor addition with a ballroom. I think he should do it.

So, Willard is fairly entrenched in this town that he built, and he stays close to home. But a lot of successful men in this town have made their money in far-off places. Adventurers, you know. They keep a fine residence in Pontiac for their families while they head out into the world, traveling and working, prospecting. Look at Charley Palmer, going up to Keweenaw for his mining investments. And Willard's brother Abiram prospecting out in the Nevada territory – what I would give to go out west on a trip like that. Or Marcus Kelsey. Now there's a man. He's mining for oil in Pennsylvania, always hopping on board ship to head over to Erie.

It's no surprise to me that all the boys are jumping into the army for a march into the southern states. What they really want is just to get away and do some camping, see the country and make some noise. I hope nobody gets hurt. I'm glad my brother Hervey is staying out of it. You know, this slavery problem doesn't really affect us here, not really, and people like me are just tired arguing about it so it will be good to settle the matter once and for all, finally. When this so-called war is over, you know what I want to do? I want to jump onto one of Mr. Lincoln's big new trains that will take me out to Nevada!

The Octagon House (Dunlap House) on Huron Street

Seeley House on Lawrence Street

Methodist Episcopal Church at Saginaw and Judson Streets.
Construction started in 1861.

A VISITOR'S STORY,
"Arcade"

AS IT turns out, the Arcade was the right place for lunch.

You don't remember this place from your last visit, but apparently it thrives with great popularity among the townsfolk for meals and meetings. Swan and Allen, Proprietors, so the sign said outside the door. Apparently this place is in "Lord's Block", next to the Crofoot building, and it's definitely part of the downtown scene. On this particular Thursday there must be two dozen customers taking up almost all of the tables, so it is noisy enough in here with various conversations, laughter, the clatter of plates and flatware being set down or removed, and the sporadic scuffing of chairs being pulled in or out of position. There are three waiters per your count, dodging about at a brisk pace. Their aprons could do with some laundering, decorated as they are with various colors of stains, apparently not a concern for the restaurant manager.

It's much more boisterous in here than what you were expecting, coming in from the street, and you like it immediately. All the activity, the aromas, the talk, the faces and multifarious expressions—you want to join in. Wainscoted walls and a coffered ceiling, all painted white, help to enable the buoyant atmosphere that prevails. You can see that many of the chairs are not matching, though the haphazard mix of styles somehow enhances the comfortable feel of the place. There's a large, black Franklin stove in one corner of the outside wall to your left, its pipe extending straight up almost to the ceiling until it elbows toward the wall. No use for the stove today, but it lends a worthy appearance nonetheless. Then at the other end of the interior is an expansive bay which accommodates a couple of billiard tables—nobody is playing just now—the presence of the tables alone testifying to livelier times that will come at later hours.

In the dining area the tables by the large windows overlooking Saginaw were fully occupied, as one might expect, so you look around the scene before making your way further inside. A glance down to the floor on either side of the door divulges several spittoons, apparently made available for customers to take to their tables if they wish. Let's just not dwell on that idea for now, though it is a common indulgence of the times that you'll have to abide. And the houseflies! A number of them—no, make that a fair multitude—are buzzing freely about the room, hovering over tables, shadowing the waiters. Nobody seems to pay much attention to them, beyond some desultory hand-waving to shoo them away. You had forgotten that fact of town life, as you now review the logic of the busy street conditions just outside, where all those horses and their *production* will beget flies by the thousands, accordingly, and many of those flies will find their way into the Arcade along with everyone else. You notice that the restaurant staff have hung strands of flypaper here and there, and some bunches of feathery asparagus leaves, high overhead, to attract the flies away from customers. It's difficult to tell whether those measures are working or not.

By the time you have sauntered in a few steps from the door you have caught the attention of a trio of young men, of respectable appearance, seated around a square table which leaves the fourth side available. "Have a seat, friend!" is quickly offered, in true hospitality, and you sit down to find yourself quickly acquainting with these good sports. All are curious and delighted to learn of your out-of-town visitor status; introductions are exchanged rapidly in the lighthearted manner of long-standing friends, and your own order of lunch is made on your behalf then and there, by dint of some peremptory words to a waiter intercepted by your new companion opposite. That settled—now on cue they all look back upon you for *ex post facto* agreement: frizzled beef with a muffin?

"Yes, that's fine." (albeit more food than you intended, but why not?)

And your drink? "Yes, a shrub drink alongside will do."

You're still a little on guard, the whole meal situation having developed so rapidly, but everyone seems genuinely easy going, and it's better than eating alone. By the looks of their plates your hosts have already finished most of their lunch, and at the center of the table a large tureen is filled with empty oyster shells. Apparently satisfied with the meal just consumed, the men are content to sit a bit longer sipping from their mugs and entertaining a captive audience as well as each other. A waiter glides by and plunks down your beef plate, rather indelicately, along with a fork and a cloth napkin which is probably not fresh; the food looks presentable, nonetheless, and you're inspired to venture a compliment about the professionalism of the Arcade wait staff.

Your hosts don't agree, genteelly.

"Oh, really? Your thoughts, fellows?"

"Hmm, can't see the professionalism."

"Agreed—fails the test of observation! Your shrub may be in jeopardy, but let's not rush to judgement."

And now they all want to hear more of your story. Where are you staying? "Hodges House." Is there plumbing there now? "Yes, there are central water closets in the halls, on both first floor *and* the second floor." . . . "Indeed, it's quite a premium for a first floor room;" . . . "No, I'm happy where I am . . ."

And so on. Names are exchanged, glibly, at this point almost as an afterthought. The fellow across from you is introduced as Lewis Drake, and on your right is George Mathews. The man on your left, you then learn, is Daniel Thurber, and when you respond by asking whether he is related to Horace Thurber, a prior acquaintance, you're intrigued by the round of chuckling and rolling eyes that you seemed to have induced. Daniel then clarifies, or rather confesses, with a gracious smile that Horace really is his father. Oho! And here the other two friends offer opinions in a more respectful tone: "A good man, Horace." "A pillar of Pontiac." You mention that you expect to see Horace this afternoon, and a reception put on by the McConnell family at their home at four o'clock. This news brings wide smiles and glad returns from all three: "Of course! Why, we'll all be there ourselves!" with all manner of remarks on what to expect and whom to look for at the party. It's unanimous: an event at the Mc-Connell's is definitely 'some punkins'. If anyone knows how to stage a big show, it's Cleantha McConnell.

"A bonnie *hoose* for a grand celebration, laddies!" exclaims George, and he leans forward to add "Of course, I'll be at ease in any house that offers a private privy."

"Hah!" rejoins Daniel, "especially after three months in Ann Arbor."

Lewis Drake, photo

"Luxury!" declares Lewis, across the table, glaring at his friends in mock sternness. Now he turns his eyes directly at you. "Say, do us all a favor," he says in a more congenial tone, "and keep Thurber senior diverted, in case a certain young lady should need the full attention of Thurber junior here." Daniel responds with a mild snort in protest, also looking at you while he cocks his head at the others in a don't-pay-any-attention-to-them manner, but George is enjoying the embarrassment. "All for the best, Danny boy," he says, still chewing on a cut of beef. "You can't assume your old man will eventually come around on this one."—George now also turns his look towards you with an aside—"Love conquers all, that sort of rot. Won't work with old man Thurber. He's strictly business."

Daniel lets the topic end there, with a grin, and you're gratified to have stumbled into the good-natured fellowship of this table. Your

University of Michigan 1855
by Jasper Francis Cropsey.
Bentley Historical Library, Public Domain

own meal is placed before you, making you a full-fledged participant in the meal and the ensuing conversation, and the group's background starts to come out. It turns out that they are students at the University of Michigan, home from Ann Arbor for the summer, and have been lifelong friends growing up in Pontiac. Actually Daniel spent only one year at the University and then last fall he transferred to Union College in Schenectady, so the gathering here at the Arcade is something of a reunion for the three of them. From what you're hearing, you can tell how being together will allow them to discuss the war, that is, more intimately discuss whether to join it and enlist in the army. That question won't be resolved here in the noisy Arcade just now. It's more comfortable and far more amusing to discuss their prospects with the young women in town, especially Daniel's attraction towards some girl in the high school. And who is she?—not revealed, never mind, no need to pry.

You would like to hear more about old Horace Thurber, by the way, knowing who he is and the importance of his business in town. What is he involved in nowadays, in light of Pontiac preparing for the war? The friends deliberate for a few moments, glancing at each other, until Daniel shrugs off the topic with a brief recap on Horace's latest investment in a new wool factory, which now seems to be exactly what's needed for war production, wouldn't you know it, wonderful timing . . . yes, he's busy with that, mostly . . . no further aspirations for Michigan politics, though.

Lewis breaks into a cheerier tone, asking your opinion on the frizzled beef, and at any rate what you think of the Arcade in general. But he's not listening, and he abruptly interrupts you:

"Boys, is this not the very core of Pontiac, right here!" he proclaims, and George then rejoins with a toast to "Best oysters in town! Bottom fact!" which is received heartily with all mugs hoisted—they're all drinking ale, you surmise, not shrub. Daniel looks around to catch the attention of a couple of army officers at a neighboring table, and he playfully hoists his mug again in a gesture meant to invite a like response, but the officers only look back for a moment, indifferent, before ignoring the college boy altogether. "Well, I reckon *they* aren't much fun," he says facetiously, turning back to you with his eyebrows raised.

Lewis agrees, "Sure, and they may as well find more suitable dining down at the Ogle House, *n'est-ce pas*?" He turns to you with a playful wink. "Fewer bumptious types to contend with, I think!"

"Oh, far fewer bumptious ones, you see!" George echoes loudly, having just gulped down a swig from his mug which he now bangs down on the table, rather brusquely in fact.

It might be better for all to maintain a little more composure, with lower voices, which everyone seems to sense. Accordingly the conversation moves to the war, and whether any of these three will be enlisting in the army.

"Not likely this year, anyway. I'm comfortable enough *in mufti*[18] this summer."

"We'll be waiting see if the governor comes up with the money for an extra regiment—the army already has all the men they need for now."

"True, by the time we get there, the action will be long over with, and who wants to stand around in southern heat doing guard duty?"

Everyone having clarified their wait-and-see attitude, the talk now turns to what plans are next for the afternoon. George asks whether you need a ride to the McConnell's, which you decline, explaining that you still have a couple of errands to run, and you may have to check back at the Hodges House for any messages. The boys for their part need to finish their meal here and head over to the railroad depot where they will be meeting a fourth companion, Joe McConnell, the new soldier boy coming home on short leave to be the very guest of honor at his own family's reception. And, you imagine, the object of much curiosity among his friends.

"Joe's a good boyo," Lewis says. "He'll do jim-dandy as a fighting man."

---

18 In mufti – in civilian clothes.

George picks up on the idea. "He's had his eye on the army for a long time, ever since high school when he was completely enthralled by the Italian War. Read everything he could get his hands on. He could tell you every single French and Austrian unit that was at Solferino."[19] He brandishes his fork in small back-and-forth waves to emphasize his last point.

Lewis adds, "Oh, I think he's just taken in by all those pictures in the 'Illustrateds'[20]. Why even bother reading the articles underneath, when all you need to see is an image of crowds of jubilant southerners screaming defiance? Joe goes all in for the inflammatory stuff, I'd say."

Daniel takes a turn, "Yes, the news was making it hard for him to keep his mind on schoolwork at Union," and then he adds, smiling, "Inflammatory? Like that sketch of the fire at the Willard Hotel, and Ellsworth's fancy Zouaves climbing all over it? You have to admit, a story like that can inspire a young man."[21] He snatches up a last piece of muffin from his plate and pops it into his mouth.

"Oh, good," Lewis says airily, "Now that they've saved the Willard perhaps they'll put on another luxurious 'peace conference' and solve

---

19   Solferino in northern Italy was the site of a major battle in 1859, a strategic victor for a Franco-Sardinian allied army over the Austrian Empire. Subsequently Italy wouyld evolve into a fully unified, independent country.

20   Frank Leslie's Illustrated, and Harper's Weekly: two national publications that included sketches and artists' renditions of major news events.

21   In Washington a few days earlier, across the street from the Capitol Building the famous Willard Hotel caught fire from an adjacent smaller building. The fire was successfully contained, in spectacular fashion, by the men of Colonel Elmer Ellsworth's "Fire Zouave" regiment, camped nearby, who rushed into action. Note: "zouave" is a type of military uniform with baggy red trousers as worn by elite units in the French army; and the regiment's nickname included "fire" as most of the men were New York firemen in civilian life. Colonel Ellsworth was also a personal friend of Abraham Lincoln.

all our problems in real style. Give ole' Tippy Tyler one of their best rooms to let him think he's still wanted." [22]

"Doubtful," replies Daniel, holding up his mug before taking another drink. "The old men are done playing nice."

"Well, the 'Illustrateds' are all for marching south to give the rebels a whipping, might and main." George says, "Makes you wonder, though, who's in charge nowadays—Lincoln, or Horace Greeley."

All nod in agreement. An extended pause ensues until Lewis declares, "Well there you are, gentlemen, *et donc voilà*. Time well spent!"

And with that pronouncement your social gathering is finishing up, short and most satisfying, as the four of you push back your chairs

Colonel Ellsworth's "Fire Zouave" regiment saves the Willard Hotel in Washington, May 1861.

---

22 The "Washington Peace Conference" was held at the Willard three months before, in February 1861, when 131 leading politicians convened in a last-ditch effort to negotiate a compromise to avoid war. Former President John Tyler ("Tippecanoe and Tyler too" campaign slogan from the 1840's) was still active in politics and presided. The conference achieved nothing, and Tyler went back to Virginia where he was later elected to the Confederate House of Representatives.

and rise to prepare for leaving. George reaches down for his mug and takes a final, emptying belt; then as the mug bangs down on the table he overtly concludes his approval with two words for you, "Monstrously fine!" You offer to cover your part of the bill, but George is already moving towards the main desk and Daniel graciously waves off your gesture.

"Not to worry, friend. We'll let George put this one on Papa's tab." Lewis further reassures you that George Mathew's family—and the huge mill that they own and operate in town—has plenty of resources to spare. Daniel gives a wink and adds that it's George's turn to provide lunch anyway. All good to go, now, and your party makes its way back to the front door.

This movement itself becomes somewhat haphazard, while the boys are caught here and there to greet other friends. During this delayed exit you notice another table, closer to the billiards side, where there are two black men as engaged in their meal as everyone else. They could be father and son, both well dressed, although the older man is wearing a clerical collar and so perhaps they are not related. Bully for the Arcade—they'll accommodate any and all paying customers, Black or White. Move along a little further, now just about at the door, but there is one last interruption as two customers walking in are recognized by your college boys, and so another fleeting conversation becomes requisite. The new arrivals are slightly older, a married couple you assume. You overhear the woman calling the man "Marcus" whereas he is perhaps with facetious formality calling her "Mrs. French." She has caught your attention as evidently an outgoing sort, and witty, judging by the laughter that adjoins whatever she is saying. The Arcade's door had been left slightly ajar, until a man's voice from a nearby table bellows out "DOOR!!!"—apparently in deference to letting in any more flies—and Mrs. French deftly nudges the door almost shut with her foot, without even looking away from her partners. The impromptu meeting quickly disjoins with a round of affable farewells, too quickly for you to be introduced, but no matter, you can always ask about them later at the McConnell's if you want.

All in all, then, you seem to be getting along fine. It was very help-ful to talk with Levi at his store, then run into Elkanah up at the court-house, and now the college boys here at the Arcade. You're getting a good head start on the social scene before going to the McConnell reception, and treated to a fairly good lunch to boot. You never know what to expect during these visits, so it's always nice to feel accepted.

VENTURES

"*OHHHH, THAT'S* good," Hervey Parke said after a nod of approval, having set down his clay mug on the small table by his chair. It was pleasant enough just to start the day out on the porch in the fresh air of the morning, but a serving of buttermilk added just the right touch. He looked over at his brother-in-law Marcus Kelsey, seated in the other chair, who glanced back with raised eyebrows as if to confirm that Hervey had enjoyed his drink. "That was a good idea, Marcus. Thank you." And the two men sat quietly, relaxed in their chairs and gazing out over the yard, the road, and the town fairgrounds beyond.

Marcus picked up the pitcher of buttermilk. "No reason to rush. Another round?" to which Hervey responded with another nod and held up his mug at the offer.

"Maybe just half a pour."

And why not? The drink was creamy, and tasted fresh. It was nice to have something of a treat while planning out the day. There were also muffins available, still soft enough from yesterday, but Hervey had declined the offer, not really hungry for anything to eat. He was using his free hand to feel over his beard below his chin, out of idle habit, as if to check for any traces of spilled drink.

"Marcus, when did you want to leave for town?" he asked. Hervey

Hervey Coke Parke

remembered that Marcus had an appointment for lunch at noon, and the point was to see whether his brother-in-law might be able to run an errand in town beforehand. "Really, any time" was the answer, and Hervey's request was duly scheduled: he wanted to send a telegram to his wife, a short message just to confirm all was well and his return home to her was on schedule. Marcus assured him now that he would be glad to stop by Johnny Hall's office at the depot and send the wire, and after a sip from his mug he added, "Have you heard from Frances? When is the baby due?"

"July."

"July? Oh, you'll be back in plenty of time. First one's always late anyway."

Both men understood the chief concern behind Hervey's need to be back up north in Hancock, at Frances' side, during the final weeks of her pregnancy. It was in that same town, years ago, that Hervey had witnessed his own sister die from childbirth, leaving Marcus a widower with the couple's other 2-year-old daughter to care for. It was too delicate a topic to talk about with Hervey, now that his wife would soon take on the ordeal of delivery, her first. Apparently there was no news from Hancock, and of course there wouldn't be, now only two days into this business trip. But Marcus sensed that he shouldn't dwell on the matter as he knew Hervey only too well to misread his outwardly calm demeanor. Marcus and Hervey knew each other quite well, as way led on to way, from working together many years in the mining industry up north, managing companies and keeping the books.

And so he changed the subject: "Hervey, how is that little Grace Episcopal Church faring, way out there in Clifton?"

"Oh, doing well, thank you, doing well."

"I see. Still a beacon of hope for all those roughnecks, working so far away from their devout families and parishes and all. And with you now gone for the more genteel life in Hancock, I trust the new senior warden will keep the place alive."

Hervey didn't mind taking a few irreverent remarks about the small church he had helped to establish in the little mining town. Moreover it was remarkable how long the protestant parish had survived at all. Clifton was a rough place. Miners—my lord, what a rowdy crew. Yesterday evening after dinner Hervey and Marcus had enjoyed reminiscing over the old times, the stories, the mishaps and outrageous capers, and the many colorful characters who came to mind. The two men had not seen each other for several months now, since Marcus had left Hancock to resettle back in Pontiac, bringing his little daughter with him. The girl was already 13, Hervey's niece Clettie. Plainly said, Marcus had accomplished a lot in this new life of his, establishing himself in Pontiac life and business, largely due to teaming up with Elkanah Comstock to make one of the town's biggest banking houses. And he had remarried and started a new family—though the new couple had to prevail through the anguish of losing two of their three children in sickness. Only a daughter had survived, now 5 years old. Yesterday evening in the parlor as Hervey was observing the Kelsey household bring the day to a close, all of them seemingly happy and secure, a word came to mind that might best describe his friend and brother-in-law: irrepressible.

This morning it was still amusing to have an irrepressible brother-in-law press on with more family talk.

"And how is your bride finding life in the far north?" Marcus asked next. The question was polite, somewhat loaded, the deeper interest being an assessment of how Fannie Hunt, Hervey's society-girl wife, had survived her first winter in a wilderness town like Hancock.

"All in all," Hervey began tactfully, still looking out over the yard, "for a politician's daughter she manages quite well. You know, she already had some familiarity with the Upper Peninsula, well, Sault Ste. Marie at least. Fannie spent a lot of time with her father while he was posted up there for a year or so. She was 16 . . . 17, I think. The woman has a more adventurous spirit than you might think."

Marcus nodded in agreement, thinking to himself, *Well, she married you on the fly, anyway, over in Port Huron. Now there's some adventure, my impetuous friend.* Hervey's marriage announcement had come in the form of a post card to the Gazette, which duly relayed the news to the public, and everyone was fully intrigued to greet the new couple when they stopped in Pontiac a couple of weeks later. Then off they went to Hancock, in the wilds of Keweenaw.

It was fitting that the two men sit on the porch this morning and enjoy a quiet interlude. After breakfast Marcus' wife Mary and their housekeeper Hannah had left to shop for groceries, taking the little one, Ella May, along with them. And Clettie was off to school, so Hervey and Marcus had the place to themselves. The time had come to plan out some next steps. For, as tranquil as things may have appeared at that time, each man had been pondering his own ambitions, actively calculating the prospects for their next ventures. In large part this was the reason for Hervey's visit, to talk things over. Both were inclined to help the other explore new ideas. Marcus was older, now 41, clean-shaven, a father and landowner, remarried and well established in town but always ready for some new endeavor;

Hervey was 33, with a full beard, a father to be, ready to embark on a long-prepared plan.

They were businessmen, each with a vision for a major investment.

Hervey needed contacts and references, and potential sources for funding his venture when the time came. His aim was establish a new manufacturing company, one that would produce medicines, balms, and pills in large volumes. This was a new industry that was emerging to provide with standardized and affordable treatments, any curative products that the public might need or want. Already there were companies starting up in Brooklyn, like Pfizer and Squibb, as well as various agencies for importing pills from England. The time was right to start a supplying company here in Michigan, especially as the country continued to expand westward. The populations growing rapidly in the new western states, and the new territories beyond the Mississippi presented a sure market needing more and more of the medicinal products. And now the country's new president was pushing for railroads and telegraph service all the way to across to California—it was easy to envisage a business taking in orders and loading products onto those westward trains.

But for now, all of this grandiose idea was nothing more than two men on a porch ruminating over their prospects, in confidence, over a pitcher of buttermilk.

Of course, there was also the war coming on. The northern states were raising their armies to march south, and armies needed supplies, and that meant medicines. The military would also need copper, of course, for making cannons and other armaments, but copper mining was always an unreliable business, as both men had seen from their years together up north in Hancock. They talked about this, until Marcus elaborated on his take on the war demands:

"Well, perhaps the action would only happen in Virginia, and only for a few months, but nevertheless the New York drug companies would be preoccupied with supplying the army and its bureaus. There's bound to be some sizeable orders for, say, morphine for the wounded. Laudanum for the . . . well, to help the stomach deal with an army diet. And quinine, for malaria, once all the boys start setting up camp down there in the South. There'll be a boom for these remedies, no doubt, but only a temporary boom, and enjoyed by the New Yorkers while they completely forsake the new western markets. I think you're on the right track, Hervey, whatever they do about the war back east. You'll get the jump on them out here."

Hervey took another sip of his buttermilk and nodded. "Could get the jump, yes. It would help if Lincoln's treasury man starts issuing those federal demand notes. Good currency in Washington, good in Detroit, good out west."

"It would be nice," Marcus agreed. He was still mulling over the whole concept of building an entire shop equipped to manufacture medicines. And he was amused, also, by the measured tone of his brother-in-law as he spelled out all of the logic of the plant, the new industry, and the growing demand for the products. The prospects for this venture were truly inspiring, more like exciting, even as they were being drily spelled out in methodical discourse by this thoughtful, say reliable, man of business. *Yes*, Marcus thought with a slight smile, *he'll need a partner or two with some pluck and blarney to round out the appeal.* He was about to reinforce the notion, for Hervey's benefit, that he agreed how it was a good time to get out of the copper industry and come back down to Pontiac. But Hervey spoke up first:

"Yes, could be some busy times ahead. By jiminy, *Monsieur le Marquis*[23], you appear to have kept your dance card full over the past year. Let's see: running a banking house with old man Comstock, peddling opium and "Joe Moses" pills with Doc Bagg and Abe Parker, serving as a delegate for the Republicans, American Express agent, and local

---

23   Hervey pronounces "marquis" as "mar-KEE" in French, facetiously.

agent for The Cosmopolitan Art Association . . . What else do you do around here?"

Hervey had been opening a finger on his hand for each activity, and Marcus kept nodding with a smile at each one listed, and most affectedly as Hervey finished off in some flourish in pronouncing the words 'art association'.

"Well, there's also Clettie. And fixing up this new home of ours."

"Oh you definitely need a new job, brother," Hervey laughed in response.

He wanted to know more about Marcus's latest project, but first there was a personal topic to cover, which was the question of why Marcus had sold the Parke homestead on the south side, to move up here by the fairgrounds on the north side.

"So that's it for the old farmhouse, then. You and Clettie were there for how long, what, a few years at least."

That place had been more of a refuge for Marcus, to be honest, after his first wife had died during a snowy March up in Keweenaw, and the distraught widower showed up first at his brother's house in Pontiac. His brother Sullivan had arranged for Marcus and Clettie and to move in with old Captain Parke and his wife Mercy in their modest homestead on the Saginaw Trail south of town, through a reasonable family connection, the Captain being an uncle of Marcus's deceased wife Cornelia, Hervey's older sister. The elderly Parke's had room to spare, and they welcomed the prospect of extra help and some liveliness around the house. And gradually, life started over for Marquis Kelsey—"Marcus" as Hervey called him, his brother-in-law.

Poor, dear Cornelia. Marcus and Hervey had both witnessed the quiet tragedy as she slipped away. There it was, long ago, another time. Family stories.

"Now tell me, what's your reason for moving out of the farmhouse?" was Hervey's question.

Marcus shrugged a shoulder. "Oh, you know, the old stand was a little shaky, a little crowded. It may have been a nice spot to build on, back in the day, parked there by the Trail, the town still small and peaceful and all. But down there we had the railroad running pretty close just behind us[24], and I simply tired of waiting through 30 seconds of racket every time a D&M rolled by. You can imagine. And

Original Parke homestead near southern limits.

then, in the front yard, you have the Trail getting busier and noisier, especially with that toll gate only yards away. Sometimes you'd get a lot of wagons backed up in line to get through, people bickering over the fare, or slouching around our fence. Mary and Mercy used to fuss over it. And now and then you'd have some guttersnipes[25] come to help themselves at our well and then run off with the bucket."

He continued: "No, up here, this is a good neighborhood. Newer homes. The town is filling in on this north side. We're not far from the Wisner estate, up the Turnpike, and the Richardson grounds, and the Comstock's. It's nice. And from here it's easier for Clettie to walk over to Union School. More of her friends live around here anyway."

Hervey nodded approvingly, taking in all the points, while inwardly he was contemplating whether Marcus and Mary may also have

24 The Detroit & Milwaukee Railroad track runs parallel to the Saginaw Trail, about a half mile to its east, northward towards Pontiac. As the Trail and the railroad approach Pontiac the railroad shifts westward until it transects the Trail at the southern end of Pontiac's city limits, and continues northward but now on the Trail's west side. Captain Parke's farmhouse on the Saginaw Trail was just south of this crossover, thus closely situated between the Trail, on its front, and the railroad in its rear.

25 Guttersnipe: a homeless child.

wanted to get away from the farmhouse, still grieving over losing their two little boys. It was a time to start over, somewhere else.

"Hmm, yes, of course."

Marcus appreciated his guest's discreet inquiry.

"And I might add, Hervey, your sister has been a great help. She's up here a lot, looking after Clettie and Ella May, helping to keep this place clean and stocked. Mary's been rather sickly, you see. And now especially when I'm away on business for a week or so, it's good that she's keeping Mary company."

Marcus was talking about Sarah Abigail—Sallie—, Hervey's younger sister, who had married last year but still lived rather independently with time to spare . . . for whatever reason. Hervey could understand his sister's need to be doing something useful.

"Oh yes, no doubt my little sister can enliven any place she walks into," he agreed.

Then there was the matter of the gold watch, which Sallie had misplaced, or lost, during one of her visits to the old homestead. A notifycation was placed in the Gazette offering a reward, but to no avail.

"So, apparently no one ever turned up with her gold watch," he asked.

Marcus rejoined, "No sir. It's been over a year, now. That watch is gone for good. It was an engagement present, I think?"

Hervey shook his head idly. "I think, yes. Or a Parke family piece, I can't remember. Well, it was somebody's heirloom. Not anymore. Didn't do much to bolster the engagement, I suppose . . ."

Marcus then remembered something else about Sallie that he needed to mention:

"By the way, Sallie told me that she wanted to bring over some old books of your father's, to leave them here for safekeeping. Just so you know. One of his medical textbooks and a prayer book. Some personal notes. It's fine with us to keep them here, unless you want to take them up to Hancock."

It was a nice gesture by everyone to have the books stored away in Pontiac, even if they weren't particularly valuable heirlooms. Someone might want them in posterity. Hervey's and Sallie's father, Ezra Parke, was the first medical doctor to settle in Oakland County in the old wilderness days, so there was some history to it. The doctor and Hervey's mother both perished in a plague some fifteen years ago, and since then Hervey and his three brothers had all moved away from the county. Nobody had followed Ezra's footsteps into the medical profession.

Now in Oakland only Sallie remained, and her situation was not completely settled as to where she might end up with her husband. Should Hervey take the books with him back to Hancock? Before Ezra died, Hervey did have some medical instruction as a student at the Bloomfield Academy, so there was that connection, whether or not it meant anything. At the moment, however, Hervey was more intrigued by the idea of Marcus assuming that Hervey would likely be returning to Pontiac in the near future, such that the Parke family items may as well stay here.

"Hmm, that's interesting. May as well keep them all at your house. I'll take a look at them tonight."

"Listen, Hervey, I don't think you need to worry about Sallie spending so much time here. There's nothing untoward about it."

Hervey made no reply and only nodded his acknowledgement. Marcus's gratuitous comment about Sallie was impulsive, of course, but not provocative necessarily, and Hervey was willing to let the matter drop. Any further argument about Sallie would only foster more defensive behavior anyway.

The two men sat and looked out on the yard, and each took another sip of buttermilk. Out on the road there were two riders on horseback, approaching each other in opposite direction, slowly, until finally they intersected and reined up for a conversation. Did Marcus recognize either of the riders? He squinted and offered his opinion that the one on the left was Sheriff Beardslee, a neighbor, probably on his way to work. Not much of an occurrence worth observing. But it seemed to induce Marcus to make one last remark about the situation with Sallie:

"And if that irascible husband of hers shows up today looking for trouble, Beardslee and I will make sure that he finds it."

The forewarning was aimed at one Mr. John French, Sallie's husband, a bookseller who travelled extensively and might possibly be arriving in Pontiac later today. There was sufficient gossip in town to affirm that French was a jealous man who strongly disapproved of his wife spending any time with Marcus Kelsey, such that the inevitable confrontation between the two men would have to be highly dramatic and newsworthy. Possibly all the feelings of ill-will were entirely overblown, but the rumors were entertaining nonetheless, especially in a town generally impassioned for war.

Hervey felt no need to concede anything further about John French, and only responded with a vague nod and took a sip from his mug. Then after enough of a lull had elapsed he broke the idleness on the porch to talk about this new thing, this mining for oil.

"So tell me about this new oil business of yours," he said, to broach the topic. It was now a year since Marcus had left his successful partnership with old Elkanah Comstock at the banking house to join another group of Pontiac men in pursuit of opportunities in Pennsylvania in the new oil-spring region. Then last September after his wedding, when he had last seen Marcus, at that time Marcus had just returned from one of trips to see the derricks and review his claims. "You know, you were showing a lot of spirit back then. I was actually envious. Here was a man taking charge, I thought, and breaking out. Mining for oil, imagine that. Do you reckon on staying with it?"

And so on. Marcus was happy to talk about the venture, starting with a tactful clarification that the business was more a matter of drilling, not mining, and he told Hervey all about the geological aspects, the derricks and storage methods, and the uses of the oil product. Hervey also wanted to know about the area where all this industry was going on, north of Pittsburgh, what type of terrain was there, and what the living conditions were like in that area. It was a lot of questions coming from a discreet, moderate man. *Well, he's clearly fascinated,* Marcus thought, *and maybe he's thinking beyond Hancock, after all.*

And the way Marcus described it, the region around the drilling grounds was quite rustic, similar to what Hervey and Marcus had experienced years ago when they worked together at Clifton. For this new venture in Pennsylvania, Marcus had joined a partnership that had created the "Michigan Rock Oil Company" that was drilling near a place called Oil City. Companies like this were setting up rapidly in this area, a 20-mile stretch along "Oil Creek" valley, with more and more derricks popping up everywhere. The whole valley was becoming one long shantytown to accommodate the booming business with all its new workers moving in, and conditions were rough, as Hervey might well imagine. But the business prospects were well worth the hardships; the oil coming from these wells was far, far cheaper than using coal tar to make kerosene for everyone's oil lamps. And whale oil?—never mind that. Whale oil had become an absurdly expensive luxury compared to kerosene which is just as good a fuel anyway.

"Yes," Hervey smiled. "I saw the cartoon in Vanity Fair—marvelous. Bully for the whales, I think!"

Marcus would have explained further some difficulties his company was facing, due to the desperate shortage of barrels needed to store and ship the oil—they were calling this kind of oil "petroleum"—to move it out of the valley to market. He decided to leave those details out for now.

GRAND BALL GIVEN BY THE WHALES IN HONOR OF
THE DISCOVERY OF THE OIL WELLS IN PENNSYLVANIA.

"Say, Hervey, after Frances has delivered, and the child is growing
hale and hearty, it might be the right time to bring your family back
down here. I mean, if you're really going to pursue this medicine business."

But Hervey had reverted back to his usual pensive state, and he
gave only a thoughtful nod in reply. For now, that was that. The men
resumed their gazing for a few moments, content to remain silent with
so many ideas having been covered. Hervey put his mug down on the
porch floor and, leaning back on his chair, began to rub his hands and
fingers over both his eyes. Marcus watched him doing this for a few
seconds and asked, "Still itching like yesterday?"

"Oh, yes, the same. Like every time I come back to Pontiac, I mean,
to this area. I sneeze, I scratch. And then I'm fine again. I don't know
why I get like this, but it just seems to happen to me when I'm here. I'm
sure I'll be fine this afternoon." Uttering a quick groan, Hervey pulled

away his hands from his eyes and sat motionless, evidently forcing himself to keep his hands on the armrests.

"I'm sorry, brother," Marcus commiserated. "After all those years up north with nary a touch of hay fever—ah, but down here Pontiac never forgets how to torment your poor old nose. Can I fix you some ginger tea?"

"No, no, it'll calm, soon. I'll be right as rain. Honestly, though, this place . . ." Hervey muttered, and exhaled slowly and deliberately, closing his eyes and blowing through his mouth.

"You know, Sarah Abigail was telling me that the McConnell's have some butterbur plants in their greenhouse. Have you tried mixing those roots into a tea? It can help with the sneezing."

Hervey knew the lore about butterbur, and he appreciated an earnest suggestion from his brother-in-law. "Petasite roots," he answered, nodding. "I've tried them. No, it helps a little with the nose, but doesn't relieve the dryness in my eyes. Besides, they can cause some mischief in my digestion."

"Mm-hmm," Marcus acknowledged. He didn't know what *petasite* meant. "Well, let's enjoy the fresh air while we can. I figure the mosquitos will be taking over in about a week."

"Early June, I should think," Hervey agreed. There was something else he meant bring up, figuring that now was as good a time as any. "How about yourself, Marcus? One might say, you don't look as robust as I remember from last year. Maybe all that travel to Pennsylvania is pushing the limit, don't you think? With everything else you do here."

Marcus plainly wasn't worried but didn't mind accommodating his guest. "You're right, the life is still a bit rustic out there in Oil City, but that's exactly why no one has bothered with all that oil until now, I imagine. Out in the middle of nowhere, just like all that copper up north in Michigan. That's always where the money is, out in the middle of nowhere. You see, riding a boat over to Erie isn't much more strenuous than sitting in a steamship going to Keweenaw. I can manage. I'm heading out to the oilfields again in a few weeks with one of my partners, Charlie Pittman."

"Yes, I remember him. He runs the clothing store in the National Block, doesn't he?"

"Still there, and doing handsomely. One of Comstock's better investments. Comstock got him a seat on the school board, too. You know, you might want to stop by Pittman at his store sometime if you're interested in making some local connections around here."

Part of the reason why Marcus would not be going to the McConnells' reception this afternoon was a meeting he had planned with Pittman to review their efforts to find barrels for sale in Pontiac and Detroit. Barrels that they would send off to Pennsylvania to move the oil. But that was another matter. At this point he preferred not to dwell on the oil venture any further but move on to address more practical matters, such as a program for the day ahead. He launched into laying out a schedule.

"So. Let's plan this out. You and Clettie need to be at McConnell's by four. And you want to take her to go see McConnell's big new church beforehand, say at three. So we should pick up Clettie at school by two thirty, which gives you plenty of time to make it from Pike Street down to the church. I could drop you off at the church and get back to see Monty Bagg at the store. The two of you could just walk to the McConnell's – it's only about a quarter mile from the church. You probably won't have time to visit the old Parke homestead. Now, back up, our lunch with Comstock at the Tremont is at noon . . . by the way, I trust you'll enjoy the oysters. They just got in a fresh keg from Crawford's. Anyway, that means we should be leaving here for Tremont's at eleven thirty. We'll need the surrey for the three of us; Jonas will have it ready. Are you taking an attaché case for the Comstock lunch? I could keep it with me after dropping you off at the church."

That seemed to cover it. The two men drank down the last of the buttermilk in their mugs as a final gamut of subjects was addressed: Would Hervey be wearing the new shoes he just bought yesterday—a handsome pair but not yet broken in; better take some small cloths for cushion; also, at the Union School, Marcus would introduce Hervey to Miss James, head of the girls' department, who should gladly allow for Clettie's early dismissal to spend time with her visiting Uncle Hervey Parke. The school's address is on Parke Street, after all. And when Hervey and Clettie got to the church they would see that the outside is almost finished, but it would interesting to know how the chancel and pews inside were being laid out.

"The church is a huge improvement for that Methodist Episcopal crowd, compared to the little place they use now on Pike. They've raised an impressive amount of money to get it started, and a lot of the dough coming out of McConnell's pocket to be sure. Oh, and look for their pastor, Samuel Clements, probably at the construction site right now with all the workmen . . ."

Marcus paused here but couldn't think of anything further, except to wind up the day's planning by confirming Hervey's next overnight lodging, which would be at the Palmer house. "So then, from the Mc-Connells' you'll be heading back to the Palmer's with Charley?"

"Yes, even if Charley doesn't make it to the reception, I'm sure Charley junior will be there. Anyway the Palmer's are expecting me. Someone will get me there, or I'll just walk. It will still be daylight when this wingding ends." Hervey was looking forward to rejoining Charley Palmer this evening, at Charley's home where he would spend the night before leaving for Detroit on Friday. Charley was something of a kindred spirit, having invested in copper mines

Charles Palmer

up in Keweenaw, requiring extended travel there while maintaining a household here in Pontiac. Charley had recently been in Hancock and had accompanied Hervey on the *Pewabic* for this trip home; he had to remain in Detroit today and would not likely arrive in Pontiac for the McConnells' reception. Apparently the mines were paying off quite handsomely this year, and by the way, Marcus had heard that Charley was considering buying a big house on Huron Street from the widow Myrick. He asked Hervey whether he might find out more about it tonight.

For today, then, all of the plans seemed reasonable, in particular the lunch meeting with Elkanah Comstock that Hervey was most anxious for. Good. Settled, then. Hervey promised to be ready at 11:30.

S.S. Pewabic, Great Lakes passenger liner.

Marcus stood up from his chair and arched his back in a stretching motion as he gazed out towards the road. He watched Sheriff Beardslee bring his horse to a leisurely trot, heading south towards town, and he had to stifle a cough before he could smile and speak his parting words to Hervey—"Very good, sir!"—and walk back into the house.

Hervey remained on the porch, sipping the last bit of buttermilk from his mug and taking in the sights of Marcus Kelsey's neighborhood. Another thought came to mind as he sat alone. He was musing over something that Marcus had said earlier about his wife Mary being "a bit sickly." Poor woman: there was no doubt about Mary feeling perfectly dreadful. Hervey suspected, as Marcus suspected as well, surely, that Mary may well be pregnant. It would be too early and untoward even to mention the idea, of course; nevertheless good hope was at hand. Over the past years Marcus and Mary had lost two baby boys while only little Ella May had survived. Wouldn't it be wonderful to see this family overcome their losses and continue to thrive, peacefully, even in these uncertain times with the war now impending.

Whatever Mary's condition might be, Hervey understood why Marcus and Mary would not be attending the McConnells' reception this afternoon. Other guests would politely inquire about Mrs. Kelsey's health, of course, but Hervey was prepared to say little about it. A tactful forbearance on the matter should suffice.

George Mathews

I haven't seen much of Danny Thurber and Joe McConnell since everyone came home from school. And, of course, Danny's been in mourning for his mother. He hasn't been seen much around town these days. You should understand that Danny and Joe are close chums. We were all at Ann Arbor together until Danny and Joe transferred over to Union College in Schenectady for the year just past. They're also fraternity brothers – Delta Phi – both at Ann Arbor and still on at Union. Thick as thieves. You know, their fathers are poles apart, politically, but the families have managed to stay friends true to form. Meanwhile Joe has taken a shine to Danny's sister Sarah—why not?—that girl has to be one of the most beautiful young belles you'll meet in Pontiac. You can bet the two of them pairing up like that has helped keep the Thurber and McConnell nabobs compatible socially.

What I'm seeing now is Danny's turn at romance, and wouldn't you know it, I think he's smitten by that Carrie Holley girl. There you have it, proof again that opposites attract. Moody rich boy meets vivacious daughter of hard-working family . . . but ain't love grand, so they say. Carrie has grown into an exceedingly attractive young woman, don't you know, and even if Danny will never admit it, she's just the spark to get him to break out and start enjoying life, about time! I'll say this, too: if Danny-boy botches his chances with Miss Holley then I'll be there to jump in and try to steal the scene myself. Who knows, this spring with the war coming on, anything and everyone is up for grabs.

As for the Mathews family, yes, that's the name you see on all over those mill buildings down by the river. We're bound to be top-drawer name in Pontiac for a very long time, the way things are going. Every year Father keeps adding another mill. We'll mill anything you need: plaster, lumber, grist, wools. Not to forget the blacksmith shop, and the distillery. It's business, boyo, and a thundering lot of it!

Two bartenders, Pontiac.

A VISITOR'S STORY,
"Wine and Candy"

BACK ONTO the street in front of the Arcade with your transient group, everyone needs to let their eyes adjust to the sunshine, and the boys are still blinking as they see you off with handshakes and genial expressions of "very nice to meet you" and "see you at McConnell's," but in a few moments it's fitting for you to turn away and make your way back across Saginaw to the Hodges House. There are a few passing wagons to negotiate around, and some "fresh" spots on the road to avoid, before you regain the boardwalk opposite and think back on the lively time you had at lunch. And how fortunate was it, to meet up with the three younger fellows, all from families that you're sure to encounter later today. What fine young men, so open to welcoming a lone traveler into their circle. And how about you—did you likewise acquit yourself well enough to make a good impression on *them*? You face around for one more wave goodbye, but there you see them walking away along the Saginaw boardwalk, already passing Butterfield's Dry Goods, up the street beyond Pike. Two of them, anyway, George and Lewis. You recall them mentioning that they would be going to Morris's Livery, around the corner on Lawrence Street, to rent a carriage.

Ah well—you proceed into the Hodges lobby, happily anticipating this afternoon's reception all the more, with all the personalities and stories waiting for you there. You only have one day for this town, and it appears you'll be making the most of it. Right now you just want to inquire at the front desk for any news or messages, although there's no reason to expect anything, but there's a couple ahead of you, checking in, so you'll have to wait for minute or so. No hurry. An idle thought comes to mind about the McConnells' party, how it might actually represent something larger than a typical social gathering. Being the first event of the warm springtime season for most of the guests, it's a rally of sorts, a chance for everyone to assess how life will carry on in this time of war. The crowd will be eager to talk, to reacquaint, to gossip, and meet new visitors like yourself.

The clerk at the desk is not the same one you spoke with earlier, and you're reluctant to delve into small talk with this one just now. No messages? Very good, thank you—so once again you're out the door to take care of a couple of errands, as you've been meaning to pick up a few gifts to take to the McConnell's. There should be some stores down to the right, southward along Saginaw. The locals still refer to that particular stretch of commerce as "The Old Stand".

Wait – what was that? A strange background noise causes you to stop and look back towards Pike, but there's nothing to see as the sound comes echoing down the street, as if, in the distance someone has poured a bagful of tiny steel balls into a tin bucket, causing a metallic rattle that lasts only one or two seconds. Aha—it must be rifle fire over at the fairgrounds where the militia units are training. No one around you seems to share your curiosity about it, so after a moment's hesitation you start walking again, although come to think of it, it might be interesting to go up there to see the campground and parade formations, if there's time . . . but right now here's your first stop, in front of Address no. 4, the storefront for Turk's, Pontiac's best-known grocer. You walk in and discover wide selections of fruits, vegetables, and various foodstuffs; it shouldn't take long to find something here. You wander your way through to the spirits section, looking for an imported sherry or a wine suitable to present to the reception hosts. There is no sherry but they do have some Chautauqua wines from New York that should do the trick. So that's fine—you take their best recommendation, and ask whether they might deliver it within the hour to McConnell on Church Street. The manager of course knows that house very well, indeed the reception event itself, so the arrangements are readily set down. Good. That's that. Let's see—still plenty of time to get yourself to the party.

You leave Turk's and turn right again to continue southward on the boardwalk, but after a few steps you slow down, inspired once again just to take in the view of the wide thoroughfare, and it brings you to a standstill as you watch the wagons passing by. It's surprising how many there are. Every few seconds another hitched team and wagon, then another, and another. They crisscross before you, with a few going left-to-right southward, but by far most of the traffic is northbound. Some of the northbound wagons are empty, but most of them are carrying freight, or family possessions, and you suspect that these must be heading further inland, to Flint or Saginaw, wagons filled with crates, furniture, and tarps made lumpy in covering all manner of items underneath.

And dreams, too. The people in those wagons are carrying dreams of a life ahead. A destination, a new home, new daily work, new friends.

All this commotion in the street, though nobody around you seems to be impressed by the scene. The sound of the horses' hooves is fairly constant, and the rumbling of the wagon wheels repeats in a crescendo-decrescendo cycle as they pull by. What other sounds do you no-tice? Steam exhaust hissing from a machine shop, probably Dawson's shop around on Pike. A cartwright's hammer pounding metal in some wagon shop. A fiddle being played in second floor room somewhere. A peddler shouting "Rags!" further up Saginaw. And somewhere down along Water Street there is some sort of carpentry work going on, by the echoes of saws and hammers and indistinct voices. Either they're extending the boardwalk or perhaps yet another storefront is going up.

Resuming your walk you start to inhale deeply to renew your focus on your next errand—but stop, no, not good, you're breathing in a full dose of pungent odor of horse excrement that has accumulated below a hitching post nearby. Let's just get past that one, shall we? After a few circuitous steps, holding your breath, you look up to find that you are now in front of address no. 3, a bakery store. Or so you thought. This used to be Crawford & Holley, a confectionery and baking busi-ness, but through the windows it appears as though the shelves are empty and some of the tables are covered with sheets. Hmm, the door is locked, too. You take a step back on the boardwalk to look down the row of storefronts, and presently a man's voice calls out, "They've moved!"

You look back towards the Hodges House. There he is, the hotel clerk with the wire-rimmed glasses, standing outside the front entrance, apparently on break or assisting a guest outside the hotel. He sees that he has your attention so he walks toward you so that you might hear him more clearly. You speak to him first.

"Crawford & Holley?'

"They moved the business across the street." He points across Sagi-naw and a few doors down to the right. "It's just Crawford now."

"Ah yes, I see it. Thank you!"

"Very good, sir." The clerk smiles obligingly and touches the brim of his cap.

So that clarifies that. You take a few steps along the boardwalk before alighting onto Saginaw—here's a good, clean spot—and begin heading over to the east side, towards a big storefront sign that reads "J. T. Crawford."

Yes, this is definitely the place you were thinking of. Through the windows you can survey the pastries, breads and candies, which bring to mind that you were also thinking of contributing a box of jelly beans for the McConnells' children, so you're happy to venture inside. And you'll have to inquire about John Holley, who used to be one of the store partners. Along with Levi Bacon, the merchant you saw this morning at McConnell and Bacon, John Holley is another acquaintance from an earlier visit to Pontiac. Is Holley still in Pontiac? Let's find out. You walk in and close the door behind you, causing a "ting" from the coil spring shopkeepers bell to accompany the rattling of the thin plate-glass window on the door.

A young shopgirl stands behind the counter, courteously waiting while you look over an assortment of candy jars, and she comes around to approach only when you ask aloud whether Holley is available.

"Yes sir, that's my father, but he no longer works here. The bakery is now run by Mr. Crawford alone." She perceives how this news is something of a disappointment for you, and she adds encouragingly, "May I help you with anything?"

So, jelly beans.

"Oh, yes," and with a genial manner she promptly leads you over another table with an array of canisters, and once there, upon her tactful recommendation you select a half-pound mix of blues and yellows.

J. T. CRAWFORD,

CONFECTIONERY AND BAKERY,

E. side Saginaw, 4th door below Peninsular Hotel,

PONTIAC, MICH.

Manufacturer of all kinds of Confectionery, Pies and Cakes, at wholesale and retail. Orders executed with dispatch, and delivered to all parts of the city. Also connected Ice Cream and Oyster Saloon Cream and Oysters in their season.

Advertisement in Loomis & Talbot's 1860 City Directory, p.13

Returning to the counter, she prepares the box and writes up the sale, and you strike up some conversation and learn that she is Carrie Holley, 17 years old, with one year remaining at the Union public school. In the afternoons she helps at Crawford's store, or in her mother's millinery and dress shop over Butterfield's store up the street—and a woman there is teaching Carrie how to operate stitching on one of the new Braman sewing machines! It's amusing how the girl is at once verbose yet considerate in manner. She offers to deliver the candy to the McConnell's herself, since she will be taking some other items over there anyway, accompanying the driver in Crawford's wagon.

"Of course. Why not?" You're delighted by her thoughtful gesture. "Thank you, and please do. Say, I just bought a bottle of wine at Turk's which they're supposed to deliver to the McConnell's, too. Ask them if they'll let you take the wine along with the candy." You cock your head just so, for emphasis: "I believe the manager would be glad to afford a small reward for your trouble. I'll let him know." Carrie readily approves, and the girl's eyes seem to widen a little, revealing her enthusiasm for the plan. Hah! You give her a wink, and she winks right back at you. No muggins[26] allowed in the John Holley clan.

Two more customers have just walked in the store—a couple of boys making a stop for candy on their way home from school—so it's time for you to move on, despite your wish to talk more about Holley and his wife's millinery business and the sewing machines. Ah, never mind. But you stand at outside the store entrance for a few moments and you think: well now, that was interesting. What a cheerful, gracious young lady. So that's John Holley's daughter. She knows the McConnell's. It's always intriguing to pick up on various connections in these towns.

So far so good. The party at the McConnell's should be interesting, if you can prevail over the burden of knowing very few of the other guests. You will have to take the initiative in good measure to meet people. But you're ready for it, your spirit bold and buoyant, thanks to those college boys back at the Arcade. Now that you think back on that crew it's unfortunate you didn't "test the table" for a response to some rowdy poetry, just to see if anybody knew a few lines of Robert Burns—even if the lines were written some eighty years ago:

Give him strong drink until he wink,
That's sinking in despair;
And liquor good to fire his blood,
That's pressed with grief and care:

Those are the first four lines, anyway. What was the rest, now . . . it always takes a minute to remember a couple of those scotch words . . . ah yes, now you have it:

---

26   Muggins: a naïve person, one easily duped.

There let him booze, and deep carouse,
With bumpers flowing o'er,
Till he forgets his loves or debts,
And minds his griefs NO MORE.[27]

In a crowded saloon everyone would wait to join in reciting the last line in unison, shouting the last two words 'no more' with ale mugs hoisted up. But in a place like the Arcade . . . chances are, few of the patrons there have ever recited anything by Bobby Burns. Too bad—it's good verse. Especially for young men soon to face major decisions about love and war.

---

27   Robert Burns, "Scotch Drink," 1785.

DRESS-MAKER

THE WOMAN sat by herself at a desk in her workshop, actually a large work table being used as a desk, where she had cleared a small area to lay out a plate for her lunch. She had just finished her portions of salted lamb and a potato salad mixed with dill and parsley, and she was about to crumple up the parchment paper covering her lunch plate, the same paper she had used this morning to wrap the food to take to work. But she also had a peach, which she may as well eat now, she decided, so she would leave the pit in with paper before throwing it into the garbage bin at the back of the shop. There was no need to get up just yet, and there were a few things to think over as the pace of the workday started to resume for the afternoon hours.

The woman sat quietly, which she would do now and then, knowing the value of taking the time to keep herself on an even keel and her schedule well planned. Simply put, she had to. This workshop was her business, a dress-making and millinery enterprise that had thrived for many years in Pontiac's commercial center, under her name as sole proprietor, Marion Holley. And as usual, this year's spring season promised to be another exciting one for Mrs. Holley and her many, many favorite clients in town.

Today's lunch break had been a welcome respite, much needed on a busy day like today that would be spent entirely in town without going home at midday. The break started out with Marion and everyone else walking downstairs from the shop in a group, out onto Saginaw Street, and after the employees had walked off in various directions to do whatever errands they had, Mrs. Holley stayed behind to enjoy a few minutes of idleness in the fresh air. There she stood in front of Butterfield's dry goods store, her eyes closed, breathing deeply and shaking out her achy hands to let them recover after a long morning of working indoors. Today she had brought lunch; some days she might walk back to her house on Parke Street, if the weather was clement, or on other occasions join with her husband who also worked in town. So: another lunchtime. Let's allow a little more time just to stand under Butterfield's awning, stretching her back, and relaxing her hands and fingers in deliberate shaking motions, before returning upstairs to her shop.

The springtime sun had now crested the tops of the buildings across the street, shining down on half of Saginaw, the side closest to her, while the boardwalk over on the east side still lay in shadows, making it difficult to see over there without putting a hand to one's forehead for a visor. Not that there was anything in particular she expected to see. The sounds and smells of Saginaw Street were no different today, reliable, many horses and wagon wheels, a busy Thursday. There was always movement on Saginaw. The scene somehow inspired Mrs. Holley to join in, just to walk across to the other side and take part in the activity. Any excuse would do. Why not go see if anything new was in the window of Allison's jewelry. And while there, take a look nonchalantly at who was walking in or out of Mrs. Goetchius's ("Frau Goetchius") dressmaking shop, her reputable competitor.

C   C

MRS. HOLLEY
Begs leave to inform the
LADIES OF PONTIAC,
that she has just
RETURNED FROM NEW YORK,
WITH A SPLENDID
STOCK OF MILLINERY GOODS,
of all kinds, Sashes,
NETS ALL STYLES,
AND
Headdresses.
Steel Spring Skirts, all Sizes and Prices.
Dresses and cloaks made after the latest F
Fashions
Pontiac, Oct. 4, 1860.

PONTIAC, APRIL 9, 1860.
———:o:———
Mrs. Holley.

Is now receiving spring Millinery direct from New
York every week, Lady's wishing bonnets can get
them either silk or straw, also girls flats, boys hats
and Lady's caps, a good article of

STEEL SPRING HOOPS

always on hand old straw bonnets bleached and done
up in the best possible manner, also,

DRESSMAKING,

In all its different stiles done with neatness and per-
fection or

NO PAY WILL BE EXPECTED,

MRS. HOLLEY, will be glad to see all her

LADY FRIENDS

who have patronised her so generously during the
last year and as many more as may find it convenient to call.
REMEMBER THE PLACE,
over Butterfield's Store.

WEST & WILSON

SEWING MACHINE

John C. Hall, Agent, Pontiac.

With fingers unwearied and fair,
    With eyes of joyous appeal,
The good wife sits in her easy chair,
    Driving her treadle and wheel.
        Stitch! stitch! stitch!
    With fingers of iron and steel,
As with a voice both merry and free,
    She sang at her treadle and wheel

DESCRIPTION OF THE MACHINE
AND STITCH.

We ask attention to the following points of ex-
cellence in West and Wilson's Machine:

1st Its simplicity, and the directness with which
the power is communicated to the needles. This is
the great desideratum and in this we claim a decided superiority over all other machines.

2d. The needle and needle bar are both straight,
and the mot on direct; the needle bar is attached
to a small wheel driven by a larger one, instead of
to the long arm of the lever as in most machines
with power upon the short one. The latter ar
rangement necessarily makes the motion of the
needle both circular and weak, while the former
gives strength and directness

3d The great power and directness of the motion
enables us to sew all fabrics, from gauze to four

And so began her brief foray to the east side. *Why not—that's the style!* A few forthright strides later and there she was, standing in front of Allison's and considering whether to go into the store.

There was no way of knowing, of course, but this little detour had set the stage for making the day a much more interesting experience.

"Good afternoon Mrs. Holley!" The cheery greeting roused her from her dull assessment of rings and watches, and she turned to see two young men approaching from the corner of Lawrence. It took a moment to recognize the smiling faces of Lewis Drake and George Mathews.

"Lewis, George . . . gentlemen . . . and a good afternoon to you!" she replied. How nice to see all the young men home again for the summer. "On your way to feed yourselves at the Arcade, I presume?" The quick deduction brought out full smiles and modest acknowledgments from the two of them.

Lewis was first to respond. "Yes ma'am, indeed we are," and turning to George he added, "There you are—first names once again. Certainly, then, this isn't Ann Arbor we're in, for real." His eyes were wide open in mock surprise.

Marion took up the levity by nodding back approvingly, lips pursed and hands on her hips, while George spoke up to explain the matter further:

"We're just on our way to pick up the Honorable Mr. Thurber—Daniel, that is—for a bite at the old haunt, and confirm to ourselves that the place is still standing."

Mrs. Holley started to respond with an assurance that the Arcade was alive as ever, but she realized how the boys' attention had focused behind her, so she turned around to see for herself. Wouldn't you know it, there he was, Danny Thurber coming up to join them, having just emerged from his father's store on the boardwalk.

Another round of greetings was made, including a cordial nod and hello from Daniel to Mrs. Holley, and the college boys politely edged their postures as if ready to continue on to lunch. But Daniel then stopped and asked, "All went well, then, with the new baby?" The question was posed a bit awkwardly, but the intent was kindly. The boy was asking about Mrs. Holley's sister-in-law and the birth of the baby girl just this past Tuesday.

"Yes, everyone is just fine, thank you for asking, Daniel."

"A little girl, then? What name are they giving her?"

"Marion."

"Oh! Congratulations! I mean to say, that's very nice – you have a namesake. . ."

And with that Mrs. Marion Holley announced, "Yes, isn't that something!" to which all three young men readily expressed their agreement. A pause. Marion then asked, "So, I suppose you're all getting ready to enlist?"

Daniel's reply "No . . ." was inflected as if asking a question himself.

George added, "No. We're still watching and waiting."

The look in their eyes revealed how they really did not know how to answer, but no matter, it was appropriate now to continue on their way. Marion watched them off and made a slight wave. What a threesome. *They're probably all arguing over this with their mothers at home. I wonder what will happen to them. They're all good boys. What a shame if they all leave for the army just when they're needed most on the social calendar.*

The short encounter was enough to kindle warm feelings, because it was by and large a happy time, and quite something, that her younger brother and his wife were naming their third child after her. Little Marion Thatcher, plump and cooing in the pink of health. Yes, this was very pleasing. *I have a niece, and she's named after me. Well, you see, with everything else going on in the world, this is a good thing.*

Marion was deeply happy for her brother Erastus and her sister-in-law Fannie and their growing family. Three children now—two nephews and a niece. A fine family. Somehow she had always felt that Erry would do well. Even if he was something of a fastidious type, for a lawyer, prone to meddling in details. But he was handsome, and had married well, attaching himself to the Richardson family. And apparently Erry had personality sufficient to convince the nabobs of Pontiac to elect him as Pontiac's first mayor. So you had to admire the man. And his wife. Fannie was younger, still only 30, sturdy enough to withstand childbirth, God be praised. And she was smart, and she clearly appreciated Marion's success in managing a dressmaking business. It helped keep things compatible. Marion had left word that she would pay a visit to see Fannie and the baby this evening, after work, since Erry would surely be out late on "mayor" affairs, which was understandable, given that the delivery had gone so well. Probably the most valuable service Marion might provide would be some needed diversion for Baby Marion's two older brothers—the little imps should be ready for some mischief with their auntie.

Marion Holley

Marion knew she ought to get back to her workshop studio to have her own lunch, frugal repast that it was, so she crossed back over Saginaw to Butterfield's store and went directly to the staircase leading up to the second floor. Here she was pleased to find that she wasn't even breathing hard—always a reassuring sign for a woman her age. And already her mind was active, starting with how she might visit Fannie and the baby later today, given all the tasks to be accomplished beforehand. She had begun to recount a number of "to do" items as she was climbing the stairs: a home dress for Mrs. Crofoot needed clasps repositioned on the back; three new gowns just received needed the hoops inserted; and those bleached bonnets still needed final adornments. *Hmm, still won't have the hoops done today. Not if I have to spend an hour at John Bray's studio waiting for ambrotypes[28] . . . we may have to get those gown images tomorrow.*

Before taking out her lunch here in her shop front-room, Marion sat down at the reception desk to look over her diary. There were various plans and appointments to consider, but she freed her mind for a short pause and raised her head to look around at the rear studio, where, through the open door she could see her assistant Lucretia examining a bonnet that she was working on.

"Lucretia," she said, using the simple stating of the name as a greeting.

"Ma'am," came back the response, with an appropriately cordial smile.

"Afternoon, Mrs. Holley," came a second reply, from another employee Fanny who had leaned into view from the left side. Her intonation was slightly cheerier, and her smile a bit wider, as if to emphasize how both of them, the two assistant milliners, were aptly on the job and all was in order. Marion nodded her acknowledgement and returned her attention to the diary. No worries about Lucretia and Fanny. Marion was always satisfied with their handiwork. It was an arrangement that had worked out well—the two of them were unmarried women in their twenties, from decent families in Lapeer County. Marion had contacted them through her church, the Congregational, and now they boarded at the Holley's home in Pontiac, such that their

---

28   Ambrotype: an early form of photographic image.

wages were commensurately lower, and this had greatly helped the business keep pace with its expanding volume. It also helped to have Lucretia and Fanny on hand to help care for Marion's aged aunt, and a young nephew who had moved in last year from New York–yes, her household had become quite populated. In a way, it reflected the spirit of the town, busy and getting busier.

Fanny's skill as a seamstress was adequate, certainly, but her personal taste in reading material was another matter. Just last week Marion had found in Fanny's room a copy of the "Malaeska" book, left on top of the chest of drawers, and this was a bit disappointing although understand-able. *Oh, no, not you too, Fanny.* Malaeska was all the rage, especially among young women and schoolgirls, one of these new so-called "dime novels" purveying only silly stories and laced with risqué ideas. Marion wasn't convinced that this sort of tripe was acceptable or even moral for youthful

Malaeska: The Indian Wife
of the White Hunter

Mrs. Ann S. Stephens

readers. Of course all of her daughter's girlfriends like Emma Adams and Fannie Pittman were surely reading these adventure books and talking among themselves like some secret society. So then and there Marion decided she should leaf through a few pages of Malaeska and sure enough, it didn't take long to figure out the gist of the "adventure": a white huntsman in the forests of old New York has a tryst with a Mohawk maiden which produces an illegitimate half-breed child, and all sorts of passionate despair is the result. *Oh, for heaven's sakes.* Fanny was instructed to keep the book only at the shop, that is, away from Marion's daughter Carrie—a futile measure, granted, but at least maintaining a principle in the Holley household in defense of worthier literary standards.

When Marion had first arrived at the shop this morning she had been looking over some bolts of materials and she was actually gratified to see, tucked away on a windowsill, Fanny's copy of *Malaeska*, dutifully kept here and away from the house. Marion had to smile to herself at the flights of fancy set loose out of a dime novel, like a Pandora's box; nevertheless, there was something not right about it, *un certain malaise*, that the younger generation would consider this sort of subject matter to be ordinary entertainment. For a few moments she wondered whether she might borrow Fanny's copy to read the entire story, just to stay familiar with what her daughter and her friends were being exposed to.

Now for some lunch. Marion set out a plate on the desk and pulled out her parchment paper with the lamb and potatoes. *No, the ambrotypes really should be taken this afternoon.* It was all well and good that her dress-making business was running full tilt, but it was becoming quite burdensome to schedule all the activities. Priorities always seemed to be shifting, like this one—squeezing in some time to obtain images of recently completed gowns. True, the image copies were proving very useful for promoting her services, but of course it meant time and money, as well as yet another argument with her daughter Carrie to get her over to Bray's studio and pose for before the camera. Oh, you couldn't blame the girl for losing interest in standing around on the platform for an hour or so, wearing one of *her moth-*

er's creations, which always called for some ad hoc adjustments for the fit, meant to last just for the one session. And then the finale—the actual picture-taking—while standing frozen for 10 to 15 seconds, no back brace, holding her breath. Too much tedium for such a lively, pretty girl. It was well and good that Carrie already spent so much time, most days after school, working in Crawford's candy shop down the street. *Well, that's life for our busy little threesome. The Holley's are workers—ask anyone in town.*

Bray's daguerreotype studio had been helpful so far, and Marion felt good about utilizing modern techniques, in the form of photography, for advertising her business. And it was nice that Carrie's curly-haired schoolmate Fannie Pittman worked at the studio in the afternoons, just like Carrie at Crawford's, as the two of them were good friends and usually walked together to their jobs after school. The Pittman's were a good family. Charlie Pittman operated a popular clothing store on the corner of Saginaw and Lawrence, and his daughter Fannie worked for John Bray, the brother of Mary Pittman, Charlie's wife. All family-connected: the girl's job at the studio was to assist her uncle with his customers, or "sitters," and prepare everything for each picture—things could become a bit playful when the customer was Carrie. But that was all right, and making things that much safer for everyone.

Marion finished her lunch, and the peach, and was still relaxing at the desk when the shop door opened and she looked up with a satisfied grin to see Mrs. Frances Mercer, another of her assistants, walking in ready to begin her afternoon shift. Frances worked part time in the afternoons, as an instructor for women who wished to learn how to operate Marion's new "West & Wilson" sewing machine. As an added service being offered at her studio, the lessons had proven to be a real coup for bringing in new clients. What had started out as only a few appointments for select Lady Friends, when the machine first arrived, soon had so many customers asking for lessons that Marion hired Frances to handle all the instruction responsibilities. This activity quickly turned into higher demand for dress materials, with all the Ladies eager to ply their new skill in making their own garments right there in the shop, especially nowadays with so many colorful fabrics now available, thanks to the new aniline dyes. Oftentimes Marion found herself cautioning against ordering a style perhaps a little too gaudy for public view, advice that often fell on deaf ears among her more enthusiastic customers.

Frances began settling in, removing her hat and gloves while peering in through the rear door to survey the scene in the work room where the machine was set up. Good-afternoons were exchanged courteously, and yes, Frances already had lunch, with her husband. Marion asked, "So, it will be Mrs. Darrow for her 1:00? How is she coming along?"

Frances replied with an accommodating grin, "Well, it *is* easier when she brings her daughter. Emily is the quick learner. Oh, and I think they'll be looking to buy more of the mauveine[29] after today. Augusta may have to start over on the dropped shoulders, which is fine for her—she just loves fussing with all the purple silks."

This brought a knowing smile to Marion's face as she returned her attention to her diary and the day's schedule. Another happy customer. And an important one: Augusta Darrow was a member of the Ladies' Sewing Society, so an ability to operate a West & Wilson was a matter of prestige. Prestige for her, promotion for Marion. This extra business for the dress-making was helpful, in fact something of a relief, as the millinery side of Marion's business was subject to much competition

---

29 Mauveine: mauve-color dye. Affordable synthetic dyes for fabrics, "aniline dyes," had become available in the late 1850's. Mauve, magenta, and fuchsia colors were among the earlier dyes, soon followed by blues, greens and yellows, etc. The original process creating mauve was discovered by 18-year-old British chemist William Perkin in 1856—it was an unintended side-effect of his failed experiment trying to manufacture quinine.

these days. That, and the effect of Mr. Lincoln's war on the South, felt immediately by the lack of available cotton fabrics. Nothing but wool, wool, wool from her suppliers. Marion had hoped to find sources in Cincinnati for lighter cotton wares for the summer season, but that market was fully closed off. New York prices for wool meanwhile were going up as the state governments were grabbing everything they could for the army's uniforms. *Well, let's trust that it won't be this way much longer. Most of the soldiers volunteering must already be outfitted by now.* In any event, maintaining customer relations with Pontiac's best families was the best insurance. And it didn't hurt to have a brother who was also the mayor.

Prestige mattered in this business, particularly with her customers all being women of means. Prestige would only be maintained as long as these women felt confident in Marion's ability to provide hats and gowns that were unquestionably the latest in fashion, pattern and color. Ensuring the prestige had led Marion to make an annual trip to New York, taking Frances along with her, where the two of them could fully immerse themselves in finding the best materials and learn the latest styles and techniques. The expertise gained in New York was always emphasized in Marion's advertisements in the Pontiac newspapers, ad copy which reliably appeared in every issue. Marion very much enjoyed making those trips to New York. The train rides were comfortable, and although it was possible to reach New York in two days, the women preferred a slower itinerary with two overnights, in Cleveland and in Elmira where Frances had kin. It was still a problem getting out of Michigan; there was no direct line between Detroit and Toledo so the trains had to go all the way west to Jackson before turning south to Ohio. For that reason, adding a third day to their overall travel time was usually a good plan. Regardless, though, Marion felt the yearly expedition was worth every penny.

Of course, it was always refreshing just to visit the cosmopolitan world of New York and catch up on the latest in *everything*, and walk the endless avenues and enjoy losing themselves in the sheer immensity of the city, if only for a day. They hadn't yet seen the new Central Park, as too much time would be spent going all the way up to 59th Street and they were reluctant to climb aboard those filthy omnibuses. But they always managed a visit to Haughwout's big department store on Broadway and Broome so they could ride the Otis passenger elevator up and down between floors, nonchalantly standing inside amid the crowd but inwardly fascinated by this new marvel of scientific invention. This was the new American world, a life with machines: huge elevators like this one, or harvester machines like her husband John was selling back in Pontiac, or little sewing machines like the one Frances was operating in the dress shop. Marion embraced all of it, and her customers were only too glad to associate with a woman of modern times.

Prestige also meant forsaking the requests from leading families to outfit their sons in proper officers' uniforms, now that the war was underway. No, Marion would not attend to men's clothing, instead producing solely for the women as always. It wouldn't help to stray from what she did best. Moreover, the business was difficult enough just as it was, with hats and gown fashions evolving ever more quickly with each season in these hectic times. As for a young officer needing a handsome uniform, let the boy's mother come in and sew one together using the West & Wilson machine, although she really ought just to take the boy down to Detroit for a proper order.

For now, look away, a busy afternoon lay ahead. Marion decided to work first on the hoops for the new gowns, and walked into the work room where Frances was already busy preparing the West & Wilson. Marion paused for a moment to survey the room, particularly the new rack that her husband had installed along the left wall, where a number of unfinished gowns were suspended on the new hanger devices that

Marion had brought home from New York. This hanging arrangement was a wonderful recent innovation, allowing for much easier access to the gowns and bolts of fabric; nevertheless, everyone was still bothered by the thought of the moths having easier access as well, so now with the return of warmer weather Marion and Frances would pack their wares every night into cedar chests, just to be on the safe side.

The room appeared to be in acceptable order, and after a quick sigh Marion took to clearing one of the large worktables to make room for the first gown. The thought of the New York prices was still bothersome. The business should still manage, even so. Marion was expecting to look over the accounts—probably there wouldn't be time today, but as soon as she could sit down next with Sarah Thurber, the young schoolgirl who was helping with the bookkeeping. Sarah was already home for the summer from her seminary in Monroe[30], returning early to Pontiac after her mother had passed. Such a tragic loss. The Thurber household was still recovering, and Sarah's father Horace being a good friend, Marion had extended the gesture of taking on Sarah more as a means to help see her through these dismal times. Besides, Marion was fond of the girl. Sarah was a very good soul, well-meaning, intelligent. And, she had taken a course in bookkeeping at Monroe, naturally, being a daughter of the foremost dry goods merchant in Pontiac. It was a good, no-nonsense school down there in Monroe, as far as Marion was concerned. Her own daughter's teacher, Almira LeRoy, whom Marion admired greatly, had graduated from there some five years ago.

Mrs. Darrow should be arriving any minute. Marion didn't look up from her arranging the gown on the table as she asked aloud to Frances, "Is Sarah coming today? Or is it tomorrow?" Frances was concentrating on readying a spool of silk thread for installation on the machine, but replied that it might not be today, as this afternoon was the big reception at the McConnell's, as she recalled Augusta mentioning

---

30   Monroe Young Ladies' Seminary, in Monroe, Michigan, south of Detroit.

at her last session. "Mmm," Marion agreed, thinking *yes, Horace's family might be making an appearance there, if enough mourning had been observed*; moreover, the reception was not slated as a gala celebration, just a late afternoon affair for speeches to see off some more soldiers to Detroit. Really, though, Sarah could stand to improve her personality – not convincingly vivacious for a girl that pretty—and the coming social season would be an especially important one for her, motherless or not. Gloomy old Horace has a beauty on his hands, but he should be the last to see it.

But here Marion's mind diverted to a new train of thought, pondering the implications of the Thurber's attending the reception. If Horace was going, and Sarah his eldest daughter was going, then Daniel Thurber would surely be along as well. *Hmm, just out there on the boardwalk Daniel hadn't said anything about the McConnell's but of course their encounter was only a short one. . . .* And, Sarah had once let slip (actually it was a remark she had made to Frances) that Carrie had admitted to having feelings for Daniel. Marion had heard, herself, some months back from Mary Thurber (God rest her soul) how her son Daniel had been asking about Carrie. Apparently Daniel and Carrie had re-acquainted themselves at one of those "Bell Parties" held at the Wisner mansion during last Christmas season, when Daniel was home from college. So, perhaps there's something to it. And Marion had to admit, that *was* the point of getting Carrie invited to a society event at the Governor's, wasn't it so, now that her daughter was coming of age, truly. *And Daniel seems to be a good boy, even if a bit tongue-tied.*

The problem was, for now in more practical terms, did this mean that Carrie might skip the modeling appointment and instead slip away to the McConnell's to meet with her beau again? *Sicut cervus*[31]

Now that would be just the sort of caper that Marion's conniving brother Erry would enjoy arranging. Erry had hired Daniel for the

---

31 Sicut cervus desiderat ad fontes aquarum: "As a deer longs for springs of water.: (Psalm 41 Latin text).

summer to work with him at the Town Hall, supposing this would help his friend, poor old Horace, in a gesture similar to Marion's taking on Sarah . . . But come to think of it, both Erry and Fannie have been mentioning about young Thurber and his fine, serious character. Ah yes, this was starting to add up. So that's why Carrie had insisted on working this afternoon at the candy shop, so Erry could arrange for her to make a delivery of sweets to the McConnell's. Of course! *Oh . . ., Marion thought, perhaps I'm overthinking all of this . . . but I should make a quick run to the candy shop just to confirm, anyway. Hmm. Johnny Bray could postpone his daguerreotypes another day, I suppose, but it would still be quite an inconvenience for the both of us.* Marion had paused in her work, and was gazing absentmindedly at one of the other new gowns still hanging on a large rack. It was satin, emerald green. *Wouldn't Carrie look simply stunning posing in something like that.* And at this point it occurred to Marion that she had meant to start the afternoon's work with Mrs. Crofoot's clasps in the silk taffeta, but never mind, she would get to those later.

The candy shop. That used to be the other Holley family shop, when Marion's husband John had tried his hand at yet another storefront business, this time candy and confectioneries. Six years ago John had joined into a partnership with Jack Crawford, by buying out the share of Jack's previous partner Bill Burr, so the new partnership of Crawford & Holley was thus underway, already well known for their sweets and bakery items at Crawford's store on the Hodges block. And for the most part the enterprise hummed along adequately. They also made attempts at expanding the business into oysters, and dairy products, but those forays didn't last very long. One investment that did pay off was the cracker-making machine that Bill Burr had originally installed, and still brings in a good flow of cash to this day.

But in any event, after only a year with Crawford & Holley, John Holley wanted out. There were just too many opportunities for other products, larger products, in a growing market like Pontiac in a time of so many new inventions and innovations. Especially farming equipment. John became the local sales agent for companies that made harvesters, combines, mowers, milling machines—and so far this stock and trade seems to be the ticket. He's had several lucrative contracts for the new Kirby harvester-mower, *my goodness, manufactured in Buffalo and shipped all the way to Pontiac.* His sales relations with the farmers is good, as apparently her husband has a knack for tact and integrity, so collections have not been a problem. So far so good for the Holley family, she had to admit.

After John had sold out his partnership at the candy shop, he and Marion still maintained a good social relationship with Jack Crawford, and in due course Jack was happy to take on young Carrie as a clerk in his shop, still operating at The Old Stand line of stores under the Hodges House. Carrie enjoyed working there (her friends probably enjoyed having an "in" at the candy store) and Marion was gratified to see her daughter keep busy after school in the afternoons, learn the trade, make a little money of her own and learn how to spend it and how to save it. Too bad for Crawford – his next partner after John also didn't last long, leaving less than a year later to set up his own grocery business across the street. That's business. In Marion's opinion, Crawford must appreciate having Carrie Holley work in his store, if only to show some stability in the community for his customers.

Crawford wouldn't be at the store this afternoon, Marion realized, as Carrie had told her yesterday that today he would be visiting Mathews Mill to schedule flour deliveries. That meant that only George Curtis, the other clerk, would be at the store while Carrie was minding the counter, and George would stand in for her if she needed to leave for any reason, no questions asked. Marion could see this all happening. *Yes, I'd better get Carrie over to Bray's before she steals away to McConnell's, before 4:00 if I can.* "Frances, I may have to step out later today for an hour or so. You'll be here, won't you?"

"Of course, Marion."

As for John Bray, there was really nothing to worry about, by the bye, but Marion couldn't help feeling just a bit leery of him, something of a caustic, jumpy sort, his personality at once genial and dismissive. The man wore a wig and laughed at his own obtuse jokes, which most of the time were difficult to follow. And apparently he was something of a charity case for the Pittman's—Bray could barely support his wife and three children. Poor as Job's turkey they were. The children always seemed sickly; and the family had already lost three children in years past. Marion was glad to support his business, by whatever indirect means it might help his family, and Bray did good work with his camera, after all. He would do a lot better if he could offer *cartes de visite* pictures, smaller, cheaper images that were produced several on one sheet, all identical. These were becoming quite popular, and it was a good bet the demand for them would grow with the war coming on, the boys all wanting to pose in their uniforms. Ah well, Bray was still unwilling to make the investment in one of those new multi-lens cameras, reluctant to find the money, or the time to master new equipment, or both. His loss.

Then there was the matter of his politics, and his past. That is, years ago, and before marrying into the Pittman family, Bray had emigrated from England where he was known for inflammatory publications calling for government reforms to improve public welfare and business practices. In a way it wasn't difficult to conjure up an image of the impoverished writer, dedicated to his social causes, always reading or lecturing, and careless of his own health. Marion's husband said that Bray was a "socialist revolutionary" or something to that effect.[32] As far as she could make out, socialism was only a European problem,

---

32 John Bray's pamphlet "Labour's Wrongs and Labour's Remedy" is quoted at length by Karl Marx in his 1847 work, "The Poverty of Philosophy."

where philosophers and writers would obsess over working conditions of people who labored in mines and factories. Here in Pontiac nobody seemed to care much about it, except John Bray. He was still writing and talking about workers and labor, even as America was preparing to wage war against rebellion and slavery in the South. Nevertheless Marion supposed there was room enough in Pontiac for "all kinds" including an odd duck like John Bray fumbling around in his attic studio.

It was all part of what kept life interesting and busy, in town in the city, with politics, ideas, and inventions like cameras and sewing machines. And Marion rather enjoyed the busy life, with all the tasks and scheduling and problems mixed in with the family businesses. Usually there was *too much* to keep track of. She had been arguing with her husband, just yesterday at dinner, about the need for installing gaslight fixtures in the workshop, which would enable more work to be done after dark, but the cost of connection to the city's new gas system was still quite significant, and it may be worth-while to wait a few months more, at least while the summer days were still very long.

Handling money was something her husband could do well, for the most part, although one or two of John's priorities were continually a subject of anxiety in the household. These days an ongoing sore point was his donations to the Congregational Church, specifically for the construction cost of the church's massive steeple which apparently might even bankrupt the Pontiac congregation, or so the rumors went. The steeple certainly mattered, admired by everyone as the most visible feature over the town's entire skyline, as grand as any of the spires ascending throughout Detroit, and yet, sometimes Marion wondered whether the elders had stretched the funds and the loans a bit too far for such an ambitious project. The greater glory of God was one thing; the cost of a man's prestige was another. Then again, as Marion well knew, prestige was a fact of life that could inspire a greater good as well, and regardless, there it was, a magnificent steeple and landmark.

But it was costing a lot of money in many households including the household of John and Marion Holley.

Business decisions, household matters, money worries . . . overall, of course, things were finally settling together nicely for the family in Pontiac. Both businesses were running smoothly, sufficient for Marion to start teaching Sunday school—*fishhooks! It's already been two years now* – and to be sure, the past year had been their best ever since they had arrived from cold, hilly Vermont. Michigan was more frontier-like, and more practical. Pontiac kept up with the times: Marion still remembered how her imagination was so stirred by hearing that the Wisner mansion had its own furnace heat coming right up from the basement. Carrie had come home from the Bell Party all impressed by the big eight-sided room with its grates in the floor where the warm air gently came up. No need for an awkward stove, or a big smoky, ashy fireplace. *Wouldn't it be nice to have something like that in our own home . . .*

Marion realized with a self-effacing grin that she had been fidgeting with the gown on the table all this time while her mind wandered over these haphazard thoughts. And by now the entire gown was fully straightened out over the table surface before her; it really was an attractive square print, with a striking red color in the pattern. It reminded her of a dress she saw last Sunday at the Pentecost service in church. As Marion looked over the fabric admiringly, the memory of the Pentecost service led to yet another distraction, as she now

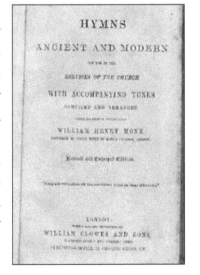

remembered a special task that she had set for herself: prepare the music for her next Sunday school lesson.

Sunday next would be Trinity Sunday—what sort of school lesson might work best for the children? Marion had been looking for a way to talk about the Holy Ghost, and she still wasn't convinced that the assigned Scripture readings would hold their interest for very long. A better lesson, she thought now, might be simply to get everyone singing that new hymn "Holy, Holy, Holy! Lord God Almighty," It had just been published in the Anglican Church hymnal. Even though Marion had only heard it once, by chance, played by Mary Merryweather in the parish hall last Sunday, she knew the tune was easy to sing, and the words were marvelously simple. Tomorrow, Friday, she would walk over to Allison's jewelry shop to see if they had the hymn book in their Jim Drake stock, or if necessary run over to Cleantha McConnell's and ask whether the

Methodist Episcopal Church choir might lend a copy for a few days. Cleantha should be in a position to return a favor, after all, since Marion had purchased for her that elegant little china plate for dainties at the Haughwout store in New York during the trip there last year. Prestige has its costs.

Perhaps John is right, Marion bowed her head as she tried to free her mind of schedules and hymns and lesson plans. *Perhaps the Sunday school teaching is spreading me a little thin.* Every day too long, it seemed, and every week too short.[33]

One thing was for sure, however: daily life was about to change greatly, now that Carrie was going to graduate from school. And now along comes Danny Thurber, a fine boy, not really the impetuous "Lothario" type, one might say. Are these the dreams of her daughter, to be courted and married into top society like that? *I should ask Fannie Thatcher how serious this really is.*

Marion raised her head, took deep breath, and went back to work measuring the gown on the table, and counting her stock of steel spring hoops, and worrying about Carrie eating too many sweets and ruining her teeth, and thinking about rescheduling the daguerreotype session at Bray's, and the benefits of gas fixtures in her home, and wondering whether all those college boys especially Daniel were going to volunteer for the army, and whether that meant a proposal for Carrie this very summer.

But for all those worries, perhaps it was just as well that Marion could work and thrive, safely and with purpose, and avoid the one threat that was always there in the back of her mind that troubled her the most. In two years Marion Holley would turn forty, "twoscore" years. The number seemed old to her, vaguely, in an age that was some-

---

33   "Holy, Holy, Holy" hymn included in the hymnbook "Hymns Ancient and Modern" published in London in March, 1861. The tune used for this hymn was "Nicaea," written by John Dykes in that year, to accompany the words written by Reginal Heber in the 1820's. The hymnbook, edited by William Henry Monk, also introduced new hymns such as "Abide with Me" by Monk, "Onward, Christian Soldiers" by Arthur Sullivan (later of Gilbert & Sullivan fame), and "Eternal Father, Strong to Save," which would later be adopted as the navy hymn, by William Whiting. The book organized hymns into sections, some according to the church calendar, others by various sacraments or feasts. It also popularized the style of attaching the word "Amen" at the end of a hymn.

how unfair to a capable woman who still wanted to pursue happiness, day to day, season to season.

Frances had turned around and was looking at her from the West & Wilson table. "Can I help you with anything, Marion, before Mrs. Darrow arrives?"

POINTS IN TIME

A BUSINESSMAN walked across Saginaw Street, pausing once
to wait for a carriage to rumble past, then a second time as a trio of
horses was being led along by an unhurried stablehand. This was at the
intersection of Saginaw and Pike Streets, at the moment fairly crowded
with traffic, and as the businessman crossed the street he was mindful
to stay on the inlaid planks of the crosswalk. He was trying to avoid
getting street dirt on his new shoes, a tact which required a few evasive
sidesteps around pedestrians coming the other way, but he managed,
aptly conferring a few peremptory nods and grins as he went. Finally
reaching the far side he hopped up onto the boardwalk, deftly slipped
through another knot of people on the corner, and was then able to
continue freely down Pike Street, eastward, to his next appointment.

There was nothing particularly noteworthy about the man or how
he made his way across the street, and no reason why anyone might
look at him twice or think about where he might be going. He was
dressed in a fine, dark suit and, like many other men on the boardwalks that afternoon he had a long beard and wore a top hat, rendering

his immediate appearance as both respectable and rather nondescript on the busy streets. He carried a leather attaché case, well-worn yet presentable for a business meeting, and thin evidently, as if it must be practically empty.

If someone had actually spoken to this man, however, they might have been quite surprised and amused to hear what was on his mind. These were his thoughts: *What a remarkable change in only a few short years. This street was once nothing more than a trail through the woods, and this exact place where I am now walking—this was once a quiet passage, under tall trees. No loud voices, no horses, no sounds hardly at all.*

This train of thought was well-masked, naturally, and the expression on the man's face gave no indication of an imagination wandering free like that in the middle of a busy intersection. Quite the contrary: he had all the look of an alert, objective-oriented businessman *en route* to his next appointment. And by the time he was striding down Pike Street his momentary lapse of focus was gone and his mind was back on track with the regular pace of time and events. What mattered to him now was that he had just concluded a meeting during lunch with a banker in the Hodges House dining hall, and as it turned out, the few documents in his attaché case were never even brought out anyway. The meal was pleasant, and the banker cordial, but whereas this interchange had succeeded in establishing a sound professional connection, the prospects for meaningful investment were simply not attractive enough in terms of available funds and business locations in the area.

So that was that. However, the man was not altogether disappointed by this outcome. The lunch meeting was only introductory, worthwhile if only for a brief exploration of opportunities in Pontiac, and in the end his original expectations favoring Detroit had not changed. Accordingly there was now no reason to remain in Pontiac another day, and the man was resolved to book a ticket to Detroit on tomorrow's morning train. This afternoon he would inform everyone of the change in his travel plans, which should not come as a surprise or cause any undue inconvenience.

The rest of today looked to be a bit more carefree, for the entire afternoon had been reserved for family and friends at a large social engagement an easy walk from the center of town. To that end the man's next appointment was at the public school, just a few blocks further on Pike, where he was to pick up his 12-year-old niece and bring her along to the party. It had been several months since he had been in town to see all his relatives and he genuinely looked forward to the gathering. It should be a good time. As far as he knew, everyone was in good health, and there would be much news and catching up to do, as usual, and encouragement to shower upon the younger relatives sprouting up. His sister would be at the party, too, which was good; her new husband would not be there, which was better still.

And so the businessman kept up his pace as the day continued to unfold, hour by hour, like an "ever rolling stream" of ideas and cares for the future. The man had just sung that very phrase a few Sundays ago in church, in a hymn that always reminded him of singing hymns with his mother when he was a boy.

Time had been streaming along indeed, for many years back at that same spot where Saginaw crosses Pike. It flew rapidly for some people, and crept slowly for others. But unless some major change was being made to the surrounding landscape, which was seldom, there was little to recall about walking through this place, in whatever era, whether it was a quiet forest path or a noisy city street. People came and went, preoccupied with what they intended to do next, careless of any future beyond their dreams, content to flit along as free as a ghost.

Just for the record, today at that same spot a few other ghosts would also be passing through not long after the businessman. Each of them must have had thoughts and ideas, all private of course, yet still worth exploring to see how they might have interconnected with one another. For example, a young man was soon crossing Saginaw but in the opposite direction, having just said good-bye to two other young men near the southeast corner. The three of them were childhood friends who now attended different colleges, far away from Pontiac, and they were all home again for the summer. They had just enjoyed a reunion at lunch in a nearby saloon, as cheery a time as it could only be; their convivial mood had stayed with them out the door and onto Saginaw where they chose to walk in the street, down next to the boardwalk, so all three might walk along side by side until they reached the corner at Pike. There they parted company, as our young man turned left to head down Pike to his home on the west side of town, and his two friends continued on Saginaw towards Lawrence on another errand.

At this point the young man who crossed Saginaw was not much concerned with history or changing times. It barely mattered to him that he was again walking through his home town, among familiar buildings, familiar sights and sounds, seeing one or two faces that were also somehow familiar, if only vaguely so. His passage here was routine, and in any event, hardly opportune for lofty thoughts about the Past and the Future. In a setting like this the young man would only think about his personal circumstances, Here and Now.

There were a number of things in his life that he felt he ought to assess more deeply and dispassionately, personal matters, the kinds of problems that he knew could not be solved. The most painful of these: that his mother had died, only weeks ago, and his father was still distraught over it. The most bothersome: that he was unhappy at college, and he did not like his studies. And the most confounding: that it seemed all of his friends were hooked on going to war, including his best friend who was rushing off to army life. What to make of this war, then? Back at college his classmates had been marching and drilling on the campus grounds with all the enthusiasm they might show for a club exercise or a sporting event. Here at home, however, the bearings were far more serious. All of Pontiac, and Oakland County, and the entire state seemed hell-bent on invading the South and "saving the union" while all the boys were signing up for 3-year enlistments! Three years of living in barracks, or tents, and tramping on muddy roads in the rain ... for this young man it didn't seem the most worthy ambition. Could he somehow find the same passion and fervor for rallying with the crowd, despite all his doubts?

And then there was the girl. He could forget everything else, manage all other burdens, and think only about the girl. If only he might court her openly and fair. But no, it just wasn't proper, for now, and he wasn't completely sure that a girl like that would even fancy his advances. No, there must be another boy that she favored anyway, or so he thought. And his dismay had led him to doubt his own appearance, self-conscious about his own jawline which seemed grossly prominent in the mirror. He envied his best friend at college for his height and more martial bearing. *No, don't show your cards to the girl just now*, he told himself. *Better wait while your family is still mourning your mother, and while men are still enlisting. Things might settle down. Just make sure you land that position working for the mayor—so no one could blame you for staying out of uniform this summer if you were working at the Court House.*

These were the burdens on his mind, as the young man left the intersection and faded from view, walking westbound on Pike. He left behind no traces of this mundane action in a mundane location. In future years someone else would have to imagine his experience, what it felt like to cross a busy thoroughfare, what he saw and heard around him. At the time, the details had no meaning.

A short time later another person has approached the same intersection, walking up Pike from the east side to cross westward over Saginaw just as the young man did earlier, practically retracing the same steps on the wooden crosswalk. This new arrival is a young woman, actually still a schoolgirl, who upon reaching the other side of Saginaw abruptly turns left to pass the front door of the big hotel there on the corner. She's nicely dressed, wearing a shawl over her shoulders, and a smartly-tailored skirt, brown leather gloves, and a small oval-shaped hat, unadorned and perched slightly forward. She walks along at a smart clip, and like any youthful person she is able to look freely about while moving along, attentive to every person and every building she passes.

It's interesting how this passer-by has been looking upon the same features of the intersection, as the young man did before her, yet with an attitude markedly different. In her case the familiarity of the buildings, the store-front windows and the signs, and the consistency of the flow of traffic up and down Saginaw—all of this lends a feeling of security and strengthens the girl's spirit. It is a world that she embraces readily without ponder or comparison, with "gladness and singleness of heart" like the scripture she has said at home[34], part of her family's grace before dinner. Here she is striding along buoyantly, heading towards a retail shop where she works most days after school, like other girls in her class having similar jobs. So, this high school student is younger than she appears at first glance, swishing along like this in the public view. It's a successful ploy on her part because that is exactly what she means to do, which is to look older.

It is especially important to look older today, because the girl has a specific goal to pursue after work: to go to a large reception party in the late afternoon at the home of a prominent family of Pontiac. The girl has not been invited but neither has she been purposely uninvited; she plans to attend anyway, alone if necessary, and just blend in with all the guests. And the reason for being there: *he* will be there. A certain young man will surely be attending as a good friend of the host family, and the girl cannot miss this chance to connect with him there at the

---

34 "Gladness and singleness of heart:" from the Book of Acts 2:46 (King James Version).

party, as she has before at other social engagements, and convey once again how she favors his company. And, discretely but plainly, convey her maturity. The boy is on the shy side but still handsome, and his depth of good character is very attractive, in her mind all the more so because he seems so unaware of it.

True, the underlying goal is to find the right partner. But shouldn't that fit with trying to keep life moving along gently, throwing in a small caper like this from time to time? Let her school years come to end, as they will soon enough, giving way to love and marriage. It needn't be so worrisome. Friends at school were always assuring her that she was fair and fine, so she ought to be able to transition into married life successfully. Her mother's expectations, however, were not as clear, moreover vaguely perplexing, as though detractive of marriage while encouraging her daughter to have loftier dreams, ideas about what she could accomplish beyond a home and family. Then again, the mother constantly frets about finances, politics, and social connections—all the issues that are never resolved to her satisfaction. What she doesn't see, meanwhile, is that for her daughter the only thing that counts now is marriage. Marriage is the next step, the key to security and acceptance in society, and freedom—freedom to pursue the full life.

But so far this day is going fine, with early dismissal from school, and arriving on time for work at the store despite a brief stop at home on the way. That part was a little iffy although it worked out. All she needed to do was quickly change into her corset to wear it underneath her school clothes before going to work at the store. No one would take notice at work, but afterwards when she changed into a dress for the party, voilà, that's when the undergarment would serve its purpose—to add that extra measure of maturity. And just as she hoped, when she had stopped in at home the only person there was a young housemaid who was kind enough to help her put on the corset and retie the backside. Fortunately, for things of this nature the maid could be relied upon for secrecy, that is, if Mother learned about the corset then she would immediately suspect the plan to run off to the party. Not that the garment itself is particularly "inapproprié"; after all, it was her mother who had surreptitiously placed the corset in the girl's wardrobe in the first place, last year on her birthday. No, there is no reason for anyone to fuss over any of this.

The fit is snug but not uncomfortable; the effect is rewarding. As the girl walks up Pike Street her back is straight, her shoulders are back and her chin is up. It's no trouble to glance down and mind her steps; she has grown up in this town and is very accustomed to the shapes and crannies of every street and boardwalk, every intersection and crosswalk, especially in the commercial area. She misses one detail: the flower boxes outside Linabury's general store at the corner of Pike and Saginaw, which today offer a nice display of purple geraniums, each box holding an impressively thick bunch of the wildflowers. But Linabury's flowers are a reliable feature, customary and expected, except in the dead of winter; moreover, today the decorations are completely upstaged by a gaudy flare of red, white and blue bunting which has been nailed up all around the window frames. *That* is what commands attention. The bunting catches her eye, and it's fun and colorful, and it signals that these are days when a person could get away with anything, so you may as well try.

The girl comes around the corner at Saginaw and continues down the boardwalk towards the storefront where she will report in to begin her after-school job; but meanwhile, seconds after she moves away from the corner, out in the street behind her there are two more people worth noting. These people are riding in wagons going in opposite directions on Saginaw, and the moment comes when they draw near in passing by each other in the middle of the intersection. One wagon is a cabriolet, the other a surrey. In each wagon there are two men, a younger man handling the reins and an older man beside him, riding passenger. It's the two drivers that deserve a brief consideration, since they know each other, say well enough to wave amiably as they go by. Neither will become famous or leave behind much in the way of a biography for others to reference; nevertheless these two ghosts really did live once, and pursued happiness and cared about their futures, until their time faded away along with the rest of the community. As their wagons roll past, there is time here to capture a few similarities and contrasts in their lives so far.

Both men have lived in Pontiac only a few years, having been raised in far off lands mired in poverty, in former lives now completely abandoned. Both now have settled in well with their new surroundings, but they still feel a need to impress everyone here that they are being overlooked, and are capable of much more accomplishment and prestigious work. The driver of the cabriolet takes care to hide an Irish accent when speaking, something he fears will prevent his finding better employment. He has resolved that the best, quickest way to improve his lot in life will be through the army, fighting bravely in battle and returning home as a hero. No stranger to a scrap now and then, he is cocksure about his toughness, and during the idle moments of his workday he dreams of a day when everyone will look upon him with surprise and admiration.

The driver of the shay is not as concerned about bravery or legend but he is just as obsessed with improving his stature. He is a black man, who grew up a slave but now works for an *employer*, the rich man sitting next to him. The world has changed so much around him as a freedman that it's hard sometimes to figure out how to get along properly. A lot of what he does—organizing his work day, spending his free time and his own money—has been one personal experiment after another. So far nobody seems to mind. Apparently, all his employer requires is to see a calm face and hear a confident answer, so, the best way to do this and keep his job secure has come through learning to read, and reading newspapers and simple books. The ability to read, to become lettered, has always been a goal that the former slave had in mind since he arrived in Pontiac, and now it is slowly happening. It still feels biggity to learn about the world by reading what *he* wants to read, *when* he wants to read it, instead of relying on lore and traditions spoken aloud by the older people. And apparently his employer seems content with his progress.

The salutes exchanged by the drivers are smooth and nonchalant, since the two men are accustomed to these brief encounters. Only one other passer-by near the corner even notices the gestures. This is a woman on the eastside boardwalk of Saginaw who is in the company of two gentlemen in conversation, though she is not paying attention. She recognizes the rich man in the shay, a distraction which leads her view to the drivers; she enjoys the subtleness of the drivers' communication. And from there her focus next lands suddenly right in front of her, on the young girl in the shawl walking along the boardwalk. The girl doesn't notice the woman, in that brief moment, but the woman recognizes the girl as the daughter of her friend the dressmaker. She knows the girl's mother, pointedly admiring her accomplishments as an independent woman running her own business despite being married. She should do something like that herself, since her own marriage has not a happy one, and she very much regrets the loss of her earlier freedom. Someday, perhaps. The sight of this girl walking past—so content, so oblivious—depresses her spirit to think of her own future, in contrast, holding far less promise. At least she can look forward to this afternoon, when she'll be seeing an older brother at a family reunion party—he's only visiting Pontiac for a day or two. Unfortunately she just missed seeing him walk across the intersection a few minutes earlier, the bearded man with the empty attaché case.

Sometimes a sampling of these stories and dreams from times past might be appealing, especially when a number of interrelationships can be discovered among the people who were there, at a certain point in time in some ordinary, inconsequential location. The place is still there today, inviting anyone to imagine walking side by side with those who once lived there, and hear the noises they heard, and smell the aromas and odors they knew, and talk about whatever it was that mattered at the time. They were earnest in their hopes and ambitions, like anyone today, and they must have felt as though the world around them was at its peak in terms of comfort, order, and modern technology. How lucky to be alive in 1861.

These sentiments could not be better exemplified than in one more person who is on the scene, a man who should be singled out just to have a better understanding of what is going on. He's visiting from out of town, purportedly to look over some available real estate, but his true interest seems to lie in meeting and observing various people around town. Nobody seems to know him very well, though some have met him before. He's a congenial sort, and well-mannered. He's actually quite engaging. And evidently he has the means, and the wherewithal, to get along with top society. There he is, standing on the boardwalk in front of the Hodges House, apparently about to enter but pausing for one more look at all the people on Saginaw Street. Strange fellow. Perhaps he fancies himself like a ghost in that Christmas story by Charles Dickens, able to look down upon scenes that took place in some far-away time, as if recast on a theater stage. Very imaginative, granted, but actually not so far-fetched for those times, an era of spiritualism and séances, mysticism, and trick photography.

But in real time, of course, everything that has occurred at Saginaw and Pike will soon evaporate from memory. Nothing *happened* there. The intersection is not hallowed ground. Now the first man, the businessman who had crossed Saginaw with his clean shoes and his well-worn attaché case, is nearing the school where he will collect his young niece for the afternoon reception party. For no particular reason he starts to sing a tune, discretely to himself, as he walks along Pike. It's a full verse from that St. Anne hymn, the one that had popped into his head back at Saginaw Street:

"Time, like an ever-rolling stream, bears all our years away;
They fly, forgotten as a dream dies at the opening day."[35]

---

35 5th verse from the Anglican hymn "O God, our help in ages past" with lyrics taken from a poem by Isaac Watts. (St. Anne melody harmonized by William Henry Monk.)

Charles Draper, Sr.

I can explain this briefly. There are two newspapers, both weeklies. There's the *Gazette*, published by Myron Howell, which has a liberal bent and favors Lincoln and the Republicans. Then there's the *Jacksonian*, published by Gus Baldwin, more conservative and favoring the Democrats. Now: Howell will be at McConnell's reception, and Baldwin won't. Clear so far? But keep in mind that our political affiliations in this town don't mean animosities, necessarily. Howell will tell you that all Democrats are appeasers and soft on slavery in the south. Baldwin will tell you that the Republicans are all war-mongers and zealots parading around in their nighttime Wide-Awake demonstrations. No, not so stark as all that. But you can appreciate how Howell and Baldwin sustain a healthy amount of subscription business.

As for me, I am a Republican and I am anti-slavery, for the West, for the South, for anywhere. I don't know whether my boy Stuart will be going to war over this or stay on at the University, but the choice is his to make, and I will abide by it. And you can see this for yourself: Michigan is going to war, and Governor Blair will raise regiments for this war, and Pontiac boys will join these regiments in swarms. So all this time, remember, in these times of excitement and political passion, who am I working with, every day at my law office? Who is my law firm partner? Augustus Baldwin. You see? We are not at each other's throat. We ply our trade and we discuss issues after hours. We each of us respect and esteem the other. And we pray Godspeed for Joseph McConnell, and for my son, and all the boys.

I'll tell you something else. Most folks around here are cock-sure that all Lincoln has to do is show a little muscle and the South will back down. Me – I'm not so sure. We're going to meet a Confederate army, in some form, and I'll wager they're just as cocky as we are. I read an article about a ceremony at the military academy at West Point, where they allowed a third of the cadets to pack up and ride right out the gates, and return home in the South, where they'll soon be commanding enemy forces. Can you imagine? A ceremony! How very *gallant* of them. No, I think we'll all regret this terribly. But there you are – *Alea iacta est.*

Courthouse on SW corner of Saginaw and Huron streets.

Ira Butterfield.

Ice! Ice! Ice!

SCOTT & CLARK

RESPECTFULLY inform the citizens of Pontiac and vicinity that they have purchased the large

Ice House of Swan & Allen,

and are prepared to furnish that decidedly cool article - ICE - to customers on liberal terms during the coming season. Orders solicited and promptly attended to.

Pontiac, May 5, 1859.   775tf

A VISITOR'S STORY,
"To Church Street"

HAVING PURCHASED the candy at Crawford's Confectionery it only took a minute to duck back into Turk's Grocery to advise the manager that Crawford's shopgirl would be coming to pick up your wine purchase and deliver it to the McConnells' party herself. Those matters settled, you're back again on the boardwalk of Saginaw Street to resume your walk to the McConnell house. The bells of the Congregational church are just now ringing out the half-hour chime, an assurance that you should still be able to make the reception with plenty of time. You could head back into the Hodges House and call for a cabriolet, but no need, the walk will do you good on such a fine day. A minute or two later you're passing the Astor House hotel on your left, and now you've reached the bridge over the Clinton River, where you came into town this morning on the cab.

Back then you hardly even saw the Clinton as you passed over it; now on foot it would be interesting to take a look over the side rail, especially on the east side of the street where, if you remember correctly, the river widens into the large retention pond. So you cross Saginaw to the Astor side and step up onto the boardwalk to take a look, and yes, the big pond is still there, a calm basin of dark water with a traces of breeze enough to cause a few glints of sunlight. And at first glance the pond presents a pleasant sight, where the river has expanded out to an area as big as three acres, curving around at the far end to the left, on its way north again to where it will pass under the power wheels of the big companies along Mill Street. It's a nice view for the guests on the upper floors of the Astor House too, you imagine. Further down on the near shoreline some people are sitting under a tent, more like a sunshade, enjoying a picnic it would seem.

You recall how Elkanah Comstock earlier today at the courthouse had mentioned that the City had cleaned out the brush and over-growth. Evidently the project was a success. It's too bad there's not much in the way of landscaping around the banks of the pond, nor is there any pedestrian access leading down from where you're standing, up here on the street. It is, after all, just a functioning mill pond, not anyone's dream of a recreational area. No trees, either.

For that matter the longer you look out over the pond the less appealing it becomes. That is, despite the breezes, most of the water's surface is smooth and stagnant, and the dark color is better described as a murkiness. You begin to notice patches of lighter discoloration—definitely some unnatural material dumped in somewhere—and here and there an empty box or some other debris is floating motionless in the distance. No, this is not exactly a city attraction. Useful, though, for the small breweries and the marble cutter businesses upstream behind you, unloading whatever waste they can into the river. Polluting the water, one might conclude, is not a big concern for the public, a public that has little leisure time anyway to spend relaxing in a fancy municipal park. There's lots of open countryside all around Pontiac for anyone planning a picnic. Then there's the fairgrounds, and plenty of natural lakes just west of here in Waterford.

Leaning on the bridge rail as you consider the purpose of a big mill pond like this, you can't imagine a more picturesque future for it. Quite the opposite—most of the townfolk probably consider it nothing more than an eyesore, albeit a necessary one for the mill businesses. Such are the times, and modern priorities.

You're done with this panorama and about to move on, but you stop to look again at the area below the Astor Hotel where a number of people are idling nearby a standalone clapboard structure, a stable probably. It's an odd scene that has caught your attention: a real display of poverty, more to the point, a collection of indigent types in a tattered, sorry state. From the rough, vacant grounds below a few of them look back at you as if hoping for some response. There are a couple of men over there, and a family here, and further on, a group of Ojibwas[36] sitting on some decrepit chairs talking with—or ignoring?—a few children standing before them, perhaps teasing them. All in all, it's a distressful sight if not disturbing. The clothes are dirty, clearly worn out, and you see sacks on the ground by the family which must contain everything they own. Their expressions are doleful, resigned, and it makes you wonder what happened to them. Are they pioneers heading inland to the lumber settlements, who ran out of money? Or are they waiting here for a husband or son to send word, and funds, to come join them at some inland settlement? Look closer at that family sitting under the tent—no, that's no leisurely picnic. Apparently there is nothing for them to do today, and nowhere to go for any particular reason.

With you on the boardwalk a large man is leaning with his back on the railing, his arms folded, with all the look of a town constable. As you walk past him, he nods slightly with an assuring smile as he touch-

---

36 Ojibwa, or Chippewa, native Americans.

es a finger to the brim of his hat. Apparently the pond is a valid place for a constable to keep an eye on things. This morning during your ride in you weren't aware of any vagrants in these surroundings. In fact until now you haven't seen or heard much about the needy in Pontiac, or anyone facing hard times or whatever misfortunes. The only recourse for food and shelter must be at the various churches in town, as there are no city organizations or alms programs there to help.

But there doesn't appear to be any trouble here, or much of anything going on, really, so you may as well continue on your way to the McConnell's. As you resume walking across the bridge there's a cabriolet going down the middle of Saginaw in the same direction, and you look up to see "Morris Livery" stenciled on the side and sure enough, the driver is Andy O'Brien. It looks as though he's on his way back to the Pontiac depot to stand ready for the next train arrival. Andy doesn't see you, but he sees the constable and signals a greeting with an inane, toothy smile. "Top o' the morning to ye, Constable Foster!" he exclaims in full Irish lilt. You glance over at the constable and see that he's grinning back at Andy, actually leveling something of a serious stare which seems to say *Yes, boyo, I know who you are. Move along now.*

You keep yourself moving along, too, over the bridge now and passing a few more shops and storefronts. Across the street are a couple of businesses quintessential for the times: Peach's farrier shop and Fisher's Livery. The sign for Thomas Peach also touts his saloon business—perhaps a competitive feature for customers needing to pass some time while waiting for a horse to be re-shod? Could be a prudent business strategy. Beyond those buildings comes the shriek of a whistle of a train pulling into the depot, or perhaps passing by, on the Detroit & Milwaukee "D&M" line out of sight from here. (Oh—that may be the train that Andy O'Brien meant to convene with.) This stretch of Saginaw has less and less commerce, and presently the boardwalk comes to an end as well. There's still a remarkable amount of traffic out on the street, rolling north towards town, and the planks and gravel have started to appear on the street surface, something you remember from your ride in this morning. And now you can see how the paving is good for the wagon wheels, although for you on foot with today's fair weather it's best to keep to the side on the hard-packed earth.

Moving along upslope there are a few more trees now, lending a modicum of shade, and after a few minutes you come up to Church Street[37] which you will want to cross before turning left towards the McConnell's. Hold on a moment—you'll have to wait while a shay coming behind you is turning off of Saginaw onto Church at a fair clip. You can see there are three passengers, a young man with two young ladies, most likely on their way to the McConnells' reception. The man driving is speaking with serious purpose, even as he glances back at you and offers a brief nod in a courteous gesture. The face of the woman sitting in the middle is partially hidden by her bonnet, and you just get a glimpse of her eyes—she's quite young—so a pretty face remains a mystery as the rig rolls by. And you only have a second to see the other young lady, at the far end of the seat, whom you think you might recognize . . . Isn't that the Holley girl from the candy shop? She's looking off to the opposite side. Well, if that was her, let's hope she's bringing the bottle of Chautauqua wine you ordered.

So far this afternoon your walk through the town has yielded a number of interesting encounters, thinking back on it. Levi Bacon and Elkanah Comstock—those two you hope to see again at the McConnell's. Not only are they highly entertaining characters but if you're tactful enough, they could help you find out a lot more about the younger people you're here to track down. Then, the three college boys at the Arcade, and the intriguing Mrs. French coming in with her gentleman friend. You look forward to seeing them at the party, too. And that outgoing Carrie Holley working in Crawford's, even though

---

37   Church Street will later be renamed Auburn Avenue.

only a brief contact—all of these meetings have already contributed towards making this a worthwhile visit. This is the kind of material you'll need for rendering a thorough report, what you were sent here to do.

Proceeding now across Church Street you can see a block further south on Saginaw where construction of the new Methodist Episcopal Church is underway, a busy site on a workday afternoon. As the cab  driver said this morning, the church is going to be a good-sized building. This much is evident, judging from the numbers of workmen deployed around the large foundation area, and all the wagons parked about, and the various scaffold assemblies that are

Schoolhouse at Church & Parke

starting to take shape. The work site is far enough away such that you can't hear much of the commotion there, other than some desultory pang-pang-pang hammer noises, while you continue to walk down Church into what is a quieter residential area. At the end of the first block you cross over Parke Street where an old one-story brick schoolhouse still stands at the corner. The McConnell house will be another quarter mile further down Church; there is no need to hurry, and in late May you can enjoy the chestnut trees and huge elms, in full leaf, and the leisurely swishing of their branches overhead in the afternoon breezes. The yards of many homes have forsythia bushes adding more greenery, their spindly branches having lost all the yellow blooms of early spring. But now there are some lilacs coming out here and there, offering a touch of color to uphold your sense of the season well underway.

Still standing at the corner of Church and Parke, the pause has allowed you to notice a couple approaching on foot, from the south along Parke Street. They are well dressed; you wonder whether they might be on their way to the McConnell's reception just as you are. The man has a long, dark beard, though he appears young, and is accompanying a girl in her teens, perhaps his daughter. Without stopping his stride he pulls out a silvery pocket watch on a chain which he glances down upon and then deftly snaps it shut.

Why not wait for them? As they draw near, you can see from the man's expression that he might be inclined to exchange a friendly greeting. The girl stays close by him, without expression, tactful, making only short glances your way, but the man's eyes are attentive, amiable, under the brim of his top hat. You extend your hand for a shake, and he likewise, and the introductions are easy and pleasant. His name is Hervey Parke, the girl is his niece Clettie, and yes, they are going to the McConnell's. It's only natural for the three of you to finish the walk together, and so you all set off again, walking along the side of Church Street. Initial conversation is only pleasantries, mostly about the good weather for the reception, and about the church worksite – it turns out that Hervey is a relative of the McConnell's, and Willard McConnell is one of the principals leading the church construction project. You are soon impressed by your new acquaintance, this well-mannered gentleman, his tone courteous yet somewhat careful, conveying good character. Hervey for his part seems interested to hear that you an out-of-town visitor, just as he is, which he is glad to explain a bit more.

He is in town for only a few days, on business, making calls on contacts in Pontiac and Detroit to arrange inventory purchases and credit arrangements for his company in the Upper Peninsula in Hancock. It's also an opportunity to attend the reception and see more of his extended family—Mrs. McConnell is a cousin, her father and Hervey's father being the well-known Parke brothers who were early settlers in Oakland County. Hervey was born and raised in Birmingham, just a few miles south of here, and as a young man he clerked for some time at the McConnell and Bacon store in Pontiac. It brings a smile to you both, then, upon your divulging how you also know Levi Bacon quite well and, agreed, he is truly an engaging character.

The girl is then further introduced to you as Clettie Kelsey, and she is 12 years old ("Almost 13. My father and I have the same birthday, July 13."), the daughter of Hervey's brother-in-law who lives on the north side of town. As reserved as the girl is now, you surmise she must be only biding her time politely before a chance to frolic with various McConnell cousins at the house. Hervey explains how the two of them had just now been down to see Willard's new church site before going to the McConnell's. *Oho, how fascinating for the young niece*, you're thinking with due skepticism. You would like to learn more about Hervey's family, and about the pioneer Parke brothers, but for now some small talk is best, and having noticed Hervey's slow pace and the exceptional shine of his black shoes, you catch his eye and serve up a casual query "New shoes?" Hervey catches your meaning and he nods and mouths the word "Ouch" quietly, moments later adding, "Balmoral boots. For the reception. Marcus sent me over to Lull's shoe store in town and I got them yesterday." With a smirk he adds, "I suppose this isn't the best time or place to break in the right-and-left. But, you know, there's always a cost for good impressions. And if balmorals are good enough for Prince Albert then they're good enough for me." Of course your Grace, you joke in reply. It's no trouble to accommodate him with a slower, more deliberate pace.

Conversation subsides for a time, and the walk down Church Street becomes a quiet passage, save for the horse-drawn ice wagon that moves slowly opposite towards town, mostly empty after the afternoon deliveries. Together with Hervey you exchange nods with the driver and handler men sitting up on the buckboard seat, as you peer at the stenciled lettering underneath as the wagon rolls past: "Scott & Clark, Ice House." Then behind the wagon your attention is drawn upwards, overhead, by a scattering of maple whirligig seeds as they spin down from the tree branches overhead. Springtime it is, with all of its enchantments. *A time for everything, and a season for every purpose under heaven,* so the psalmist wrote way back when.

Your threesome saunters along, and you can't help but ponder the quietude of this setting, the trees, the ice wagon, the impressive landscaping around all the homes, all of it starkly contrasted by the tension and excitement of national events that will define these febrile times. The war has finally started, so tensely expected, and at last the waiting for it is over. The Southerners have fired the first shots, bombarding a federal harbor fort in Charleston into submission, and with this the gauntlet has been thrown. Pontiac will now go to war practically as a celebration, and today at the McConnell's it will be no different if a bit more formal, and cordially conveyed.

After all, the very purpose of this reception is to celebrate the Mc-Connells' son Joseph, who has just joined the army and is now embarking on a military career with an enlistment for three years. From what you read in the Gazette and picked up at the Arcade, his regiment will be training in Detroit for several weeks until they are ready to travel to Washington and assemble with the rest of the army there. Like those boys you saw on the train this morning, Joseph must be enjoying a few days' leave at home before he returns to the Fort Wayne barracks to start his service. And this leave will also give him the chance to attend, tomorrow, a major social event in Pontiac, the wedding of his own commanding officer, the renowned Colonel Israel Richardson, to Fannie Travor. So it's one big "to do" after another. What a time of pride and such excitement for the McConnell's, and the Richardson's, and all the landed pioneer families in Pontiac.

"And what do you know of Joseph McConnell," you ask Hervey.

He's about to answer, but three carriages just then are clattering by on the street, distracting him for a few seconds, and while still watching them he replies, "Oh, not all that much. On this trip I did meet Joseph a few days ago at the rail depot. He and a group of friends were walking out from the telegraph office, and we chatted for a minute or two. All good folks. Someone's younger sister was tagging along."

He goes on, "I reckon there's a number of these college boys home for the summer, keeping time with their friends' younger sisters, within the social circle of the area's better families." Hervey exchanges a glance with his niece, who can't hide an embarrassed smile, as he adds "Someday, Clettie, you too might discover romance among the friends around you, too." She looks away, as if distracted by something she sees across the street.

Almost there now. You can see how the carriages are turning left into a field opposite the McConnell house, as directed for the event no doubt. You start recounting all the people you're about to meet. Let's think . . . Willard and Cleantha McConnell, the hosts. They have two grown sons: Parke, the gold rush prospector, and Joseph, the new soldier; and three younger children. Then there's Willard's brother Abiram, a doctor, who went with Parke out west on the goldrush. And then the elders: Cleantha's parents, old Captain Parke the surveyor, and his wife Mercy. Who else will be there? Dignitaries such as Governor Wisner, Colonel Richardson, and attorney Morgan Drake (no wonder Levi Bacon was anxious to attend the party!). Joseph's friends from college—both University of Michigan and Union College—and likely some other comrades already enlisted in the army, or about to go. And any number of other family children and cousins invited to keep the young men occupied.

Some of the family names are identical and need to be sorted out.

"Hervey, let me make sure I have this correct. We'll be seeing Mrs. McConnell, who is your cousin Cleantha. And her father will be there, your uncle, who also has the name Hervey, right? Captain Hervey Parke."

"That's right. You can use my full name if it helps—Hervey Coke Parke."

"I'll take it! So, then . . . your father's name?"

"Ezra Parke. But my father and mother died many years ago."

"I understand, yes, of course. And the McConnell's also have a son named Hervey, don't they?"

"They do. He's the oldest. He goes by his middle name, though, 'Parke'. Parke McConnell."

"Thank you, sir. This is helpful," you say, and Hervey grins and makes a slight nod as if happy to oblige. But you have one more name to cover: "And then, your niece here, Clettie. Her formal name is Cleantha, correct? Like Mrs. McConnell's name?"

Hervey laughs, agreeably. "The same. And you'll probably find more Clettie's at the party. The name seems to run in the family."

You're now finally approaching the corner of Paddock Street where you are nearing the outskirts of town, and here stands the McConnell house on a large property on the right side of the street. So, just as El-kanah was telling you back at the courthouse, the house really is 'quite something' for this small town. You stop for a moment just to take in the sight, which doesn't surprise Hervey, who is glad to wait along-side patiently while you admire his cousin's homestead. His hands are clasped behind his back, and his expression conveys a *yes-it-is-quite-nice* opinion—even though he's been here before here many times, cer-tainly. And the young Kelsey girl seems content to fiddle with a whirl-igig that she picked up earlier, trying to pry open its seed pocket while she waits for us.

It's an inspiring sight, this big, two-story house, set back on high-er ground up from the street. Brick stucco, Italianate Villa style. Tall windows finished with elaborate woodcut moldings. Front entrance framed by a wooden, ivy-covered portico which also supports a balus-trade for the second-floor balcony above it. Heavy, curvy corbel brackets below the roof, itself topped with a decorative parapet. You can see that there is a large wing extending off the back end, and in the yard to the right there is a detached green-house with glass walls. In the front yard the most prominent feature of the landscaping, spectacular outright, is the two flowering crabapple trees. They're still in full bloom in late May, most of the blossoms having turned white although many still have their pink color, and the overall effect is just beautiful. What a thrilling first impression they make for the arriving guests. No doubt about it, this place

can easily accommodate a major social event, which makes you realize what a privilege it is to be invited here.

The approach from the street is rendered all the more grandiose by having a short, separate lane leading off from Church Street, running parallel but sloping upward onto the higher ground so that a wagon might deliver passengers closer in front of the house at about the same level. Once across Paddock you can now veer onto this lane and use a sidewalk that has been laid in alongside, running in between the lane and a low, wrought iron fence over a retaining wall that borders the McConnells' front yard. It's a nice touch, you think, adding a fence to define the other side of Church Street, over a huge expanse of land also owned by McConnell, as far as you've heard, where you can see a large open field apparently being used today for parking several carriages belonging to other guests.

You reach the point where the lane meets the front walkway of the house, where the fence has a gate anchored between two handsome newels. Today of course the gate has been swung wide open, and Hervey proceeds to lead you and Clettie up three stone steps before the newels, through the gate and onto the front walkway towards the door. At this point you can hear from the windows the voices and sounds of the party already underway. Several guests have also gathered in the yard on the left side of the house, which is a good sign—if the temperature is somewhat warm indoors then you might still enjoy the cooling afternoon breezes in the yard. Either way, the cheerful tones and laughter from inside and out are good clues that the event is off to a good start.

When you have just cleared the gate you pause to see what is going on behind you, where a large coach has pulled up in front of the house, and as soon as it has come to a stop by the gate its side door is thrown open and four young women come bounding out onto the stone landing step and jump down to the sidewalk, one by one. It's amusing to watch them hastily gather themselves for some final primping before climbing the steps through the gate at a lively pace, all the while immersed in silly banter and laughter as quickly overtake your own group on the front walkway. Good friends all, of course, they appear to be 17 or 18, and naturally attentive to how their appearance at this reception will be regarded by all the college men and soldier boys. Looking back at the coach you see the words "Mathews Mill" stenciled in large white letters across the black sideboard, so a fair conjecture is that someone's daughter has asked papa for the use of the carriage to bring a few lucky friends to the reception. Somewhere in all their giggling and rapid dialog you catch the words "Oh, Julia!"—spoken in feigned admonition—could that be Julia Comstock, Elkanah's niece, and who are the other three? You'll have to ask later. As they scamper through the opened front entrance ahead of you, perhaps both you and Hervey are musing over the idea of four young women arriving at such an event without a chaperone. How about that, these changing times—you and Hervey trade glances with a shrug—though it is, you suppose, still daytime. Well, no matter. "Shall we go in?"

Now it's your turn, and, ready for both cordial introductions and witty diversion, you venture through the door to meet the families, the friends, and our intrepid new Union soldier.

McConnell House on Church Street in 1861.

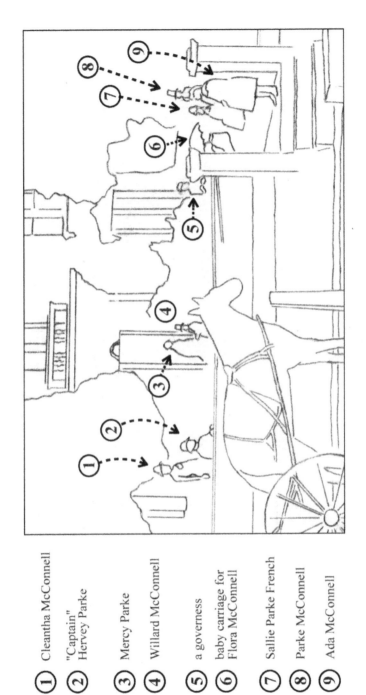

1. Cleantha McConnell
2. "Captain" Hervey Parke
3. Mercy Parke
4. Willard McConnell
5. a governess
6. baby carriage for Flora McConnell
7. Sallie Parke French
8. Parke McConnell
9. Ada McConnell

CHANCE ENCOUNTER

CARRIE HOLLEY walked out the front door of Turk's Groceries and turned left to head up Saginaw Street towards Bray's Daguerreotype & Ambrotype Studio[38]. Her spirit was up, her pace quick and purposeful, and she was heartened to be moving along freely in the mid-afternoon sunshine. How nice to get away from her work at the candy shop, after only an hour or so behind the counter, and how gratifying to have accomplished the first two parts of her plan in such short order: first, at Crawford's candy shop his regular clerk George Curtis had agreed not to tell anyone about her leaving early, although her absence wouldn't matter much anyway since George's wife Mellie would be coming to the store soon and could fill in for Carrie.

Then second, just now at Turk's Groceries, Carrie had succeeded in retrieving for her Visitor the bottle of wine with little trouble, other than abiding yet another clumsy flirtation by Billy, the skinny, deliber-

---

38   Daguerreotype imaging was more popular in the 1840's and 1850's. Its resolution was superior but would only produce a single image on a glass plate. Ambrotype imaging became available in the 1860's; its resolution was adequate, it required less time sitting still for an exposure, and it could produce several copies on paper. Finished images could be provided to a customer ("sitter") within an hour.

ate clerk who never failed to remind her that he would soon be enlisting in the army, and would Carrie agree to come see him in his uniform when the moment came for him to leave for Detroit to join his regiment. A tactful "we'll see" with a reassuring smile sufficed to defer the suggestion and politely grasp hold of the wine, and so Carrie made her way out posthaste onto Saginaw's boardwalk, her cotton drawstring bag now heavy with the wine bottle in addition to the wrapper of jelly beans meant for the McConnell's. Now it was on to Bray's Studio where Fannie Pittman should find something for her to wear instead of this calico school dress.

She had to stop for a minute outside the main door of the Hodges House while several well-heeled guests were crowding the boardwalk—apparently having finished with lunch at the Hodges, they were *en train* to climb on board the three cabriolets parked for them just there on Saginaw, the gentlemen holding the ladies' parasols and purses during the risky maneuver of managing hoop skirts through to the cab seating. Carrie wondered whether she might see these couples again at the McConnells' reception. And, as the daughter of one of Pontiac's premier dressmakers, she couldn't help but take in a quick assessment of the ladies' attire, the fit, the hem work and the shoulder seams, and the embroidered buttonholes (very elaborate).

But enough of that. The fashionable group at last completed their loading and Carrie's path cleared for her to proceed along Saginaw, cross over Pike Street and revisit the more-appealing realm of tall buildings of central Pontiac. Bray's Studio was half a block further on, in that stretch of buildings that everyone still called "The Old Stand," actually occupying a top floor above Phelps's Jewelry Store. Carrie wove her way past other, less hurried pedestrians who occupied the boardwalk, her mind focused on the next step in her plan, the plan that, back in Miss LeRoy's classroom in an excited whisper Emma Adams had called an "afternoon caper."

There were some tricky parts in the task ahead. The change of clothes had to be accomplished quickly, allowing Carrie to leave for the reception before her mother arrived at Bray's for the photography appointment; this assumed that Fannie would already have a suitable dress ready for Carrie, and that no other "sitters" would be at the studio waiting to be photographed. Also, Fannie should have found a way to persuade Mr. Bray, her uncle, to postpone the Holley's session altogether, since Carrie would not be available to model her mother's dresses. Finally, there was the matter of transportation to the McConnell's. Carrie was hoping to borrow Mr. Bray's carriage, and Fannie along with it as a driver, to go to the McConnell's with the premise of delivering the wine and the candy. If Bray's carriage was unavailable, then Carrie would have to go back to Turk's, now fully dressed for a party, and cajole the lovelorn Billy Frederick into driving her to the reception with some fimble-famble about it being a routine delivery errand.

The idea that all these complicated steps might actually happen was adding up to an entirely implausible caper was not particularly bothersome, not for now. Rather, what mattered was the sunny weather, and the fun of thinking ahead on all that needed to be done, and the final prospect of seeing Danny Thurber at a big reception. These were happier, busier thoughts. The world around her may be unraveling into war, and graduation, and social standing, and all manner of doubts and worries, but today was meant to be different. Today she was free and mischievous, setting out to discover all that could be accomplished this one afternoon on her own.

Now here's the door to William Phelps's Jewelry, where Carrie turns and enters in by rote, just as she has done so many times before on her way to an ambrotype session with her mother. Inside there was only one person, Mr. Phelps himself, seated behind his window counter and reading an "illustrated," and he looked up to give Carrie a pleasant smile and a nod—no greeting was necessary, knowing that Carrie will be proceeding directly to the stairs along the side wall that lead to Bray's studio upstairs. And, as usual, Carrie was quick to shut the door behind her, in reliable deference to Phelps' policy of minimizing the number of houseflies gaining access to his store. Carrie likewise would hardly notice any of the merchandise about the store, all of it long familiar to her, the clocks and watches, the rings, the silver service items; also the picture frames and pendants that should complement a customer's newly-purchased photographic image from the studio. The little store was quiet except for the tick-tock of a mantel clock, somewhere, and the muffled street noises coming from outside. As Carrie mounted the staircase steps, clutching the bannister in one hand and her bag in the other, the clatter of her shoes was that much more pronounced in the snug stillness.

The doorway at the second floor led into a hallway with another flight of stairs up to the third floor. Another round of rapid clack-clack-clack of shoes on the steps and there, finally at the very top as Carrie reached the small landing, still holding on to her drawstring bag, when the door marked "Bray's Studio" was swung open by a smiling Fannie Pittman, apparently alerted by the boisterous steps which heralded her friend's arrival. Carrie wasn't really short of breath, despite the exertion needed for the stairs, but there was a moment of trepidation—a closed door meant that a photographic session was underway (and please enter quietly)—until Carrie could take a few steps into the room and realize that, no, this was not the case. Fannie and her uncle had simply neglected to reopen the door after the last customers had left. Carrie could perceive from Fannie's tacit smile that the coast was clear to move ahead with the plan of outfitting Carrie for the McConnell's party—no other sitters in the room needing Fannie's attention, and her Uncle John fully absorbed in organizing his inventory of materials and various smelly chemicals.

The studio's main room always had a cheery, artistic feel to it with plenty of daylight coming through the big, wide skylight built into the ceiling, as well as from the front-wall window with its top in a roman arch shape. Carrie knew the room well, and everything in it, the tables, the cupboards, the tripods and pedestals, the tools and the jars of iodine and other smelly chemicals. On a sunny day like today the ambient rays revealed the dust particles lazily floating mid-air, which only seemed suitable, in the way that it further enhanced the feel of an exotic, third-floor atelier. And for now the place was quiet, even quieter than Phelps's shop downstairs, the studio being so far removed from the street noises below. Bray was leaning over a worktable off to one side, examining an assortment of small glass wetplates, intently enough, judging by the way he was idly drumming his bald head with the fingers of one hand.

Fannie Pittman

Fannie beckoned to Carrie to follow her the rear of the studio, to the waiting room which also served as an expansive wardrobe closet. The two girls quietly walked single file around the backdrop structure, which faced towards the front, its tall wooden screen reaching almost to the ceiling. Its raised floor was covered by a section of carpet, dark green with a pattern of light-colored octagonal shapes. The screen was painted light blue, which didn't go well with the carpet but it didn't matter—the photography images being only black and white, the main purpose of the backdrop was to provide an unobtrusive contrast with the sitters' clothing and their faces. Just now on the setting there was a single carved wooden chair with an upholstered seat, accompanied by a head vise "brace" on a tripod behind it. But off to the sides there were many more props and accoutrements available, upon request, including a small table, a decorative newel with a section of balustrade, a pedestal, some stools, vases, and a selection of framed paintings. There was also a curtain rod fixed overhead, extending far out to either side and holding drapery at the ends that could be pulled into view to enhance an image if deemed necessary.

All of these items had been placed and replaced haphazardly around the back of the studio, and it was generally recognized that this was Fannie's domain, managing the props and suggesting their usage in backdrops that the sitters might like, that is, adding an artistic touch to the images they produce. It was a creative part of Fannie's work that had always impressed Carrie. As the girls made their way around to wardrobe entrance, Carrie was looking over the various furnishings and paintings and couldn't help but remark once again on the appeal of the image-making:

"Fannie, don't you just love setting up for the pictures? It's almost as if you were arranging the stage for a play, or a tableau." [39]

It was an idle comment but this time, unexpectedly, it drew a direct answer. Fannie stopped while she was opening the wardrobe door, and had turned around to look back at Carrie to express her opinion:

39   Tableau: "tableau vivant," a static scene on stage using live actors to pose motionless in recreating a famous painting.

"Truth be told, I wish there were colors. We can make pictures only in black and white, and sometimes I think that they only look like dreamy shadows. Like those ambrotypes that Uncle John makes of me—I look like a ghost, not a real person."

They continued on into the wardrobe, a long, narrow unfurnished room that extended all the way to the building's rear window and served as an oversized closet, with one section near the door reserved as a waiting area with several small chairs. Noticing that no one else was in the room, Carrie offered a more apt reply:

"I'm sure I could take up portrait painting, after graduation. I'd be so pleased to capture your true likeness—in full color. Which do you prefer, m'lady? Oil, or water color?"

"Either, just as long as you leave out the cleft in my chin."

Carrie picked up on the wishful teasing and feigned an artist's serious expression as she regarded her subject's face, saying "Hmmm" while rubbing her index finger over her own chin. It brought out an "Oh, no help from you . . ." with a resigned nod of disagreement from Fannie, smiling as she walked directly towards a line of large cedar chests further back in the room.

As she lifted open the top of one of the chests and began rummaging among the dresses that were draped inside, she added one last comment:

"Still, I hate to think of my grandchildren years from now looking at images of me, all pale and morose. That's not really who I am. Who we are. We're young, and alive and . . . colorful."

"And full of fancy piffle?"[40] Carrie answered, trying to make light of an unanswerable worry.

But Fannie only continued: "What does it matter, in the end? We'll all end up as ghosts anyway, I know," she said, picking through more clothes deeper within the cedar chest. "Some fancier than others,

---

40 Piffle: trivial, nonsensical talk.

I reckon." Then she found the one dress she had in mind, and carefully pulled it out for a full view. It was blue sateen, in a promenade style, good condition, and passable fashion. She held it up, turning it round to show front and back, and maintained a silent, inquisitive expression until Carrie presently spoke up to confirm "Yes, it's perfect."

Of course it was. Carrie had worn the dress once before, when her mother was still in the process of designing and completing it for one of her customers. In the end the dress was rejected, and after receiving payment for the cost of materials her mother had donated the dress to Bray's wardrobe. It was a close enough fit and the color was a close match for her blue eyes. And, as both girls knew, no one had seen the dress before in public. Coming out from the chest the dress still carried a slight smell of cedar and lavender, and otherwise nothing offensive was noticeable, or would be, after an hour in the fresh air. Yes, this would do nicely. Carrie found a table to put down her wine bottle and the candy, then took the dress from Fannie and headed to go behind the screens to change, while Fannie then picked out a 3-hoop crinoline

from an assortment behind the chest. With luck she wouldn't need more than a minute or two to pin the hem snugly around the bottom hoop.

And indeed, a few minutes was all it took. Fannie stepped back examine the overall fit, and shrugged raising her hands, palms up, as if to say voilà – done. Right there in the empty hush of the wardrobe room, Carrie Holley had fully transformed from calico-clad shop girl into an attractive invitee for the McConnell reception. For the moment, however, none of this was particularly surprising and there was no reason to stand around and admire the girl's graceful appearance, or the very determined look in her eyes. There now remained only the last step in Carrie's plan, which was the need for a carriage ride, preferably more comfortable than a delivery buckboard but less ostentatious than a fancy shay.

It was potentially a setback in the caper. Carrie looked at Fannie and said, "Bray's wagon not free, I suppose?"

"Alas, Cinderella, you have no ride to the ball."

Both girls were thinking how loathsome it would be to have to recourse to Billy Frederick to borrow Turk's grocery wagon.

"I'll just walk to the McConnells."

"Not in *that* dress you won't. Let's go round to Morris' Livery and I'll hire a cab on my uncle's account. I'll go with you. We'll settle the fee later, somehow."

"Yes, or maybe Turk's will cover for me!" Carried agreed enthusiastically.

So that was what they would do. Carrie retrieved her packages and waited while Fannie closed down the cedar chest, and then the two of them walked back into the studio where they both noticed the time—still several minutes before 4:00 —on the mantel clock that was wedged among the ledger books on a cupboard shelf. Her uncle was now standing by the tripod-mounted camera and looking over his appointment book, and as the girls made their way towards the studio door Fannie casually mentioned aloud how they needed to leave, just for a few minutes. Bray didn't look up from his book as he replied "Very good. Oh, can you pick up a couple eggs at Stanlake's, if he has any,[41]" and then he glanced over at the mantel clock and added, "And you will return promptly, please. It's still a clear day outside, and with

---

41   Egg whites were used for their albumen content in developing ambrotype prints.

the light this good we're sure to have more customers come stumbling in this afternoon."

True enough, but the girls' spirits were much too high to worry, and Fannie confirmed a quick "I will, Uncle John" and led the way out—no need to belabor the request for now. Best just to leave quickly, before her uncle noticed Carrie's promenade dress and could ask whether her mother might be coming later. So: two girls, full of life and fancy piffle and definitely colorful— nothing like the lifeless, ghostly photographs Fannie worried about—clattered down the steps and were soon walking out Phelps's shop onto the boardwalk of Saginaw Street. Carrie was always amused to hear Bray's English accent, how it differed from the Irish accents she occasionally heard spoken by housemaids and errand boys. Moreover this time she had been very impressed by the intensity of Mr. Bray's expression when he was mentioning the eggs and the afternoon daylight, so ironic as if he meant it

Fannie Pittman with her uncle, John Bray, photographer.

only jokingly, and on the stairway down she asked Fannie, "Is your uncle really a revolutionary? He doesn't strike me as a dangerous man."

Fannie only shrugged her shoulders and answered, "I don't think so. He doesn't talk to me about politics. He's very much against the war, though. That much I know."

They might have discussed this curiosity further, but now they were outdoors again— and a sudden, pleasant contrast it was, after working in the quiet of the third-floor studio and wardrobe room. Amid all the usual sights of pedestrians and sounds of passing traffic, with the commotion amplified here in the valley of tall, brick buildings, somewhere there was a brass band playing "Hail Columbia". The band had to be up by the courthouse, and the song's rousing strains were echoing all the way down Saginaw. Fannie and Carrie couldn't help but quicken their step to match the rhythm of the march, which made them laugh at their own silliness, but despite the patriotic intent of the music it was a more personal gratification that came over them, in congratulation on their secret pursuit and success in getting Carrie to the McConnells' grand reception, at last.

They were approaching the intersection with Lawrence Street where they walked past the big National Block building at the corner—National Block included Pittman & Herrington Clothiers, the store managed by Fannie's father, with its two display windows siding directly at the boardwalk. But there was no reason to pause and look through the windows just now, while the girls blithely skipped around the turn to head down Lawrence Street, and just as they came around the corner a cheerful voice called out a greeting which made everything come to a stop. "Fannie! Carrie!" It was Julia Comstock, a dear friend they had not seen for some time, but that voice was unmistakable, no matter how unexpected the time and place. And there she was, seated in a barouche carriage that had parked by the boardwalk. "Julia!" the girls answered in unison, impulsively veering immediately towards the side of the barouche. "When did you get home?"

Julia was a former schoolmate of theirs at the town's Union School, but for the past school year she had attended the Female Seminary in Cleveland, and the girls hadn't seen her since Christmas. Running into her now on Lawrence was a surprise though not entirely—all the girls at boarding schools should be coming home for the summer about this time. Fannie had also known Julia for many years growing up, as both the Pittman and Comstock families were members of the Baptist Church up at Huron Street. Julia had always been a popular figure among her friends. She was a happy, busy character who always seemed to be running some sort of activity to get everyone together. And no different now, having perked up immediately from her sitting quietly next to her uncle Elkanah Comstock in his family's barouche. The gentleman seemed glad for some distraction, too, and he imparted a deferential nod to the youngsters, his finger touching the brim of his silk top hat, in response to the respectful good-afternoons and quick curtsies proffered by Carrie and Fannie.

Julia quickly introduced her friends, while her uncle took a second look at Fannie and, recognizing her from church, he inquired about her father Mr. Pittman and whether he was soon to be traveling out to Pennsylvania with Mr. Kelsey to inspect their oil field investments. "Yes, Mr. Comstock. I believe they will go together in June, if Mr. Kelsey regains his health." Carrie was impressed by Fannie's answer, the way it sounded so measured and knowledgeable. Comstock and Kelsey were banking partners, of course, so Fannie's polite mention of Kelsey's health was at once cordial and familiar. "Right you are," Comstock agreed, "and I recommend they choose a restful cruise on the lake to Erie, and avoid the railroads. The trains are all filled with soldiers these days anyway." He seemed pleased to be speaking to this attentive schoolgirl. Fannie said "yes, sir" and curtsied again (rightly so, Carrie felt, since Fannie's father and Elkanah Comstock both served on the school board). Thereupon the three girlfriends were now properly released to launch into a highly animated exchange of catch-up news and chatter and planning, while Elkanah looked on with an amused grin and exchanged an acquiescent glance with the carriage driver, a dull-faced man who had turned around to see about all the talking going on behind him.

It turned out that the Comstock's had been waiting in the carriage for Julia's guardian Mrs. Goodale to return from a brief stop at Pittman & Herrington's where she needed to pick up a pair of summer blouses that had been fitted for Julia's younger sister Emma. For whatever reason the errand was taking longer than expected, which was the likely reason why Elkanah was holding on to his pocket watch, its gleaming gold chain drooping down from his vest button. Julia and Carrie and Fannie could easily converse over several topics in short order in the meantime, with a shared awareness that the meeting would end as soon as Mrs. Goodale returned.

For the girls, as delightful as the reunion could be, there was also an underlying issue that went unspoken even though it begged clarification. That is, Miss Julia Comstock and Miss Carrie Holley were both attired in fine dresses suitable for an occasion, for example, an afternoon reception at the McConnell's. But no one felt as though they might ascertain politely anyone's immediate plans for the afternoon, or invitations, or otherwise, in their reluctance to cause embarrassment or gossip, especially here while they were reacquainting after a long separation. Surely the McConnell's house was Julia's destination; however, she only mentioned how she was on her way to Fannie Mathew's home to join some other Cleveland friends who had also recently returned to Pontiac. And Carrie for her part would only drop a hint that she was posing in another of her mother's gowns at Bray's studio, same as ever. No further details were forthcoming.

The issue didn't seem to impair everyone's cheer during their encounter, all in all, but yet another incident arose on the scene then and there on Lawrence, as a smaller carriage was slowing down before proceeding into the Saginaw intersection. Julia interrupted the current conversation with an abrupt holler of recognition, "Oh look! It's Danny Thurber! And Sarah!"

The smaller carriage—it was an open shay—pulled up to stop directly alongside the Comstock's, and sure enough, its two occupants were Daniel and his sister Sarah, the two of them fully *soigné* and unmistakably bound for the McConnells' reception. And not in mourning clothes, either, which was noticeable but acceptable all the same, it having been several weeks since the funeral for Daniel and Sarah's mother. Here and now, admittedly, the handsome bonnet worn by Sarah Thurber made her appear much more mature than her 15 years, but then again, how could it fail to enhance a face that pretty to begin with. Very *à la mode parisienne*, Carrie thought. And Daniel was looking quite fashionable too, in a new waistcoat style, sporting a grey bowler hat, and look at him—acting so competently as he checked the reins and leaned forward to engage the brake.

Initial greetings were made in cordial tones, led by Daniel as he and Elkanah exchanged good-afternoons and a few other words to reveal that they had already met earlier that morning at the Courthouse. The girls, four of them now, followed with more casual talk, refraining from condolences for Mrs. Thurber but focusing on the returns to Pontiac by Julia, from school in Cleveland, and Sarah, from school in Monroe. They were all good friends, originally, at the public school in Pontiac, now gleefully recalling when they were all together last August at Julia's back-to-school party.

Daniel's mien was still very reserved, but his attention had come around to a steady look at Carrie, his expression now softened to a kindlier inquisitiveness that made her look twice in responsive curiosity. Yes, no mistaking it, his gaze was meant for her alone. How flattering, and how quietly welcome. Carrie tried to stay engaged with the others around her but soon lost track of what all of her girlfriends were chattering about, hearing only random words such as Cleveland and Monroe and train rides, while she made sure of one thing, that she lowered her chin just so and looked back and smiled at Daniel Thurber. It was the right thing to do, and now he was smiling too, watching her from where he was perched up on his carriage in the middle of the street. No one else seemed to notice this intimation shared by the two of them.

But inevitably through all the talking it became clarified that Daniel and Sarah, and Julia as well, were *en route* to the McConnell's. And as the conversation veered towards the McConnells' reception there was no way to avoid declaring what was obvious, that Carrie was going there too, and what's more, a ride to the McConnell's would be helpful. So—there was room for one more on the seat of Thurber's shay, and that was all that an instigator like Julia Comstock needed to settle the matter and direct Daniel to invite Carrie up and sit beside his sister.

The next minute passed in something of a blur as Carrie found herself complying with the suggestion, and with everyone's encouragement she climbed up into the near end of the seat. She had meant to arrive at the McConnell's on her own surreptitiously, on the premise of delivering wine and candy, and then in some innocent manner she would find Daniel there and could speak with him alone, meaningfully, affectionately, just as the two of them had done when they met before, at the Wisner's last winter. That was the plan. Suddenly all of that intricate approach was being cast aside for an abrupt pairing high up on a wagon seat, with Danny's sister in between, rolling down the middle of Saginaw street for all to see.

The music of the brass band was still audible from down the street, which now seemed rather silly. Carrie became aware of Fannie Pittman standing alongside the Thurbers' shay and talking; Fannie was wishing her a good time, and hastily adding how she would miss not seeing all the hubbub at the McConnells' house and who all was coming, but no matter—she needed to go buy the eggs for her uncle, anyway. As the shay slowly started to pull way into the intersection Carrie turned round and replied, "Yes, eggs. Don't forget the eggs." And with that, everything was left behind, as Daniel guided the horse to the right to proceed down Saginaw. Carrie waved goodbye to Elkanah, who had raised his cane in a gracious salute from his carriage.

What on earth would she talk about now, to Daniel, or Sarah, on this shay? Or should she anything at all? *Vanity, Carrie . . . vanity.* Yes, the drawstring bag with the wine and candy was there, in her lap and not forgotten. Carrie turned to Sarah next to her, and the two of them exchanged happy grins that conveyed an isn't-this-pleasant attitude, simple and welcome, as the shay passed through the gamut of Pontiac's commercial center. Daniel was silent and only made a brief, encouraging nod as if to affirm that there was nothing to worry about.

As they went through the intersection with Pike and were passing Linabury's store on the left side of Saginaw, Carrie leaned forward to peer sideways past Sarah and Daniel at the store's flower boxes filled with geraniums. It wasn't the flowers themselves that attracted her notice; rather, a memory evoked *by the flowers*, how Carrie's mother had enjoyed so much a display of purple asters in those same boxes, months ago last autumn. It's funny how a memory like that should arise for no reason, its singular feature being the experience of strolling along Saginaw together with her mother on a chilly afternoon.

The three riders sat side by side without speaking, so Carrie resolved that she ought to say something, anything by-the-by, if only to convey to the others her feelings that all was well. She remembered that her mother had engaged Sarah to work at her shop during the summer as a copy clerk. Perhaps that would do.

"Sarah, I thought you were going to be helping at my mother's shop today."

"No, not today. Tomorrow," was the girl's reply, simple and friendly. Given how obvious it was that Sarah was outfitted not for work but for the McConnells' reception, there was something tactful about the way she handled the stray question, Carrie noticed. Sarah Thurber was still as pleasant and as beautiful as ever.

"And will your father be coming to the McConnell's too?" she asked Sarah, just to offer one more benign inquiry, and leave it at that.

"Yes, . . . "—"Yes he is coming," both Sarah and Daniel replied together.

"Oh, that's wonderful, for all of you, isn't it?"

Enough conversation, then. Carrie began to relax, settling more into her seat. She began recounting to herself all the experiences of this day so far: breakfast at home with her mother, classroom work with her friends at school, minding the counter at Crawford's, changing into the dress at Bray's, traipsing along the boardwalk with Fannie. This was, admittedly, a lot for one day.

And now here she was, on her way to the big social event, a place where important questions might be asked, and new directions made clear. *This is freedom, I suppose, isn't it*—she thought, and clasped the handle on the side of the seat, and looked ahead down the street.

*Spirit of
Modern
Times*

PART III:
AFTERNOON
PARTY

Myron Howell

I've been the editor of the Gazette for some three years now – my first job since graduating from the University of Michigan. It's worked out very well. Pontiac is a great little town to run a newspaper. You get to know everybody and everything that's going on – and I thoroughly enjoy writing about it. Here at the Gazette we have more of a progressive leaning, oh yes, pro-Lincoln, and glad to see the Republican Party take over from the hapless Whigs. If your taste is for reactionary politics then go read the "Jacksonian" and see what Augustus "Caesar" Baldwin has to say. But the Gazette is where you'll find the true go-ahead spirit of Pontiac, the news – and the fun – of life in a community on the rise.

Count on it: I'll be at the McConnell's wingding today. I'd prefer to hobnob with all the college boys who will be there to give Joe McConnell a proper send-off to the army; alas, my job will be to stand around and palaver with all of the town nabobs, you know, all the founding families fit to be seen with the likes of Governor Wisner and Colonel Richardson. But Cleantha McConnell knows how to stage an event and ensure her guests are handsomely accommodated, so "Skimmerhorn" – that's me – will do his part to come and bear witness. And I think the party is to be held outdoors, a capital idea, it being May and we're all ready for some frolic *al fresco*.

You know, for all the young men – actually, myself included – it's decision time, about whether or not to sign up for this war that's started. My best friend Judd Mott is itching to join up in the lancers, and it's a sure bet they'll make him an officer. True, it's bound to be the adventure of a lifetime, but sustained camp life and riding around in the rain may not be for everybody, let alone getting shot at. The boys are strong and brave, though, and I shouldn't think there will be that much fighting once the rebels see what we're all about.

I reckon my job in all of this will be to keep the Gazette well-informed with the right war correspondents, in the right places at the right times. It's a whole new business nowadays, using telegraphic communication. The folks back home are going to want all the news from the front, as soon as the dispatches come in.

"ARABELLA MARIA. "Only to think, Julia dear, that our Mothers wore such ridiculous fashions as these!"
BOTH. "Ha! ha! ha! ha!"

Harper's Weekly, July 11, 1857

A VISITOR'S STORY,
"McConnell's Parlor"

STEPPING THROUGH the door into the McConnell house you enter into a wide center hallway that extends down the full length of the main floor, the preeminent feature being the staircase attached on the right side and leading up to a landing openly visible high at the far end. The hall must be at least eight feet wide, and its ceiling twelve feet high, making for quite the cavernous entryway, even more opened overhead by the three-foot wide stairwell cutting into the ceiling. The hall floor and the stairs are carpeted; a pair of double sconces are affixed high on the left-side wall, and triple-crown moldings run along the ceiling. Immediately on both sides are large, heavily molded doors presumably leading to parlor rooms—the door on the right is closed, the one on the left is open to a formal room where there are several people inside. Beyond the staircase there are two more doors, framed by the same handsome molding, which must lead into the dining room and a conservatory.

SPIRIT of MODERN TIMES

The first person you encounter is at the foot of the staircase—Willy McConnell, a spirited young lad, say 14, who speaks right up to greet you and Hervey and especially Clettie his cousin who is rapidly coming to life opposite someone more her age. It is not difficult to perceive what the boy means to express, how he is fully enthusiastic about the war, as he resolutely announces that he marched with his brother Joseph in the Wide-Awakes demonstration (last week, in the late evening) and carried one of the torches! He goes on to add that he, too, will be enlisting just as soon as he can, if the war is still going on, to join his brother in the same regiment. Another boy is standing by, listening impatiently—you catch his name only when Hervey calls down to him as "Master Fred"—he looks to be a few years younger than Willy, probably a cousin. Little Fred soon succeeds in pulling Willy and Clettie away to go find other children, and ice creams, and they all run off to the back of the hall, *en route* presumably to the kitchen. Their youthful excitement leaves you amused as you look after them, and in turn you're noticing more details around the hall such as the fashionable wallpaper, the handsome mahogany banister and spindles of the stairs, the frieze pattern on the side of the staircase; and you take a second look at the double sconces—probably not yet connected to the gas line, you figure, seeing how they are not lit. All in all, first impressions being what they are, what a treat it is to be invited into such a fine home.

There are a few guests further down the hall, no doubt attracted towards the dining room in search of *friandises* and proper sweets, or to explore the activity in the conservatory, but for you and Hervey the first stop is to greet your hosts in the family room to your left. Setting down your hats on a side table, for the moment, the two of you join the small company that is idling about the room in sundry conversations, and of course this is a very well-appointed room, adorned with a six-arm chandelier suspended from a large bronze medallion, very ornate and finely patterned, and a fireplace on the far wall between two window doors left ajar for entry out onto the side porch. The décor is formal yet agreeable, and fashionable with the times, as evinced right away by the bright red curtains hung from a brass drapery rod over the front window, offset by light green wallpaper with a faded floral print, and a generous assortment of framed watercolors and oils—all of it complementing well the heavy crown molding, intricately carved and painted gold, surrounding the room overhead. The fireplace deserves a second look: all grey marble over a brick threshold, its fascia fully trimmed with beveled shapes, and a single, sculpted corbel centered below the mantel. Can any other residence in Pontiac boast a hearth like that? Perhaps the Governor's mansion at Pine Grove on the north side of town. Remarkable opulence.

What else. There is a large fern spreading out from a vase on a demi-lune table, and a *whatnot* shelf crowded with small books and curios. A marble-topped table with a Sinumbra oil lamp, probably decorative only. A small Pembroke table, one drawer, with some reading materials left on it, casually tasteful, including a Peterson's issue with a stub of folded paper to bookmark an article inside. The few velvet upholstered chairs, as positioned here and there, are not crowding the floorspace. And another touch: even the andirons' front plates have been polished to a shiny copper. There's a large door on the rearward wall, which probably connects to the dining room, but it's closed, and clearly meant to be kept that way for now. Judging by the décor and refinements one might get the impression that this room is normally reserved as a private family room, opened up today by the McConnell's just for the reception. A faint aroma of cigar smoke is detectable, a lingering feature of past repairments for the gentlemen after a supper, as one might envisage.

A small number of people are hovering about, chatting with the hosts and with each other, as this venue is apparently a gateway before proceeding out to the side yard; now you can see that there are two

Capt. Hervey Parke
engraving (OCPHS)

window doors on the far side that would lead you out onto a porch to get there, and many guests ahead of you have already done just that, judging by a glimpse of the scene outside. It's only now that you become aware how the ambience of the parlor is subdued, with quiet respect afforded the elders as they receive their guests. A few men are standing by the fireplace mantel and here is where you are introduced first to an elderly gentleman, 'Captain' Hervey Parke. So this is young Hervey's uncle—you wait while the two Hervey's exchange a brief greeting before the nephew moves on to the other hosts. Captain Parke now turns to you with a kindly demeanor and dignified bearing; he uses a cane to steady his posture, evidently, judging from the strong grip of his left hand on the derby-style handle. Your ensuing conversation reveals that he has just celebrated his 71st birthday a month ago, and it is remarkable how good he looks for his age, tall and fit, lean, attentive. He impresses you as a fitting patriarch for the McConnell household.

This much you already knew about him: the Captain was one of the very early settlers in Oakland County, 40 years ago having literally walked 500 miles from upstate New York carrying only a backpack—the Erie Canal hadn't opened yet—and he established himself as the first government surveyor to map out large areas of the Michigan wilderness during the 1820's. The work exposed him to extreme physical hardship as he hiked throughout the territory, often in winter conditions for months at a time. You can sense this man's quiet confidence in his well-earned reputation for integrity and good works, and his satisfaction in the progress marked by Pontiac in his lifetime, a far cry from his first log cabin home years ago. Was he ever really in the army? Not so. His rank as captain came about because he was appointed by the government in Detroit to lead a civilian group—the so-called "Wampler expedition"—to survey and assess the wilderness territory around Pontiac. You remember how Levi Bacon once explained it to you, with a wink, how this military promotion was not exactly earned through bravery in the heat of action . . . no, in truth the title was derived simply to afford some command discipline over the civilians who were part of the expedition. Actually, from what you know, these first explorations were rugged, arduous experiences, orienteering and camping for weeks on end, slogging through swamplands, fending off clouds of mosquitos, and surviving on scant provisions and shelter. When you ask him whether he misses those days, he only smiles back without making a reply. Your question may have been a bit inane for such a man, or perhaps he simply couldn't hear you. Now you're feeling embarrassed, hoping it was the latter. This is when you notice in a corner of the room another walking cane placed leaning against the wall, having a brass derby handle like the one the Captain is using now. *Does he sometimes use two canes just to move about the house?* If so, then any talk of the old expeditions might seem all the more gauche.

Standing with Captain Parke is his son-in-law Willard Morse Mc-Connell, the host of this reception, with whom you shake hands next. You sense immediately that he is a man of sharp mind and energy, with all the mien of a "prominent merchant and influential citizen of Pontiac," clearly a man of unequivocal probity. His dry goods business continues to post sustained growth and success, and he has become a wealthy man, in this fine home he and his wife have filled with their five children. His greeting with you is gracious if not a bit measured, the kind of transient exchange you might expect from a man who is used to maintaining a tight schedule, meeting with many people. You make mention of your call on Levi Bacon at the store this morning, just meaning to enhance your introduction, but Willard seems unimpressed, and he replies only with a peremptory "Yes, very good" and then directs his attention to another guest in turn behind you. You're left wondering whether you have just made some kind of miscue.

In any event, not to worry. You move over to a corner of the room where there are two women, seated in armchairs, and you know one of them must be Willard's

Willard McConnell

wife Cleantha McConnell. The other is an elderly woman, perhaps Cleantha's mother, Mercy Parke, wife of the "Captain." They are in close conversation, so a few seconds will pass before your approach has been noted, and meanwhile you catch sight of a book lying on the Pembroke table nearby—Darwin's "Origin of the Species"—over a copy of the Pontiac Gazette, and next to a small bowl of black licorice pieces. The women's attention is at last acquired, with the help of a perfunctory introduction by Willard, and you are met with kind smiles and a brief inquiry for your opinion on Darwin's work. Cleantha seems to be looking you over with a whisk of caution, and you start to comment on the Darwin but promptly gauge there is only fleeting social interest about the book. No one really wants your full assessment just now. However, common courtesies having been duly extended, now you should be able to stand by and listen in for a few moments to conversations going on in the room.

From her chair Cleantha is talking with her husband Willard, who has his hand on her shoulder as he bends down to hear, and she reminds him how he promised to talk to Colonel Richardson about as signing Joseph to a staff position, away from the front lines. Their son is, after all, an educated college student from a fine family, capable of handling the more complex matters of the army's chain of command. Surely he would be more useful among the officers. Willard reassures her that he will see what he can do, but in any event, she needn't worry. The campaign shouldn't last very long, and it is hard to see how the southern farmers could put up much more of a fight than those poor Mexicans did in the last war.

Cleantha Parke McConnell

"Well, I worry about him," she says, and she's looking up at you, although her attention doesn't really seem to center on you in particular—just any listener nearby—"and who knows where the army might send him after this war is finished. Florida is so hot and sickly, and Utah so cold."[42]

"Now, my dear, he's a strong, healthy boy, grown up in our Michigan weather just as rugged as anywhere else." Willard follows his wife's gaze to look at you while he adds, "And Joseph is so excited about this, and he's already talking about a military career after college. With this campaign on his record, imagine such a future, what?"

Cleantha casts a quick glance towards Mercy, as if trying to reassure her mother in turn; but you can see by her thoughtful expression

---

42   Cleantha is alluding to recent military actions in 1858: Florida for the 3rd Seminole War, and Utah for the Mormon/Deseret conflict.

and furrowed brows that Cleantha is still anxious to confirm the safe handling of her son.

Willard then straightens up to resume his conversation with another couple, and you catch a few of their remarks offering more light-hearted opinions: probably all those boys with Joseph in his Wide-Awakes "battalion" are having a fine time of it, drilling and filling their minds with visions of grandeur. Like all the recruits in militia companies forming up in Detroit, Flint, Adrian—all around the state—they usually manage to have a grand time of it playing soldier, although, you hear Willard contend, serving in a militia is a serious tradition especially in a frontier area like Michigan. Besides, yesterday the army made Joseph a sergeant on the spot when he signed up in one of their volunteer regiments, down at Fort Wayne in Detroit.

Frontier area like Michigan? You muse for a moment over this idea. *Protection from whom, exactly? The Chippewa, wherever they are now? An invasion from British Canada?* But never mind—your host is apparently an enthusiast for martial preparedness. The war is coming, even to a northern state out here on the "frontier."

Here is where you overhear a key piece of news which changes your whole perspective about what is going on in the McConnell household and Cleantha's and Willard's reactions. It turns out that their son Joseph has just enlisted in the 2nd Michigan volunteers for a period of not three months, like the 1st Michigan before it, but for three *years*. Apparently this has come as quite a shock to the boy's mother. Three full *years*! The family had caught wind of rumors to that effect, that some long-term regiments were forming n Michigan and in other northern states, but the reality had only hit home this afternoon when Joseph walked in the door and made his announcement. Willard had tried to reason in his usual objective manner that the long-term enlistments meant that the government must be anticipating an extended occupation of the South after the fighting had finished. Cleantha, however, was evidently still trying to grips with this sudden upheaval in all her plans and expectations. Three years? It was a long time to live away from moral society. What about his college? And his connections in Pontiac? Were his friends enlisting for three years too?

Listening to all this, silently, and standing as you are by the two seated women, it's becoming perhaps a little awkward to maintain your courteous posture, bent slightly forward with hands clasped behind your back. A moment comes when you exchange smiles with Cleantha's elderly mother, seated before you, so perhaps you should try and divert her with a few pleasantries. You already know her as Mercy Brownson Parke, the wife of Captain Hervey Parke. She appears reserved and somewhat tired. Ailing perhaps?

"I say, Mrs. Parke, things seem to have come a long way since you first set foot in Michigan. Am I right?" Mercy smiles back and as she starts to reply you realize you have to bend down more closely to catch her words:

"Do you know that when we first came here, this property was nothing but a wooded knoll? All . . . woods. Isn't that a marvel?"

You nod encouragingly, but evidently Mercy has little interest in talking about the old days. Instead she cocks her head slightly towards her nephew Hervey, in another part of the room, as she replies that she saw the two of you come in together, and she asks whether you are business colleagues. You explain how you and Hervey had only just met and had arrived together walking up Church Street, and how Hervey had also brought Clettie along with him. You need to lean in even more to hear this woman's soft-spoken voice as she looks up at you through her spectacles to disclose some observations she has about her long-lost nephew:

Mercy Parke,
from oil portrait
(OCPHS)

"I'm happy to see him looking so hale and hearty. When he was younger he used be sneezing all the time, especially in the summertime. You would have thought he was just an indolent boy like that. But now, after all those years up in Keweenaw he looks much better."

"Yes, I think so. The climate up north must have some salutary effect."

She doesn't seem to hear you. "And little Clettie Kelsey!" she adds. "I spied her running past out in the hall. My heart is so lifted to see the girl playing with the other grandchildren." And as you keep your eyes on Mercy's face you can see a how she seems to drift off with a look of approval, vaguely, and you lean in closer to hear what she says next, quietly to herself. She is reciting: "When the Lord turned again the captivity of Zion, we were like them that dream. Then was our mouth filled with laughter, and our tongue with singing."[43]

Mercy closes her eyes with a satisfied grin, and you glean that she'll have nothing more to say for now. Too bad for you—you would love to hear her reminisce about early Pontiac and the remarkable experiences she must have had during the journey from upstate New York to resettle in Michigan. What you do know is this: that the Captain, who had already spent a year working and living in the Pontiac settlement, alone, had returned to upstate New York—on foot again—to gather up his wife and child for a final emigration to Michigan. And so the day came in a little New York village in Oneida County, after a church service with several neighbor families to offer a farewell, that Mercy and the Captain, with their daughter Cleantha then only four years old, had stepped aboard a barge on the Erie Canal,

LAKE ERIE STEAM BRIG SUPERIOR
Capt J. SHERMAN 1st AD. 18__

---

43 Psalm 126.

westward bound, bringing only a few vital household supplies such as they could carry. The young family took the Canal as far as Rochester, the western terminus at that time, then rode on wagons over the last 80 miles to Buffalo. They weren't the only ones making this journey but there were very few other travelers with them. After waiting a week in Buffalo they were able to book passage on the steamship *Superior* for transport across Lake Erie to Sandusky, Ohio, and then to Detroit in the Michigan Territory. From there the Captain Parke took his family on the last leg of the journey, inland to Pontiac, where they settled into their first log cabin homestead.

The story is compelling just to realize what Mercy and the Captain have accomplished as true pioneers, and here you are meeting them in their daughter's elegant home, in fine company. Is this a future they could ever have imagined, when they sitting together on that canal barge, watching a mule tug them along from the canal's "tow path," hoping for clear springtime weather, carefully measuring their savings allowance and food supply?

Another couple, who have been in the room for a few minutes, are starting to move towards one of the porch doors to make an exit out to the side yard, as other guests have done to join the gathering outside. These were the two you overheard speaking with Cleantha earlier, inquiring about the health of her "little baby Flo" (pink and prissy, and a good sleeper, Lord be praised). Now as they are passing you nearby it seems acceptable to extend your hand to the husband for an introduction, which he takes up gladly, and so begins your new acquaintanceship with Dr. Abiram McConnell and his wife Helen. The two of them right away seem to impart an adventurous spirit. They appear to be in their young 30's, both of them friendly and engaging, the kind of guests who can easily meet new people. The doctor is Willard McConnell's younger brother and has been practicing in Pontiac for several years. (Levi Bacon had mentioned earlier today that a number of men had ventured out to Colorado in the gold rush, and wasn't Abiram in that party? Might be more tactful to ask about that later, if a chance arises.) His wife is very attractive, and you're impressed when you learn that she is a mother of three young boys. "Yes," she laughs, "that was our Fred you ran into when you first came in." Abiram rejoins how he saw you arrive with Hervey Parke, and he asks whether the two of you were already acquainted, so you describe how you had just run into Hervey and Clettie on Church Street while they were *en route* here, having looked over the new church work site.

"Oh yes," Abiram asks, "did they also go visit the Captain's old farmhouse on the turnpike? That's where Clettie grew up, you see, until her father sold the place and moved his family into one of those new houses on the north side."

"No, Hervey didn't mention a farmhouse."

"Clettie's father is Marquis Kelsey—have you met him? Ubiquitous fellow about town, quite entertaining, at that. Is he coming here today?" Helen shakes her head no, her brows slightly raised as if to say she hadn't heard either way.

You bring up how Hervey is an out-of-town visitor like yourself, and the doctor has a few more things to say about that.

"Oh, he's always discussing business, you know, whenever he comes to Pontiac. What do you think of that long 'virgin beard' of his?[44] I suppose scissors must still be a rare commodity away up there in Keweenaw!"

Helen speaks up to override her husband's wry tone with her own observation that Hervey is clearly doing quite well, and has the best wishes of everyone in the family for success in his new business venture . . . what is it, producing medicines?

"Well, whatever it is," Abiram says, "Hervey may as well stay busy up in Hancock, since he has too weak a constitution to join the army.

---

44 Virgin beard: a beard that has never been trimmed since started.

And Willard agrees—Hervey would never survive the rigors of military campaigning, let alone the heat down south."

"But my dear, Hervey is after all a 33-year-old man, just married and soon to be a father. The military might be very interested in anybody who can supply medicines, you know. It must be heady times up in Hancock, with the government already placing huge orders for iron and copper to manufacture arms for the new armies. That's what we hear from Charley Palmer, anyway. Bet on it, Charley knows what's o'clock."

Abiram acquiesces politely to his wife's views, but you sense he is still doubtful of Hervey's future prospects. He turns to you and, with a slight cock of his head, quietly gives an aside: "Well, there he is now, talking with the Captain about yarrow and echinacea herbs that he saw for sale over at McConnell & Baines. Medicinal herbs? I don't think he's going to interest the army with plants just now." But you're thinking: *interesting idea, nonetheless.*

Abiram and Helen politely disengage at this point to continue on their way to the yard, trusting to see you again out there later. Before you head out to the yard yourself, you're thinking of looking in on the dining room, or the parlor, and other parts of the house, although where you are just now you can overhear an interesting discussion going on between Willard and yet another couple, and the Captain, and Cleantha as well, who has risen from her chair to join the group. Mercy Parke remains seated alone, and she exchanges a look that invites you to linger for a few extra minutes. You bend your head closer to hear what she has to say.

Trying to help, it turns out, is her intent, and she wants to let you know who the people are who are with Willard and Cleantha. Apparently Mercy is circumspect enough to observe how you're on your own in a room full of company. She gently touches your forearm and, with a sidelong glance at the guests in question, tells you that they are Mr. and

Mrs. Darrow. "Mr. Darrow is our Justice of the Peace, you know." And with that you comply politely, yes-of-course, and Mercy goes on say "And you see behind them, that's Mr. Crofoot behind them. He used to be a judge and he still is a big tycoon in town. I don't see his wife, but I'm not surprised, you see, they have several small children at home."

Willard has noticed your talk with Mercy and he now beckons for you to join them, and with that you are shaking hands with Frank Darrow and making a refined, deferential bow towards his wife Augusta. Willard briefly points out that he and Frank work together on the school board, and winks at you while jesting about how he's almost succeeded in persuading Frank to abandon the democrats and finally come over to the progressive party. Frank wryly responds with a well-not-quite-yet while Willard, smiling as he pats his friend's shoulder, postures himself to break away to go catch up with young Hervey Parke. Judge Crofoot, who hasn't said a word so far, likewise gives you only a peremptory nod as he moves off along with Willard.

Thus left in conversation with the Darrow's you learn that the two wives, Cleantha and Augusta, after many years' association with the Ladies Sewing Society were only recently compelled to dissolve the Society. Apparently its mission all along was to raise money to help found a women's seminary school in Pontiac, which in the end is finally recognized as unachievable, much to everyone's profound disappointment. Augusta speaks with a resigned demeanor about the Society's demise, and how their treasurer had turned over their entire fund of $500 to the new high school enterprise. Frank blinks his eyes once, solemnly, as he repeats the dollar amount[45], almost as an epitaph.

The Darrow's are motioning to each other that it's time to move on to the outdoor activity; you take this cue to offer them a closing nice-to-meet-you, then sidle once again over to young Hervey and Willard, who have just been joined by a new arrival into the room. He is Augus-

45   $500 in 1861 would be worth approximately $15,000 in year 2020.

tus Baldwin, and from the introductions you learn that he is an attorney and the editor of the *Jacksonian* newspaper. His wife is not with him and he has only a short time to visit, insofar as he wants to congratulate the McConnell's and their son, of course, but he also needs to discuss a few matters with Colonel Richardson. At this, Hervey turns to you and explains that Augustus is also the Brigadier General of the Michigan state militia, just not in uniform this afternoon—which makes everyone smile at the jest, although now you can understand how Augustus' otherwise stern demeanor would be the normal expression for him. Actually, this meeting

Augustus Baldwin

has turned out to be a pleasant surprise for Augustus and Hervey, something of a reunion: years ago when Hervey was in his teen years he was a student at a private academy in Bloomfield, and Augustus was his preceptor[46], himself a young man in his 20's working at the academy during the day and studying law in the evenings in Pontiac. Busy times, all agree, and didn't we all have our heads filled with dreams back then? Augustus is enjoying the reminiscence and takes the moment to make a quick jest at Willard about keeping Hervey out of the clutches of the Republicans—Hervey's wife is, "don't you know", the daughter of James Hunt, a former U.S. Representative and a fine, fine Democrat. Willard graciously returns the jest and assures him that Hervey has nothing to worry about under this roof, where a "house will not be divided unto itself."

---

46   Preceptor: a teaching assistant.

The topic shifts to the reasons for Hervey's visit, then from there to the current business conditions in Pontiac, specifically in response to army supply needs and how things are going at Hiram Paddock's new woolen factory. (Apparently Willard and Horace Thurber were two of the key investors in the factory a couple of years ago.) The army will be looking for wool blankets, also for grains to feed the troops, not to mention their horses, so the topic has moved on to grain prices and local farm production. The new farming machinery items are sure to come in high demand before the year's harvest seasons arrive. "Our friend John Holley must be filling up his order books for those Kirby harvesters that he sells," you hear Willard say. "When the army is buying, that means good credit terms for the farmers." Or that new reaper machine made by McCormick out of Chicago. "Have you ever seen one of those self-raking reapers in action?" comes from the Captain, who has just walked over after checking on Mercy in her chair. He goes on to relate how last year he watched one being used at Leander Taylor's farm over in Waterford. It was astounding to see an entire acre cleared in under an hour by a single machine behind a two-horse team.

His listeners all concur with this reflection on yet another marvel of modern times, and their nods of approval reflect their own habitual conclusion that now is a very good time to be alive. The Captain's last remark strikes you as a memorable one, as you consider this elderly gentleman quietly watching a technological revolution happening right before his eyes on a Waterford farm field. The reaper machine is emblematic of all the new technologies that are coming into Pontiac, great and small, affecting everything. Just look at all the newspaper advertisements you were reading this morning back at the Hodges House. You can order a big harvesting machine from John Holley, or you can buy a small can of Maryland oysters from Thomas Turk's. You can buy items that just a few years ago people couldn't even imagine.

It is flattering to be in the same room with all of these accomplished gentlemen, though admittedly they seem to have little interest in learning about you. Augustus presently moves off, walking out to the hall and the front door on his way to the yard, and he is replaced almost right away by a tall young man who now enters comes into the parlor and addresses the group to suggest that everyone should start to move outdoors to the yard, where the toasts and speeches will soon begin for our "courageous Sergeant Joe." Willard deftly interjects with an introduction for you, and here you shake hands with his oldest son Parke, whereupon you briefly recount to him how you had just been at McConnell and Baines where you found a good pair of gloves. Parke smiles in satisfaction to the news, oh-yes-thank-you, but just now he is distracted with gathering up guests to go out to the yard. The gentlemen start making motions to leave, and there is short wait while attention is focused on Mercy, who says she is content to remain seated, telling all not to fuss over it; Cleantha in turn volunteers to stay with mother, and she beckons to Parke with an inquisitive glance—did he bring the toffee candy from Crawford's?

"Yes, yes, Mother, it's already in the dining room."

"And did you stop by the post office?"

"Yes, nothing there for us today."

"Oh, and someone said something about a bottle of wine being delivered . . .?"

"I don't know." (Here you catch Parke suppressing a quick smirk.)

You follow Willard, Parke, and Hervey back to the hall you begin asking Parke about his goldrush expedition to Pike's Peak. "Oh now that was quite a caper," he laughs, saying he'll tell you more later, "but for now let's just say I cannot recommend the stagecoach ride from Iowa to Colorado—a truly excruciating mode of travel. If I ever go out west again it won't be until the railroad gets laid out for the entire run."

Once back in the hall your group is delayed by the front door, as there are a few women who are also exiting from the parlor opposite, and the resulting social encounter persists despite Parke's genial efforts to keep everyone moving. From your position behind you are, in effect, left out of the introductions, although you do overhear one woman's voice asking "Emily, have you met my brother Hervey." And chatter and chatter. After a few moments, with the group's conversation evidently not coming to a close, you decide you may as well wander off on your own to survey other realms of the first floor, that is, the open doors to two rooms off the far end of the hall beyond the staircase.

And sure enough, the room on the right is a conservatory, which you might peek into later, and on the left is the dining room, where the scene reveals various youngsters seated at the table and on the floor by the windows where there is extra space, and still others hovering around a large, ornate hunt board table set with an assortment of oatmeal cookies and slices of almond cake. Happily left to cavort about with their own company, now that most of their parents have moved on to the yard, for the young ones it's also a smart interlude to snatch up the remaining treats whenever opportune. A young housemaid is also there, the sole figure of authority to ensure things don't get completely out of hand; she beckons to you that you are welcome to come in and try one of the few remaining deviled eggs, which you do (actually, quite tasty) while she proceeds to gather up some of the empty plates still on the hunt table. And here you see Hervey's niece Clettie is seated at the main table with a plate of cookies and a small sandwich, with another girl about the same age in the next chair. Clettie has her mouth full but she still looks up with a happy grin as soon as she recognizes you.

"Well! Miss Clettie—so we meet again," you smile down, while she nods agreeably in return. "And who is your friend here?"

The other girl is polite enough to respond directly: "I'm Ada Mc-Connell."

"Ah, Miss McConnell, I'm a friend of your father. So this is your home, then. I must say, it certainly is a beautiful . . . "

In mid-sentence, however, another girl about the same age rushes in through a door—from the pantry, it would seem—and huddles close to the two girls, whispering something surely scandalous causing all three to giggle wide-eyed. You figure: well, they're having fun, and you pull up to take in what else is going on. You see Willie McConnell and his cousin Fred, the doctor's son, over by a window with another boy, ignoring everything but their ice creams, their fox-and-geese gameboard abandoned on the floor nearby. And the other children here and there are likewise occupied with their companions and their treats. One can only assume they are the younger McConnell's, like Ada, and various cousins.

As you were trying to tell little Ada, her home is truly splendid, including this dining room with its bay window, its coffered ceiling and matching wall beams topped with decorative corbels. As if the child had any idea. My goodness. And nice family touches, such as that tray on the window sill, set with a crystal decanter and silver oval-shaped snuff box. On the dining table where Clettie had been sitting (What was her last name, Kelsey, was it?) you spy a large book left alone on the corner; by cocking your head you're able to make out the title, ah yes, 'The Song of Hiawatha'. The cover is adorned with gold leaf and an elaborate floral design, and it looks quite new—a gift to Clettie perhaps.

You should return to your group at the front door, if they haven't already left, but first you want to check in on the room across the hall, which is of course the conservatory. You quickly see that is also fully occupied, but with a crowd that appears to be all young adults. As you stop at the doorway several of them turn to stare back at you, with incurious expressions that seem to convey their hope that you don't mean to intrude on their party. You take the hint, but manage a quick glance around just to see that the room actually extends all the way back to the front of the house, as one large family room, the midway point somewhat effecting two halves by the way the furniture is arranged. There's a spinet[47] in there, too, and you wonder whether it will be put to use later on by anyone in here with some musical talent. So, then . . . time for you to go rejoin the parents. Walking briskly back up the hall you see the last of your group making their exit—Willard has to follow one of the women single file as her expansive hoop skirt takes up the width of the threshold—so you're just in time to catch up.

No you won't. Just after Willard leaves through the door, three new guests slip in the opposite way, a trio of young schoolgirls, probably intent on joining the group back in the conservatory. Nevertheless out of courtesy they take the time to exchange greetings with you, and introductions, and patiently abide your exclamations of recognition as you learn whose daughters they are—all people you know. Here is Levi Bacon's daughter Molly, and Horace Thurber's Sarah, and the third . . . a niece of Cleantha McConnell, with the same first name, Cleantha Parke.

Molly Bacon; Sarah Thurber; Cleetie Parke

---

47   Spinet: an upright piano.

You jokingly feign some exasperation in sorting through so many Cleanthas and Cletties, which draws some well-practiced giggles as the girls recommend you remember this one as "Cleetie Theresa." Her father is John Parke, Mrs. McConnell's brother, and she lives just down the street. You're beginning to perceive now that this threesome is a bit younger, 15 or 16 years old or so, although at first glance they appear older by their dresses and gloves and the shawls around their shoulders. Very charming. Cleetie was making a discrete wave to her aunt in the parlor, which also provides an auspicious moment for the girls to excuse themselves to you, with slight curtsies, and go meet with the elders there.

Looking into the room after them you see that now that only the Captain and Mercy and Cleantha remain in the parlor, and the Captain gestures with a smile and points with his finger that you should hurry along. Out you go, then, through the door and down the stairs, where you turn to the right to walk towards the side yard where the most of the party has already assembled. The afternoon weather is perfect, the fresh air invigorating. The yard makes for a very pleasant setting, framed within an array of rhododendrons and largely shaded under a good-sized chestnut. And a bit chatty as well, with most everyone enjoying themselves in numerous small reunions. The happy spirit is infectious as you walk in, finding yourself suddenly immersed in the crowd of guests and a cacophony of conversations and casual laughter. This is the main event. Now you can start to wend your way around and look for familiar faces.

McConnell house side porch in later years.

AERONAUT

AWAY FROM the party on the opposite side of the street was a calmer setting, quiet enough to hear all the voices and socializing going on at the house and its side yard. On this side there was work to do, and responsibilities, that ensured a successful event for the McConnell's. This was the empty field they used for a carriage park for their guests when they came to attend a swell affair, and now it was the place for horses and wagons, and water, and brushes, and a small number of people entrusted to keep watch. David Jackson was there, the man in charge, a black man 25 years old. He was a servant of the Lord at his church, and he was a paid servant in the McCo-

David Jackson

nnell household, the family's stablehand. For an occasion like today's reception it was only fitting and proper that David should manage the visiting guests' drivers and all the activity going on in the park.

All of the drivers, and many of the guests themselves, were already well acquainted with David Jackson, a good man at his station. For some years now he had been living in the McConnells' barn behind the house where his chief job was to tend to a pair of horses and the family's carriage and the surrey. He had his own room inside the barn, neatly constructed using planked boarded walls and a ceiling, and furnished with a bed and a trunk for all his belongings. Beyond the normal stablehand duties, as a member of the household David worked day-to-day with Eliza the English nanny, and Mary the Irish scullery maid, whenever help was needed with specific tasks involving repairs or heavy lifting. There were also errands to run for Johnny Hill, McConnell's assistant for his business, who occupied a room in the south wing of the house which was also an office. All of these folks got along just fine, though perhaps with an occasional to-do with Eliza who also served as the cook and could be a might bossy in the kitchen unless Mrs. McConnell herself happened to be there.

These were good days for the household help, and no less for Jackson. The daily activities around the house had become more interesting now that the warmer weather had returned and the family was having more social calls. Visits meant news. Nowadays Mr. McConnell and the two older sons always had lots of news about the nation and the coming of war, which they readily took time to talk about with Jackson. And for all that time his employers were talking about Fort Sumter, and Confederate States, and war supplies and business, and Joe coming home from college to enlist, and President Lincoln said this and said that, Jackson listened and listened, and he just couldn't get over it: so they really were going to form an army and march into the South, and go free the slaves. After so many years of talk and argue, a call for action was truly happening, and it was going to happen this summer, and hallelujah to that!

Jackson was quiet man by nature, as he had grown up this way, observant and cooperative, and unless he was with friends he would keep his thoughts to himself. He was learning how to read and write, a slow process. Mrs. McConnell had her younger children teaching both Jackson and Mary—Mary once said in private that the lessons probably were meant to help the "teachers" as much as the students, but never mind, it was knowledge gained. Jackson was beginning to read. He could read the store signs in town. He could read the train schedules posted at the depot. And some of the pages in the children's McGuffey books when they were left forgotten in the kitchen. Some of the folks at his church were asking whether the McConnell's had a copy of "Uncle Tom's Cabin" and could Jackson get a hold of it, but no, he had already seen the book at the house once before, and it was still too difficult to read. Besides, Jackson had heard that it was illegal for black people to read the book; even if that weren't true it didn't matter—probably the story wouldn't tell him anything new, so what was the point.

Then some weeks ago at the church someone had given him a newspaper article about something that really mattered. Mattered to Jackson at least. It wasn't a news report about the war, or the South, or wagons, or tack and saddle for horses.

It was a story about men who had flown through the air under a giant balloon.

This was sensational, to Jackson. *This* was what he dreamed about doing, himself, some day.

The underlying truth was this: that the news story had reawakened in Jackson a childhood memory, and an imagination all about floating up in the air. It was years ago when he was still a young boy, younger than 12 say, still working the fields with his family. In those days he had learned to sing the pass-time hymns, along with everyone else around him, and sometimes they all just listened while the older slaves recited an old folklore tale, with the storyteller pausing to let other slaves voice the speaking parts as fitting. Jackson always listened attentively to these stories while picking or digging, whatever his task was, and gradually he memorized them by dint of so many repetitions. And of all the folklore stories, Jackson's favorite was the one about slaves who could fly away into the air and easily escape from the plantation overseers. All they needed was to hear the magic words shouted out by old Toby, and join all their hands together, and float up and away in a big group into the clouds with the birds.

A few years on, after Jackson had been assigned to work in the manor's stable, he always remembered that one special story. It was the old myth that everyone called "The People Could Fly."[48] It didn't matter how the story ended, or didn't end at all. It was just an idea, an inspiration to think about how it would feel to be floating, how the earth would look from on high.

Nowadays everybody had been talking about balloons, about giant balloons that could lift a room-sized basket, a *gondola*, carrying several men a mile up in the sky. None of his friends had ever seen a balloon launch (an "ascent"), and a balloon had never been sighted in the skies over Pontiac, but nowadays there many balloons flying over different parts of the country, and many newspaper columns and sketches depicting the events. These balloons were traveling hundreds of miles over two or three days, at speeds faster than a train on the ground. There were stories about a *balloonist* in Michigan, a Professor Bannister down in Adrian, who had made several voyages in the skies over the state. The McConnell children had been talking about him. But the most fascinating story of all had only recently been reported: a Professor Lowe had floated from Missouri to South Carolina in just

---

48 This story has been put into print, with illustrations, by Virginia Hamilton in "The People Could Fly: American Black Folktales" (New York, Knopf, 1985).

one day, high enough to pass over the Blue Ridge Mountains; he had returned to St. Louis by train with his balloon deflated and packed in a crate, and now he was celebrated as a national hero. Mr. McConnell had shown Jackson a map of the country, and had traced with his finger where Professor had started and ended the trip. Jackson kept in his pocket a copy of a long newspaper article describing the adventure, which he had almost completely memorized. He had sounded out every line, asking the McConnell children for help with the new words, and explain what some of them meant.

One new word stood out especially. *Aeronaut*. Professors Banister and Lowe were *aeronauts*. This was a rallying point for Jackson's imagination, inspiring him to work through the rest of the text. He even conjured up a plan: he would master this news article, then find more stories about balloonists, and at some point he would go see a real launch. He could start setting aside a little money, every week, saving for the day when he would travel, maybe to Adrian, maybe to Battle Creek. He had to see this for himself. He wanted to meet Professor Banister and talk to him about ballooning, if they let him. Usually there were huge crowds coming to see a balloon launch, so it might be hard for a black man to get in close.

What he wanted to know more about was this: one story about a balloon journey had described how there was not only a gondola, but a sixteen-foot boat suspended below it, and in the boat there were fans that could be set to waving in circles and actually propel the balloon forward.[49] There was no sketch, but Jackson could picture in his mind what it would all look like.

A fine daydream, from time to time, and easy to fall back on during a slow moment like now in the carriage park. Jackson had been thinking back on the church service last Sunday—Pentecost Sunday—with its celebration of the descent the Holy Ghost in the form of tongues of fire floating over the heads of each of the disciples, giving them the ability to speak in other languages. For this special service the choir had sung an old spiritual, and most of the congregation joined in, including Jackson who know the song from his childhood:

God's gonna set this world on fire one of these days, hallelujah.
I'm gonna sit at the welcome table one of these days, hallelujah.
I'm gonna eat and never get hungry one of these days, hallelujah.
I'm gonna drink and never get thirsty one of these days, hallelujah.
God's gonna set this world on fire one of these days, hallelujah.

As a little boy he sang about a world on fire, and mighty acts, and he could dream of people flying away in the sky. Now up north as a grown man he could still sit in church smiling to himself as he recalled the old stories, the old dreams. And it seemed a man might live to see a share of mighty acts after all. There was a war coming soon, and in

---

49   Balloon launches had been highly publicized events, two in particular, in St. Louis in 1859 and Cincinnati in 1861. The first was attended by tens of thousands of spectators, when a four-man team led by John Wise floated skyward to begin what was to become an 18-hour voyage over 700 miles ending in Buffalo, New York. The second was a solo voyage by Thaddeus Lowe which took him overnight to South Carolina. Pioneers in balloon technology were already theorizing that prevailing winds could propel a craft across the Atlantic Ocean to Europe within a few days' flight.

town there were bands playing, and torch-lit parades, and speeches. There were acts and changes all around him. These days it was common news that people were flying—in balloons—all the time. Jackson could rightly gaze skyward and imagine the view of an aeronaut, from high in the air among the clouds, looking downwards at birds in flight, at the houses of Pontiac, at the Clinton River winding its way through Oakland County, and he wondered what a cloud would feel like if he could touch it.

"O say, David Jackson, where *aaaare* you?"

Familiar teasing brought him back to ground, a little annoyed perhaps, resuming his attention to the activity and friends around him. Other stablehands were on hand, friends of Jackson, who had driven some of the wagons bringing guests to the McConnell's. The men had finished their work for now and could spend some time relaxing by the rough-hewn wooden table in the carriage park field, still keeping an eye on the surreys, fancy cabriolets, and big-wheeled phaetons that were parked about the field and in the streets, arranged for prompt retrieval, their horses standing hitched and soothed.

Everybody had been watching Eliza who had emerged from the house and crossed the street carrying in one hand a large pail of something good to drink, one might suppose, and a sack in the other hand which probably contained the cups. Sure enough upon arrival the pail turned out to be filled with cooled rhubarb shrub, and the sack with a stock of apple fritters, which Eliza arranged open with a cheery "My good friends! Some *hors-d'oeuvres* for you!" She always enjoyed an occasion to use this latest expression from New York, with suitable pomp, which on cue elicited wide smiles and rolling-eye looks among her audience. But as the fritters were passed around and the men took a first bite, there were "mmm's" and nods of approval throughout the group.

"Right smart tastier than her rusks![50]" "Good treats today, boys!" "Much obliged, ma'am." The happy sentiment was unanimous.

Eliza was only too happy to reaffirm: "Oho! Delmonico's wouldn't bake any better!" ("Who?" "What was that she said?") No matter—the fritters and shrub refreshments were much appreciated and the men were ready for their own round of socializing, the mood buoyed up by the chatter and laughter they could hear coming from across the street at the house.

This was a group that saw each other frequently around the town. Some were white, some were black freedmen. Those gathered now on McConnell's porch with Jackson were five of the freedmen who employed full time by families or working for livery stables. More than just acquaintances through their work, these men were fellow parishioners, family friends, sharing similar stories from previous homes or previous families left behind years ago. A few of them had been born in northern free states, but most had come to Michigan from southern states; it was generally presumed that they had escaped slavery and made their way here through the Underground Railroad. But if supposing they had, they never spoke of their flight or the hideaways along the way. And for those who had come alone, without family, there was no way to know for sure whether those whom they left behind—parents, siblings, sweethearts —were still alive and well, or even in the same plantations where last seen. Some day in a dreamlike future there might be a time for visits and reunions but for now it was best just to get along with the new life, new homes, new communities, and their new church. And confide in very few people.

This particular Thursday afternoon was peaceable enough, with fine weather, with fritters and shrub to enjoy, and with a good hour or so before a return to duty when the reception would end and all the families came calling for their rides home. Jackson and his fellow

---

50 Rusk: a hard biscuit, sweetened, similar to modern day Melba toast.

drivers situated themselves around the long wooden table, some seated on its split-log side benches and few others on the table top, and some reclining nearby on the grass. Eliza left the refreshments for the men to manage, so Jackson took to pouring the shrub into the cups while the usual dialog of jokes and stories picked up again from whatever event had last brought the men together the last time. The air was still warm, even in the encroaching shade, as the sun made its way down beyond the trees in the west yard. It would be a fine, languid evening, almost summer-like. And there was also that buzzing noise—cicadas—rising and fading intermittently in the trees here and there. Calming, pleasant: der-der-der-der-der-der. Jackson recalled the McConnell's talking about 1861 being a "cicada year."

Wait, now, here's something happening. The men stopped their banter and all eyes turned towards Church Street, and after a few moments someone said, "Well, well, will you look at that." What everyone saw were two more guests walking toward the house, both of them gentlemen, and both of them black men, well-dressed, walking confidently at an unhurried pace, shoulders back. One of them appeared older, say 50, and the other was younger and just as grand in appearance. The freedmen recognized both of these visitors immediately; it was just surprising to see them coming now to the McConnell's in this circumstance. Remarkably, here was their very own pastor, Reverend Augustus Green, with his son Alfred, making their way towards the festivities along with all the high society. Jackson and all the others stood up, as a natural reaction to show their respect, and this motion apparently caught the attention of the pastor, who returned their look with a broad smile and a tip of his hat. "Gentlemen!" he called out clearly, and all the stablemen nodded back promptly. The pastor continued towards the front walk, turning his attention to another guest who had waited to shake hands and extend greetings.

"I'm telling you, Campbell," Jackson said to another man nearby on the porch, "everything happens this year."

"I believe you got that right, Mr. Dave. Abolition getting' underway, sure. Now here comes Reverend Green hob-nobbin' with top white people inside. I say we be seeing our own church, real soon, and schools, and . . ."

"And soldiering," said another man. "A whole army, marching south." He sighed, and added, "I'd go with 'em if they'd take me. I can shoot."

"Naw, no use dreaming, mister. They got plenty of white boys in blue suits as it is. You see 'em at the fairgrounds, forming up, drilling all day long."

Doubtless true. To that effect it was common to hear a thunderous crash now and then echoing from the fairgrounds, whenever hundreds of muskets were fired off together in practice. The noise was exciting; the very idea of what it meant was downright exhilarating.

They were all watching as Reverend Green started up the front walk to the main door, but suddenly all attention was pulled back in front of them when they realized that the reverend's son Alfred had separated and was striding straight towards their group in the field. The stablehands held their places in silent respect, one or two voices offering a "Welcome, brother," until Alfred came to stop just before the table and made a measured glance over each man as if he were about to speak his mind before the entire group. Jackson was fully taken by the man's appearance, especially the top hat and silk cravat, if for no reason. He had seen well-dressed black men in town before, once or twice, but never up close like this at the McConnells' house.

Alfred's first words were striking: "You boys ready to fight?" What he meant was army service, they all knew, but nobody in authority had ever come right and asked them that question before. It was all they could do to overcome their surprise with staggered replies of "Yes we are" and "I'll go" and "I can shoot." Another pause. Alfred was now glaring at them, and was nodding his head approvingly, slowly. The deep, redoubtable voice spoke again: "Well, you may just get your chance." And with that, he turned back around and strode away towards the front door of the house.

"Damn," Campbell whispered, in hushed admiration.

And so the working men went back to their cups and fritters around the table. There was little to say now, exchanging smiles and nods and how-about-that expressions. They became themselves again, perhaps less jovial, each of them pondering why a lettered man like Alfred Green would speak to them like that. Jackson was seated again at the small table, where he drank down the last swig of his shrub drink. He was still enjoying the camaraderie, subdued though it may be. He looked down into his empty cup, thoughtfully with his eyebrows raised, listening to the others, until he turned his gaze up towards the trees around the yard. He didn't mind the few last joking remarks around him ("So who else invited? Sojourner Truth[51] herself coming here to make a speech?") while his thoughts turned away, reflecting on all that might happen in the coming months. Would he really get to see the old folks once again? The old places, the old life. He wondered whether there was anyone back there who might remember him.

Jackson had never thought much about going anywhere outside of Pontiac since making the McConnell house his home. How many years had it been already? Mr. McConnell had been asking around about hiring a stablehand, and must have met with old Lizzie Forth[52] about it at some point. Word came to Jackson down in Detroit, where

---

51 Sojourner Truth (born Isabella Baumfree) was an escaped slave who became an outspoken abolitionist and women's rights advocate. In 1861 she was 64 years old, living in Battle Creek, Michigan. Two years later in 1863 she would attain wider renown when her 1851 speech "Ain't I a woman?" was published nationally.

52 Elizabeth Denison Forth (1793-1866): another runaway slave who worked for a family in Pontiac and eventually became the first African-American landowner in Oakland County, buying four lots in Pontiac in 1825.

he had just arrived "from Kentucky" that a job was there for the taking in Pontiac. Parishioners at the "Covenanters" Church[53] paid his way on a buckboard wagon, and that was that—the next morning there he was, riding up the Saginaw Trail, not knowing anyone or any places, and still pulling remnants of straw out of his shirt after having spent his last night in Detroit in a hayloft in Mr. Finney's barn.

Years ago, years ago. What a day that was.

In Pontiac Jackson was met by McConnell's son Joseph at a livery stable where the buckboard had stopped, and from there the two of them walked back to the house, Jackson carrying everything he owned in a small satchel bag. Mrs. McConnell was waiting for them, and she greeted Jackson using his Christian name, David. Here on the kitchen porch Jackson's new existence was spelled out for him: tend the two family horses, tend the wagons and the tool shed, help with the bushes and flowers around the yards, and maintain the greenhouse plants as directed by Eliza the cook and Mrs. McConnell. Jackson's room and board were provided, along with a small wage that Mr. McConnell's assistant Johnny Hill would manage for him. Jackson was too tired from his travel to understand the full impact of all these new arrangements, but he knew he could toe the mark for all these jobs, familiar enough to him already, so for the moment it was enough to keep repeating "Yes m' . . . yes m' . . . yes m'" after each instruction. And look friendly, and look honest. Finally Eliza suggested to Mrs. McConnell that they allow the poor soul to rest up before dinner, and the new stablehand was shown to his quarters in the barn.

The room assigned to him turned out to be the biggest surprise of all. Jackson followed Eliza outside and around the back end of the house, past the garden and into the barn. Inside, the stables seemed well kempt enough, and there was plenty of room to work around the

---

53 "Covenanters": a secret society within a Presbyterian Church in Southfield, Michigan, that was extremely anti-slavery and active in the Underground Railroad.

carriage area. But then Eliza showed him his quarters—separately situated as a room with walls, floor, and ceiling—and mentioned off-hand that he would have the place all to himself. Jackson was quietly astonished. The room was clean and tidy, no lock on the door but no matter, and there was even a stove by the outside wall. How about that. This was going to be a completely different life, a good place to toe the mark.

And it was. Jackson's good provenance was real and lasting. He readily mastered his various duties and quickly learned the "ins and outs" of working with Mrs. McConnell and Eliza day-to-day. He enjoyed running errands in the town, which led to new acquaintances made with other blacks, and although there were many limitations on where he could go and what he might do, nevertheless he had never been threatened or bullied. And it seemed that everybody in town knew that he worked for the McConnell's. That meant something. And even when he encountered a gruff remark or a condescending look, for the most part he felt as though white folks still respected the work that he did for them. Within a few months a more matter-of-fact measure of his independence became apparent with the arrival of freezing winter weather, when he was allowed to spend most nights at the home of his friend Campbell who was married and owned his own place. A new life for sure, this was.

People also respected the blacks' religious community, small in number but persistent, and steadfast without even a church building of their own. They held their gatherings in various homes or at an old schoolhouse, led by George Newman, a popular freedman in Pontiac. Jackson was always impressed by the way Mr. McConnell encouraged him to participate, sometimes even arranging to let them hold services in the basement of the M.E. Church[54] on Perry Street. Earlier this year Reverend Augustus Green started showing up, visiting from Canada

54   M.E. Church: the Methodist Episcopal Church.

across the river, to help Newman organize the group into a congregation of an *African* M.E. Church. Jackson was greatly inspired by Reverend Green, and the reverend's stories about Frederick Douglass in Boston, and Sojourner Truth in Michigan, and the reverend's own son Alfred in Philadelphia, and other blacks who were educated and traveling around the north preaching for the abolition of slavery.

Sitting here in the carriage park, Jackson thought over Alfred's jarring words about fighting in battle. In all honesty it was difficult to imagine wearing one of those "blue suits" and being trained what to do and how to fight. Campbell, noticing his friend's absent gaze, tried to draw some reaction by mouthing off how it would be nice to get enlisted soon, so they could march south in time to miss the next round of freezing winter weather here at home. Home—Jackson smiled to himself. Which home? "I don't know, Campbell. This whole scrap will be long over before they take us on for fightin' men. Maybe I could still join up, anyhow, to work the army horses. Or drive wagons." Campbell nodded, "Yes sir, maybe so. I reckon we get no uniforms for that mark, though. Still, I'd like to go see Mississippi again, if they go there. Hooo, now wouldn't that be something."

Campbell was right—it *would* be something. Jackson often had that daydream too, of walking around the old fields and cabins of his former life. He would be wearing the blue uniform. The people would gather around, waiting for him to say the words, magic words like the ones old Toby said in the stories: "You can all go." Then they would all be cheering and singing about the world set on fire . . . but Jackson would only watch and wave, approvingly, before getting on with his army duties that needed attention. And in camp he would write notes to describe what he did and what he saw, his own writings, to bring home to Pontiac—his *real* home—after the war ended.

Yes, this summer could bring some big changes, if a man made some careful decisions. Of course, everything hinged on whether or not the army would let the freed black men enlist. If they didn't, then Jackson would turn to another dream, a dream that had seemed possible ever since he first arrived at the McConnell's in Pontiac. He would have start a family of his own.

Jackson couldn't remember much in the way of family life in the south, other than living with the older people that he called auntie or uncle; he had no brothers or sisters as far as he knew. Up north now, life was different. If a man could support a wife and family then there was no reason why he couldn't court a woman and settle down. This was the common expectation in town and in church, that a good man like David Jackson should become the head of his own household, lifelong, and pass on his name to his progeny. The family could stay in one place, or move away if they needed, but they would always be together.

No question about it—that is what Jackson wanted, army or no army. He wanted family, in his own homestead. And why not right here in Pontiac, a town that celebrated all those "pioneer families" who settled here first, years ago. Wasn't he just as much a pioneer himself?

One way or another, this year things were bound to change—and it might happen soon. The right girl was at hand, and for all his quiet carefulness and thoughtful planning, David Jackson was also a man in love, truly, and freely. Miss Martha Parker, a girl at church, had captured his heart with hopeful eyes and a loving smile. The easy friendship between them had steadily grown into a serious courtship so comfortably that it seemed only natural to spend all their free time together, and within a few months they began to speak freely about marriage and children. There was a future now, a clear future. Jackson was close to proposing, maybe even this summer. In this new life he had become a man capable of planning his own course on his own initiative, and the time had come.

The man's carefulness might sometimes overshadow the romance of all that was happening between them, which Martha understood and actually found to be one of his more endearing traits. But as for Martha, her mind was made up. This was her man, and she would accept his proposal, to be sure. And besides the romance there was planning—wasn't that just life? So the two of them talked over what all was at stake, fully aware how it could be a little shaky. The foremost consideration was Jackson leaving his room at the McConnell's to find a suitable accommodation for a married couple to move into. Quite likely this meant losing his employment at the McConnell's as well, even if he stayed on good terms with Willard and Cleantha, but this was all for the good, anyway. His wages there would never be enough to support a new family of his own with Martha Parker.

Jackson had intimated all of these worries to his friend Campbell, who agreed with him, saying how "Marse Willard can't ever pay out the spondulicks that a family man needs."[55] True, Jackson supposed. Campbell had a good job working at Archie McCallum's sheep tannery, and could get Jackson a job there too, if he wanted. Scraping sheep hides was not an exciting prospect, of course, but there were many other less onerous tasks involved in the process of making leather. And it would mean good, steady wages. Jackson had always thought that the tannery was the most likely course; besides, there was always a chance that the army might be taking on black soldiers. If they did, then he and Campbell would immediately enlist together, never mind that Campbell was married and Jackson might be engaged by then. Probably they would be away no more than a year, and likely not do any actual fighting; but even driving wagons or toting supplies would be all right if it allowed a visit to the South.

The thing was, though, Jackson inwardly was hoping for something far different from driving wagons. He wouldn't say this to his friend, no, but what he really imagined himself doing in the army was not tending horses. It was tending balloons.

---

55   Spondulicks: cash money.

He had been running an errand for the McConnell's, to pick up purchases over at Butterfield's store, and he had overhead Ira talking with some customers about the war and how a "Professor Lowe"— another balloon professor like Bannister, Jackson figured—had been invited to see President Lincoln in the White House to talk about how the army might use balloons to float high in the air to provide a means of observing the enemy positions. And quietly, then and there in store while he waited for his packages, Jackson was totally overcome by this idea: the army could make him an aeronaut. If he joined the army, maybe the McConnell's would see to it that he get assigned to the balloon service. All the way home in the buckboard he thought about how this might play out. This was why it would be important to meet Professor Banister first, to learn more about ballooning first hand.

The young freedman started harboring this new ambition. He could do it. Why not? He could learn how to prepare a balloon for launch, lay it out on the ground and attach the rigging to the gondola, arrange the pipe to blow in the gas, and man the tether. He could read, so the army would teach him all about the equipment and the gases and what to do, and what all the jobs were in an army balloon unit. And sooner or later, the day would come when he, too, would be ordered to ride in the gondola and man the flight.

They would be using spyglasses, sure, to scan over the lands below looking for the Confederate army units. Jackson had looked through a spyglass before, when he was a boy in Mississippi. It was on the front porch of the manor with the master's son, who was using a spyglass attached to a tall wooden tripod to watch the workers digging sweet potatoes in a faraway field. The son noticed Jackson's interest and invited him to take a look himself, which Jackson did obediently, and it was a quite an experience. He could make out how people would bend over or kneel down, and stand up again, and talk to each other. He couldn't see their faces clearly enough to know who they were. The son showed the method of focusing, and explained how the curved glass lenses magnified the images far away. The barrel was round, smooth metal, with eye rings and attachment parts made of shiny brass that fit perfectly on the tripod. The fancy word for it was "telescope." Jackson never got another chance to look through it again. But afterwards several times he espied the telescope set out on the porch, on its tripod, and he overhead white folks talking about it, using words like magnify, and lens, and focus. He liked the sound of these words and he enjoyed pronouncing them out loud when he was alone. Ap-par-a-tus. Mag-ni-fi-ca-tion. Magnify. In Bible stories and songs they magnify the Lord, and in the telescope they magnify slaves far away in a field. It made sense.

Since arriving in Pontiac Jackson was still acquiring more words, words about science, and equipment, and words used in newspapers. Train schedules, and types of trains, and business words spoken by Mr. McConnell with his son Parke. Jackson could now read these words in print, for himself. It was . . . interesting. It would be even more interesting to converse with others, and talk about equipment, hydrogen gas, geography, aeronauts. How could man not dream about learning these things in the new world that was being realized all around him? Let the war come, then, and let a man prepare a man for a new life, in Pontiac or wherever. Even if the army didn't take a black man, there must be some way to join the movement and learn new skills. Jackson was ready. He knew he was smart, and healthy, and now he was lettered.

"Doggone it, Campbell," he smirked at his own conceit, "What am I thinking, anyway. Say, come along to the greenhouse and we'll pick some of that rhubarb for your wife." Campbell was glad that Jackson remembered. The other day he had asked Jackson whether the McConnell's might be growing tomatoes, but no, like many folks up north the McConnell's had little interest in southern "poison apples", as they called them. But they did have a good showing of rhubarb.

The two friends stood up and walked across Church Street towards the right side of the house, then turning the corner at Paddock Street so that they could approach the greenhouse from outside the fence, meaning to stay away from the McConnells' party in the opposite yard. They hopped over the short fence, and then decided to keep going around to the rear property, by the herb garden, where they could take a peek at the east yard where the guests were starting to gather—only a small number had appeared so far. Most folks must still be inside the house. It would be a while before any speechmaking got started. Jackson and Campbell had plenty of time to go back to the greenhouse and look over the springtime rhubarb.

Rev. Augustus Green

The McConnell's are nice folks. Willard has always been a sympathizer for our cause. These days he's preoccupied with growing his Methodist Church, of course, but I believe he is just as satisfied seeing an African Methodist Episcopal Church become established in this town as well. It's a kind gesture to allow our A.M.E. members use the old church on Perry for our place of worship. Willard also helps me get my issues of *True Royalist* distributed around Pontiac. You'd be surprised at how many black citizens in this town can read my papers.

I enjoy coming here whenever I can. Yes, I'm still living across the river in Canada, in Windsor Town. We've had a real church there for some four years now. Our biggest job is working with the British government to maintain our safe haven for fugitive slaves. I always have to be a little careful about arranging a crossing into Michigan, but once inside I can travel around openly. The 2nd Baptist in Detroit is plenty safe, and the time is right to get an AME Church, too, up here in the interior. You've met George Newman, haven't you? Tomorrow I'm meeting with the Newman's about making arrangements to hire a resident pastor. Yes, these are new times, new times coming. The help of the Church here will be crucial, now that this crusade is underway -- when our boys march down to free the south, they must bring a strong spirituality along with them.

My son Alfred has the fire within, God help him. You'll feel it if you ever hear him speak his mind. I'm so proud of his way with words. Don't you know, he was jailed back east in Harrisburg for two months on some nonsense charge, oh sure, disturbing the peace while standing up for some runaway slave they were after. Well, we got Alfred released. But truly, he's come out of there a troubled soul, and I believe he won't rest now until he's recruited an entire army of fugitives to follow him into every plantation in the south and root out the old masters. And you and I will soon witness this mighty act: in a few months our country will finally be cleansed of the scourge of slavery, mark me.

GLORIOUS MEETING.—With only five hours notice, the Republicans of this village and vicinity assembled by thousands, in front of JEWELL's PENINSULAR HOTEL last night, and listened to eloquent, stirring and appropriate speeches from Gov. Wisner, Byron G. Stout, Henry W. Lord and Charles Draper. The Wide-Awakes were out in a magnificent Torch-Light Procession, and capital and most appropriate music was furnished by Hirst's Brass Band from Clarkston. It was indeed an enthusiastic ratification of the splendid Republican Victories in Pennsylvania, Indiana and Ohio

The Douglas Worshipers also had a meeting at the Court House. attended by about 140, at which Gen. Baldwin re-repeated his well-learned declamation about "Republican stealing." It was a lame affair, and ended in a street-fight.

A VISITOR'S STORY,
"Among the Guests"

THIS IS turning out to be quite the swell affair. Mrs. McConnell has orchestrated a lively outdoor event, and it has delighted everyone. There must be some thirty people gathered in the side yard, so far, in fair weather suitable for a picnic, late enough in the afternoon to avoid the gnats and mosquitos, with plenty of room for guests to mingle or step away for an intimate discussion. The grass underfoot is cushiony. A set of folding tables has been set out with refreshments, and the yard expanse is enhanced by a few trees and islands of rhododendrons, and its periphery defined by an array of witch hazel and other bushes. And there must be some lilacs nearby, their springtime fragrance unmistakable. It is an occasion for happy faces and cheerful greetings, and hints of pleasant aromas from the women's perfumes and the men's pomades. There are smiles, broad smiles catching your notice now and then for the way they might reveal someone's discolored or missing tooth, in an unguarded, carefree spirit, only for a moment.

Here you can find a large selection of Pontiac's premier society, a posh ensemble of husbands, wives and a few older children, all enjoying the company and an opportunity to see and be seen. The women have thoughtfully opted for cotton attire from their wardrobes, as opposed to silks, and have turned out in very attractive versions of promenade dresses, some flounced, and many with pagoda sleeves. You see several instances of the new color scheme in shades of pink (How did Levi describe it—magenta? Or solferino?) which adds a nice flair to the show. And most are wearing spoon bonnets—again, the time of day is just right, the sun being low and unobtrusive. No one has brought a parasol. Their husbands are likewise taking advantage of the outdoor environment by doffing their hats; you saw the one table nearby with an accumulated assortment of top hats and bowlers. And while the older gentlemen are still outfitted in long frock coats and vests, many of those younger have opted for Prince Albert waistcoats or are sporting the newer style "sack" coats and suits, shorter with a looser fit.

Before committing yourself to any social interaction you decide to go take stock of the foods and treats that have been arrayed on a couple of tables draped with linen. There you find various samplings of dried fruits, licorice and maple sugars, with small cups to carry them away, but for now you are mostly attracted to the beverage table. Bowls and bottles; let's take a look. First off you notice that your contribution to the event, the Chautauqua wine, apparently has not made it from Turk's to this table. Perhaps your gesture was not deemed appropriate? It appears that no other wines are set out, whereas the beverage table is dominated by large punch bowls, including a large silver one on a tray in the middle, and two lesser, ceramic bowls at the ends. Probably the big silver bowl holds the alcoholic punch, while the ceramics are for serving shrub or switchel[56] to any guests who prefer a more benign af-

---

56   Shrub beverage: berry juice and vinegar, sweetened with sugar or honey, reduced and combined with carbonated water. Switchel: water and cider vinegar, seasoned with ginger, sweetened with molasses or maple syrup.

ternoon refreshment. You don't see any sweet cider, of course, not this time of year. Let's play it safe and avoid the punch for now, so, taking up one of the larger drinking cups, you choose to start with the switchel. Now having suitably equipped yourself for social discourse, you can take a few moments to scan over the company. It is a cheery scene, noisy even outdoors with a cacophony of voices and polite laughter, further animated by the ladies' fans fluttering here and there. The fresh air itself seems to induce a casual rapport among the crowd.

From behind you comes an exclamation loud enough to be audible over everything else, "Reverend Green!" You turn around to see Willard extending an excited hello to, what's this, a black gentleman, handsomely attired and evidently an honored guest. Interesting. The reverend is accompanied by another black man, his son from what you can overhear, and by Mrs. McConnell, who must have escorted these new arrivals into the yard. Willard is outright boisterous in his greetings and questions for the reverend: thank you for coming, how was your trip, how are things with the B.M.E. church in Windsor and tell us about your Pentecost service, did you bring an issue of The True Royalist, so this is Alfred—I read your speech in Philadelphia, let me find our Reverend Samuel Clements and introduce you two . . . and so on. It's surprising to see Willard so uncharacteristically animated. Reverend Green is likewise just as affable as his host, and his deep bass voice booms out counter-greetings with questions such as "How's my favorite tenor?" and you can see him turn around to no one in particular as he adds, with a wink, "Best voice in any choir in Oakland County! Well, loudest anyway." And right away both Willard and the Reverend are staring into each other's face, eyes wide open, singing in unison the word: "A-a-a-m-e-n-n-n!" [57]

Following this abruptly comical reunion there are one or two onlookers who are introduced to Green and son, and then you, too, are

---

57   A new Anglican hymnbook, first published in London in March, had formalized the practice of singing "Amen" at the end of a hymn.

brought forward to shake hands as well, apparently at random, but no matter. Reverend Green is quite used to being introduced, which is to say you are immediately impressed by the charisma and grand manner. He is easing into this social setting as much as anyone, but you do sense a serious side to him, and his son, a certain forbearance in both of them. Soon the McConnell's are leading their newcomers deeper into the crowd, and you still hear the Reverend's loud, sociable tone as he meets with other guests. Definitely not "low-profile." And this is definitely an abolitionist arena, here in the McConnells' yard, judging by how nonchalant everyone's reaction is to his inclusion on the guest list.

In the aftermath of such a grand entrance you now find yourself standing with two younger women who, like you, are just as amused by the scene they just witnessed. You're not properly acquainted with the two of them, but under the circumstances you should feel safely beyond reproach to start up a conversation, if only to comment further about Reverend Green. Which you do, starting with "Well, *that* was a splash."

"Indeed, sir. The Reverend cannot fail to be conspicuous, wherever he goes."

The witty remark brings a smile to your face as you turn to the women, who both rejoin with nods of approval, and so a congenial talk might now be opened. Having introduced yourselves you then realize that these women had been in the hallway earlier, with the group by the front door chattering away and blocking your exit with Willard and Hervey; and that the woman who first spoke up is in fact Hervey's sister, and conversely she remembers observing your arrival at the front door with her brother. She is Sarah Parke French, and her companion here is Emily Darrow (who looks a bit wan, consistent, you might think, with the girl's diminutive frame), whose parents are Frank and Augusta whom you met in the living room—ah yes, yes. The three of you proceed with agreeing that the reception is a fine time; that the

McConnell's are most accommodating hosts; that the weather is like-wise as accommodating and did you hear the cicadas this morning; that the war is certainly becoming a reality; that Colonel Richardson is here in full uniform; that a round of speeches will be made later, probably using the porch as a dais. You mention that you don't see any soldiers in the yard just now, that is, Joseph McConnell or his college friends, and Emily explains that the young folks are all indoors in the McConnells' family room having their own party, but they should be joining us in the yard at some point for the ceremonies.

"I should say, it's curious to see the Colonel here, and in full array, which is even more curious," Sarah says. "I wasn't sure whether Michigan's most famous farmer even kept an old army uniform in his trunk any more. But he seems to have cleaned himself up nicely for society's sake."

"Today at least," Emily adds. "And he is, after all, the man in charge of all our soldier boys, including Mrs. McConnell's fair-haired boy Joseph. And behold! Our hostess has opened her home even unto the biggest Billy Goat Gruff, now when it truly matters."[58] It's difficult to tell whether Emily's tone is derisive or approving.

Sarah changes subjects to compliment you on your gloves ("very handsome—are they new?") then asks how long you have known Hervey, and when you clarify that you only met him this afternoon she seems interested to apprise you a little more about her brother's story.

"I haven't seen him for a while. He comes down from Keween-aw from time to time, sometimes with Charley Palmer—do you know Palmer? He's another 'iron ore' man. They're all making good money up there nowadays."

"So your brother owns a mining business?"

---

58 Emily is referring to the children's tale of the three Billy goats who cross a bridge owned by an evil troll. The story was included in a collection of Norwegian folk tales, published in English for the first time in 1859.

"Oh, no, he was just managing the books for one of larger companies, the Cliff Copper Mine, for many years, but then a couple of years ago he ventured into business with a partner to set up a hardware store in Hancock—that town is the nearest thing to civilization up there, you understand—and it seems to be working out. Well, I assume so, anyway. Hervey isn't the type to regale about his exploits. But he keeps going back to Hancock, and last year he took a bride up there with him."

"I see, so your brother just married last year—someone he met up there?"

"Mmm, no, a young lady from Pontiac. Maybe not really a young lady—more like his age, around 30 or so, from a very good family, though. The Hunts, don't you know. Her father was a politician in Washington. He just died a few years ago."

"I'm sorry, I'm not acquainted with the family. But I have heard about the coppermine country in Keweenaw. Rugged area, it would seem. Let's hope the new bride is as inclined for the pioneering life along with your brother. So, she's in Hancock now, I gather?"

"She is, and she is *expecting*, wouldn't you guess, and the baby is due very soon now. You know, we're all a little on edge about it. There's some sad family history in that town, going back to when Hervey first went up there ten years ago."

"Ten years! He's been working there that long? What happened?"

Sarah pauses and gives you a quick once over before continuing the story—but after all, she was the one who said 'sad family history', not that you're prying.

"It was after we lost our parents in an epidemic—they both died in Birmingham where we all lived—and we had an older sister who had just followed her husband to the mining country by Lake Superior. It was a pretty rudimentary existence up there at the time as you can imagine, but there was plenty of work and besides, the lake air is better for someone like Hervey, you see. He never stays healthy here in Oakland surrounded by all these woods and swamplands. So they invite him to join them up in . . . where is it?"

"Eagle Harbor," Emily puts in. "On the Keweenaw Peninsula." Her tone is a bit insistent, or sardonic, more accurately, as if to imply that Sarah ought to be able to name the obscure location by now.

"Eagle Harbor? I thought he said Clifton," Sarah says, her eyes open wide. "Heaven forbid I muddle my mining towns. But yes, Keweenaw. And so he went. *Et donc voilà*—just like that."

"Wait, now," you ask, trying to follow. "That was a 'Kelsey' your sister had married, right? Hervey is here with his niece Clettie Kelsey who came with us to the party."

"Yes, Marcus Kelsey," Sarah says in an offhand way. "The girl is Hervey's niece. Isn't she a darling? She was only a toddler when Hervey arrived in Keweenaw. But the tragedy was that the girl's mother, our sister Cornelia, poor thing, up and died when her second child was born."

"Oh, my goodness," you reply, sympathetically. *Yet another young mother lost in childbirth*—is on your mind as Sarah continues.

"It was a baby girl," ("Eva," Emily puts in) "And it all happened just after Hervey had moved in with Cornelia and her husband Marcus. Can you imagine?"

Despite her words, Sarah's telling of her brother's misfortunes seems rather dispassionate, as if it were information that she had recounted many times to others.

Emily speaks up again, "You see, the reason Hervey went up there in the first place was to assist with Cornelia's confinement period after the birth."

"And he stayed on, anyway . . . ," you venture.

"He did. First he helped Marcus make arrangements for Cornelia's burial back here in Pontiac, and have Clettie and baby Eva move in with another family," ("the Murlins"—Emily again) "yes, on their farm in Waterford. Then—he goes back to Keweenaw, on his own, where he takes a job with Cliff Copper, way out in another little mining town on the Lake Superior shoreline. Hervey must have been one of very few educated men living out there with all the miners. Plenty of leavened bread up there.[59]"

"Heavy winters up there, too, but I reckon the work goes on year round in that sort of business."

"It does. 'Cool breeze off the lake', as they say. Meanwhile, Marcus didn't stay long afterwards, and he came back to Pontiac for good. He picked up his daughters and they all moved in with the Captain and my Aunt Mercy at their old homestead not far from here. So, since then, things have worked out well for Marcus Kelsey. He's become quite the popular townsman. Eventually he re-married and moved into another place of his own on the north side. I don't see him here in the yard, and it's too bad. He's a man you should meet."

Cornelia Parke Kelsey
(Parke family archives)

"Kelsey? Yes I should, certainly." Sarah is glancing at you with a quick nod, her brows arched, which seems meant to convey her admiration for Kelsey's depth of character. You nod back in agreement, but this story has you thinking again about Hervey. The point is, Hervey had witnessed his sister's dying from childbirth, out there in the wilds of Keweenaw, and now he has his own wife up there in the same predicament, possibly. He doesn't seem to be particularly worried about it, as far as you can tell.

"I trust Hervey will be getting back to Keweenaw fairly soon?"

---

59 An allusion to 1st Corinthians 5:8. Emily is suggesting that the miners' community was not exactly morally impeccable.

"Actually he and his wife don't live in the mining town now. They moved into Hancock, where his new business is. It's more inland, a real town, similar to Pontiac from what he says, with a real doctor or two."

Emily interjects again: "I should think a respectable daughter of Judge Hunt deserves as much." She looks askance, shaking her head slightly. "I know I would."

"Yes, of course. Well, I wish them the best." You realize how that last remark sounds trite even though you mean it sincerely.

Sarah has finished her narrative about her brother Hervey, apparently, and she breaks off to chat idly with Emily, who had been biding her time and looking somewhat distracted as Sarah rolled out the now-familiar story. You have a chance to observe Sarah with more of a detached perspective and now you realize something, what you had suspected all this time, that this was the same woman you espied at the Arcade earlier today, and what's more, the man you thought was her husband was actually Marcus Kelsey, the hapless widower returned from Keweenaw. It makes you wonder whether Sarah and Marcus are a couple themselves, and if so, shouldn't Marcus be here at the McConnell's too?

Be that as it may, it's also more understandable why old matriarch Mercy Parke was so content to watch Clettie Kelsey running about with Molly Bacon and the other children—today's reception at the McConnell's is a far-reaching reunion. Far reaching? You're trying to picture Hervey's winter existence in an isolated settlement, snowbound, the wind howling in from the lakeshore ... and at this juncture Sarah and Emily, "Mrs. French and Miss Darrow," are ready to move on, and you bid goodbye for now, thanking Sarah for her interesting account about the Parke's. Inwardly you can't help but assess whether you have acquitted yourself adequately as a fully engaged listener in return. Probably you could have been a notch more animated but regardless, Sarah does come across as someone who would be challenging to keep up with, whatever the topic.

By yourself now, you can take another sip of switchel, tasting its slightly vinegary bite, and reflect a bit more on Hervey Parke's situation. Not for long, though, as standing in the middle of an outdoor party will present so many distractions all around you. And you notice, suddenly, a face in the crowd that doesn't seem to fit in well with all the others. Over there, a man is standing some ten yards away, by himself, and he seems to be staring straight at you. Look around to your right and left, and then back at the man—no, he is definitely focused on *you*. His demeanor is not threatening, and now he begins to show a grin as if he were an old acquaintance who perceives your predicament, that is, that you don't recognize him. Strange. So far, no one else at the McConnell's has looked at you in such a manner. Let's drink down the last bit of switchel and then go over and introduce yourself, or rather, reacquaint yourself with this unfamiliar man.

But just like that—he's gone. You're left looking around the crowd . . . no sign of him. Fine, then. So, where to turn now? There's Cleantha McConnell again, still looking as worried as when you first saw her in the parlor. She's speaking with another woman, presumably a friend who is there to help, as they both quickly scan over the situation and each refreshment table. Everything seems to be going smoothly, as far as you can tell. You could approach the two women as a probe to see whether they might be receptive to let you in to their conversation, but just then you overhear Cleantha speaking closely to her friend, saying something like "Oh dear Lord, he's not coming *here*, is he? Today? A man like that is capable of—" And upon noticing your presence, Cleantha turns her head to give you a quick, polite smile; nevertheless, it's clear she would rather not speak with anyone else but here friend at the moment.

Back off a step or two, with a respectful nod back at Cleantha, and to her friend. You might wonder who *he* is, that Cleantha seems so worried about—oh, just local gossip, likely. Let's just look around some more for any other society notables you might interest you. Aha, yes, there's someone—it's Elkanah Comstock, who gives you a brief nod in return though he is engaged in conversation with Horace Thurber, the hardware merchant who you saw walking to work this morning. And Michael Crofoot, again, talking with another couple. Thurber, and Crofoot and . . . it comes to you now: these two were part of the original four investors in the Pontiac Gas Works, along with McConnell and Levi Bacon. So they were the men who just "lit up" the city last winter with a retort house and the installation of pipes, street lamps, and already many indoor gas lights. Articles in the Gazette were particularly enthusiastic about the project—really anything that modernizes Pontiac. The work did encounter a few setbacks during final completion, due to severe weather, but despite all that the project prevailed and the service was initiated at last. The gratified citizenry certainly can only admire their civic leaders for this singular accomplishment, as the gas lines continue to extend out from the town center and more and more households link up to this modern convenience.

Elkanah has separated away from his speaking with Horace Thurber. He holds a plate of dainties in one hand while his other hand fumbles over the food that still remains on it, and his stance suggests that he might appreciate hearing a remark from you, so long as it's something quick and witty.

"Fine vittles. Plenteousness within the walls, wouldn't you say?" Let's see if Elkanah picks up on your alluding to the old Psalm.

And he does, of course. His response is to hold up a small cheese biscuit and, pursing his lips while displaying a mild grimace he thoughtfully disagrees:

"*Plenteousness*? I should think we'd say 'prosperity', for this palace of merry Methodists anyways!" He glances up at the McConnell house and starts making his way towards the beverage table.[60]

"Either way, I'm glad to be here . . ." you answer back, although Elkanah probably didn't hear you.

Just as you hoped, this event in the yard is providing a chance to circulate and shake hands with some of Pontiac's well renowned figures, for instance Moses Wisner, the former governor, whom you glimpse in a nearby cluster of guests. Wisner completed his term last January and has returned to his law practice, working out of his mansion north of town on Saginaw; he's an outspoken admirer of Abraham Lincoln and is most enthusiastic about the war, as everyone knows. You see him talking with Augustus Baldwin, also with Colonel Israel Richardson, who is eminently recognizable in his formidable full-dress uniform and his glowering visage under a wide-brimmed hat. The Colonel is a West Point man and a hero of the Mexican War who had retired to a life of farming in Pontiac (or was it law?), but now in his mid-forties he is returning to military service to command a volunteer regiment—Joseph McConnell's regiment – in Detroit.

Governor Wisner

Wisner and Richardson have buttonholed McConnell for a few words, and you decide to sidle in close enough to hear the discussion: will Pontiac be raising its own regiment, like those in Detroit . . . can Wisner secure enough funding for it from Governor Blair or Senator Chandler . . . the campground would be set up at the fairgrounds . . . plenty of material for uniforms right here from the carding mills . . . and so on. Wisner quotes a Latin phrase, "Suscepit Israel," which seems

60   From Psalm 122 "I was glad when they said unto me". The Visitor quotes the old
       English prayer book version, and Elkanah counters with the Baptist Church version.

to be a witticism that the colonel appreciates[61]; Richardson in turn is jesting that Wisner had better keep an eye on Pontiac's saloons, especially the Tremont and the Arcade, absolutely off-limits to the recruits. McConnell is evincing hearty agreement, as he adamantly asserts that no debauchery brought on by 'tree bark' spirits will be tolerated on the streets of our town. You can't help but think sarcastically, *yes of course, and good luck with that.*

Col. Israel Richardson

There's little chance that you'll be welcomed into this imposing group to share in their high-level conversation, and your cup of switchel is empty, so you look around the yard for something else to do. Still no sign of that stranger, the staring man, so maybe it's not worth worrying about. Who else is here, then, that a visitor might latch on to?

There's another bunch that appears friendly: you spot the shop girl you met earlier, Carrie Holley, who has apparently been invited to stay on at the party after having delivered your wine and the jelly beans from Crawford's. She's engaged in conversation with two gentlemen, though she has noticed you also, and now the two of you exchange an "OK" sign confirming her er-

Carrie Holley

Erastus Thatcher

61 Suscepit Israel: from the Magnificat (Luke 1:54-55 "He has helped his servant Israel"). This is a play of words on Colonel Richardson's first name.

rand was duly completed. You then gesture that you would like to join her circle, and she readily beckons for you to approach. Introductions proceed, and the next thing you know, here you are shaking hands with Honorable Mayor Erastus Thatcher, who turns out to be Carrie's uncle. Well now, there's a mild surprise—so the vivacious shopgirl runs in a larger society, it turns out. Now you begin to appreciate more her poise and grown-up composure. And there's a second discovery going on here: the girl has also changed attire into an elegant dress for the reception, of course, and the transformation is remarkable—that same shopgirl has become an attractive, captivating young woman in society. You can only smile to yourself about this unexpected turn as you introduce yourself and converse along with these new acquaintances. Meanwhile you're learning more about Thatcher's story, that he is in fact the very first mayor of Pontiac, now that the town has incorporated, following upon his prior service on the board of directors. He is an attorney, seemingly quite the intellectual, but soon exhibits a personality, oh, perhaps needing a little more character. (It's distracting how he keeps looking left and right about the yard while talking with you.) Carrie for her part is much more engaging and direct. And yes, it turns out that the manager at Turk's did come through with some recompense to Carrie for delivering the wine, which she confirms to you before you can ask about it. One comment by the Mayor seems peculiar: asking his niece about whether or not her mother knows she is here, the niece answering "Yes, I think so," which sounds a tad evasive. She also seems to be quieting down, in deference to letting others speak, in particular the other man who stands beside her.

This other man—younger, very well dressed, in fine posture with his hands held behind his back, his expression somewhat distracted— is Daniel Thurber, who was one of your lunch partners at the Arcade. He seems glad to shake your hand again here at the McConnell's, though his manner is more cordial in this current circle. It turns out that there's more social connection here. Daniel and Joe McConnell are college roommates, now at Union College and during the previous year at the University of Michigan which was before they both transferred to Union. The two of them have also been Delta Phi fraternity brothers at the chapters at Union and at Michigan. "Yes," he says, "today's honoree and I share a long history."—this brings a nod

Daniel Thurber

of affirmation from Thatcher. You would like to hear more about McConnell, but Carrie starts explaining how Daniel may start working for the Mayor this summer, which seems to render Daniel somewhat unprepared to comment, but the young man is plainly beguiled by the suggestion, or by the girl herself, whatever she says. Moreover the Mayor is glad to play along as he offers a could-be-so reply, provided that Daniel doesn't follow his friend Joseph into the army. Carrie and Daniel have been casting quick glances one at the other at different times, you've noticed, and following the Mayor's words Carrie now faces Daniel with a look of isn't-that-right, as though expecting his reassurance that he wants no part of the war.

Daniel admits to having no plans for now, though it may not matter since the whole fracas will likely not last more than a few months. He adds that Joseph, however, may end up making a career of the army, knowing his taste for adventure in faraway places, definitely inspired by all those stories he heard from his grandfather the surveyor captain. This is the most that you have heard Daniel speak, at the Arcade and now here, and the first sign of any personality. His comments have also provided enough information for Carrie, evidently, and her attitude of casual indifference seems to resume. You look again upon the Mayor for more discussion, but Erastus only smiles and holds up his glass in salutation. Well then, there we are.

Daniel excuses himself to go find Joseph—you surmise he's one of the friends slated to come out later and preside with toasts and presentations. Carrie and Erastus likewise use the moment to break away to investigate new refreshments just laid out on the side tables. Here is an opportunity for you to return to the beverage table for a refill, and this time you go for the shrub, which turns out to be a fairly tasty drink, rhubarb flavored, still cool, and not overly sweet. Like the switchel it has that slight twinge of vinegar which has a way of enhancing the rhubarb. It's good. This is also a moment to realize again how much you're truly enjoying yourself in all this company. Despite the occasional hint of, say, a strained relationship here or there among the guests, as you've been led to understand, nevertheless the overall ambience of is that of civility, of mutual respect, soundly upheld by everyone.

You do spot a slight lapse in comportment, on the part of two other guests, amusingly. It's a husband and wife couple standing near the silver punch bowl, along with one of the McConnell servant girls, and they all seem fixated on the ornate silver ladle which the girl is holding up. Aha, it must be curiosity on the part of the wife to identify the maker's mark on the back of the ladle, as engraved into the silver. But the nearsighted woman cannot read the mark without the help of the girl, you're guessing. They're trying to be discreet, but apparently the wife and the girl are not adroit enough for the husband, who starts to show some impatience with them. A mischievous thought arises: perhaps you should sidle up and ask them the name of the silver maker?

Never mind. People will always be curious, and from time to time they shalt covet. Somehow it makes you feel all the more at ease, despite your situation as an outside visitor.

Being at ease, of course, is exactly when "the unexpected" can befall, and it comes now in the form of a figure approaching on your right

... that's him, that's the face. *So we meet at last.* It's the Stranger, a man in his forties, you might say, well dressed, full beard; one of the few men in the yard still wearing his top hat, which is dark brown like his morning coat. He seems very intent on speaking with you as he walks up, and you turn to face him directly, a bit confused at first, but there is no cause for worry. The man's expression is amiable and he seems to sense your embarrassment, as if he were about to explain away some misunderstanding, and he wears pince-nez lenses before his blue eyes which further suggests a conciliatory demeanor about him.

"I should say, you seem to be enjoying yourself adequately," he starts without introduction. His presupposing tone is unexpected and not helpful.

"Have we met before, sir?" you reply, cordially.

"I believe not. But we may be kindred spirits." Again, cryptic. This is awkward.

A brief pause. The face is friendly but serious also. You need to stand pat and listen as he continues.

"I saw you checking into the Hodges. I'm staying there myself. From what I understand, you're here to investigate Pontiac. I'm glad to help you with that, if you're interested."

"I'm sorry—I didn't catch your name. You are ...?

"A friend of the family, you might say. And a correspondent for the Detroit Free Press. I'm really here on assignment to land an interview with one of Pontiac's more mysterious figures, John Bray. Do you know him?"

No, you don't, other than recalling how you saw his name stenciled on a doorway on Saginaw. It was a photography shop. How is that a mystery, you'd like to know.

"Can't say that I do. Is he here in the yard?"

The man has no interest in your question, however, and only proceeds to lay out some stunning remarks. "I would only wish to recommend to any visitor to this town not to become so enthralled to assume all is well here in this modern Eldorado[62]. It's not as if all pioneers are saints, you know. Pontiac has its darker sides, less than civil, we might say. Of course, this is top society at hand for the McConnell's, naturally, and most every one of them can take pride in all their accomplishments. But there's a lot of money at stake now, a lot of money. A lot of land that quickly gains value, and the chancery lawsuits that follow. Ready labor, risky investments, winners and losers, plenty of characters fit for an American rendition of Thackeray's Vanity Fair."

You're thinking of walking away at this point, but the man's bizarre tirade may be worth hearing if only for a minute or so. He's definitely no one you know, so what does it matter? He perceives now that he has your attention, your curiosity at least, and as both of you gaze over the crowd he continues his commentary:

"Such marvelous times are these. Fortunes rise and fall with frightening rapidity, so they say. You can't blame these families for indulging in their luck so far. What do you think of that old map-maker Captain Hervey Parke, presiding over all this success? Leave it to the chief surveyor to set the stage and get a street named after him. Sure it's a tough go out there, tramping around in the cold wilderness, hauling your surveyor chains and living off the land. But if you survive all that, when you come back you're in for a lucrative reward, at 10% value of each square mile sold. 10%! Not bad, hmm?"

You don't really know how to reply, but regardless, the man keeps talking, his tone growing more implacable.

"How many of these fine gentlemen are also widowers, their first wives lost to childbirth? How many sturdy pioneers here, and their children, struggle with health problems and little vices? All this clothing they wear is probably hiding all manner of skin problems. Now you can see for yourself why they never smile for a photographer.

---

62   Eldorado: utopian society depicted in Voltaire's Candide, 1759.

And you have to wonder about a troublemaker like John Bray in the middle of—"

"—Right, then, that's enough!" you break him off. This warrants a sustained glare showing your irritation. The man's crassness is tiresome and out of place, and you turn to head back to the drinks table. "Good day to you, sir!"

He's not following after you, but you can hear him call out one more oddly cynical remark: "By the way, Elkanah Comstock is here. You might ask him about his sister-in-law Elizabeth, the poor widow with three daughters. Why wasn't she invited here this afternoon? Is she that much of an inconvenience to the Comstock's? And why are Elkanah's nieces being raised not by their own mother but by the Goodale's—Mr. and Mrs. 'de bonis non'? Ask him that one."

These remarks cause you to stop and give the stranger one last look that's at once quizzical and dismissive, before leaving him behind. What an obnoxious, presumptuous fellow. He evidently likes to show off his thorough familiarity with all the local gossip. You weren't ready for this sort of distraction, vaguely inimical as it was. And no, you're not acquainted with Mr. and Mrs. Goodale.

This calls for a retreat back to the refreshment table for another round of switchel, on your own, and it's here by the punch bowl that you strike up a chance conversation with Parke McConnell who is also standing by the table, having just refilled his cup—actually a crystal goblet. You have the impression that he is as amused as you are to be in the yard, as he scans the scene to note which friends and neighbors have made an appearance. The two of you take a couple of steps away from the table, and you take the opportunity to ask again about his goldrush experiences, and what must have been a dauntless stage coach ride across the plains to get there. But Parke still seems disinclined to talk about it, which is disappointing; nevertheless, remembering that you're from out of town he is kind enough to offer to point out some of the key players, some of whom you have not yet met.

He starts with Charles and Mary Draper, making their way back towards the refreshment tables from the far side of the yard. Charles is the prosecuting attorney for Oakland County, who last year served as one of the town trustees along with Levi Bacon, during Pontiac's last year before incorporating as a city with a mayor. Last October after one of the larger war rallies he made a speech at the Peninsular Hotel in celebration of recent Republican election victories across the

Charles Draper and Augustus Baldwin, law firm partners, Draper a Republican and Baldwin a Democrat.

nation, an event still much talked about. It's interesting how a leading attorney like Charles Draper can share his law practice with a political opposite such as Augustus Baldwin, but it seems to work. And there is Elkanah Comstock, school board director ("Yes, we met earlier in town.")—and Abram Mathews, owner of the large grist mill business. Morgan Drake, another prominent attorney, is also in the crowd. He is a solicitor in chancery[63], like most of the attorneys in Pontiac—Parke leans closer to you to opine, more discretely, whether Morgan's relationship with Abram Mathews may still be a bit awkward, following

---

63 Chancery court: resolutions of real estate disputes and inheritances.

the Wesson affair[64] that you have heard about. In some ways Pontiac is still a small town experience.

An elderly woman is next identified, Mary Ann Hodges, chatting with Augusta Darrow. Mrs. Hodges is the wife of Ira Hodges who owns your hotel. "Yes, the town matriarch. I see." She also is, or rather was, president of the ill-fated Ladies' Sewing Society that Augusta told you about, earlier in the parlor.

"The Darrow's are a fine couple," Parke goes on. "Augusta is learning to use the new sewing machine—for a woman her age, patently adventurous I say—and her husband Frank is the commander of our Masonic fraternity. Oh—and over there, there's Myron Howell, no surprise, from the *Gazette*. Howell used to be a teacher up at the school when he first came to Pontiac, and he stayed on to take over publishing the paper. He gets around town a lot, as you might expect. I'll wager this Friday's issue will include a detailed report on this gathering in the page 3 'Local and Miscellaneous' column."

Good point. Perhaps you could ask Levi Bacon to mail a copy of the paper to you that includes an account of the McConnells' reception . . . But you haven't seen Levi anywhere, so far. He must still be at the shop. You'll have to remember to ask him about the *Gazette* when he gets here later. It would be useful at this point to have a written recounting of all of the society figures that are steadily expanding your cast of connections in this community. But now you're reminded of something else that's been on your mind.

"So that's Myron Howell," you observe aloud. "You know, I was thinking I might ask him about something I saw today—some people I was watching down by the Mill Pond. Poor folk, clearly. Vagrants, or people just down on their luck." You have Parke's close attention now, a look of curiosity as well, so you continue, "And I was wondering:

---

64 A year ago Morgan represented Sewell Wesson in his successful lawsuit against Abram's wife and in-laws, the Whittemores, causing them to sell off eight property lots in a public auction.

where do they go at night? Or in bad weather? Is there any public relief for them?"

"You needn't worry, friend," he says. "The churches will take them in for the night, especially if they're just families waiting for a father to find work. There are a few charitable societies, and St. Vincent's offers a lot of food and shelter from what I hear." Parke has been looking directly at you, as if to assess whether you're satisfied with this information, and he adds, "If you're interested to learn more about it, you should go talk with Gus Hovey over at his drug store. He also serves as the town's 'Superintendent of the Poor'—stands to reason, since he knows everyone's business around here."

"Gus Hovey . . . at Dean and Hovey Drugs, on Saginaw. I know where it is."

"It's the place to go for the latest talk on anything. Walk in there and you won't miss Big Gus. He's a big fellow. A 250 pounder at least. He knows all the benevolent societies, and he'll connect them with a family that needs passage on an empty wagon going up to Flint or further inland if that's where they mean to settle. But I agree with you—when you see those people dawdling around the pond it looks a bit dismal. Truth be told, though, we have had very little trouble . . . "

"Quite the cast of characters, I'd say," a familiar voice calls out nearby, and you turn to see that it's young Hervey, your fellow out-of-towner, coming to join in.

"Agreed!" you answer, impressed that he has read your mind, or your reaction anyway, at learning so many names in succession. Hervey shakes hands with Parke McConnell who in turn means to introduce you by asking whether you have met his cousin Hervey, and you explain how the two of you had arrived together, sharing a walk up Church Street with Hervey's niece—who was it? ("Clettie Kelsey" Hervey says)—and that you understand Hervey is also a visitor to Pontiac, from his home in . . . ("Hancock"), yes, the Upper Peninsula. Parke responds with a good-natured smile and compliments your ability to recall, and then both he and Hervey advise you not to bother with memorizing the entire clan—too many Parke's and Hervey's and Cleantha's—and today it will suffice just to keep track of the McConnell side. Fair enough, you accept the challenge. It's confusing, but an amusement nonetheless.

For the sake of confirming what you know, you reiterate how Clettie Kelsey is the daughter of Hervey's brother-in-law Marcus Kelsey, the widower whom you just heard about from Sarah Parke, Hervey's sister, a few minutes ago. Hervey affirms that you've got it right, but then comes a curious turn. When you follow up by asking whether Marcus is also a guest at the party, Parke McConnell answers with a smirk, "Not likely. But if we need to find out, we'll only need to ask Sarah." Hervey only smiles and shakes his head dismissively, and his brief flinch clearly shows how he would just as soon ignore his cousin's caustic remark. You're left wondering whether there's another story there, though it wouldn't do to pry further into it just now.

Parke bids leave to check on his mother at the house, and then you're about to see whether Hervey would have more to say about the life up north, when Hervey starts first with his own suggestion. The McConnell's have an extensive garden plot just beyond the rear yard, which he has been meaning to see, and he's joining a few other guests to go back there now, and would you be interested to see it yourself? Hervey's sister will be on hand to describe all the plants and flowers. "We won't be gone for more than a few minutes—come on, let's take a look."

"The garden—just the thing! Gentlemen, may I join you?" a voice cuts in from behind Hervey. The speaker steps forward . . . it's Myron Howell, the expressiveness of his face both cheery and inquisitive, with a slight overtone of presumption.

"Mr. Howell, why of course," replies Hervey, and you throw in a nod accordingly.

"Opportunity knocks," Myron proclaims. "A truly *cultivated* man would want to inspect the grounds." The pun succeeds in evoking a casual grimace from Hervey, and the three of you set off through the crowd for the garden. Myron has to detour to set down his empty plate upon a table, and during this brief pause you see Parke McConnell off to the side. Parke is just about to start climbing the steps up to the side porch but apparently he has noticed you heading off in company with Myron, and he wants to signal to you a warning, you surmise, about talking with a newspaperman. He points a finger at Myron and then holds the finger up to his lips, in a quivering motion as if to say "shush!"

Oho, Parke must think that you'll be asking about the vagrants at the Mill Pond. You smile back and hold up your hand: message received, not to worry.

HERB GARDEN

"*I SUPPOSE* it's just you and I for the tour," Daniel said to the woman, standing at the threshold of the McConnells' garden. Of course she was also a guest at the reception, like himself, and she was finely dressed, most noticeably by her fashionable, wide-brimmed hat, low-crowned with wide silk ribbons. The two of them had been waiting there in case more people might join them, and this interim was proving slightly inapt because it *was* just the two of them and they were not formally acquainted. They had nodded hello, and for a minute they had each been observing the garden entryway with its arched arbor framework, now thickly covered with ivy, and the small bench to one side, whitewashed, of a simple design with a backrest. The bench could seat two people but for now, unoccupied, its only purpose was uphold a decorative style. Not far off, the McConnells' reception party was in full swing just around the house in the east yard, where the sounds of many conversations blended into an ongoing din of indistinct voices, punctuated by an occasional laugh or loud exclamation.

"I'm Daniel Thurber, by the way," he decided to add, just to ensure courtesy.

"Yes, we may have met before. I'm Sarah Parke French."

Daniel nodded back, and both resumed their waiting postures, appropriately separated by several feet. Daniel looked down and used his left shoe to shuffle a small stone sideways under the bench. Meanwhile Sarah had raised up both her arms so that her hands might reach behind her head, presumably to adjust a hairpin; her posture struck Daniel as a bit laconic for a lady in public, more so in that she seemed completely oblivious to any such perception. He appreciated how Sarah had announced herself using her full name, including her middle name Parke, as if to help him identify her within the overall McConnell clan. She was likely several years older than he, and by the look of her she was by nature alert and well-meaning, her dress and her hat stylish enough for even a college man to take notice.

He had intended to stroll through the garden alone for a few minutes of solitude, but Sarah had been there at the arch already, and as he approached she asked whether he was part of the group expected for a viewing. No, no he wasn't, but of course he would be glad to tag along. What other recourse was there, anyway? Besides, after a short while he would need to return to the house for a small, private meeting with his friends. Another minute or two had passed quietly. Apparently this Mrs. French felt no compulsion to talk, thankfully, and Daniel could let his thoughts drift back to the carriage ride he had shared earlier with Carrie Holley so close to him. What amazing luck, suddenly out of the blue, to be riding along, practically alone with her. *Could she tell how tense I was?* Daniel was still regretting his utter inability to impress the girl in any meaningful way, let alone convey any affection. He just drove the shay. *Why didn't I just SAY something?* Well, then again, his sister was there, too, sitting between them. It would only have been awkward, whatever was said.

In such moments as these, beset in silent frustration, Daniel's usual recourse was an appeal to the poet, just to recite something, anything distracting, learned in a saloon or a college class:

But whom to love, and whom to treasure,
Who won't deceive us in the end?
And who'll be kind enough to measure
Our words and deeds as we intend?[65]

You are hopeless. Once again, the same old foible, or so he felt. But the words were soothing at least.

He now looked up to see a group of men coming around the house towards them, so he spoke up to announce, "Ah, there, perhaps we have a few more participants headed our way."

"That's my older brother, Hervey Parke—the one with the beard," Sarah rejoined, "along with Myron Howell and his moustache. I just met the other gentleman. I think he's a business association of Willard's. He seems very curious to know more about the family. He's friendly enough, though."

Her information mattered little, which she sensed, but she continued. "My brother might interest you. He likes herbs, that is, herbs used for medicines. I told him he should see the McConnells' plot, since they cultivate many of those plants here. I can show them to you, if you're interested."

Daniel replied with a noncommittal "Yes, perhaps." He was looking at the three men, and he remembered her brother, and his beard, last year was it, at a dinner party at the Widow Hunt's home. Hervey and the Hunts' daughter had just married, and Daniel and his parents had been invited for a dinner in their honor—Daniel's father Horace having known the bride's late father as fellow Democrats. The dinner was formal and not much fun. He remembered Hervey being cordial

---

65   From "Yevgeniy Onegin" novel in verse by Alexander Pushkin; translated from Russian.

and gracious but not saying much; at one point he asked Daniel about his studies at Ann Arbor, and showed genuine interest by his sustained conversation, which was flattering in light of Hervey's otherwise quiet nature.

Sarah acknowledged the newcomers cheerily, making a special point of greeting Howell as "my dear Mr. Skimmerhorn" in deference to the *nom de plume* that the journalist used occasionally for comical editorials; whereupon observing simply, "So—call it a fivesome. Shall we proceed?" she led the group single file under the arch and on down the main path of the garden. The arch, with a camellia bush on either side, was the only structure marking the edge of the plot which was otherwise fully open, but this was distinctly the correct way for visitors to commence an inspection of the plot. Once "inside" the garden properly, the next detail was to pause for a round of introductions, which went quickly as the formality was for the most part superfluous. Various light facts were clarified, for example, that Hervey and the Visitor were fellow out-of-towners; that Daniel had shared lunch at the Arcade with Visitor earlier today; that Howell's mother had fallen ill again and that his brother had just joined him at the Gazette to take over some management duties. And as it turned out, Hervey did recognize Daniel from that dinner a year ago; he also offered condolences on the loss of Daniel's mother. And Daniel noted how Hervey had addressed his sister using a longer form, Sarah Abigail.

The group resumed its pace down the center aisle while Sarah Abigail made a few remarks about the garden such as when Mrs. McConnell had started it, how Eliza and Jackson had brought in new ideas for more plantings, and how the garden had evolved into its current state of making the left side only flowers, and the right side only herbs. Her last observation about the split between flowers and herbs was not meaningful, especially for Daniel, in that there weren't many blooms to help him identify one plant from another, except for the patches of purple crocus flowers and yellow daffodils to his left, whereas everything else around him was just small and green. It was still May, after all. But he listened patiently while Sarah Abigail pointed out areas destined to produce late-Spring blossoms of hyacinths, calla lilies, peonies, bleeding hearts, and others. The herbs on the opposite side, as far as Daniel cared, all looked like low-lying jumbles of tiny leaves, the various types mostly indistinguishable to him, even as everyone else thoughtfully looked over the spreads.

He realized that his mood had turned a bit dour, after having upheld a friendly appearance through a number of conversations in the side yard, mostly with his father's friends and associates, all of them offering condolences for his mother and repeatedly wishing him well. *Maybe it's the season*, he thought. *I don't do well in Spring. Never have.* Springtime was an in-between time, when farmers were planting and everything was changing and people caught colds and schedules remained . . . unresolved, until the weather finally gave way to a consistent summer pattern. *Another Spring, and here I am: I'm not in school, I'm not in the army, and the only girl I want doesn't seem to be interested in me. I don't really know what I should do.*

On both sides of the aisle the plantings were fronted by a border row of budding marigolds, showing only faint hints of yellow-orange blooms yet to open. Daniel knew that marigolds were put there to deter any deer sniffing around for a nighttime bite. And the cat: there was a cat sitting in the sun at the far end of the aisle, keeping an eye on the strollers while the tip of its tail curled and uncurled to touch the ground by its front paws; Daniel figured the cat's assigned duty was to hunt down any marauding chipmunks, such that together with the marigolds, the garden was well protected from deer in the night, and rodents during the day. *So far it seems to be working. So that's the story of the garden. Fine.* Meanwhile Hervey's fellow visitor was apparently impressed by the garden's overall dimensions, declaring that the plot must be at least 20 by 30 yards; no one else seemed interested in hearing his estimates. Daniel weighed how much longer he might remain with the group before politely making an exit for the house.

The tour, however, had by now devolved into Sarah and Hervey drifting ahead and carrying on their own private discussion that focused only on the herbs. Daniel followed, and behind him came Myron and the Visitor, the two of them discussing some other guest at party, a "stranger" that the Visitor was keen on learning about. When asked whether he might know the man in question, who said he worked for the Detroit Free Press, Myron mockingly replied how, no, not at all, and don't you see? Your stranger is probably a Pinkerton[66], in town to sniff around and keep tabs on someone like . . . who is that eccentric photographer we have on Saginaw . . . John Bray?"

Myron's assessment seemed to evoke a measure of enlightenment, judging by the way the Visitor blurted out "John Bray, hmm?" with echoes of do-you-really-think and yes-of-course. A little embarrassed by his naïveté, too, enough to change the subject—Daniel next heard the Visitor reciting out loud the names of the same flowers that Sarah Abigail had mentioned earlier—obviously an attempt to show off his attentiveness just to ingratiate himself to someone in the McConnell-Parke clan. But then the Visitor stopped and now he was glancing back at Daniel as if expecting to initiate more idle chat. *Oh no, he wants to continue our meeting at the Arcade.* The solution for avoiding this was promptly realized: Daniel showed a tactful nod to the Visitor, while he quickened his pace to catch up to Sarah Abigail and Hervey, which worked, as Hervey was just then retracing his steps back towards Daniel, intent on sharing some fascinating information.

---

66   Pinkerton agents: from an investigation agency founded by Alan Pinkerton, started in Chicago and originally hired by railroad companies to provide security services. During the Civil War the agency expanded into military intelligence for the Union army and counter-espionage activity.

"Daniel, this really is a remarkable cultivation. And the fact that the plants aren't overcrowding, that's good. Now, you see these herbs all along here – this area is entirely medicinal. Look at these. They have cayenne—good for stuffy noses, and thyme—good for sore throat, like bee balm teas. Catnip, over there, and peppermint—they help with indigestion, and colicky babies. Foxglove, for heart pains. And echinacea, there with the pink buds—you can tincture it with alcohol and make a salve for skin infections. And this, this here, this is ginger root—you can make a rub for muscle aches."

There was a short pause while everyone gazed down at the herbs, and Hervey sneezed, once and then almost again, but he pulled out a handkerchief in time to block his nose. Sarah commented aloud, "Aha, the joys of springtime." She could have been referring to her brother's sneezing, or to the sight of a number of butterflies that were flitting about the echinacea plants, or a dragonfly hovering low over the edge of the pathway by Daniel's feet. Hervey looked up at his sister, "No garlic, Sallie?"

She shook her head, "Not here. It's with Eliza's kitchen herbs over there." Sarah Abigail—*Sallie*—pointed further down the garden where there was a cross-aisle cutting toward the side. And here, Daniel began to wonder whether it would be acceptable for him to address Sarah as Sarah Abigail, or perhaps Sallie. "Mrs. French" must still be the safest route.

Hervey stepped a few paces further along the aisle, focusing on an array of slightly taller herbs, the first being a large clump of green feathery stalks. The Visitor hazarded a guess: "Dill?" and Hervey corrected him, "No, this is rosemary. It has that fair aroma, as you know, but it's also useful for preserving foods. I also saw it used with steam vapor to purify the air in a hospital up north, for the miners, trying to alleviate consumption[67]. I don't know whether it was effective as a palliative to reduce suffering."

"Hmm," remarked Daniel, in an approving 'I-didn't-know-that' sort of tone. Hervey's observations were turning out to be fact rather interesting.

A short silence passed while Hervey seemed lost in thought, until he said "Up north we had to cultivate our own medicines. The herb gardens were still a serious business." Then he looked back on all four his listeners as he meant to emphasize one last observation in his lecture, motioning an arm over a section of herbs that had long, skinny stems topped with clusters of tiny white flowers. "*This* is yarrow," he announced, upon which Sallie also nodded and confirmed, "Yarrow." Daniel knew yarrow, and its uses, but he had never seen it in plant form in a plot. Hervey went on: "Doctors are using it more and more, as a very helpful salve, for treating cuts and scrapes, reduce bleeding..."

"—Battle wounds...?" Howell interjected.

"Yes! An astringent. It's very useful for the military. Better than lavender for staunching blood flow in..."

Daniel understood why Hervey had not finished the sentence. The gruesome image of a treating a bullet wound wasn't really appropriate for polite company.

Sallie spoke up so as to open a more genial topic, that of Willard McConnell's interest in medicinal herbs, not only for augmenting the local supply to the community but also for encouraging more study among local doctors of the curative properties, that is, for science. Howell added that, actually, it was Willard's son Parke McConnell who agreed to expand the apothecary business at his store, although there really wasn't much money in it, of course. Hervey agreed, also expressing his opinion on the need for more science in medicine, and his misgivings about the public's reliance on "blue mass pills" and cure-

---

67 "Consumption" in later years would be identified as tuberculosis.

all elixirs that probably contained dangerous amounts of mercury, or opium, and little else.

Curative properties. On this note the conversation was wrapping up on a more serious course, in a vague sense more appropriate. A short pause followed while everyone scanned over all the garden, herbs and flowers, in silence, and the sounds of the party were again noticeable, even as a breeze caused a swishing sound in the high branches of the trees nearby. No one seemed motivated to continue the tour and examine the kitchen herbs further on; perhaps it was time to start making their way back to the reception. Daniel then said aloud how he should join his friends up inside the house, and Sarah offered to accompany him, just to peek in and make sure the young folk were behaving themselves.

The five began slowly edging back toward the arbor entryway, and Hervey came alongside Daniel to have a few extra words. "Too much lecture?" he began.

"No . . . it's interesting," Daniel replied with a shrug, then a nod.

"Well, it is an idea that I have been pursuing—whether it would be viable to produce medicines on a large scale, with consistent quality, from herbs, from whatever. Especially now, with the army preparing for war."

"Yes, of course. Supplies are a large part of it. Armies need drugs along with everything else. They were talking about this a lot at college."

"So, then, for you: soldiering, or staying a student?" Hervey's inquiry was to be expected, given the context of a social event honoring Joe McConnell's enlistment. It came across as just another topic for the sake of small talk.

Daniel glanced up and straight ahead as he walked, his hands in his pockets, as if he meant to look distracted. "That's the big question this summer, it seems."

There was no need to pursue the matter further; clearly the choice had not been resolved yet. The group was now filing out under the arch, and here was where one final question brought Daniel to the point of becoming truly annoyed. It was the Visitor, again: "Tell me, Daniel, who was that girl I saw you talking with earlier, in the yard? She's here with Mayor Thatcher, right? Carrie, I think. Very attractive. Is that the girl your friends were talking about at lunch today?"

"Um, yes. I know her family." Subject closed. *Yes, dumley, even _you_ noticed, didn't you.* Daniel continued through, under the arch.

The company now paused to exchange some good-bye's and see-you-then's as their little group was about to disband. Sallie stopped to take her brother's arm and mention something she had just remembered: "Hervey, before you leave this evening, I want to show you those old medical books of father's, the ones Aunt Cleantha has here in the house. I think we should keep them, don't you? Even if they are outdated and useless to anyone, the books should stay in the family. Do you want to take them with you back to Hancock? I just want to make sure we all know who has them."

"Yes, Marquis was telling me about the books this morning. I should think we might commend them here to the McConnell's and the Captain."

Hervey promised to find his uncle later to settle the matter; moreover he felt quite touched by his sister's kind intentions. Sallie wasn't

week with friends in this village.—A fine Gold Watch belonging to Miss Sarah Parke was lost in this village, or between, this village and M. W. Kelsey's residence last Monday. A liberal reward is offered for its recovery.—Miss. Lizzie Fitch, will entertain the

Pontiac Gazette, Jan. 13,1860, Page 3 column "Personal"

always the most sentimental about old family keepsakes. Perhaps she was still mindful about losing the gold watch at the old homestead. Hervey knew well the books she was talking about—father's old books from his student days in northern New York 50 years ago—some medical texts, a personal notebook, and an old family prayer book. Ezra the Good Doctor, meticulous in all manner especially the care for his patients. Just seeing the exquisite penmanship in his notebook was enough to awaken many memories of his discipline, his steadfast faith, his advice and high standards set for all his household. *Whatever your circumstances may be in this world, still value your Bible as your best treasure, and whatever be your employment here still look upon your religion as your best business.* It was a code of conduct worth preserving in that little book, if not to memory.

The herb garden tour was herewith finished, with Hervey and the Visitor intending to return to the side yard, where the party was still ongoing with little change in vitality; Howell had also moved a few steps apart to look back in that direction, ready to seek more interesting subject matter over there. Sallie and Daniel were both looking to go inside the house to join the younger guests at their reunion in the parlor. The moment came when everyone knew that little time was left to catch someone for a private remark, if there was anything to say, before the opportunity was lost. At least, this is what Hervey and Sallie felt, brother and sister, and each had something they wanted to say to the other, away from the others.

Hervey went first. "Sallie, any word from your husband? He's doing well with his bookshop, I should think."

The inquiry was well-meant; so far today nobody had mentioned anything about Benjamin French, and Hervey still had only scant information about the state of his sister's marriage beyond knowing that Sallie was still in Pontiac while Ben worked as a salesman based in

Washington, D.C., coming to Pontiac once a year on sales trips in the summer.

"Doing quite well, thank you. The 'French and Richardson Books and Stationery Store' still presides over the literary world of Pennsylvania Avenue."

"He'll be here again in July?"

"Same as last year. That's what I hear from him. We won't see an advertisement in the Gazette about it for another month or so."

"Hmm. Fine, then. So, do you plan on removing to Washington with him this time 'round?

"We'll see. Eventually, yes, I suppose."

"You know, I was talking with Marcus this morning and . . . "

"—Yes," Sallie interrupted, "I spoke with him, too, at lunch today at the Arcade." She then added with a mischievous grin, "You know, *frère*, there's nothing untoward about it."

Hervey knew that this was all that his sister would impart for now. But he noted how she used the same phrase exactly as Marcus had said it this morning, about 'nothing being untoward.' Interesting. Hervey also knew that Sallie would take her turn, next, as he expected one of her habitual parting remarks, the kind meant to stoke the imaginations in people she encounters only briefly.

"But enough about sales figures and lonesome husbands," she said, ready to change the subject. "I must say, Hervey, an idea heartens me, that you might return from the wilds of Keweenaw with your loyal, beautiful wife, and start making medicines—something you seem to know about—down here. And start making money, too. You've wasted enough time up north, I think. Take a lesson from Marquis."

Her brother only reacted with a grimace, really only feigned, to appear hurt by advice which Sallie had voiced more than once before; meanwhile Sallie turned her attention on Daniel. "The only thing getting rich in Hancock," she said, "is that beard of his. Well, how about you, Mr. Thurber? A little facial hair, perhaps? A handsome college boy like you could sport more of the wisdom of the ages."

The men all exchanged glances and Daniel's eyes widened in amusement.

"Well, perhaps I might at that. What do you think – a Van Dyck?"

Hervey nodded thoughtfully, and the Visitor agreed, "Yes, Van Dyck, definitely!"

"It could help you make up your mind about things," Sallie added quietly to herself. But Daniel had heard the cryptic coda and he started to wonder the woman knew more about him than she let on. He thought of pursuing the matter by asking what exactly she meant by that, but as the twosomes where separating, Sallie turned again to her brother and called out, "Oh, and Hervey . . . "

"Yes, Mrs. French?" her brother paused and faced around.

"I'll want to hear more about your meeting with our Mr. Comstock. Marquis says . . ."

"—Yes, when I see you inside," Hervey interrupted, with a congenial nod, and then continued on with the Visitor.

Sallie and Daniel meanwhile had reached the other side of the house where they might enter via the side door to the pantry, and from there proceed to the hall and on to the parlor where the younger guests were having their reunion. Daniel was thinking about what kinds of hors d'oeuvres might still be available inside, but as he followed Sallie on the kitchen porch she suddenly stopped and looked at him, waiting for his full attention, and then offered this off-hand advice:

"I think, Daniel, the army can wait. Go back to college. These friends of yours signing up for three years are going to regret it, after the war is over—by next summer, the way I see it."

"Well, you may be right about that . . ." he replied hesitantly, surprised by the personal remarks. Sallie's brows remained furrowed, her expression confident that her observations were warranted.

"And that girl is too young for you. Don't rush into anything this summer."

"Hmm-hmm." More peremptory advice—not prepared for that. *Does everyone here think I've taken shine to Carrie Holley?* Daniel thought to himself, more annoyed than embarrassed.

And he could see that Sallie was enjoying the moment. She was looking up at the trees and listening, apparently, to the buzz of the cicadas, and she said, "What I really like is to see people coming to proper conclusions about what to do next in their lives, which is best done *after* mingling at a large wingding like this one. Don't you think?"

Daniel quietly walked along and felt no need to respond further, anyway, as his guide had already turned to look over at the large greenhouse some thirty yards out in the west yard. She was grinning as she straightened up and put her hands on her hips, ready to call out to someone and interrupt what they were doing, and Daniel looked, too, to see what this was about. Over at the greenhouse, with a mustering of tall sunflowers in front of it, two black men had just walked out from the entrance.

It was Jackson, the stablehand whom Daniel knew well, with a friend. Apparently the two of them were just leaving, probably returning to their duties across the street at guests' carriage park, and now they also stopped and looked at Sallie on the porch, Jackson smiling and waving hello, his diffident friend standing by holding a large, cloth sack. No doubt the sack was filled with a quick harvest of some produce out of the greenhouse.

"Well, I trust you left some of the rhubarb for the rest of us," Sallie exclaimed, loud and clear, although by her tone she was jesting, mostly.

"Plenty more to go!" replied Jackson, with a bigger smile now as he slapped his friend's shoulder in a gesture to mean *don't worry, let's just get back to work.*

Sallie looked on, also smiling, her next remark for Daniel: "He's a good man. He grew the rhubarb. He should take as much as he wants."

Daniel rejoined, "You know, you don't often see him smile like that. Serious sort. Smart, though. He's taught Joe and me everything we know about horses."

"And *we* have all had a hand in teaching *him* how to read—a quick learner, I have to say. He's a runaway, you know, so there may be reasons why he doesn't smile a lot. You never know."

"True," Daniel agreed.

"Knows his way around vegetables, anyway." Sallie added, her voice echoing in the pantry as the two of them went inside.

Erastus Thatcher

I'm encouraged to see another social season getting underway with this reception, despite all the war fever. It's too bad Kelsey isn't here – he's quite the character. Have you spoken with Abiram McConnell, or Myron "Skimmerhorn" Howell from the Gazette? Likewise very amusing types, but don't take anything they say at par value. There's plenty of foolery and frolic in this town, if you're looking for something more engaging than those ponderous debates up at the Courthouse put on by Draper and Baldwin -- I mean, really now, "Are we indebted mainly to the Puritan element of New England, for our national prosperity?" Fascinating topic. Toss me an opium pill and maybe I'll go.

Here's an item for you: behold our redoubtable Colonel Richardson over there in all his finery. Have you heard the full story behind his coming engaged? Well apparently he had been betrothed to another Pontiac woman, but when the girl learned that the Colonel would be away on military campaigning for a three-year commitment, she demanded that he shorten his service to three months. This condition was totally unacceptable to the colonel, of course, but the girl refused to consent. So then and there at her doorstep he broke off the engagement saying, "Very well, Madam, there are others who will. Good Day!" He called for his hat, crossed the street, and offered himself in less than ten minutes to a girl whom he had never seen but twice before, Miss Frances "Fannie" Travor, and she accepted. So there you have it, fine decisive action in these whirlwind times. And no time to wait – the wedding will be on the 29th in Detroit, and will surely be quite the affair. And perhaps Fannie will take to simpler camp life in a tent anyway, after such a gala.

Ah, springtime. I have to admit, it's great sport to "pair off" the lads and lasses here. You saw my niece Carrie totally captivate young Thurber, my otherwise sober-minded clerk? I can see a future in that match, and bully for him. And our court jester Lewis Drake with the Mathews girl. I caught that one. Some good money there. How about Joe McConnell with Sarah Thurber? That's what Carrie tells me, anyway. Perhaps Sarah is a bit young, but there's a war on, you see. Their fathers may be at odds, but youth reigns impetuous, you know especially nowadays.

The Courthouse

P. Y. M. ASSOCIATION.

The Pontiac Young Men's Association will hold its next session at the Union School House, on Wednesday eve'ng, March 8th, 1854.

The following *Question* will be discussed.

Has *Woman,* a greater influence on the destiny of mankind, than *Man.*

SPECIAL DISPUTANTS.

AFFIRMATIVE.	NEGATIVE.
Martin Marix,	Junius TenEyck,
J. M. Alden,	W. C. Palmer,
E. Thatcher,	B. G. Stout.

Before the opening of the debate an Essay will be read by J. Barritt, Esq.

The public are respectfully invited to attend.   I. M. RHODES, Sec'y.

A VISITOR'S STORY,
"Talk and Hearsay"

THE YARD party is still in full swing with a "fund of conversation" as you and Hervey return from your tour of the McConnell's garden. In fact, the overall ambience here seems even more jovial than before, mostly in response to a new round of appetizers that have been set out on two of the folding tables, and these have succeeded in attracting a cluster of hungry guests around each one. Hervey has made his own way over to Elkanah Comstock to resume some conversation; as for you, let's go take a look at the victuals being offered on one of the tables.

With a little deft movement you can slide through the barrier of happy, chattering guests, and it's a fine sight, truly, all the "dainty dishes" of foods arranged in larges plates around the white linen-topped table. What's more, it's gratifying to see the ample sufficiency of dainties still at hand. There's a bowl of salted nuts; a couple of plates with vegetables, one with radishes nicely cubed, and the other with short cuts of asparagus mixed with cheeses. You also see oatmeal cookies, deviled eggs, candied beets and candied carrots, and what looks to be a rhubarb pie with only two pieces left. The largest offering happens to be just before you, in two large china tureens, one with its top removed to reveal a chilled potato salad—it's still half full, with two silver spoons leaning on the rim inside at the ready. The potato chunks are shining with oil, and vinegar of course, and there are small bits of ham mixed in, by the look of it, and a modest sprinkling of dill to complete the appeal. *Mmm, by all means* let's pick up one of the small guest plates, a fork and a linen, and start with a serving of *that*. You might come back later for some of the pie or the candied items.

Now you can move away from the table, guarding your plate carefully to avoid having it knocked or tilted over in close company. Finally the chance comes to taste the potato salad, and true to form, it certainly is delicious. There is no place to sit down to eat so you remain standing while feeding yourself as graciously as you can, along with everyone else. Actually it is helpful to be left alone at this stage, conversing with no one and enjoying your dish as you survey the scene at your leisure. Somewhere above in the trees comes the sound of a chickadee, its rapid wicka-dee-dee-dee-dee call offering a lulling overtone to the collective commotion of the party below. Men and women around you are talking about the war, and the army, and the prospects for various young men in local society; your chickadee is charming none of them this afternoon.

It's only a short interlude, detached as you are from everyone else, but then as you wipe your hands on your linen napkin and you finish swallowing the last bite of the potato salad, another guest intervenes— it is Abiram McConnell, the doctor and one-time gold prospector, offering the favor of thwarting your awkward solitary status in the midst of a party. He holds a cookie in one hand and a shrub drink in the other.

"I noticed you coming back from the garden. What do you think?" he asks.

"Very impressive, for a household garden. Apparently there's no trouble with local wildlife coming 'round to help themselves to a meal—I reckon the deer don't like the wire fence."

"Oho, no they don't. And later on, when the lavender plants are up, it will be another reason for them to stay away. A deer doesn't fancy making his legs all smelly for the wolves."

Lavender—so that was what all those sprigs were, at the base of the fence.

"Yes. Interesting."

Abiram continues, "Seems to protect the grounds well enough. But I think the deer just don't like getting too close to the house and the stable. How about all those herbs—did you see those?"

"Indeed. The herbs were the main attraction, you might say. Your cousins Hervey and Sarah Abigail imparted an extensive tuition on all of them. Hervey seemed particularly keen on the medicinal uses."

The medicinal angle drew an appreciative response from the doctor, his eyebrows rising upwards. "The old curatives. It's Parke McConnell's idea, bringing more herbs to sell in his store. It's good to have a reliable apothecary in town for this stuff. I buy a lot of his herbs for my practice, for treating patients' aches and pains, the more ordinary complaints."

"I believe people will ask a doctor to cure just about anything that feels bad, these days."

"There's more and more of that, you're right, but it's understandable. What I don't like is all this obsession with the opiates. People just want to swallow a pill without even knowing what's in it, whether they're sick or not, and they'll believe anything they read about it. It's dangerous."

"Well, I'll wager a pill in a bottle would convey a lot more science than some dried peppermint leaves in a jar."

Abiram laughs slightly and admits likewise. "Agreed—the people want modern treatments for modern times, and they have the money to pay for it. Whatever smacks of *science*, that's the ticket. Nowadays they're a little less inclined to boil roots into a tea. But you know, I am starting to see more bona fide products like ointments, and liquid extracts, coming in from these new companies in New York. I'll put my faith in German chemists to conjure up the new remedies."

He goes on to opine about how the people here are becoming too weak-willed and too ready to jump for treatment of any perceived ailment, compared to what he experienced out in Colorado, during the goldrush, where people managed to survive in far more primitive conditions. And despite the fact that he and his friends never struck it rich, there was another, more subtle reward: as a doctor out in the West he often had to ply his trade as best he could with few supplies and using very pragmatic techniques. In that regard the whole adventure was profoundly valuable and Abiram would do it all again if he could.

It's an interesting glimpse into a national event, the goldrush, deserving more attention, and Abiram's long diatribe also let you understand why his nephew Parke McConnell had been less than enthusiastic to tell you much about the "expedition"—nobody got rich, and the party all returned home to Pontiac no better off than having spent a few months sightseeing in the western territories. It may well be that Pike's Peak is a sensitive matter, one of those family stories that may be acknowledged but preferably left unsung.

How about another matter, or two, that you're also curious about . . .

"I say, Doctor, might I ask, do you know the news correspondent from Detroit who is here today as a guest? I understand he is pursuing a story about John Bray, a photographer here in town."

"Newspaperman, from Detroit you say? I'm afraid I don't know him, but I'll wager Myron Howell knows him, if that helps. And if there's a story to be reported about John Bray, yes, that stands to reason. Bray is something of a character. He writes about politics. Before he removed to Pontiac he was a correspondent himself, in Detroit. And he's a born Englishman, don't you know. Is Bray a friend of yours?"

"No, we're not acquainted really, not at all. It was only something I overheard another guest talking about. Oh—another thing . . . there's a Mrs. French, Sarah Parke French. I was talking with her earlier. She's Hervey Parke's sister. And is her husband here? I believe his name is Marcus."

This is a leading question, that you put to Abiram, and wholly disingenuous of course, as you have already heard all about Marcus Kelsey. What you really want to know is: who and where is this Mr. French? And: is there anything more to learn about Sarah and Marcus since seeing them walk into the Arcade together at lunchtime.

"Ah—Mrs. French's wayward husband," Abiram says with a smile. "Now that's something you're more likely to read some day in the newspapers!"

Is that so? Now *this* should be an interesting *trouvaille*. You're all nonchalance, but you press Abiram to explain a little more, which he is glad to do.

"No, not Marcus," he begins. "You mean Benjamin—Benjamin French. An impetuous type, on a similar order as Sarah, as a fair impression. Their marriage last year was likewise an impetuous action, I would say comparable to the wedding that's in the works for Colonel Richardson in Detroit next week. You know all about that one, I should ask?"

"Not fully apprised, no," you smile back, "other than to hear of the suddenness of the Colonel's . . . change of plans. But it is wartime, after all." Actually it could only be ironic to hear Abiram's ideas about suddenness, or any acts of impetuosity, in light of his own record of jumping onto the "Pike's Peak" bandwagon.

"Yes, suddenness always helps to ensure a dramatic marriage. And for the Frenches the drama began soon enough when Benjamin went back to Washington for his work as a bookseller. Sarah stayed behind here in Pontiac just to prepare, as I heard it, for a permanent resettlement to follow. As it turns out, their temporary separation is still unresolved, and indeed has not changed after one or two visits to Pontiac made by Benjamin to check on the health and well-being of his wife."

"I see. I take it Sarah spends most of her time here under the protection of the McConnell family."

"Yes, and it's fitting that you say the word 'protection,'" Abiram adds, affirming your hunch. "The man's heart is touched by fire, as they say, and he definitely fits the mold of a jealous husband."

"All the way from Washington?" you interject.

"Jealous . . . Better I should say: prepossessing. I think French by now is simply embarrassed by the whole encumbrance of having an absent wife out on the Michigan frontier. His visits to Pontiac are nothing more than an excuse to see for himself if Sarah is still living here." Abiram leans in little closer to add, "And what people are saying now is that the situation has become downright dire."

"Oh? And how so?"

"The man is dangerous," the doctor says, nodding as if to agree with his own statement. "and irrational. And he's just the sort of fiend to take inspiration from the Danny Sickles affair[68] to see his way out of this sort of . . . grievance."

---

68   Daniel Sickles affair: two years ago in February of 1859, Daniel Sickles shot and killed Barton Key in the middle of the day in Lafayette Park, across from the White House in Washington, DC. Barton Key was district attorney for Washington (and son of Francis Scott Key) and was openly having affair with Sickles' young wife. Sickles was a U.S. Congressman from New York, notorious for his hot temper, his former ties to Tammany Hall corruption, and was himself a widely-known philanderer. In the sensational trial that followed, Sickles was acquitted based on the first usage of temporary insanity as a legal defense. Sickles fully reconciled with his wife publicly three months later; but, now scandalized and having lost all prospects for a future in electoral politics, with the outbreak of the Civil War he turned his ambitions to a military career and was active in raising four regiments in New York City for the Union army. In May 1861 Sickles was put in command of these regiments, known as the Excelsior Brigade.

For the first time you feel the tenor of your little conversation with Abiram take a turn towards serious attention. Alarming, honestly. Murder in broad daylight being dismissed as "temporary insanity" was no longer some fantastic scheme for courtrooms back east but a real possibility even in frontier towns like Pontiac.

"You think so? Temporary insanity might work for the general of the 'Excelsiors' in New York but it's doubtful for a bookseller intent on shooting someone out here in Michigan, don't you think?"

"I think anything goes in a courtroom nowadays. It doesn't matter anymore what the law says, if you have a gun and enough money for a fancy lawyer. And never mind the lawyer—it's the gun that matters most now, whether you're in Bleeding Kansas, or Harpers Ferry, or a gold mine in Colorado, or in drill formation right here in our fairgrounds."

Abiram was laying out all this piece of mind in calm, sarcastic tones. He looked away, over the people around him, as he continued, "I know this man French. I've treated him, you see, and I know his ailments. And from what I've seen, I can tell you this: that Ben French is just as deranged and dangerous as Dan Sickles ever was."

"You know, when I was in the herb garden with Sarah, I remember her saying that her husband would be coming to Pontiac again this summer, probably in July. Do you think he might . . ."

"—No, here is what you don't know, apparently. The fact is, everyone is expecting French to arrive *today*. You see, he might turn up any moment at this very reception."

"Really," is the only response you can offer, more as a statement than a question. How strange to think that this benign, peaceful social gathering could be spoiled by the appearance of an unruly, threatening intruder. What would it bring? A confrontation between the Frenches with loud, angry words shouted. Guests scattering away, or moving

Daniel Sickles murders Philip Key in Washington, Feb. 1859

in to prevent physical harm or even violence. Hah!—Myron Howell would love it, no doubt noting every detail to report in his paper.

A question comes to mind. "So, French would have to arrive by train, at the depot, wouldn't he?"

"Most likely. We'll see," Abiram says, turning to you directly. He seems to enjoy the notion of an imminent spectacle, and the emerging worry on your face that he has evoked. "Then again, the rumors may be all wet."

It takes some effort to keep nodding amiably at Abiram while trying to belie how affected you are by those rumors. Good grief, French could be lurking about with his pistol just behind the stable, or in the trees beyond the herb garden, right now for all we know. But you can still keep your composure and chide yourself for believing everything you hear, as an out-of-towner anyhow; and clear thinking leads you to perceive the underlying issue here—a love triangle involving French, his wife Sarah, and this Marcus Kelsey that no one wants to talk about. Hah, there it is again, that ever-amusing hang of putting two and two together.

Food for thought it is, as you scoop up a last deviled egg from your dainty dish, while the doctor takes another sip of shrub. At this point it's understandable that you're ready to break off your discussion, allowing you to ruminate further over this news about Sarah and her temporarily insane husband, along with all the reproachful opinions shared by that Detroit reporter—or Pinkerton agent, or whatever he was—and any other hints of troubles that you may have missed this afternoon.

Yes, it would be good to find some means for a polite 'social extraction', and presently that opportunity arises when Abiram's wife Helen steps in to interrupt, the premise being that she would like a refill to her cup of coffee—apparently there is also bottled coffee set out on the beverage table.

"Don't let him go on too long with his tales of Colorado," she adds playfully, looking at you while grasping her husband's arm, then delicately taking the empty plate from his hand. "We're all just happy to have him home, safe and sound, gold or no gold." She raises her face to look up at Abiram, her expression implying that they should move on to the table for coffee.

This is convenient for you, too. "Oh, no, please. That's fine. In fact I just caught sight of someone else I've been meaning to talk to." All well and good. The Good Doctor acquiesces to his wife's request, and your conversation with him concludes with genial assurances to see one another again before everyone leaves . . . and now you're free to think over all you have learned about the Frenches, and the cynical Pinkerton man, and dodgy sights by the mill pond, and Daniel and the shop girl and her uncle the mayor, and Hervey Parke breaking in his new shoes, far from home and his young wife, *enceinte* and alone, waiting for his return.

The best tack is to stop by the beverage table yourself and pick up another cup of shrub, if only to have something in your hands, and then gradually make your way to the periphery where one might better observe the crowd in its entirety. A maid is standing at the beverage table, carefully ladling a few extra ceramic mugs with shrub, or switchel, or whatever it is, from a large metal pail. Take a mug, thank the girl, and look around for where you might go next. There now: this should be unobtrusive enough. From here you're able to scan over the various huddles of guests engaged in discussions as they fidget absent-mindedly with the plates and cups held in their hands. One group includes Governor Wisner and Reverend Green, along with the Baldwin's; in another you see Horace Thurber and Abram Mathews chatting with the Darrow's—Emily Darrow is there with her parents, yawning, her gaze turned absently sidelong to observe other guests nearby. Yet another group has old Mrs. Hodges together with Mayor Thatcher, the newspaperman Howell, and the shopgirl Carrie Holley. And numerous other small assemblages, and still more guests idling about the refreshment tables.

Should you join in with one of the huddles, or wait here until the presentations begin? Perhaps you're mistaken, and there are no presentations planned for the event at all. This entire reception might have no particular purpose other than to extend one's personal best wishes to Sergeant Joe McConnell, who isn't even in the yard, strange to say.

Elkanah Comstock happens to be nearby, and catching your eye he takes the opportunity to ask whether you might know if his niece Julia and her friends are returning soon to the yard. You can only shrug, as if to say: no. Frankly, you don't really understand his question.

You notice Parke McConnell on the other side of the table, waiting for a refill of his mug. Let's go join him and get back to enjoying the party.

YOUNG IDEAS

JULIA COMSTOCK carefully laid down a tray of empty cups on the counter, then stood back to look at the tray, really to pause for a moment and allow herself to focus on her own composure. She and her friend Malvina had offered to bring trays back into the McConnells' pantry, as a gesture of helpfulness to Eliza the McConnells' maid. Even though it was a bit early during the reception, this task was actually providing a buffer of time to prepare for what the two girls meant to do next: make their entrance into the family room where all their friends were gathering. As if the magic of this springtime weren't already enough, to be home again, for good this time after finishing their school days at the seminary, Julia and Malvina were now about to brave another threshold here at the

Julia Comstock

Malvina Taylor

door of the McConnells' drawing room. Inside was the promise of escape, privacy and intrigue. And there, if only for a short time, they might sequester themselves for a party-within-a-party, away from parents and chaperones. There were boys in that next room, of course, an unnerving predicament, but Julia would be there in the midst of her girlfriends, conformed and proper, their fans folded up and dangling from their wrists. And with Emma, her younger sister, too. For once, perhaps this was a comfort anyway, if only by making Julia look older by comparison.

Ready? Julia exchanged with Malvina Taylor a wide-eyed glance of here-goes-nothing as they turned to go back through the dining room door. There was nothing more to primp or straighten; it was time to smile confidently and move forward. Julia wasn't as concerned about her appearance as she was about her heavy breathing – was it from carrying the tray, or was it nerves? In the dining room she espied Emma, who was holding a small sandwich while listening to Willy McConnell, and Julia made a "follow me" signal with her

Emma Comstock

free hand, to which Emma promptly complied and rallied herself away from young Will.

The three girls crossed the hall to the drawing room and, unhurried, walked in. And there they were, the boys, older, talking among themselves. Julia wasn't expecting such a nonchalant reaction but was glad for it. *Just remember to appear friendly.* The room felt warm. There were hints of perfumes. A revelation now: there weren't any seats available for her group to remain together, no, the scene was arranged for sitting or standing here or there, but spread out with everyone intermingled to promote one overall inclusive party. Julia followed Malvina to a table in the bay window area where Lewis Drake was standing with two of his friends—she knew Lewis—and she smiled methodically through introductions and the offer of a glass of switchel. Malvina took over the niceties allowing Julia to glance over the room while nodding and grinning awkwardly to Jim Goodsell and then to some other men she did not know. She could see Joseph McConnell but he was absorbed in a small clique just then; granted, she wasn't really acquainted with him either, just formally introduced once before, at a reception last summer at the Whitehead farm in Waterford.

At this point the conversations going on around her were all male voices, the boys joking amongst themselves and sounding very worldly. Julia could perceive the sarcastic overtones and double-entendres in off-hand phrases such as "I assured her I had no ignoble designs" and "his mount was rather indisposed at that very moment." It was bit uninviting, socially. And when one of boys who was wearing a militia uniform exclaimed "A deuce of a blunder, I say!" this caused Lewis to stop short, and smiling with arched brows, interject with "A *deuce*? My word, I haven't heard that word for some time, now. A deuce, you say?" Joseph picked up the tease and added "Oh, *dash it all*, Lewis, let the man decry in peace!"

Julia wasn't impressed by the sarcasm, and she stopped listening to look around the room. It was very spacious, running from the bay window, behind her, all the way to the window in the front wall of the house at the other end. There was light aplenty coming in from three windows along the side wall, such that it made for a cheery feel to the place, despite all the ponderous wainscoting, built-in cabinetry and heavy curtains. Julia had been in this room before and knew it well;

it was bigger than any room in her Uncle Elkanah's big home, as far as she could tell. This room was also characterized as being separated into two halves, in a way, front and rear portions, as suggested by the two imposing eight-sided columns adjacent to the walls at midpoint. The front portion had the fireplace with its glossy fascia of green tiles in a brick-like pattern, framed by wooden casing; the rear portion had the Connecticut wall clock that had just now chimed the 4:30 half hour in the Westminster theme that Julia could hear behind everyone talking. There was a large barometer mounted on a wooden frame by the rear door. There were all sorts of family items and artwork throughout, but for now the most noticeable feature was the placing of two large armchairs under the midpoint arch, in a way establishing a limit and corral most of the guests in the rear portion. With a dozen or so people gathered in this part it helped create a certain intimacy, and there was an alluring feel to it, here in a secluded area with her friends, consorting with all these sophisticated older boys.

The faces all around her were well-familiar, and the voices, but the mood of the room was somehow taking on a more audacious quality. It was the girls—they, too, appeared more mature, at least a few of them who had removed their shawls to reveal dress sleeves so short that they barely draped below their shoulders. *My goodness, is it really so warm in here?* And small actions, barely noticeable, now seemed fitting for this venue, like the way in which the girls would remove their gloves, finger by finger, while settling blithely in a chair or speaking frivolously with a neighbor, as the boys looked on with careful indifference, evaluating the dainty hands and feminine ways. Fannie Mathews handled these mannerisms very easily; young Molly Bacon was not as adept.

But Julia's dissipating thoughts were suddenly broken off as she caught sight of something that really didn't belong here: a wine bottle. Across the room Fannie Mathews was sitting with Joe McConnell and some others, around a small table, holding crystal glasses, and Joe was just setting down a bottle of red wine on the table. He must have just poured the glasses, including Fannie's, and Fannie's calm smile was, pardon me, simply not appropriate. *They're drinking wine? And hard cider, maybe?* Julia couldn't help glancing over to see the smiles, the sippings, the grown-up behavior. She wanted to nudge Malvina and share her observations but checked herself—*don't be such an ingénue.* She began to feel self-conscious about the style of her dress, whether it appeared too plain, and whether she looked too immature for this company. *But just look at that Molly Bacon flaunting her bare arms like that, in mixed company! How can her stepmother let her dress like that?* Supposedly the family room party was "in bounds," so arranged by the McConnell's, and Julia recalled how Mrs.

Fannie Mathews

Molly Bacon

McConnell in the receiving parlor had told them all to "scoot back there and enjoy yourselves for a while." But the wine was admittedly a bit forward, actually, if not altogether unnerving. Apparently Fannie's older brother George, standing nearby in another group with Ella Draper, hadn't noticed or wasn't worried, and after all, Fannie's 17th birthday was just two days ago. But Julia resolved to decline, if offered any spirits, and so would her sister Emma.

Nonetheless it was exhilarating to be here in this large, stately room, to engage in various discursive conversations with friends and friends' connections, away from school, unchecked by chaperones. A new idea came to mind: perhaps the time had come to grow up. For her, for her friends, for everyone here. The adult life was coming, this summer certainly, after graduation, and now was a good time to focus on one's behavior, compatibility, and reputation. *These boys will soon be off for the army, and when they come home, how will they look at me?* Julia pondered over this idea while she glanced at faces around her, at Joseph McConnell, and Lewis Drake, George Mathews, Stuart Draper, and Jimmy Goodsell. She really didn't know much about them anymore, since she had been away at school in Cleveland for so much time, and so she resolved now that she would reacquaint herself with all of them, one by one over the summer.

For that matter, Julia realized she didn't know much about men in general, let alone the eligible bachelors such as these. They were expected to go forth into the world and establish themselves in careers and become husbands, and they would need partners to help them create homes and families. Somehow everyone should be paired up, eventually, whether they stayed in Pontiac or moved elsewhere, the country growing ever bigger as it was. This had always been an underlying message in her classes at the Seminary, that the graduating women were destined to become the wives of future civic leaders, and in that regard the girls' preparation was meant to impart practical knowledge and the skills for building a community. *That* is what a bachelor would find attractive in a prospective bride, a future partner, an ideal wife like . . . like Mrs. McConnell, or Mrs. Hodges, women that Julia admired, who had gained social prominence and respect without any formal education. *Ah, but the world is a lot more complicated today.* So much more science, and inventions, and medicines—and such changes in the way that people think and live. In her Mental Philosophy class Julia had studied John Stuart Mill's "Essay on Liberty," most of which was a bit dreary, but her teacher Miss Haven had finally stirred all the girls' attention when she described how Mill had acknowledged the influence and contributions made by his late wife Harriet Taylor Mill. That was the interesting part.

A partner, then. An attractive partner. What does a young man want by way of a partner? This had become a nagging thought, something never clearly addressed at the Seminary, and at home the only advice she heard was that it was not something to worry about, that because she was well educated and proper, held herself well and was industrious then nothing else mattered. But Julia still worried, sometimes. Was her face pretty enough? She tried to assess her appearance objectively, but there was no way to judge, really, in the way of pictures or art. The French women depicted in the "La Mode Illustrée" pictures were the only consistent standard. And of course it was noticeable how the boys seemed to favor the Thurber girls, and that Carrie Holley. But it was vanity, only vanity, to compare oneself like that, and worry about her chin being too small and her eyebrows too large. In the end a good man would be looking for a wife, not a fashion image. And as for matters of intimacy, a good man would take of that, too, and make sure everything went as it should. Julia had never talked with anyone about the mysteries and rites involved in marital relations, but she had faith that she would be ready to let nature take its course when the time came, like everyone else.

Whatever opinions the crowd might have of Julia, her looks and her character, what counted most to her was the enchantment of the gathering itself, that everyone was here in this attic cavern, enjoying each other's company and rekindling old friendships. This was her group, her generation, all coming of age together. Julia had always relied on the definitive nature of this group, ever since she and Emma were orphaned, in a sense, having lost their father nine years ago, and with their mother almost fully estranged from their home life. Uncle Elkanah had placed them under the care of Mrs. Goodale, on Perry Street, and helped arrange for their schooling at the Cleveland Female Seminary. Social acceptance of the Comstock girls was thus sustained, and it would grow from there. At Cleveland Julia had become good

friends with Malvina, another Pontiac girl.
Malvina had transferred to Cleveland from
the Monroe Seminary, which in turn led to
another connection, Sarah Thurber, who was
Malvina's schoolmate at Monroe. Sarah wasn't
here but Julia had run across her earlier in the
yard. She was younger but somehow more earnest, and likeable, to Julia. Maybe they shared
something of a higher bond, too, both of them

Lewis Drake

living without mothers. *Oh good, there she is—*
Julia noticed her standing alone, looking out
the window by the far corner. *Poor Sarah. I'll
find a quieter time to ask how she's getting along.*

Julia thanked Lewis Drake as he handed
her the glass of switchel, his gesture having
pulled her attention back matters at hand.
She knew Lewis well enough to be on guard
for his wit and his blarney talk, but as more

Stuart Draper

people drew her in, Julia felt increasingly at ease with the small talk,
the questions about school, the vacation, which boys were home from
college, who else might enlist, had anyone seen Larissa Lockwood,
and so on. Of course it was easy to express true feelings about the
excitement of being home and seeing everyone again, yet marveling
over the realities of the town preparing for war. How exhilarating it
was, everyone agreed, to see so many men in uniform walking about
town, to hear parents arguing and citing newspaper articles, and
marvel about the call-to-war demonstrations. Julia overhead Fannie talking with Stuart Draper, wondering aloud if the southerners
were just as excited and doing the same things, which was a strange
thought. How could they know anything about raising an army, and
why would they even dare to fight back at all? Julia had never met

anyone from a southern state, and having read "Uncle Tom's Cabin" she felt little need to travel there.

So far only Joe McConnell had actually enlisted in the army. He was at Union College in Schenectady, with Danny Thurber although a year ahead of him, having just finished his junior year. Julia tried to imagine more of the boys around her doing the same, leaving college to join the army, wearing blue uniforms, marching in formation, shooting muskets and swinging sabers. It had already been several weeks since the President's call for volunteers in April, and since then most of the talk about the boys enlisting had been josh and boasting; but the tone had changed today with the news from Detroit that, starting now, the enlistments meant joining the army for three years. That was a long time to be away. Everyone seemed to be much more respectful of anyone who would volunteer for a serious undertaking such as this, and now, when Julia looked across the room at Joseph, watching him converse with friends, he looked older, more commanding, somehow. Even though he still had that same friendly grin and that steady gaze locked on whomever happened to be speaking to him at the moment.

And so Julia's boyfriends would become men, and her girlfriends become women. Everyone appeared ready for it, and Julia was beginning to feel proud just to be among them. A notion came to her that she ought to consider how she personally could participate in war preparations, getting involved in supplies or medicines. Perhaps she could start a club at the Seminary; then again, she would be graduating in a month anyway. No, she would have to wait until summer, if there was still a need for anyone's help at that point.

Well, well, oh well. All of that seemed vaguely far away. For now the boys had only to prepare the speeches they would make later, in the yard, before all the guests. Joseph didn't look nervous; he seemed rather admirably self-possessed, not so brash as Julia remembered him. Probably they would all be called downstairs again soon enough, which was too bad, because this occasion was becoming exceedingly fine. The discourse grew a bit more orderly as the various separate gatherings gradually melded into one large group, everyone more comfortable and enjoying the ambience. A little more fresh air would be nice, but Julia stayed fully absorbed in the company nonetheless, even as she unfolded her fan and put it to use. There was witty humor, and there were awkward faux pas, and there was gossip. And someone had asked whether The Honorable Lewis Cass would be coming later, which drew scoffs and ridicule, and rejoinders that Wisner and Richardson would have little to say to that old *doughface*[69] anyhow. Besides, Richardson's wedding will be in Detroit, not up here in Pontiac, so don't expect any bigwigs today.

Mostly, the discussions were interesting. Did anyone know this Fannie Travor that Colonel Richardson was marrying . . . Who was down in Detroit when the 1st Michigan paraded at the Campus Martius and received their colors . . . Is Joseph going to Detroit tomorrow on the same train as the Colonel . . . Why wasn't Alfred Green invited up here with us . . . Is Joseph's father going to let his new church be a stop on the Underground Railroad . . . Were there any cricket matches being organized for the summer . . . Is our *highbrow* Mr. Howell out there now in the yard . . . Did Danny's father really speak to his wife at a séance . . . We should organize a picnic at Orchard Lake like last year's . . .

Julia listened attentively and tried to add a word here and there, although it didn't seem as though she could garner much response. The war talk was strangely benign. There was some banter about how much fighting might actually happen, and the dangers of combat—one of the uniformed Flint boys made a boorish remark that a man in combat was less likely to die than a mother in childbirth. This produced only an awkward silence for several seconds, until someone else tried to joke

---

69   Doughface: northern politician having southern sympathies.

about "Well, there's a pregnant pause for you," but his crass pun only made matters worse, with all the girls' eyes downcast in hushed embarrassment. Lewis finally rescued the impasse, asking briskly "Oh, come now. Is life really worth the trouble of so many questions?"[70]

"Here, here!" a few voices answered enthusiastically, and several glasses were raised. Lewis could sense how everyone was ready to steer away from anything morbid. "So what's our formal opinion about the wines?" he asked, and a more congenial dialogue was thereby restored, welcomed by all, on a topic that piqued Julia's interest much more than she might let on.

She would not learn much about wines just now, it turned out, as her attention was taken away by two newcomers who were entering the room, Daniel Thurber and an older girl that Julia didn't know. The girl was a young woman, more accurately, and probably the oldest person in the room. But she apparently was not at all self-conscious about her age, or being out-of-place; quite the contrary, she was completely at ease and ready to join in. Daniel introduced her as Joseph's "Cousin Sallie" whereupon Joseph uttered a mock warning of "Uh-oh, look out now, everyone." This of course focused all expectations onto how Sallie would retort to his remark, and she didn't disappoint, reaching for clean wine goblet and coolly announcing "Time you all learned a thing or two from a *real* chaperone." She brought the glass near the bottle Joseph was holding and added "Dear Cousin, decant away, I pray thee." Whereupon Stuart Draper and Jim Goodsell exchanged a mischievous look as if to say *Should I? Indeed, you should!* And then Stuart stood up with a smile, his glass raised, and began reciting a few lines in French from Voltaire:

Charme de prunelles, tourment des cœurs, lumière de l'esprit!

---

70 Lewis is quoting from "The Three Musketeers" (Alexandre Dumas, 1844) where an impatient Athos is complaining in his typically insouciant attitude, "So let us go and get killed where we are told to go. Is life worth the trouble of so many questions? D'Artagnan, I am ready to follow you."

Je ne baise point la poussière de vos pieds,[71]

Many in the room, if they had graduated from Pontiac's Union School, knew right away (with a groan) that this quote was from Mr. Howell's French class, and was a perennial requirement for memorization and recitation. Before Stuart could finish with the next line, his sister Ella and Jim joined in to recite in triumphant unison, eyes fixed on Sallie:

Parce que vous ne marchez guère![72]

The French pronunciation being muddled as it was, the nostalgia was great fun, and cheers and raised glasses were the boisterous response, with Cousin Sallie no less gleeful along with everyone else. Sundry conversations resumed now with heightened daring and spontaneity. Joseph wryly observed how reassuring it was to have a French-speaking chaperone on hand who could read Madame Bovary[73] and was thus no stranger to the avant-garde ideas coming out of Europe; and Sallie only stared back at him, grinning with a wouldn't-you-like-to-know defiance in the midst of ooh's and oho's voiced by the boys nearby.

But Sallie was only shaking her head with an impish grin, and her gaze landed straight at Julia (momentarily flattering, in a way) as she said, "Don't be impressed by these popinjays trying to speak college French—they still have a lot to learn."

Jim Goodsell's retort was to stick out his tongue back at Sallie, playfully, drawing some laughter, and Julia impulsively turned to look down the far side of the room to check if any chaperones were there to

---

71 "[You are] a charm for the eyes, a tormenter of hearts, a light for the spirit! I can't even kiss the dust under your feet." The quote is from Voltaire's novel <u>Zadig</u>, from its introductory salutation. The context is sarcastic while still lightly entertaining.

72 "Because you hardly ever walk at all!"

73 Madame Bovary, by Gustave Flaubert, published in France in the 1850's was immediately recognized as a literary masterpiece but was also attacked for content that was considered obscene. A translation of the novel into English would not be published until 30 years later.

disapprove of all this misbehavior. But of course there were none.

Julia had never heard of Madame Bovary, no matter, but she was still quite taken by Sallie's presence in the room, and couldn't help making several furtive glances to observe the woman's style and finesse. There she was, laughing and conversing ably with everyone, nimbly sipping wine from her goblet, throwing out comments like "abstemious types always make me nervous." And how intriguing to find out that Sallie was in fact a married woman, Mrs. French, a rel-

Sarah Abigail Parke French, "Cousin Sallie"

ative of the McConnell's. Someone had asked who brought the bottles, and Joseph had surmised that it was Cousin Hervey Parke, visiting from up north, but Mrs. French said no, the wines had been delivered from Turk's, she thought, on behalf of some other out-of-town guest who came with Hervey. And she added that her straight-laced brother Hervey would never have brought wines or spirits to a gathering such as this. So . . . gradually Julia also picked up that this Mrs. Sarah Parke French was temporarily residing here in the McConnell home. She was extended family, then, the lively outsider with a sharp wit and not shy to show it. Did she have children? It wouldn't seem likely. At one point Julia tried to ask Dan Thurber surreptitiously whether there was also a Mr. French at the reception, and could only smile at his soft reply, "Best not to inquire."

George Mathews then brought up the topic of a building a third floor atop the McConnells' house:

"Say, what do you think of it, then? Joe says the Old Man wants a ballroom in the attic."

Sallie's eyes went wide. "Yes! I know! The Mr. and Mrs. have been talking about it. That is, the Mrs. has been doing the talking, and Mr. the listening."

"Could be a messy undertaking," Joseph rejoined. "As long as I'm safely in Virginia somewhere when they start tearing off the roof of this place." He glanced at Stuart and double-perked his eyebrows as he took another sip from his glass.

Stuart's turn: "Might be fun. I reckon from a third floor window you'd have a view all the way to the courthouse cupola. I say: build up. If an attic ballroom is good enough for a lumber baron in Bay City, it's good enough for a nabob in Pontiac."

"Agreed! Just ask Augustus Baldwin," Sallie spoke up again. "His ballroom was quite handy a few times last winter. And can you imagine my Aunt Cleantha finding room in here for that crowd if it had rained today? Bit of a squeeze, n'est-ce pas?"

Such a predicament was easy to visualize, and all agreed on today's good luck with the weather. Julia wasn't interested in the prospects of the McConnell's adding a third floor as she was in watching Mrs. French and wondering whether or not it would be acceptable to remove her own gloves, although it was probably too late for that by now. But a broader conversation was starting to pick up, and someone mentioned the toffee candies from Crawford's . . . oh yes, others speak up, they're absolutely fizzing, a fine treat, and wasn't that Carrie Holley who brought them earlier—or do you mean *delivered* them? . . . Isn't she joining us . . . I think not . . . she was speaking with Mrs. Darrow in the yard . . . yes the store used to be called Crawford and Holley but her father left that business to Crawford years ago . . . Carrie just works there now after school. And so the discussion went. Malvina remarked how Mrs. Holley certainly kept her daughter busy, and someone else rejoined how the entire Holley household was very *enterprising* (Julia knew the word meant to imply "overly ambitious")—although, by the way, wasn't it a bit pretentious for Carrie to pose for those daguerreotype images for her mother's dressmaking business.

The talk slipped into gossip about Carrie, and Fannie Pittman and Emma Adams—the public school girls with afternoon work in town—caricaturing them as business tycoons-in-the-making ("Not fair!" Julia tried to speak up on the girls' behalf). Julia knew Carrie well and was very fond of her, and admired her style and tact, which she said aloud when she could. Others within the group began to agree, which then led to a question from Lewis aimed squarely at Daniel, whether he had seen the pictures of Carrie and wouldn't she be quite the catch. "After all, you and your sister brought her today, didn't you?"

Daniel sloughed off the inquiry with a smirk, well-yes-of-course, but no, he hadn't seen any images of Carrie wearing her mothers' gowns. Julia espied Daniel shortly afterwards glaring back at Lewis in what could only be embarrassed resentment, and thus it dawned on her that Daniel and Carrie would actually make a very attractive couple. *Of course! Am I the only one to see that?*—she looked around the room. She wondered whether Carrie Holley was already friendly with Daniel Thurber. Or had something just happened between the two of them today? Julia's face brightened as she took in a quick breath: *Maybe I'm the one who started this, back at the National Block when I told Carrie to get into Daniel's carriage.*

Julia was fully enthralled by the prospect. Shouldn't she do more to help make this match happen? Daniel and Carrie. Julia didn't really know that much about Daniel Thurber personally, except that his mothered had died and he had three younger sisters; but then again she had always thought of him as very well-mannered, smart, and that despite his reserved nature he was a robust, active sort who loved horseback riding. That's the kind of romantic gentleman that Jane Austin would write about, the kind who couldn't fail to see the finer qualities in a girl like Carrie.

As for Carrie, Julia hadn't seen her for some time before today, not since Christmas as she recalled, although they had exchanged some let- ters—the two of them had been good friends at the Pontiac Union School before Julia left for the Cleveland Seminary. Of course, Carrie had never mentioned anything about romantic in- terests in her letters. But Carrie should definite- ly be made aware of Daniel's feelings, especially now before all the boys went off to enlist in the army. Then—a hesitation: *Perhaps I should find out more about Mr. Thurber, before I approach Miss Holley.* Julia resolved to have a talk with Ella Draper, her class- mate at the Seminary, knowing that Ella's older brother Stuart was a close friend of Daniel.

Ella Draper

Various tacts and ploys now kept Julia's mind occupied, quietly un- noticed, while all the others around her chatted and quipped. Probably everyone was ready to wind up the "salon" party anyway, as Julia figured that almost an hour had already passed. This seemed to be a general understanding, that the group's presence downstairs was ex- pected, if especially relied upon for the boys to regale the older folks with some clever *badinage*, and of course the ingratiating patriotic exhortations. A momentary silence befell the room and Lewis Drake said aloud *"Comme il nous faut, copains!"*[74] making the pronouncement definitive that it was time to go. Julia was fine with this, the air getting somewhat "close," and she had noticed some dampness on the faces around her. Despite the fellowship and intimacy, enjoyable as it was, she was looking forward to rejoining the main event outdoors in the fresh air. And just on cue—who should appear at the door but young

---

74 "As we must, my boys!"

Willy and his cousin Fred, bringing official tidings that the hour for speeches had arrived. "Well there we are," someone said. The younger set stirred to action and began to stand up as Joe McConnell dismissed the messengers with an authoritative "Well done, Willy, run back and tell them we'll be right along."

Julia rose from her chair and prepared to move along with the rest of the party towards the door to the hall. The girls were snatching up their gloves, their fans and their muslin shawls, but several gloves and fans were dropped off on a sofa by the door—evidently there was little concern for the need to carry them back to the yard and the world of parents. The open space of the yard would be welcome, and there was also the intriguing matter of the speeches—what would these college boys have to say for themselves, out there in front of everyone? Julia hoped they would rise to the occasion with some worthy oratory and not squander the moment with their tomfoolery. After all, Joseph McConnell deserved respect for his solemn endeavor, and the dangers that must lay ahead. But Julia understood that her sentiments had no weight in the midst of this lighthearted, insouciant, flirtatious crowd.

A sudden opportunity: the group's movement into the hall had brought Julia side-by-side with Daniel, momentarily. She stopped her fanning. He looked upon her, with relaxed eyes and a genial grin; obviously he recognized her and it would be fine for her to say something in passing, just to be polite.

"Good luck with the speeches, Daniel."

"Thank you, Julia."

"It must be a proud day for Mr. and Mrs. McConnell."

"Yes, of course." Daniel widened his grin and looked down towards the floor, but then moved his eyes upward to look straight ahead as he walked. Julia wanted so much to say something about Carrie, but she didn't. There was no way to couch the matter smoothly with anything the group had joked about earlier. She couldn't think fast enough, and the moment was lost. Daniel moved on further to take up with his colleagues while Julia could only wish she had made more of an impression. No one should see her sigh, she thought to herself. *But I must confess he is quite a handsome man.* Perhaps showing some bare arm would have helped. Fair to say, a sleeveless dress in this warmth would be nice. *No, it's just not proper.* Mrs. Goodale wouldn't approve, moreover, frowning upon any sort of style she deemed *outré* for a schoolgirl. Carrie's mother would never agree to it either, certainly.

So that was that. Julia slowly made her way towards a door to the hallway along with everyone else, and presently Malvina Taylor came beside her, and the two girls proceeded together arm-in-arm. Julia turned an inquisitive look at Malvina, and a smile, and inquired with just one word: "Well?" Malvina returned the smile and replied *sotto voce,* "You know, I was expecting to see more uniforms."

Malvina Taylor

Of course I know all of the Cleveland girls – I'm one of them! -- even though my family home is a mile west of Pontiac on a farm in Waterford. Before he took up farming in Michigan, my father was a teacher, and he and my mother have always stressed the importance of education. I used to attend the female seminary in Monroe, where I met Sarah Thurber – she is so pretty and gracious – and she has a shine for Joe McConnell, I'm sure of it – Joe is her brother's best friend. Then last year father put me and my sister Libbie in the Cleveland Female Seminary, which I think is a better school. It has nicer surroundings, and the school building has piped water indoors. They teach more mathematics and sciences, and they have much more apparatus to help us learn the sciences. I take a class on bookkeeping, as father says it is especially important. And, he likes the classes they teach on politics and economics, but I don't see why those subjects are so important except to make us girls sound intelligent when we ask our future husbands how they vote in elections.

There are a lot of Pontiac girls at the Cleveland Seminary. Let's see: Julia Comstock and her sister Emma, Fannie Mathews, Ella Draper, Larissa Lockwood, Libbie and me, and Mary Bacon. Eight of us. We're all home for the Spring recess. This time it's especially helpful to be home and see all the boys once more before they go off to the army for the war. Isn't it exciting? I can't wait to see everyone at the McConnell's! Then after the party I'll be staying tonight with Julia Comstock at the widow Goodale's house. You know, Julia is the smartest of all of us. She's so generous and always helping people. She should be a teacher after she graduates. I think that's what she wants to do. She lost both of her parents, some years ago, so her uncle pays for all of her schooling.

Local and Miscellaneous.

PONTIAC, SEPTEMBER 30, 1859.

☞ We are requested to give notice that the Rev. Mr. Sawyer of Farmington, a Universalist Minister, will preach at the Firemen's Hall next Sunday evening, commencing at 7 o'clock. The public are respectfully invited to attend.

PERSONAL.—Another installment of Pike's Peakers has been received back into the pale of civization by the return to their homes of Isaac I. Voorheis, Wm. Morris and T. C. Beardslee. Their countenances look familiar, and seem none the worse for wear.——Alfred Williams, an old " salt" (not sailor) of Pontiac, is stopping at the Ogle House.——Pontiac returns to the University this week, John E. Colby, of the Junior Class; Stuart Draper, Lewis Drake, Joseph McConnell, Daniel D. Thurber and James H. Goodsell of the Sophomore Class, and also sends Charles H. Taylor, to the Freshman Class. Abundant success go with them.——Our young friend, E. G. Comstock, is about to leave us to accept a situation in a Detroit business house.——It is hinted that our enterprising Bookseller, Geo. H. Smith, Esq., intends bringing back from New York, in addition to his usual stock of Goods, a—wife. There, we came near telling of it.

Jenny Lind
1820-1887
"The Swedish Nightingale"

GOOD BYE.—A goodly gathering of the young friends and relatives of Joseph McConnell and Dan D. Thurber, who are about to enter Union College at Schenectady ; and of Misses Mollie Bacon, Fannie Mathews, and Julia Comstock, who were leaving at the same time for the Cleveland Female College, met at the depot on Wednesday afternoon to bid them a hearty good bye and a God speed, as they leave home and friends to enter upon the noble work of finishing up their school education. It was an occasion of interest.

Cleveland Female Seminary

318

A VISITOR'S STORY,
"Speeches and Prayers"

"AHA, HERE come the boys," says Parke, as the two of you turn to look up at the side porch platform where a number of young men are filing out of a door from the living room, the room where you had first met the Captain and his wife Mercy. You recognize Daniel Thurber among the "boys"; he is speaking closely to another, taller one in the group, and the two of them share a laugh. Is that . . . ? "Yes. That's my brother Joseph," confirms Parke. "You'll have to excuse me—duty calls," he adds, and heads over to the porch stairs to join the assembly.

For the next several minutes you stand alone, shrub drink in hand, feeling perhaps just a little awkward and solitary, exchanging polite nods with a few non-acquaintances. Soon enough, however, your attention is drawn over to observe another group, a covey of pretty girls walking into the side yard from around the front. They must have detoured out the main door of the house while the lads were gathering in the living room. It's a close-knit group of schoolgirls, no doubt the daughters of many of the guests around you, and among them you recognize Julia Comstock whom you saw earlier when you first arrived. So there they come now, a merry little company, self-conscious about making such an appearance but showing no intention to disperse among their parents. You can imagine how they could otherwise be quite frolicsome, but for now they must constrain themselves to uphold a more demure look, especially before the boys. Nonetheless there's no denying how their display is in sharp contrast to the conventional dress of their mothers here in the yard, as the girls sashay along freely in their "artist gown" dresses, their hair rolled-up and bedecked with strands of flowers à la Jenny Lind. And why not?—the free spirit of a school recess may as well be fully indulged, especially in May.

And just as you're standing there enjoying this ostentatious processional, who should show up next to you but Carrie Holley again, also looking on with a knowing grin. "And here comes the *arrière-salle* crowd," she comments, her tone . . . envious perhaps? *No*, you think, *she's only amused just as you are.* "I think," she goes on, "the college boys and seminary girls must have had their own private party somewhere inside the house." She keeps her eye on both groups, the boys on the porch and the girls nearby below them.

"Duly chaperoned, of course," you tack on, in support.

She shows a wry smile, "Probably so." Then she adds, "No gloves or fans—they must have left them inside. Might have been getting a little warm in there. At least they remembered their shawls."

You ask whether she knows any of them, and at last she turns her face towards you full on with her answer: "Of course. I know all of them. This is my home." And with that, a knowing smile. Her short, direct reply was only an offhand pleasantry, of course, but then it strikes you how these few words have conveyed her kindly spirit, and a happiness just to be here, to be in this company. It's enjoyable, and it makes this young woman all the more charming, along with her lovely smile and graceful manner which impressed you earlier when you met her with the Mayor and Daniel Thurber. You nod back, and make sure to exhibit only a proper, detached attitude, despite realizing now how captivating she truly is.

And while Carrie seems content to stand by and answer questions on who-is-who, why not allow yourself to be charmed a minute or two longer? You're obliged to turn your look once again on the *Jenny Lind* coterie so that you might ask discretely: who are those first two girls, arm in arm—is that Julia Comstock? "Yes," Carrie says, leaning her head slightly sideways to follow your lead, "I think the other girl is Malvina Taylor, from Waterford." And she points out a few more: there is Fannie Mathews, the mill owner's daughter, and Ella Draper, the attorney's daughter, and two of the younger girls, Malvina's sister Libbie, and Molly Bacon. You mention how you had met Molly Bacon earlier, and then you nod towards the men hobnobbing on the porch, to the tallest one among them, saying that he must be Joseph McConnell, correct? "Yes . . ." And the fellow just behind him—that's your Daniel Thurber again, isn't it? But this time Carrie makes no reply as she looks steadily upon the porch. No need to distract her from what she sees now, your sidelong glance tells you. She's looking straight at Daniel.

Joseph McConnell

The young men are still milling about on the porch, which seems designated to serve as a stage upon which they might address the guests in the yard before them. Of course that's the idea. The porch has been decorated with a stretch of bunting, dark blue with a line of large, white stars interspersed every foot or so, hung just below the porch roof, and you notice a further embellishment in the form of two large flower pots placed at the base of the corners, each crowded with yellow daffodils, which nicely accentuates the springtime setting for the oratory to come. Aha, and there he is—so, that's him, Sergeant Joseph McConnell, our honoree and top attraction. You think that you have seen him before—where was it—yes, on the train this morning, when everyone was getting off the car at the Pontiac depot. He must have been returning home after enlisting down in Detroit. Up there now with his friends he does strike a handsome appearance, tall and self-assured, with blue eyes and light brown curly hair. You have learned from someone—his brother Parke, was it?—that on Saturday he'll be returning to Detroit for official mustering in with the 2nd Michigan. So, the young man will be in uniform soon enough but for now he's still a college boy in civilian attire in his morning coat.

Amid his entourage he clearly enjoys the teasing remarks that you glean the others are making, even as he strives to uphold a proper serious demeanor, his arms folded and chin down, but he cannot stifle a quick smirk with raised eyebrows at some of the ribbing. A few of the fellows have attended the reception dressed in trim, grey military tunics, with brass buttons and chalk-white bands passing diagonally over the right shoulder—must be Joseph's friends in the Flint Union Greys, in a uniform of sorts. One might imagine them all parading about in those Wide-Awakes demonstrations. And probably some of them are the older brothers of the "seminary" girls Carrie was pointing out earlier. Standing close by are Daniel Thurber and a few other college chums, you might guess, including Lewis Drake and George Mathews who were at the Arcade. Lewis has been exchanging glances with George's sister Fannie, which you can see is evoking caustic remarks from his colleagues. It's an amusing idea, that the yard party might serve to disclose some potential matchmaking among the various families' younger folks, with all the conjecture that goes with it. And so once more you scan the social arena, observing the friends and relatives and all the other well-wishers. Even Hervey's little niece Clettie Kelsey, and future soldier Master Willie McConnell, have succeeded in slipping away from the other youngsters to come observe their elders' animated behavior.

You can sense how the crowd around you gradually perceives that arrangements are developing for a round of oratory that will cap the event, and everyone begins to quiet down and draw closer to the porch. Presently Willard McConnell steps front and center to marshal the audience, proceeding with a few ceremonious remarks to introduce his son and the others in his retinue. In turn, one of these, like Joseph not in uniform, starts off by stirring the crowd to laughter with some witty denigrations about the sergeant's performance in college – presumably this is Lewis Drake, Morgan's son, and a friend from Joseph's years at the University of Michigan where they were both members of the Delta Phi fraternity. Lewis is having a fine time regaling the audience with college stories and goes on to recount how, for junior year, Joseph along with Dan Thurber had transferred to Union College in Schenectady, New York.[75] There, as Lewis suggests with feigned reverence, Joseph would learn all about the Dutch Reformers and experience the "old country" where the McConnell's originated, and "solemnly stroll about Jackson's Gardens" with all of Union's brainy engineers and future generals.

Lewis's oratory rolls into full swing, leaning towards Joseph but keeping his eyes locked on the audience, "And how did our 'alpha' chapter out there compare to Ann Arbor, by the way? Surely much more refined, with decorum to spare . . . maybe not enough for Union's old Eliphalet Nott, a hard abolitionist when it comes to fraternities. But not to worry, everyone, Old Joe has seen the light and has rushed back to old Pontiac . . . You did manage to finish your junior year stud-

---

75 Union College is where three fraternities, Kappa Alpha Society, Sigma Phi Society, and Delta Phi were founded. These three are known as the "Union Triad" of college fraternity "alpha" chapters.

ies, didn't you Joe? . . . (here he raises the back of his hand close to his cheek as if to speak covertly) . . . just in time to become a real soldier and grab all the glory before the rest of us can march off!" This draws some laughs from the other young men, particularly Daniel Thurber and George Mathews. The embarrassed sergeant shakes his head with a wry grin while some in the audience chime in with other spontaneous heckling, and you cannot help but admire the wit and the convivial mood that prevails.

Joseph's older brother Parke steps forward to interrupt with his own comment, pointing his thumb towards Joseph while he says to the audience, "No, really. Can you see this *Mick* spending time behind a sales counter and trying to make a sale? Not for five Yankee minutes, I think!" More laughter and catcalls rejoin in answer, while even Joseph himself shakes his head and shapes his mouth as if to say "No." You look over at Willard who sees he has caught your eye, and he gives you a lighthearted wink. Also while you briefly scan over the audience you see Lewis Drake's father, attorney Morgan Drake, and his mother Sarah (standing nearby Governor Wisner) also appear to be enjoying the entertainment. Actually you have met Morgan once before, and his older brother Thomas Jefferson Drake, both of them attorneys. Morgan works for the railroad, and Thomas is something of a retired politician, not here at the reception – too bad, for he is still very popular for his sarcastic wit. Morgan's son Lewis, along with Daniel Thurber, has just finished his sophomore year of college; if Lewis and Daniel will both be returning for junior year, you can appreciate how the Drake and Thurber families are spared from that underlying anxiety about the war. Lewis in particular still has an innocent, boyish look about him, and his friends on stage have caught him exchanging glances with Fannie Mathews out in the audience, which evokes some chummy ridicule as he tries to wrap up his presentation with aplomb.

Daniel steps up next to speak, and he starts out with some hesitation, first offering a general thank-you to all the guests who have attended on such short notice, then congratulating Mr. and Mrs. McConnell on the achievement of providing to the military an outstanding recruit, brave and strong, wise and skillful, and a dear friend to "many of us here." It's apparent right away that Daniel will not continue the glib or witty pace as the previous speaker, but he seems to warm to the task and there is an earnest sincerity in his words which resonates well with his audience. Just as impressive is the brevity of his remarks, brought to a close unexpectedly soon, but for the first time in the yard drawing a round of applause. At that point Joseph McConnell steps forward and puts a hand on Daniel's shoulder, and when clapping has died down he addresses the crowd with a few words of his own:

"A good friend, ladies and gentlemen!" And spotting Horace Thurber he adds, "There you are, Mr. Thurber, those expensive lessons in rhetoric at Union seem to be working!" The crowd approves with a burst of laughter, almost as if they had been holding back for a lighter moment, and although you can't see Horace you can imagine him enjoying all the favorable attention, letting go his normal, cautious restraint.

The festivities continue with more presentations made by two of the uniformed comrades in the Flint Union Greys. These turn out to be more formal and less entertaining while duly congratulating of the honoree. We do learn that the Greys, like other militia units in the region, have been rolled into a state regiment, the 2nd Michigan Volunteer Infantry, as "Company F," where Sergeant Joseph McConnell has likewise been assigned. Not far from your place in the audience you see the mill-owner Abram Mathews and the somber-faced Charles Draper beside him. Mathews is saying something in quieter tones (as best he can for all his self-confidence) and if you edge a little closer you can also catch his words to Draper. ". . . They're all big, strong boys. I have no doubts about their courage. But all they care for now is the camping and parading—you know, most of them have never been outside Oakland County. Well maybe some of them have seen Detroit. If it comes to a real fight, though, let's hope they'll stand up to it . . ."

Draper is nodding grimly as he looks up at the speakers. "Well, if anyone can whip those boys into fighting trim, it's Dick Richardson. I just pray he won't lead them into some heroic charge that gets half of them killed. He's a rough number."

It's striking to hear these subdued opinions in contrast to all the bravado that has pervaded throughout this event.

As the slower segment on stage rambles on, you look beyond the ensemble and see Captain Parke leading his wife Mercy quietly out onto the porch to stand behind the others. Is everyone around you as impressed as you are, that the elderly couple are making this effort to stand together for the event? A finale of sorts seems to be at hand. Reverend Samuel Clements has stepped up from the yard to join the group, accompanied by Reverend Green and Willard McConnell, and a brief conference ensues with the Captain and Mercy. Reverend Clements then turns to address all the guests with a call to prayer. All heads bow, all eyes close, and all hear the Reverend's words spoken aloud in steady, earnest cadence:[76]

> ALMIGHTY God, the Savior of all men, we humbly commend to thy tender care and sure protection, these thy servants who have come forth at the call of their country, to defend its government and to protect its people in their property and homes. Let thy fatherly hand, we beseech thee, be over us; let thy Holy Spirit be with us; let thy good Angels have charge of us; with thy loving kindness defend us as with a shield, and either bring us out of our peril in safety, with a heart to

76 This Collect is from "The Soldier's Prayer Book" published in 1861 by the Protestant Episcopal Book Society, Philadelphia.

show forth thy praises forever, or else sustain us with
that glorious hope, by which alone thy servants can
have victory in suffering and death; through the sole
merits of Jesus Christ our Lord. *Amen*

The prayer concludes, and, after a respectful pause, here is where
Joseph McConnell now steps forward to preside, thanking all for their
encouragement and best wishes, with a nod to his parents, his friends,
and finally to Colonel Richardson, thereby graciously introducing
his commanding officer. Aha, you're thinking, this might revive some
exuberance in the crowd. Sure enough, the Colonel in turn responds
with just a few words—as succinct and peremptory as reliably in character—warning the southern "home-spuns" to look out, and now a
toast to victory for the regiment, "To the regiment!" he shouts, and his
words are echoed by all voices. Governor Wisner pitches in with his
own stentorian "Here-here!" likewise refrained; all glasses and cups are
raised. Here you are, surrounded by friendly, welcoming people, and
together with them you have just raised your cup to salute the brave
men going forth. A moment for communion has arrived, embracing all
their fellowship and their disagreements, their kindness, their conceits
and envies. All drink now, and during this brief hush you're aware of
the sounds of a cicada, and a song sparrow, and the calming hush of
chestnut branches in a gentle breeze.

Close by to where you're standing, a man's voice then makes a quiet
remark, "Llama"-*something-something*, reciting words in a foreign lan-
guage, presumably, just barely perceptible; you glance up from your
bowed head posture, curious, and see that it must have been Horace
Thurber who said them, his eyes still closed. Even more curious, a whisper reaches your ear from the other side—it's Willard McConnell offering you a helpful hint, "It's from a Psalm, I think, that he likes to

memorize in the original."[77] You cast a quizzical glance back at Willard, who grins slightly as he leans closer to add "Horace used to quote freely from 'Macbeth' and 'King Lear', but more recently he's taken to learning Bible passages in original Hebrew. Or Greek, I suppose."

Everyone remains still for a few more moments until the respectful stillness might elapse, which it does, as if signaled by some generally agreed protocol. Conversations resume, less boisterous than before though steadily regaining new life. The party will be concluding as well, after a bit more time presumably, but for now the yard regains its previous commotion while the presenters descend from the porch to join with friends and family. Your helpful guide, Carrie, has been drawn away by another girl with George Mathews (who recognizes you with a friendly wave) to go comingle further into the crowd, and so you're alone again and you may as well make your way to a refreshment table to refill your shrub cup.

You'll have to wait your turn while Horace Thurber and Morgan Drake are doing the same ahead of you. There's a moment now recall what you know about Thurber, from times when you had met Horace and his wife Mary. This morning when you first espied Horace striding along Saginaw Street he was looking a bit grim, or so you imagined, and here at the McConnell's he still appears somewhat tight-lipped and withdrawn, not exactly the gregarious type. Come to think of it, for the Thurber's, both father and son, as well as Horace's three daughters, these days must be especially trying—the McConnell's reception is the first social engagement they have attended since Mary died, only six weeks ago, and everyone is pleased to see Horace and Daniel again in public life. You've overhead a few exchanges where people have offered condolences and encouragement. And here you have Morgan Drake complimenting Horace on his store's fine new look, which you glean is

---

77 "Lamah rag'shu goyim": translated from Hebrew, "Why do the nations rage?" Psalm 2, verse 1.

the result of a project to replace the roof and add a few enhancements on the building's exterior.

The polite deference being afforded to Horace is noteworthy, given what you've heard about his reputation and past frictions experienced by several people. Horace's political history as a democrat in a town that is becoming more and more republican could only be discouraging. You know that several years ago he ran for the office of state senator, unsuccessfully, and there were scathing attacks in the newspaper leveled against him, accusing him of being pro-slavery and politically corrupt, and allegedly skimming money from public funds for railroad development while he was county treasurer. Perhaps Horace's involvement in local real estate transactions, and careful management of his hardware company's finances (that is, strict credit terms and collections) would inevitably result in some parties feeling slighted, victimized by Thurber as if by an Ebenezer Scrooge character. But regardless of selected enmities, there is no denying Thurber's status as a major proponent for the town's expansion. His friend Mayor Thatcher is also a democrat, and you can see how Horace's son Daniel might be fostering closer relations by securing a position over at the town hall.

Horace Thurber

Here in the yard, meanwhile, the chatty socializing is still going strong. You have your shrub in hand, and in the fluctuating ebb and flow of company you find yourself next standing with two of the schoolgirls, Horace's daughter Sarah and her friend Fannie Mathews. You remind Sarah that you saw her earlier, in the hall, with Molly Bacon and another friend, which Sarah doesn't really remember; and Fannie, when she first arrived in the Mathews Mill wagon, which likewise doesn't conjure up much of a response. Sarah listens patiently as you recount what you know about the extended Thurber clan, how they still reside in the Monroe area, south of Detroit, where they first settled in Michigan, but when you remark in jest how she must assuredly be well chaperoned by aunts and uncles in the vicinity, her only response is to glance at Fannie and then look back at you, unimpressed, and answer, "Yes, sir." This leaves an awkward pause, so you proceed to inquire about the girls' school life at their two female seminaries, Fannie at Cleveland and Sarah at Monroe. Even though the two girls would clearly prefer to mingle with just about anyone younger than you, especially any of the "young lions" nearby the porch, nevertheless you have touched upon an agreeable topic, apparently. The girls glance at each other enthusiastically and then launch into describing their dormitory rooms, their routines and rules; and rapid listings of their classes, which actually surprise you somewhat for their practicality, having a good dosage of sciences, civics, and health upkeep. It would be nice to delve further into the seriousness of this level of education, but here you realize that your discourse has burdened these youngsters long enough, and so with congenial laughs and a nice-to-meet-you they both graciously slip away towards . . . wherever.

Ah, well. That's enough of trying to catch a dialogue with younger sons and daughters, elusive as ever. The insights about the school programs are interesting. In any event the yard activity is winding down, as you perceive how the yard occupants are beginning to ebb towards the house for a last round of goodbyes before departure. You can lower your emptied cup now, and find a place to set to it down on one of the tables, and then find a place for yourself in line with the others. Our parting words on the way out may be heartfelt, or courtly, but it's all been great fun, never mind those base imprecations uttered by that intrusive newspaperman at the beverage table. He seems to have disappeared anyway.

A MEASURE TAKEN

"TIME TO go, Carrie."* Mayor Erastus Thatcher had waited for a break in the conversation that his niece was having with Julia Comstock and her uncle Elkanah, before walking up to make an interjection while smoothly preempting Elkanah's attention with a handshake. Carrie and Julia looked at each other with weak smiles to reflect their disappointment, although it was clear that the party was winding down, and Elkanah probably needed to begin his ritual of cursory goodbyes to as many friends and associates as he might during his exit.

"Very good, Erastus, you'd better get your niece back to her post at Crawford's. Oh, and be sure to get in touch with me soon about our arrangements for graduation. I trust Hizzoner will have some worthy words for an address to this year's crop."

"Count on me, sir," the Mayor replied with a reassuring nod. Carrie noticed that her uncle already held his hat in his other hand, ready to depart.

Elkanah was still grasping the Erastus' hand as he smiled to Carrie and added, "They're all going to miss you, young lady, next year at the school from what I hear."

Elkanah was the superintendent of schools in Pontiac and it wouldn't matter to him whether Crawford's shop was already closed for the day, obviously. Carrie only needed to accept the compliment with a promise not to be a stranger, her reply coming as gracefully as only natural for her, and all smiled and left it at that, having no reason to complicate things with opinions on the very uncertain prospects for any eighteen-year-old single woman after high school, beyond working part-time in a candy store. And so the company parted, their see-you-soon's cheerfully said, and Elkanah headed back to the table to fetch his top hat while Julia went to join her seminary classmates who had gathered on the porch with an intent to maneuver the college boys into a last round of socializing inside the house before everyone would be called away.

And Carrie was left standing with her Uncle Erastus, who like El-kanah should also be taking the opportunity for some "glad-handing" as he left the party. The expected rout would be to make his way up to the porch and into the McConnells' living room, ultimately saying goodbye to the host and hostess in the hallway by the front door. But Carrie was curious to see her uncle appear rather ambivalent to all that normal protocol, as he suggested instead that they may as well leave straight from the yard and cross over Church Street to retrieve his pha-eton for the drive home.

He's worried about getting me home late, and what Mother will have to say, she thought. True, there was no cause for embarrassment about leaving work for a social event at the McConnell's. In any event she wouldn't be home much later than as if she had walked from Craw-ford's as usual. *Why would any of this be some big secret?*

A minute or so later, having signified their departure with a few silent nods and smiles to various acquaintances in the yard, uncle and niece fell in with several other couples who began crossing the Mc-Connells' front lawn. Making their way to the front gate they had to skirt around the lower branches of a flowering crab tree, where the fragrance of the blossoms was still a delight for anyone passing nearby. The lingering aroma would distract them only for a moment, however, as Erastus and Carrie made their way to the gate and down the steps to the private lane, then further down to Church Street to cross over to the carriage park on the other side. Erastus was keeping his eyes looking ahead as he mused aloud, smiling.

"So, Miss Caroline Holley, I understand you brought a bottle of wine to this august occasion—good initiative on your part, I must say."

Carrie heard the sarcastic edge to his tone. "No, no, not at all! The wine was just a delivery for a customer from the store, well, actually he bought it at Turk's and just wanted it delivered along the candies he bought from me."

"Uh-huh," Erastus answered in affirmation, though evincing some skeptical amusement.

They began crossing the street, and Carrie didn't try to explain any further, coping with the alarming thought that she had made some sort of faux pas without realizing it. *The wine? It was just a delivery. Is that such a scandal? And this is why I'm being ushered away like some misbehaving child!*

"Oh, no, not to worry," Erastus added, sensing his niece's apprehension. "I know you were just bringing a bottle to, uh, make things legitimate. Truth be told, I was impressed by the ploy. You'd make a good politician. Runs in the family, after all."

The compliment didn't help. Then again, the delivery from Turk's was a ploy to come to the reception unobtrusively, albeit uninvited—her uncle was right about that. Also, she had been berating herself for her reluctance to join her friends in the family room party, an extra measure which would have been a little forward, perhaps. But now she felt reassured that her caution was justified, after hearing her uncle's chiding remarks about the wine. Yes, it was just as well she stayed in the yard.

"Uncle Erry, why did we have to leave so quickly?"

They had reached the carriage park across the street, and Erastus stopped to. He wanted to say something, and Carrie could sense that a peremptory remark was coming, that her uncle was somewhat bothered by the question and only meant to put the topic to rest, counting on his niece to understand. He waved a hand by the side of his face as if to brush away a mosquito.

"Anyway, you need to be careful around holier-than-thou Baptist types like the Comstock's. Elkanah—we needn't worry about him, as he's seen enough of the world to take a joke. But a do-gooder like Julia might draw all sorts of untoward conclusions."

Trailing a few steps behind her uncle, Carrie rolled her eyes sarcastically. There was nothing bad about Julia Comstock being a Baptist, for heaven's sake. *You needn't worry about my friends like that. We're more grown up than you think.*

But then Uncle Erry came to the point:

"Carrie, your mother and I . . . we just don't want you to get your hopes up, you see, trying to fit in with the swells.[78] No odds, you see."

Now the girl started to grasp the meaning of all of this. The matter wasn't the wine. It wasn't her formal dress and it wasn't about missing an appointment at the daguerreotype studio. It was all about Danny Thurber. *Society crowd? I shouldn't try to fit in with the society crowd! What is my uncle talking about?* Carrie felt a sudden wave of exasperation. *Should I be embarrassed?—no, there is no reason for that.* Two things came to mind: one, her uncle couldn't understand her feelings,

---

78   The swells: high society.

and two, she needed to have a serious talk with her mother. And then three, there was no use arguing about this with Uncle Erry for now.

One more worrisome thought arrested all her attention: had she put off Danny by showing up in the McConnells' yard?

Carrie and her uncle now stood at the makeshift entrance to the carriage park, along with a few other guests, and before them a small group of stablehands stood ready to go and lead out a carriage as requested. There were some twenty carriages arranged in the park, a few of them in short rows but most of them randomly stationed. The idea was to have the stablehands do the retrievals so that the guests might avoid stepping on anything indelicate in the grassy expanse.

As the two of them stood waiting, Erastus turned away for a moment to greet a man sitting on horseback at a standstill nearby, who had been quietly surveying the park and the people coming across from the house. It was Clark Beardslee, the county sheriff, a lean, taciturn man in his fifties, wearing a bowler hat and seated as self-composed as always on the saddle of a red roan.

"Mister Beardslee," the Mayor called out, touching a finger to the brim of his hat.

"Your Honor," came the reply. The two men nodded to each other, and with this one succinct communication it was confirmed that the public security of the McConnells' prestigious event had been duly monitored as anyone might expect. Carrie likewise turned towards the sheriff and he nodded to her as well, recognizing her as a friend of his son Henry in the same class at the Union School; in response she made an impromptu curtsy, a reflexive motion that she instantly regretted, berating herself for acting like a simple schoolgirl in her fancy dress. Probably no one else noticed her curtsy, but the embarrassment would make her resolve not to say anything about the wine, or her friends, or fitting in with the 'swells'.

Erastus was trying to catch someone's eye to make a request for his carriage, until one of the hands who was leading up someone else's horse called out to a colleague behind him, "Yo there, balloon man! Customer waiting."

Whereupon the other man stopped his tending to a nearby team of horses hitched to a four-wheel coach, and stepped towards Erastus and Carrie, his eyebrows raised in expectation for their request.

"Balloon man?" Erastus asked instead, amused.

The man smirked in return, good naturedly. "Don't pay no mind that foozler[79], sir."

"But you like balloons? You know about ballooning?"

The first stablehand called over, "Oh, he's a first-class *aeronaut*, he is."

Again the balloon man smiled at Erastus to explain, "He's an old friend, just helping. I'm in charge here."

This made Erastus raise his eyebrows, too. "Oh? I see. You work for the McConnell's, then?"

"Some time now. I take care of the horses, the wagons. And the greenhouse."

"And you are . . . ?"

"Jackson, yes sir. I can read. That's how I learn about aeronauts, especially Professor Lowe."

"Aha—Professor Lowe[80]." Erastus was nodding his head, and paused for a few seconds, as if he had an idea about Jackson's interest in balloons. Carrie looked down and muttered an "oh, no" to herself imperceptibly, still sullen about her uncle's obnoxious remark about not being fit for top society. How typical of him to strike up an off-hand

---

79 Foozler: a clumsy person; a bungler.

80 Thaddeus Lowe, a self-educated "professor," had completed a balloon voyage a month before, widely publicized, having launched in Cincinnati and landed in South Carolina. Although the Civil War had just been declared, the local southerners who had captured Lowe after his descent resolved to let the professor return to Cincinnati, having recognized him as a non-combatant civilian scientist—and not a spy.

conversation with a stablehand. Like any mayor, anywhere, he would talk to anybody at any time. This could get tiresome. *Let's just go home.*

"Tell me, Jackson, do you know who I am?"

"I know you're Mayor Thatcher, sir. Your honor."

"Very good. Let me tell *you* something, then. Perhaps you would be interested in making some extra money, working for me on a city matter. It involves balloons."

Jackson straightened his back and steadied his eyes on the mayor, and waved downward with his right hand to call off his friend who was already walking off, anyway, toward the wagon of another guest. "Sure. What can I do for you?"

"Well, Mr. Jackson, here's the story. Are you also familiar with Michigan's own aeronaut Professor Bannister?"

"Oh, yes, of course, your Honor. Professor Bannister flew from Adrian to New York, few years back."

Erastus was growing steadily more encouraged by Jackson's response. "New York, yes, well, Buffalo anyway. Didn't end well for Bannister's assistant, did it?"

"I know the story, yes sir."

"Well, as it turns out, Professor Bannister is coming to pay us a visit here in Pontiac. He still lives in Adrian, and I happen to be a friend of the mayor of Adrian—who, by the way, runs a big dry goods store down there, just like McConnell and Bacon—and he told me that the Professor is looking to find someone to build a special wagon for his balloon supplies, actually to carry the gas he uses to fill his balloons. And as you know, that's something we do here in Pontiac, we make wagons."

Jackson shifted his posture, still listening very intently. He couldn't make out what the Mayor had in mind for him. Carrie appeared to be listening, too, although her mind was now recounting all of her behavior at the party. By now she was convinced that she had made a complete fool of herself in front of all of Daniel's friends.

Erastus went on: "Thing is, I believe Professor Bannister is also in need of assistants who can help him with the equipment for operating his business, that is, setting everything up for a launch, that sort of thing. And all the men he had in Adrian are all going off to join the army, leaving him without any trained workers, you see?"

Jackson was stunned by this prospect. "You think he would train me? Oh, I know I could man the balloon, sure."

"So, first off, you know horses and wagons, don't you?"

"Top man for that, your Honor."

"And you're not married, are you? And McConnell could let you go work for short periods with Bannister, wouldn't he?"

"Oh, yes sir. He'll let me." This conversation was not the time or place to be mentioning Martha Parker.

"Then it might work out. Do this, then. Ask Mr. McConnell if you could take some time away next Wednesday afternoon to meet with us at Willard Palmer's wagon shop. Tell him you need to do this for the mayor. And tell him that Mayor Henry Hart from Adrian will be there, too."

"I know the shop. I'll be there, your Honor."

"Done. See you then."

The conversation had ended, but Jackson remained standing there anyway.

"Um, we'll need the phaeton, over there, with the bay horse."

"Oh, yes sir. Right away!" Jackson turned and hurried off to bring the phaeton.

Carrie and Erastus watched, and presently Carrie felt her worries about the party easing, in comparison to the stablehand's interest in balloons which was itself interesting. And this might be a good time to sound attentive and say something encouraging. "I think I know

Mr. Jackson," she said, "from his coming into Crawford's on errands. Daniel says he's a good man. He came to the McConnell's a runaway."

"Not surprising." Erastus inhaled a breath and nodded as he looked at his niece and mulling over his plans for next week.

"Uncle Erry, what was that all about?"

"Oh, just a vision I have. I would love to see a big balloon launch taking place in Pontiac, and I think we should try to impress Bannister to bring his balloon here. We have the county fairgrounds with plenty of space for a big crowd. Wouldn't it be a grand sight—thousands of spectators flocking in to watch an ascension in Pontiac just like in Adrian and Detroit?"

"Of course." Carrie hid her grin by looking away, amused and impressed by her uncle's devising yet another scheme to promote the city. "But the fairgrounds are all taken up with the army camp," she suggested.

"True. But we could also stage a launch right here in this field, for that matter. I've also heard that Bannister couldn't get the quality gas he needed in Detroit, and I should think that Horace Thurber and his group could provide good stuff from their new works over at the Circus Grounds. I don't know much about this special supply wagon that Bannister wants, but I'm sure Willie Palmer could put something together for him. Or maybe Charley Parsons. So we'll see. We'll see."

Jackson brought up the phaeton, leading the horse by the halter, and Erastus and Carrie climbed aboard. Erastus took the reins and exchanged a nod with Jackson that meant to convey "see you on Wednesday," and the phaeton pulled out onto Church Street, turning right to head back to Saginaw. By now there were many other carriages in front of the McConnells' house waiting to pick up passengers, making for slow progress until the phaeton had cleared the congestion. Carrie was seated on the left side of the seat such that she could peer directly over the groups of guests still milling about in front of the house. She caught sight of the Thurbers—Daniel and his sister Sarah, and their grim-faced father Horace—but she was hesitant to call out to them. And nearby was Lewis Drake, talking with Fannie Mathews. Then she espied Julia Comstock, who was standing with Malvina Taylor, both of them all smiles and wide open eyes and waving back fitfully.

And so for Carrie Holley the main event of the day was over, her part in it anyway. The phaeton slowly pulled away from the McConnells' house, and their yard, and Carrie's friends, and all the rapture of moving about among such gracious guests. A sigh, a smile, a last look back at the house. One more errand needed attention, to return home still wearing the dress and explain things to her mother. This should not be too difficult, but whatever scolding might ensue wouldn't matter, not on this day. Besides, her uncle would be there to help smooth things over. What did matter above all else was that she had managed to see Danny Thurber at the party, and speak with him, and be seen by him in this dress. That much had been accomplished. Now it would be acceptable, when the two of them met again, to speak of matters closer to heart. It was only a matter of devising a next time.

"Uncle Erry, are you going to hire Daniel Thurber for the summer?"

"Yes, that's what I'm thinking. Do you know whether he'll enlist in the army?"

"No! I mean, no he won't."

"Well, the young man certainly shows promise."

"I hope he stays."

"I know you do. Remember, Carrie, the Thurber's are still in mourning."

Carrie nodded in agreement to show that she understood, and looking back at the McConnells' house she was feeling happier with the way everything had turned out. Really, could this day have been any better? She saw that Julia and Malvina had stopped their funny waving; in fact, the two of them were now talking with, with . . . Danny Thurber. What was he doing? Carrie watched as Danny quickly strode past the girls and hopped down onto the street, evidently intent on catching up to her Uncle Erry's phaeton. She touched her uncle's arm, who looked around and then straightaway pulled up the reins to come to a complete stop. In a few seconds Danny was standing next to the carriage on Carrie's side.

The young man was all smiles. He waited to speak while he caught his breath.

"Mayor Thatcher, may I address Caroline?"

Erastus only nodded back, grinning and gesturing with an open hand towards his niece, clearly satisfying the protocol for Daniel to continue, which he did, turning to her directly. "Carrie, my father would like to invite you to a dinner at our home, later this month. You and your mother and father. We, I, we still need to agree on the date."

"Of course, Daniel, we would love to come!"

"Good. It's settled, then. I'll tell Father."

Erastus couldn't help but lean in: "Let them know the date as soon as you can."

"Yes, of course. How shall I . . . "

Carrie understood the hesitation and said, "Come see me at Crawford's. That would be easiest. I'll be working there next on Saturday afternoon."

Daniel nodded yes, enthusiastically. "Yes, I will. Wonderful. You know, my family is just starting to come alive again."

"I see that," Carrie agreed, with a patient smile.

A few seconds of silence followed, until Erastus announced, "Well—off we go, then!" The phaeton started to pull away, and Carrie and Daniel waved each other goodbye.

There were still other carriages around them, heading in the same direction, but the phaeton made it through to the open street soon enough, and Carrie finally turned around to sit forward in her seat as Erastus allowed the bay to clip along at a slow trot.

A minute later Erastus spoke up again. "So, how about that? *Deus ex machina*—you're never ready for it. But there it is: your bold *inamorato* [81] wants your company for dinner, mother and father in tow."

"My bold *what*?"

"He's a good lad, if a tad impulsive. I'll tell you what. How about if I arrange for just you and me to make that dinner date? I'm sure there'll be a business matter or two for me to discuss with Horace Thurber over a fine meal."

"Yes, over a fine meal," she replied, absently, still completely dumbfounded by the conversation that had just taken place, and Daniel's invitation to the Thurber home for dinner. How direct and assertive he was, as her father would call it, "a fine measure of a man." Would it be all right to talk about this with Emma Adams and Fannie Pittman on the way to school tomorrow morning? No, too soon, she should keep it to herself until the date was set and everything was arranged formally.

Both uncle and niece sat quietly, watching the houses pass by, thinking back on all they had seen, and said, at the party in the yard. Cicadas in the trees overhead provided a steady, high-pitch hum to entice a leisurely mood in the late afternoon air. Erastus was satisfied with the idea of inviting himself over to Horace Thurber's house, taking his niece along for good measure. He also had it in mind to summon the newspaperman Myron Howell to the balloon meeting on Wednesday. Carrie for her part was thinking how she might refrain from mentioning the Thurber invitation to Emma and Fannie. No doubt her friends would need to hear all about the Cleveland girls and their flimsy frocks so boldly exhibited—"lacking in definition," her mother would say, even for our high-spirited times. *What on earth are they learning at*

81 Inamorato: a man in love. Inamorata: a woman in love.

those seminaries? And where did they find those summer dresses—Detroit, must be.

Truth be told, it's always more fun share dreams with like-minded people.

Cleantha McConnell

The reception? All told, I think we did very well. We had to prepare quickly, especially to get all the invitations out, but the affair itself wasn't really all that elaborate, not much more than a few tables set up in the yard. Providence had granted us good weather, praise God. And my cook and the maid were both absolutely indispensable for making the dishes and drinks, and I'm satisfied with how it all went. Joe and his group came through with the oratory, and Reverend Greene arrived in time, and Cousin Sarah didn't insult anyone, and there weren't any serious altercations over in the drawing room, as far as I've heard. Out in the yard there were a few faces I couldn't recognize, and there was that misfit friend of Levi Bacon nosing around, but no harm done. You have to trust people.

So it went well. And wouldn't you know it — everybody came. The secret is: stage your event when everyone is so pent up that they're ready to celebrate anything. We have now done our part for the social season, and I don't see another reception here until the war is over, when we all welcome Joseph home again, I'd say next summer before he goes to his next assignment. He's enlisted for three years, you see. By then I would expect Colonel Richardson will have made Joseph an officer. Imagine my son a commissioned officer! The first ever for this McConnell clan in America.

We have been making history here. We built this town, we are building our church, and we will free the slaves, with God's help. These are no longer just dreams. This is our legacy, our descendants' legacy, set forth by all of Pontiac's pioneers that you saw gathered at the McConnell house on a fine spring afternoon. I pray that our children will understand how they are a part of it, already, and will prove as worthy.

A landau carriage

A VISITOR'S STORY,
"Return to the Hodges"

GUESTS ARE beginning to disperse back towards the house, some towards the front entrance, others ascending onto the porch and into the living room. The party is winding down. The younger folk disappear first, rapidly, surely looking to re-congregate inside and enjoy some last minutes away from parents, who are still making their way to return their glasses and shrub cups to the tables. Overall the timing is good—as the afternoon daylight starts to wane, gnats and gallinippers[82] are already coming back to reclaim the yard. You're not surprised to notice someone's hand waving before their face, or hear somewhere a slap on someone's neck accompanied by a mild imprecation amid the conversations around you. Now unencumbered of cup and napkin, and in step with the crowd's gradual migration towards the house, you encounter once again Hervey Coke Parke—and has he enjoyed the reunion with family? "Oh, yes," he smiles, and he asks for a quick moment to turn around and say a few words to one of the younger

82 Gallinipper: mosquito.

men still on the porch, apparently confirming arrangements for a ride home. He turns back to you to resume with "Yes, it appears to have been a most successful afternoon." You both know his true meaning, in that you were alluding as much to business contacts as to family—"Yes, it's been a fine visit with everyone." You append another polite inquiry about the new shoes: are the balmorals cooperating?—this is met with a low groan and grimace, so you both acknowledge his predicament with resigned shrugs, together. As the two of you edge along with the crowd it might be a suitable moment to learn more about Hervey's family and his years up in Keweenaw at the copper companies.

The tact pays off. Hervey seems to appreciate your cordial tone, and there is after all some time for "how it all began" stories, albeit briefly, starting with his father Ezra arriving in Oakland County a year behind the Captain. Ezra was the very first doctor to practice in this region, and in those early days he also served as post-master and the town clerk, and started the Methodist Episcopal Church here in Pontiac. His wife Rhoda, Hervey's mother, was renowned throughout the county for her singing at church services and other occasions. In due course the couple built a fine home in Birmingham, some six miles south of here down the Saginaw Trail, and there they raised their six children. This was the prosperous life, but it all ended abruptly when both Ezra and Rhoda died in an epidemic of erysipelas[83] fifteen years ago in the winter of '46; since then, the family has dissipated about the country, Hervey and Cornelia north to Hancock, and Hervey's three brothers off to California. His younger sister Sarah Abigail, who was showing us the garden earlier, is the only sibling still in Pontiac, although she herself will likely be moving soon to Washington to rejoin her husband, a certain Mr. French.

You surmise that there is no use in asking Hervey about Ben French, based on what you heard about from Abiram McConnell ear-

---

83 Erysipelas: an acute skin infection.

lier, so you ask him about his new business, and it's nice to see his face brighten in response as he rejoins with a "yes, Parke & Rainey Hardware" and, raising a finger as if quoting a company slogan, "servicing all the copper mines in Keweenaw." The full story is that after ten years in Clifton (a little settlement by "The Cliff" mining operation), he was ready to remove to a larger commercial center like Hancock and Houghton, twin towns growing rapidly on opposite sides of the Keweenaw waterway. And then last year he returned to Pontiac briefly when he proposed to Fannie Hunt, the daughter of the late U.S. Congressman James Bennett Hunt. (Ah, now you begin to perceive that Hervey's new bride—from a well-to-do Michigan family—would probably enjoy life much more in Hancock-Houghton than in the wind-swept wilds of Clifton . . .) So, now

Hervey Coke Parke

things are coming along very well. He cocks his head to you sideways to remark on how Hancock is much more civilized, and growing rapidly, a lot like a Pontiac. It will do nicely for his wife and child, and in terms of business prospects the success of his venture almost assured.

You nod back in agreement. Well, certainly he must know the region thoroughly after all those years. Really, ten years? With a quick laugh Hervey admits that life was bit crude out there, in a land of hard-drinking, roughneck miners. A good number of them immigrants from Finland, too. "I'm not sure the Know-Nothings[84] would

---

84 Know-Nothings: a reactionary political movement that was both xenophobic for its stance against immigrants especially Irish Catholics, and progressive in its advocacies of abolition, labor conditions, and women's rights. From its formative times as a secret society, if the members were asked whether they adherents to this cause, they were advised to reply "I know nothing."

feel that comfortable about it," he adds with a grin. (Yes, you can imagine.) But then he surprises you with an anecdote about how he and some colleagues actually established a small Episcopal Church parish in Clifton, some years back, (starting churches being a family tradition, it strikes you), although now it seems unlikely to remain active for much longer. There simply aren't that many Episcopalians in the town, except for a few managers hired from Cornwall, England, who are practicing Anglicans. But almost all of the miners working out there are Catholics, coming from Irish and French Canadian families. Grinning here with a small gesture of that-was-that resignation, Hervey finishes by noting how, on the whole, he didn't mind "roughing it" too much, and he greatly enjoyed building his career in managing the finances and business relationships for the big companies forming in that area.

Hervey suggests that you come up to see him and Fannie in Hancock sometime this summer. "You know," he adds, "it's only a 2-day trip from Port Huron. The passage is quite pleasant, by steamship on the lakes, and especially easy now that the canal locks are operating at Sault Sainte Marie, connecting Lake Huron with Lake Superior. And the weather in Keweenaw is wonderfully refreshing—not so humid and stuffy as in Oakland in the summertime. And, there are far fewer mosquitos pestering you up there in the cooler air !"

The two of you have been following along with those guest who have chosen the route up the stairs to the porch to re-enter the house. Once on the porch this "recessional" movement is impeded by funneling through the door into the living room, although this affords more time for mingling and greetings, and this interlude is now being enhanced by the sound of piano music emanating from the conservatory inside—someone is playing patriotic tunes to accompany the singing of a few talented guests. Ernest renditions of "Hail, Columbia" and "God Save the Union" regale and will surely bolster the spirit of everyone seeing off Sergeant McConnell, and Colonel Richardson, to The Call. You overhear Elkanah Comstock behind you affirming to another guest that his granddaughter Julia is leading the chorus.

Watch out there !—a deft sidestep and you dodge a couple of the children, Clettie Kelsey and Freddie McConnell, on their way slipping back through the crowd to go fetch dishes from the yard (likely complying with an elder's suggestion as a means to earn more dessert treats in the kitchen). Hervey calls after Clettie to be more careful, but she's already disappearing down the porch steps. It brings to mind once again a comparison of the two young cousins, Clettie Kelsey and Molly Bacon, their lives and futures, both of them granddaughters of the pioneering Parke brothers, two girls who had lost their mothers early in life. You ask Hervey whether Marquis Kelsey ever arrived at the party, and Hervey only shrugs to reply that, no, Kelsey must still be working. You mean to ask another question, about his experience with medicinal herbs, but just then the piano music changes to a rendition of "Oh! Susanna" which evokes a few catcalls from people around you in the hall. ("No southern music allowed!" and "Stop that now!"). Are the protests only in fun? You call out: "That's not Dixie! That's Stephen Foster, you know, he's from Pittsburgh. He's a northerner!" But a man turns back to glare at you, and replies, "Then he shouldn't be writing songs about Alabama, should he!" *Good gracious, the man is serious,* you're thinking, and you opt to nod your head in acquiescence.

Abiram McConnell, the doctor, now sidles in to join your conversation, and he wants to know how Hervey's brothers are faring in their goldrush in California. You learn that, as it turns out, they're not panning for gold but they're all in Nevada for the silver, at the Comstock Lode mining boom. Not silver miners themselves, they've been selling mining supplies for a few years in Virginia City and doing quite well. Abiram rejoins that he understands the copper business in Keweenaw isn't too bad either, drawing a smile from Hervey, and aren't those Ezra Parke boys quite the adventurers after all. Hervey remarks on how different the life is up there, in Keweenaw, with most people still preoccupied with the mining and building, whereas his return to Pontiac immerses him back into "war fever" and all the tension and preparations going on here for the impending march on the South. Again, the war talk. Abiram agrees that it has all gone too far, for his liking, and you would have thought we could abolish slavery through peaceful progress, without splitting the country.

"But now," he goes on, "you have John Brown and his maniacs in Harper's Ferry rousing up the entire South, and free-staters out west are actually running around shooting people . . . I guess everyone's spoiling for a fight. Lincoln wants 75,000 men – that's a lot. Can we really afford that? I don't think the entire nation sent half as many troops down to Mexico. Well, whatever happens, it shouldn't take long for the army to march into those "confederate" states and root out the rabble-rousers and settle this thing quickly. Richardson is a good man and should keep our boys out of too much trouble. I'm sure Willard would like to see his son safely back in college after it's over."

You hadn't meant to change the topic but now there's little opportunity left to ask these gentlemen about something still on your mind:

"Say, I was wondering whether Clettie's father Marcus ever made it to the party. Did either of you see him?"

Hervey and Abiram glance at each other, and Hervey shakes his head no. Abiram sees fit to clear his throat, for effect, and suggest that "You might want to ask Sarah Abigail just to make sure." You notice Hervey throwing a stern look at Abiram. That's it, then—you may conclude that Mr. Kelsey and Mrs. French are involved, in some manner. It may be a minor mystery worth pursuing, later perhaps. For now, however, you should just maintain an unknowing, pleasant look.

When you finally reach the inside of the living room you spend another minute or milling about, and then decide to drift away from Hervey and make your way towards the hallway and around towards the conservatory. And while passing through, you're gratified to see that Levi made the party, too, now chatting with the Captain and Mercy in the parlor opposite. But first here's a chance to peek into the conservatory and observe most of the younger set gathered by the spinet, ably played by Fannie Mathews, Lewis Drake at her side, Stuart Draper and Julia Comstock singing in duet, Daniel Thurber and Carrie Holley together, looking on. The song is quieter than the rousing numbers they played earlier. You recognize the tune "Cora Dean," simple and easily melodic, standard fare for Stephen Foster, and apparently not bothersome to northern sentiments. This is Foster's latest popular release, and Stuart and Julia have to read the lyrics off of the sheet music on the spinet as they sing along. A moment: this scene strikes you as wonderfully sentimental, a tableau surely to last in nostalgic memory. How does that old phrase go?—few things are as peaceful as a late-afternoon sunray dappled and swirling in the window of a well-furnished room.

But you catch yourself gazing, and turn back towards the front entrance thinking time-to-go, and say your goodbyes, and thanks and congratulations to Willard and Cleantha. The Captain and Mercy receive you next; they are gracious but perhaps a bit fatigued, understandably; a few genteel words and a deferential handshake suffice to move you along. At this point only a few departing guests remain, and in short order you have your own turn at the threshold with Joseph, finally, to grasp his hand and wish him all the best. Up close, now, you realize how confident he is, as he looks at you briefly, straight in the eye, and thanks you for coming. His nod and smile are polite enough, but there is no hiding a more serious nature and ambition. You turn and proceed out the door, convinced that Joseph McConnell is fully capable of that military valor which will doubtless enhance the legacy of his proud family.

Well, that's that. Out the door, and here you are abruptly alone, moving along among all the guests heading down the front walk and out onto the street. You have had a most satisfying time, and surely in the pleasant evening ahead you will enjoy reminiscing over the party, and new friends made, and interesting things said. Judging from what you hear around you, most everyone shares your favorable opinion. So: it is only 5:45 and still bright outdoors as you turn down Church Street back towards town to the Hodges House. Half an hour more on foot and you'll be relaxing back in your room.

Back in the street there are several carriages waiting, single rigs probably rented from the liveries, and many people are milling about, saying goodbye and making their way in and around the horses and carriages. Other guests have crossed the street to the field opposite where the McConnell's had arranged a livery park for the party. At the moment there is one carriage, a phaeton, that has just exited the field and is slowly passing from right to left to get around the clogged area, and you can see that its two passengers are Mayor Thatcher and Carrie Holley. Carrie is waving at someone nearby you, evidently, and you try to catch her attention, but to no avail. Best not to shout out, anyway, which would be deemed a bit uncouth. The phaeton clatters away down the street and you watch as Carrie turns back around in her seat.

But now you hear a familiar voice calling out your name from further down the street—it's Emma Bacon, Levi's wife, seated in a large open carriage, ostensibly waiting her husband's return from his own brief call at the house. You draw closer to say hello, and you recognize Emma's step-daughter Molly as she is climbing onto the rear seat. Now alongside, your greetings can be exchanged and Emma asks where you are staying in town. "Hodges House." "Oh, well, we'll be passing right by it! We're on our way to visit my family home in Waterford for the evening, so we'll be leaving town on Huron . . ." and she insists that you accept a ride back with them as far as Hodges House. Well now, this is a welcome gesture—"Why thank you, Mrs. Bacon! Gladly!" She directs you to step up to the driver's bench to sit there with her brother Richard Whitehead, evidently the teamster for this ride, who is holding the reins to the two horses hitched in front. Richard obligingly lends you a hand to grab on your way up, while Emma explains how the carriage seats will soon be full of friends and family. Oh, not a problem at all, you assure everyone. It's good to be resting your tired feet, after an afternoon of walking and standing, and . . .

But your words are preempted by the arrival of Levi who jumps in and settles next to Emma. "Well, hello there again my friend!" he offers in delighted surprise, upon his wife's introduction for you. Levi is ready to say more, but Emma is asking him about Molly's friends and aren't they coming. "Yes, yes, my dear, right behind . . ." And sure enough two schoolgirls are soon running up to join the group, and step aboard to sit with Molly in the "vis-à-vis" front seat facing rearwards towards Levi and Emma. The result is much chatter and giggling emanating from all the passengers behind you, so for now you're content just to listen while you watch Richard start off his team in a slow turnaround to head back to Saginaw Street. With a quick glance back upon the passengers it brings a smile—how nice of the Bacon's to take you back to the hotel, actually a bit out of their way home, as their house is south of town, not far from Capt. Parke's old farmhouse. You catch a few words between Emma and Levi about "and how was Mr. McConnell"—yes, Willard was in fine form, and no, he has no time even to think about joining the Masons, busy as he with his new church. ("He did tell me that as long as I'm already a member in good standing, having at least one partner of McConnell & Bacon in the Masons should suffice for now.") You deduce from this that Levi is a Mason, presumably here in Pontiac—is there really a Masonic Temple in town? You'll have to remember to ask about this when you're back at the Hodges House.

With the team now underway towards home, you can turn to Richard and offer a tactful compliment on this very fine vehicle, with its smooth suspension and plush seats for the passengers. "A landau carriage, eh? Haven't seen many of these around here." Richard nods appreciatively but still looks forward upon his team. So you add, "Was it made here in Pontiac?" This evokes a little more response. Richard, still facing forward, casts a glance sidewise towards you, his eyebrows raised, as if to approve of your interest. "The body was made in Detroit, but everything underneath it was built in Pontiac. We put it all together over at Willard Palmer's." Impressive, in your opinion. Why not try to show off a little appreciation for the technology—and so you ask, casually, whether that might include a proper Ackermann steering with kingpins and tie-rod. Richard only glances back at you with a succinct 'mm-hmm' for a 'yes'. "Well," you conclude, "It's quite good." You're thinking back on the schoolgirls, how when they got into the carriage, were exhibiting a bit of wide-eyed enthusiasm at the prospect of having a ride in a large, comfy landau, pulled by a two-horse team. Richard sees fit to add: "Well, perhaps not the same luxury Queen Victoria expects, but we like it. The two top-folds are useful, especially in winter, unless you're the driver, you see. Yes, it is a smooth ride, suitable I should say, for my pregnant sister. She likes to get out and about on a nice day."

Fair enough. In your mind you can start to put together the events: the landau belongs to Levi's wife's family, the Whiteheads, who live over in Waterford, and judging by their carriage they are likely a family of some means. Evidently they have dispatched Richard to pick up Emma and Levi and Molly for an evening back in Waterford, with a detour to the McConnell's to allow Levi to drop by and make a short appearance. One last piece to cover: "Say, Richard, who are Molly's friends, back there with us?" Richard turns to take a brief look back, himself, at the folks (still having a jolly time of it back there) as he notes offhandedly "Um, those are a couple of the Taylor girls, neighbors of ours. Malvina and Libbie. They're schoolmates with Molly down in Cleveland."

So that's the whole story behind this errand. So, enough for now—no need to pester Richard with more questions. The ride down Church Street continues at a leisurely clop-clop pace, the passengers quieter now, the landau seeming to glide under the elms and maples. A mild amusement then: Richard pipes up with a couple of questions of his own for you. "Was Joe McConnell in uniform?" No, just regular attire. "Hmm," he says. This, followed by, "Was Sarah Thurber there?" Molly answers this one from behind, "Yes, I saw her with Fannie Mathews." "Hmm," again. Oh, you ask Richard, do you know Sarah? "I know her father." You hear Levi in the back telling Emma how he saw Horace Thurber briefly at the door. "I pity Horace," he adds, "burdened with all those beautiful daughters just now coming of age, and no mother to guide them."

Richard muses quietly on this idea, muttering something about the girls' older brother Daniel probably not going to help his father much in that predicament. "Daniel is busy with his own pursuits," he says to you, as an aside.

"Ah yes," you rejoin, "I met him back there at the house, with Mayor Thatcher and his niece Carrie Holley . . ."

"Is that right?" says Richard, some irony in his tone. You both agree, grinning.

"Well, I understand Daniel will be working for the Mayor this summer," you try to clarify Richard's idea of 'pursuits'.

"What's that about Dan Thurber?" asks Emma aloud, also catching the sudden attention of Molly and her friends. Her brother Richard only sloughs off the question, but Emma presses on to recommend to you that you should talk with Daniel some time, and that despite his serious disposition he can be quite charming, very sincere. She relates how Richard and Dan Thurber have been talking about joining a cavalry regiment if they get the chance—"*mes braves chevaliers!*" Richard complies with an off-hand remark about yes-I-love-horses, but as for you, what is becoming clear is that whatever the conversation, Emma Bacon is just fully enjoying the evening ride and a chance to catch some fresh air outdoors. And you recall how Mercy Parke had mentioned that Emma is expecting, this time for a fourth child.

"And Carrie Holley was there, too?" she asks aloud. "Beautiful girl. Captivating. I know her mother. That family's fortunes have had their share of ups and downs, but just when you'd think they would have fallen déclassé at last, John Holley seems to find a new way to keep the family afloat."

Richard responds, his eyes still on the horses, "Well, whatever her family status, a quality girl like that shouldn't be wasted on a 'gloomy Gus' like Danny Thurber." He spoke low enough not to be heard by the passengers behind him.

Levi has remained silent for a while, content to relax in the landau after another full day managing the store, but he still conveys a cheerful disposition and an easy manner. That irrepressible, pleasant tone emerges anew as he asks about how your visit to Pontiac is going, and whom you saw at the party. You run off a few names, and when Levi hears mention of the Darrow's he has to break in:

"Oh, so you met Frank Darrow? Say, was there any talk of Frank selling the old Sibley cabin on Lawrence? I hear he's selling it off to a shop worker! Can you imagine?"

Emma joins in, "Don't you know, that old cabin is the first home ever built in Pontiac, and it stands even today. I hope the new owners will take proper care of the place. It's almost a monument—it would be a shame to see it become run down." Levi adds "Indeed," and then remembers to ask you about the "long lost" cousin Hervey Parke, back from the Cliffs.

"Well, sir, there he is now," you say as you turn Levi's attention towards a carriage a few yards behind, and now the two of you exchange a formal nod with Hervey. He's seated next to the driver in a small shay. Levi turns frontwards again to inform you that the young man by Hervey is Charley Palmer's son, Charley Junior. Palmer?—you ask. "Oh yes," says Levi, "quite the upper crust family, for Pontiac anyway. The son studies at the University of Michigan—he must be home for the party. There's also a daughter, Virena. She just got married last November. Big, big wedding over at Zion Episcopal. I've heard that she's in the family way—if so, it may not be going well—she hasn't been seen around town for some time now. I've been thinking about going over to see the family. Are you still in town tomorrow? I'd be glad to introduce you, if you'd like to go along."

You thank Levi for the invitation but explain that you should put off meeting the Palmer's until next time. Everyone agrees: you've already met a multitude sufficient for one visit. Emma says something about Palmer being interested in the widow Myrick house, but at this point you would just as soon let the conversation to trail off, which it does, and you're glad to relax and just sit and listen to the simple rhythm of horse hooves hitting the street. There still is some tittering back and forth between Molly and Malvina, until Emma intervenes to find out what it is exactly that the girls are snickering about, and what you hear next quickly rouses your attention once again. Apparently during the party, when the young people were meeting in the family room there were spirits being served, secretly, and most of the people there were drinking them, and silly things were being said. Molly and Malvina deny participating in the scandal, of course, and Emma and Levi are amused enough to verify whether the girls meant to say *spirits*, or perhaps it was just *wine* they saw.

"So it must have been real wine," Malvina confesses. "In crystal glasses."

"Heavens!" exclaims Levi, feigning indignation for the girls' bene-fit. "And who might have brought a bottle of wine to this little caper?"

"Carrie Holley!" the girls reply in unison. Malvina adds, "Willard McConnell said he saw her putting the bottle on a table in the yard."

A brief pause ensues—Levi and Emma must be mulling over this bit of gossip. Richard then offers an explanation, "Well, now, perhaps Carrie was only making a delivery from a store in town. You know, Turk's is right next door to Crawford's where she works after school."

Another pause. The horse hooves continue their clip-clop rhythm while a cycle of buzzing from the cicadas rises and ebbs away. Malvina says, "So she came to the McConnell's from her work at Crawford's. But I thought her dress looked very fancy—not the sort of thing she would wear to school or to the candy shop." No one has anything to say further, until Emma muses aloud with "Hmm, the wine could have been someone's gift to the McConnell's, then. I suppose there's always one person on the guest list to make an uncouth gesture. They proba-bly knew full well that the bottle would be whisked away to the family room." Levi agrees, "In short order, I should think."

Meanwhile for you this entire dialog has triggered a chilling reve-lation that the true culprit here is: you. Your purchase of a fine Chau-tauqua wine for the party has turned to be an embarrassing faux pas, despite your best of intentions. With alarm you think back on all the things you said at the house—did you ever tell anyone about your gift? No, no, it would appear you never did. But it's now even more vexing to think that your cloddish gesture may have impugned the reputa-tion of an innocent schoolgirl! No, you think, the Bacon's aren't about to pin this on Carrie, and they're certainly not in conniptions about younger folks in the house falling prey to corrupting influences, either. No, it's all just a harmless amusement. Should you confess your crime? How dashed awkward this is. Glance over at Richard—no suspicion there. But you should say something, at least.

"Yes, I think so, too. Just someone's idea of a joke. War fever, I reckon."

Emma seconds the motion with "Yes, of course. Carrie's a good girl. Was she there in the family room gathering?"

"No, Ma'am. She wasn't," Molly answers.

"Of course not," you hear Richard add quietly to himself.

Case closed.

The houses slowly pass on either side, and you notice that Emma has turned to look back on you, just to give a reassuring smile, and you nod in return, just to affirm that it's a fine afternoon. Likewise with little Molly—the two of you exchange a brief smile, in passing, and you're moved to think back on Fannie Mathews and Sarah Thurber recounting their seminary classes, causing you to imagine entire classrooms of young women taking instruction in the sciences. For them a future could . . .—but now the loud snorting of a horse catches everyone's attention, and you all glance over at a surrey that is catching up on the left side, and Molly and Malvina excitedly wave hello and goodbye to their friend Emma Comstock as her family's carriage steadily outpaces the landau. "*Au revoir!*" they both cry out, in a playful show-off spirit.

The ride then becomes mostly quiet, except for the whispered chattering among Molly and the Taylor girls in the far back. Next to you Richard seems to have settled into deep contemplation, as he needs little effort to manage the reins at this point. You can relax, too, and let your thoughts drift over the names and faces you met today. It's the younger people who come to mind, first and foremost. You had set out originally to rekindle old relationships with the parents, but now you find yourself pondering over their children's generation. There are sons about to leave college studies to go to war, and there are daughters about to finish school and cast their fate to the vagaries of matchmaking. And today you caught a number of them right at the time when they're facing these very thresholds.

Consider the two friends Joseph McConnell and Daniel Thurber. Brought together at colleges and clubs, both are scions of large, well-to-do families, and both appear to be quite serious about pursuing the honorable life, whether it leads to the army or to city politics. Interesting, though, the political differences of their fathers, one Republican, one Democrat, undoubtedly hovering over the two boys in these times that can be so divisive. And what of the prospects for all those "seminary" girls, coming out of school just when all the boys will leave for the army. You remember your talk with Fannie Mathews and Sarah Thurber, and how you espied them gazing up at the boys on the porch making the speeches. Gazing—perhaps more like *evaluating*. Will anyone be exchanging wartime letters with Sergeant McConnell? Oh, it can't be helped, such it is, the age-old sport of matchmaking. You smile in spite of your own conceit, and you lean your head back to gaze up at the branches of a beech tree passing directly overhead. But after all, Sarah Thurber is the sister of Joe McConnell's best friend Danny, isn't that so? And Danny Thurber certainly was all eyes for Carrie Holley, and she for him. Danny and Carrie, then. That's the most obvious.

Clip clop, clip clop. The landau slowly passes the little schoolhouse near the corner with Saginaw Street and starts to make its turn towards the town center. But Richard brings the team to a stop, which causes everyone in the back to look up. Strange—no other wagons are on Saginaw along this stretch. There is no need for anyone to ask why Richard stopped, as the obvious reason is a commotion going on, down the street to our left, where several people are rushing out onto Saginaw out from the railroad lane, and just at that moment we can all hear a "pop, pop, pop" noise, and Richards says aloud, "Gunshots!"

It doesn't seem real, for how could any such outburst happen in the middle of a pleasant evening like this? "Shots—do you really think so?" Levi asks. We all continue to gaze in silence at the scene, some one hundred yards distant, and now there are echoes of men's voices shouting excitedly, and no longer are people running away but a few figures are quickly striding towards the lane where the disturbance broke out. "Oh, Richard, we mustn't sit too close to whatever that is," Emma speaks up. "Let's move away. Please!" Richard still holds the reins taut, however, while he keeps his inquisitive look off to his left. The horses are snorting and twitching their ears but they don't appear to be skittish while the landau sits still in the empty intersection. And at this point another carriage rolls past us from behind and veers left onto Saginaw directly towards the action. You can see that it's the carriage that Hervey Parke and Charley Palmer are riding in, both of them holding onto their hats as their horse has begun to pull faster at a trot—why did they turn south onto Saginaw?

"Let me just walk down as far as the church to get a closer look," offers Richard, but Levi quickly rejects the idea, countering with "No, better we should get these girls home in time for dinner, don't you think?" He says this with a reassuring smile to Molly, Malvina, and Libbie. The girls have been on edge since the landau stopped, the three of them staring straight across at Levi and Emma, apparently not as curious as Richard about the ruckus down the street. And now there are two or three carriages behind the landau, likewise halted, the riders undoubtedly just as curious about what is going on. Then from the railroad station a train whistle blares twice to announce the D&M's departure, and this seems to break the stalemate as Richard finally flips the reins and his team resumes pulling the carriage, slowly northward towards town, and away from whatever worrisome event had occurred on the railroad lane. "Probably just some raw recruits getting off the train and showing off with their squirrel guns," he mutters.

Maybe he's right, or maybe it's another matter, say, some sort of hubbub caused by Ben French, just arrived in town and looking for trouble. Or maybe your imagination is only stirred up over nothing; then again, the vision of Ben French and Marcus Kelsey facing each other in some climactic scene fit for a dime novel is . . . oh, come now, it's ridiculous. You have to smile at your own susceptibility for gossip and melodrama, or whatever entertaining rumors Dr. McConnell is offering. So, we all have to admit to a foible or two. But wait, now, who is this?—a man is walking rapidly down Saginaw, in the opposite direction as the landau, and as he draws nearer you realize that he is clearly heading towards the fracas at the depot, looking grimly determined to get there fast.

"Well, there goes Constable Foster to save the day," says Richard dully, and he turns to you to add, ironically, "*That* should quiet things down, I reckon."

Yes, that should do it. You settle more on your seat and fix your gaze forward towards the Clinton River bridge and the buildings beyond. The gaslights on Saginaw are still unlit but the lights of some interior lamps are becoming noticeable, winking here and there in windows. Let's get back to reviewing the day, the party, the Bagg and Flower buildings, and all the reasons why Pontiac is still an attractive destination. It *is* an exciting time, isn't it? And there's every indication that the town will continue to prosper, in wartime and afterwards. You wonder whether Hervey Parke may be planning a permanent return to Pontiac from Keweenaw, or like you, considering a second investment here, which for him would mean producing medicines in some business partnership with Elkanah Comstock. These are the opportunities you should be thinking about, without the distractions you'll hear from the scandalmongers. When you're new in town you have to be careful of scandalmongers and grumblers.

It is not as busy along here as when you walked through before on your way to the party. You can detect dinnertime aromas drifting out from all the buildings--a yawn, contentment, all is well. No one is talking in the seats behind you; turn around to look, and there are the girls, sitting quietly and gazing at storefronts off to the left and right.

Levi catches your look and gives you a reassuring wink; next to him Emma sits upright but has her eyes closed. And next to you, here is Richard sitting fully relaxed, his legs crossed, using only one hand to hold the reins, loosely. His team knows the way home very well, probably, through the town streets. Will they know enough to continue all the way up to Huron and turn left towards Waterford, all on their own? That's something you won't get to see, in any event, since you'll be getting off at the Hodges, coming up ahead.

You're ready for some quiet time back at the hotel. And a dinner— you recall the desk clerk touting the German veal blanquettes on the restaurant's menu this evening. Perhaps you should start some writing in your room before dinner. There's a lot to cover by way of your cartes de visite, and a special note *en remerciement* to the McConnell's. They put on a fine affair, and it was just what you needed, capping off a remarkably successful day: good weather, good information gathered first-hand, many new friendships made. You have been immersed. The main question is whether or not you see a better future for yourself in this young, industrious town outside Detroit, where you continue to establish good contacts among important people. Before you walk into the Hodges you should let Levi know when you plan to return to Pontiac the next time, in early summer, so that he might expect a telegraph message beforehand.

The landau rolls over the Clinton River bridge—much more freely this time, compared to this morning's arrival—and you turn to see how the girls are faring in the rear seat. All three of them are looking back at you calmly with slight, childish grins. "Hungry?" you ask this one word aloud. Their silent nods in response are enthusiastic and unanimous. "So am I," you rejoin, happy to agree with everyone's contentment with the way this day is closing. You turn to look forward again, and when the landau reaches the crosswalks at Water Street you hear the expected change in sound, first with the horses' hooves on the boards, then followed by the wheels rolling over the same place. Look at Richard, there, sitting next to you, laconic, bored. Like the Irish cab driver this morning he's probably daydreaming about becoming a cavalryman in the army, a *brave chevalier* riding off to faraway lands. He wants "out" of peaceful Pontiac, while you want "in", even as the two of you sit together on this landau bench. It's a sure bet, however, that Richard will be the one to see history being made, much more than you will.

NEAR MISS

THE SETTING could not have been more peaceful, out in the open air on the railroad lane in the late afternoon quiet. At the far end of the lane at the depot, a train on the Detroit & Milwaukee line stood motionless on the tracks by the boarding platform, still fixed in place and clearly visible due to the lack of pedestrian crowds as relatively few passengers had exited at the Pontiac station. Only three or four carriages had been hired to transport the new arrivals to town, and in fact only the last of these was still on the lane, having not quite reached the intersection with Saginaw Street. The sun would be setting in an hour or so on the far side of the station, low enough already to start casting shadows over the lane from the picket fences and bushes that ran along either side. Granted, it was not one of the tidier, more picturesque streets in town, but this was a nice time of day nonetheless.

During the past few minutes, however, there were two men who had been waiting at the intersection while they watched the carriages approach their position and then pass by to make their turn onto Saginaw, heading into town. These men were not at all sensible about peaceful settings, at the moment, for they felt only a tense apprehension about the situation they were in, observing each carriage one by one and the people who were riding on them. They did not listen to the bland conversations, nor the squeaks and rattles of the carriages, nor the hiss of steam escaping from the train at the station platform, nor the distant rattling of a load of coal being dumped at the gas works plant. All of these mundane noises meant nothing to them, while they concentrated on their view of the lane before them.

They were expecting to spot one man in particular, and they were ready to act if he appeared.

One of the waiting men was seated in his own surrey which he had parked on the north side of the lane at the corner where it ended at Saginaw, facing towards the station, as if he had only paused there on his way to meet someone arriving in Pontiac. The other man stood alone, separately, on the other side of Saginaw. From time to time he turned around to look upon the construction site of the new church building behind him, and upon the workmen who were still there, hovering about the foundation, putting away tools and materials at day's end. But mostly his attention was directed on the railroad lane, especially when a carriage was coming out in front of him. And now as the last carriage was slowly approaching, it was time to stand ready on full alert.

The man sitting in the surrey was Marcus Kelsey, 40, a man of business, his health somewhat impaired by his weak lungs. He was a congenial sort, well-liked by his colleagues and very active in civic life, naturally gregarious, and he always strived to avoid confrontational situations and aggressive behavior if at all possible. Today, however, he found himself on a mission altogether loathsome to him, to confront an aggressive man—a man who threatened the well-being of someone dear to Marcus. The aggressor was now at hand, no doubt, riding on the last carriage coming down the railroad station lane. It was Benjamin French, from Washington, ostensibly visiting Pontiac to sell books as per his normal business routine, although his true intent this time was to find his wife Sallie Parke French in order to "settle matters" once and for all about their marital status. Marcus and Benjamin had met once or twice before. Ben French was clearly the more robust and more petulant character.

The man across the street was younger, likewise robust, and self-confident about his abilities in his line of work. He was a "Pinkerton", an agent adept at detective work and prepared to use his firearm if called for—although so far that need had yet to arise. He also knew his way around railroad offices, a large part of his job, and he maintained a number of personal contacts among railroad officials and station managers. It was not difficult for him to call upon a colleague in Washington to inquire at French's bookstore about upcoming sales travel planned for Detroit and Pontiac, and then piece together a likely schedule and arrival date. In the new era of telegraphic communication this information could be relayed quickly. It was Marcus Kelsey who had asked the Pinkerton agent a month ago to undertake the project for him. Kelsey and the Pinkerton were friends, introduced to each other years ago through Kelsey's brother Sullivan, the judge.

Now the hour had come, at last, when a face-to-face encounter with Ben French might very well happen. The logical presumption was that French would arrive in Pontiac on the 5:50 PM train northbound from Detroit, probably bringing one or two crates of books that were meant for sale at an event in Pontiac. More likely, however, this merchandise would serve only as a premise for French's visit; in that regard there had been no advertisements posted recently for such a book sale. No, clearly the point was to find Sallie and harass her in some way that would compel her to get out of his life. Whether French planned on going directly from the station to McConnell's party, or check in first at the Hodges Hotel was moot—Kelsey wanted to intercept him right at the station, and make him see in no uncertain terms how the town was on guard to prevent any sort of mischief French had in mind.

The cab continued to approach the corner of Saginaw. It was a one-horse open wagon, not really a carriage. Two men were seated on the buckboard—the driver and one other. Kelsey grew increasingly fret-ful, watching from his surrey. Behind Kelsey, the Pinkerton standing across the street grew increasingly excited about the chance for action, any second now. He was prepared to pull out his firearm and wield it, if necessary, to prove his authority.

There! Yes, that's him! –both Kelsey and Pinkerton realized at the same instant, silently, and steadied themselves. The man next to the driver was Ben French, his face showing only boredom and indiffer-ence, not yet aware of Kelsey's presence. A few more seconds—still no reaction. Kelsey now made his move. Snapping the reins in his shaking hands, he guided his horse to pull the surrey astride the railroad station lane until he stopped it in the middle, perpendicular, effectively block-ing off anyone's exit from the lane onto Saginaw.

Kelsey kept his eyes forward, looking over his horse harnessed be-fore him. He could hear how French's wagon came to a stop, and after a few seconds there came the sound of a man's boots landing heavily on the ground. Kelsey waited for the sound of boots walking towards, but nothing happened. French must be standing there, glaring at him. Why didn't French say anything? Where was the Pinkerton—still waiting across Saginaw? The sustained silence was awkward, and an-noying. Kelsey slumped his chin down, realizing the dangerous situa-tion he was in and loathing everything about it.

"Cornelia, I'm too old for this sort of thing."

The image of Cornelia, Kelsey's first wife, was very clear to him, appearing nearby like this whenever he was extremely hard-pressed or nervous. Though he had lost her to childbirth so many years ago, yet she continued to hold a presence in his life, daily revealed in the visage and the voice of their daughter Molly. It was only natural that Cornelia would be sitting next to him now, as she leaned forward to take a look at what French was doing. Kelsey felt very relieved that she was safely on the side of the bench away from French, in case French might try to do something violent.

"You'll be fine," she said, her voice quiet and steady as always. "Don't breathe so hard. Your heart is pounding."

It was time to look up again and glare back at French. Oh yes—there he was, standing next to his wagon, his legs planted slightly astride, his hands grasping the lapels of his coat and holding them openly apart. His figure was more like a silhouette as the sun was lowering directly behind him, and Kelsey couldn't make out all the aspects of his face, but the tall beaver hat on top of his head was the only salient feature anyway. It made him look all the more tall and threatening.

"He's drunk, Marcus," Cornelia whispered.

Kelsey smiled at this. *Leave it to ghosts—they can always tell.*

"What brings you here, Ben?" Kelsey spoke loudly at the figure, with as much brass as he could muster.

"Get your rig off the road, Kelsey," French snarled back immediately.

"Tell me first where you're going." Yes, the man was drunk and belligerent. There would be no defusing this showdown.

"By God I'll tell you nothing! Now get out of the way! I have a right to go where I please."

French took a couple of steps forward as he spoke; Kelsey didn't move and he gripped his reins tightly. It was amusing to see a large crate on the back of French's wagon, just as Pinkerton reckoned. So French had brought along his books, all right. The very idea of this booksale gambit helped Kelsey steady his nerve and regain a more laconic composure, although his heart was pounding away, beyond control. *Don't breathe so hard. What happened to his driver?* Kelsey hadn't seen how the teamster managed to disappear after he came to a stop. And only now did he become aware of the small number of other passers-by, people coming down the lane who had to walk to the sides to make their way around French's wagon and Kelsey's surrey.

That was the motive he needed: confront French face-to-face while there were still witnesses at hand, and act on it right now. Kelsey jumped from his seat on the side facing French, still holding the reins as he landed on the road. The horse remained calm, so Kelsey could toss the reins back to Cornelia—but her ghost wasn't there. Kelsey stared up at the empty seat, chagrined now because he had meant to tell her *Now is as good a time as any for me to give it all up, on this very spot.* Fine, then, what of it? He patted the horse's rump lightly and turned around towards the sun and the darkened figure before him, ready for shouting, or shoving, or whatever harm lay in store.

"Ben, Sallie has no bad intentions, or any desire to ruin your—"

"—Ruin yourself, Romeo!" French interrupted. The men stood two paces between them. "Last warning, Kelsey. She's my rib, by law, not yours or anyone else's. I'll handle my property as I see fit. Now lead your rig to the side, dumley, or do you really want to see me lose my mind over this?"

French was thrusting his right hand into his left coat pocket. *Here comes the gun,* Kelsey thought, *Here comes the insanity.* It was too ridiculous, but there it was, the gun coming out in the open. No chance now for civility, for talk, for settlement—just a drunk man wielding a weapon.

"Drop it, French, or I'll put a hole in you right now!" shouted Pinkerton from behind the back end of Kelsey's surrey.

French took a step backwards, startled, as he hadn't expected to deal with anyone else intervening. He looked at Pinkerton and raised both his hands up in the air, his right hand still holding the gun. He then glanced back and forth at both of his adversaries with an innocent expression as if to say he really meant no harm—don't shoot! Other people nearby now suddenly began to run past the surrey or back towards the station, while one woman cried out her husband's name and another young man leaped over a picket fence to hide behind a clump of bushes. Meanwhile Kelsey seemed frozen in place. He had hesitated to make a lunge at French, and that brief chance was now gone, so he could only stare and wonder whether he was about to see the man get shot by Pinkerton right here, right before his eyes.

What should he do now? Would Pinkerton move in now to make an arrest? Or would French really start shooting?

French is grappling!—an assailant has rushed upon him from behind, and all at once they're locked together in a struggle to grab the gun. Kelsey stands where he is, mesmerized, watching as the gun is still raised upwards but waves crazily in all directions. The wrestling goes on, as French tries to dislodge his captor's grip from around his back, and then the gun goes off—bang! And another shot—bang! The loud reports are a shock, but still the men stagger and grunt and fight. The assailant is about to bring French down to the ground, just as the gun fires off again—bang! Finally both men are down on the lane, the assailant on top pinning French beneath him, the gun still in French's hand at the end of his arm, now stretched out and rendered inert.

At this point Pinkerton moved in and stood over the two men as they lay panting on the ground, and he planted a foot on the wrist of French's hand that held the gun. The fight was over. French had spittle drooling out of the side of his mouth as he snarled through gritted teeth at the assailant weighing down on his back, "Get off me, you lousy cheat!" No release was forthcoming, however, as the assailant only shifted to a kneeling position, both knees squarely on the middle of French's lower back.

"Well done, Mr. O'Brien. Risky, but a good show," Pinkerton said.

"At your service, constable," was the cheery, breathy response from Andrew O'Brien, the driver of the Morris Livery wagon. "I caught the whiskey on his breath, and sure I knew t'would be no trouble to take the man down."

Pinkerton picked up French's hat, then bent down near the pinned man and reached over to pry the gun free from his grip. "Now then, Mr. French, I'm sure we can find a nice accommodation in town for you and your books." Then he raised his head to scan over the scene, asking "Is everyone fine and hale?" And he now looked directly back at Kelsey.

Kelsey was not fine and hale. He was staring down at his left leg, above the knee, where a hole had just been ripped into the trouser fabric. He couldn't move the leg, which suddenly felt very hot on the inside, and his first reaction was to pull away his morning coat by the lapel to look all around upon at his thigh, not so much stunned as he was curious about the sensation. Now he could see a stain of blood forming below the hole in his trouser leg, and he began to realize what had just happened. *Ridiculous*, he thought, and feeling a bit lightheaded he decided that he ought to sit down where he was in the lane. Which he did, rather abruptly.

As soon as he sat down his view of the world was blocked by a crowd of faces, all glaring at him in frightened alarm. Pinkerton was closest, and his voice was the only one saying anything coherent, are-you-all-right and take-it-easy and the like, over a vague background of other voices all shouting orders and questions. Kelsey could only nod in agreement and whisper "Yes, yes" to Pinkerton, not really knowing what he was saying. Someone was bracing his shoulders and the back of his head, which felt nice, and he was suddenly aware that his mouth was dry, very dry. Hervey Parke was now there too, leaning over him, gently pulling down the bloodied trouser cloth which had become all ripped away separate, it would appear. Had he blanked out? He heard

Hervey declare that the shot must have missed the bone, and then Pinkerton was gone but Kelsey could hear him ordering Charley to go find Doc Abiram at the McConnell's and bring him here quick. *Charley? That must be Charley Palmer.*

He began to grow calmer, oddly calmer, and he focused on Hervey and found he could say "Thank you, brother" without much effort, though his leg was beginning to ache. Hervey smiled back, and breathed and said, "This is not the good life, Marcus. No sir. I saw this sort of thing up in Clifton more than once. More than once. I think you'll be all right. Let's have Abiram take a look at you." Kelsey was about to tell Hervey not to fret over him, but then he saw Cornelia again—she was crouched just behind Hervey, looking over his shoulder at her wounded husband. She wasn't exactly smiling, nor scared; it was that steady, serene look that he always remembered, even years later.

"All for naught, Cornelia, no matter what I do."

"What's that?" asked Hervey. "Nothing you do is for naught, Marcus."

Cornelia's face became very saddened, and Kelsey could barely make out her reply: "I'm sorry for leaving you, husband. I am so, so sorry."

He wanted to comfort her, *No, no. You didn't leave. You were taken.* She always apologized; he knew that whatever kindly remonstrance he made would never help. It was always the same with her.

But Kelsey could sense that he would surely get over this and "live to tell." Now there was a strip of fancy purple fabric wrapped all the way around his thigh, tight as a belt. As long as he didn't move, he didn't feel much pain inside. Cornelia had disappeared but there were a few other faces still staring at him, people he didn't recognize. No one was speaking. What's this now?—he could see men off to the side, conferring in a group, obviously getting ready to pick their wounded comrade to put him in a wagon. There was Dr. McConnell, and Jack Foster, and Hervey and Charley Palmer, and Pinkerton. This was not going to be a pleasant ride.

"You blanked out for a few minutes," Hervey said. "How do you feel?"

"Where are we?" Kelsey murmured in return. He was lying on his back, in a wagon that wasn't moving, his head cradled on some soft material. Evidently he had been laid on the flatbed with his feet toward the front. His waistcoat had been taken off and was draped over him like a short blanket, covering his legs up to his belly. There was some form of a pillow cushioning his head; without looking he lifted a hand to touch the pillow, and figured that it must be a small burlap grain sack filled with oat seeds, probably.

Hervey was seated opposite Kelsey on the wagon with his knees drawn up and his back leaning against the frontboard. He looked down at Kelsey approvingly. "The National Building. We'll carry you up to Dr. McConnell's office."

So, then, the wagon he was in was parked in the center of town, on Saginaw. Kelsey gradually regained his consciousness and an awareness of how he had come to this condition. The sky over the buildings had turned grayish with the onset of a warm springtime twilight. Kelsey could see that a nearby gaslight was not yet lit, however.

"Your ambulance committee should be down in a minute," Hervey continued. "Marcus, be strong. That was a near miss."

"I am feeling better now."

"Good, but you look as white as a ghost. Or like someone who has just seen a ghost, I should say."

A ghost, you say. You don't know the half of it. Kelsey could only grin at the thought of it. But he wanted to say something positive about what had happened. "I suppose that livery teamster saved my skin."

"The young Irish lad. He did a good turn for us all. I'm sure Beardsley will see him carry off the palm.[85] Too bad you got caught in the crossfire."

"Oh, I just stood there, Hervey. I should have helped. Ridiculous!"

"Well, one thing's for certain—your actions saved my sister's life today."

So I lost one of your sisters as my wife, and rescued your other sister as my paramour, is that it? "Maybe so. I knew I would have it out with French sooner or later. Where is he now?"

"Sheriff Beardslee and his deputy are holding him at the station. I don't know what their plan is. I think French's books are still in that crate we left back at the lane. Charles and I will go pick them up. Maybe we'll drop off the crate at the Hodges. Beardsley took quite an interest in French's pistol. Apparently you were shot with a Smith and Wesson 7-shot revolver."

"That's good to know," Kelsey responded laconically, amused by Hervey's penchant for recalling detailed information, whether germane or utterly useless.

Hervey nodded slightly as if to convey *my pleasure.* Then he went on with another observation: "Say, lucky it was, that Charles and I were passing by on our way to pick up his son at the station, when this whole ordeal blew up. You're much too old for this kind of caper, brother."

"You may be right about that." Kelsey sensed how Hervey was making an effort to keep him distracted. Saginaw was strangely quiet, it seemed, and Hervey was speaking to him in quiet tones.

"Your Pinkerton man has a bit of dash. You know, I thought I had seen him at the McConnell's, maybe not, but then I remembered: it was this morning on your porch. We watched him riding by your house with Sheriff Beardslee. Am I right?"

---

85 "Carry off the palm": a palm leaf presented (figurative expression) as a reward for heroism or victory.

Kelsey didn't feel a need to reply, or mention anything about the Pinkerton agent's role in the 'caper'.

"And *Mrs.* French, then, is still at the party?" he asked instead.

"I doubt Sallie knows anything about what happened," Hervey rejoined, "but when she hears all about it tomorrow . . . well, I'll wager her Uncle Willard will have something to say about her current arrangements. Personally I think her marriage is ready for divorce."

"She could always plead 'temporary insanity' to the judge," Kelsey deadpanned.

Hervey allowed a slight smirk, and Kelsey started to shrug his shoulders in response but caught himself as a sharp pain emanated from his wounded leg.

Having noticed the grimace, Hervey saw fit to redirect to another idea: "And by the way—I trust you weren't planning on heading over anytime soon to Pennsylvania with your precious oil barrels. You've just been shot, you see."

Kelsey was about to agree and comment on how the oil drilling could wait, but responded instead with a more amiable suggestion: "Yes, it's probably safer to stay home and drink a buttermilk with my favorite medicine man." This proved to be the response Hervey wanted, enough for him to nod in satisfaction.

A clatter of footfalls on the boardwalk meant that the group of Kelsey's caretakers was returning to gather him up and carry him to Dr. McConnell's office upstairs in the National Building. Kelsey made an effort to raise himself into a sitting position, but as soon as his head was elevated he began to feel faint, and let himself collapse back down onto the burlap pillow. There was nothing to do but lay helpless, and his thoughts drifted, leading to memories of exploring the oil fields in Pennsylvania, where he had camped in a tent and used a grain sack for a pillow. It felt just like this one. Yes, the camping—in those early days we slept in tents, for a week or so, using nothing more than blankets and a sack pillow.

The men of the impromptu aid party were now standing around the wagon, looking on while Hervey and Dr. McConnell unfastened a portable stretcher beside Kelsey on the flatbed. Then while they helped Marcus to ease himself onto the stretcher, Hervey said something that was meant to be only another casual comment but instead stirred up an alarming idea:

"Well no doubt we'll be reading all about the shoot-out in the Gazette."

"Yes—probably next week, Monday's issue," someone else added. The voice sounded like Charley Palmer's. "Hot work for Myron Howell."

"Misery me! Nothing in the papers, please!" Marcus cried out. The last thing he wanted was any publicity about an entanglement involving himself and Ben French, and by implication, Sallie. "Hervey, tell Howell and Beardslee to keep my name out of it!" Raising his upper body up on his right elbow he then implored his friend more keenly, "Promise me!" There was a moment of silence, until Palmer's voice again was heard, saying "Understood." And Hervey rejoined with "Yes, I think we could keep you and my sister out of it." Marcus laid back down on the stretcher made an effort to say "Thank you, gentlemen" but his leg suddenly ached so much that the only word he could manage was "gentlemen."

At that moment the sound of a bugle call was faintly audible, coming from the fairgrounds camp, probably announcing "lights out" or some other military order for day's end. *How fitting for all of us,* Kelsey thought, *We'll hear the music for one more sunset.* He wondered whether any of those Pontiac Volunteers ducking into their tents for the night had ever pictured themselves getting shot on some battlefield.

So the shot was only a near miss—but it was pretty close, in a peaceful little town like Pontiac. For Marquis Kelsey, at least, it had turned out to be a rather eventful day. He wouldn't remember much about being carried through the lobby of the Hodges, other than staring up at the ceiling as it passed over him, and wanting to tell someone, everyone, how the world was going to hell in a handbasket.

Spirit of Modern Times

EPILOGUE

A DAY RECOUNTED

BY NOW everyone had returned to their homes, where nightfall would gradually transform the households into a more subdued, quieter state as they relied more and more on candlelight in the darkening interiors. Most of these people had their own houses but a few others lived more simply, residing in rented boarding-house rooms or in communal bunk establishments. In whatever kind of home they had, the day was closing for all of them in the growing darkness after sunset. Those who had been guests at the McConnell's were now returned home at last, some of them still upholding a complaisant disposition while others were feeling outright languid; they required only a light supper served up by household cooks, and then off to bed. Those who were less socially favored and had missed the party were content to retire at will, privately and frugally, burning only a single stearin candle[86] at bedside—there was no need for them to prolong a Thursday evening

---

86   Stearin candle: a manufactured candle that is more practical than a tallow candle in terms of sturdiness, duration and brightness; also far less expensive than the higher-quality beeswax candles.

by lighting up their parlor room with a big oil lamp, only to incur the additional expense and cleaning that came with it.

Eventually in candlelit bedrooms in all of the homes there were people settling in to ruminate over the day's dealings. Several of them recited prayers, murmuring the names of loved ones living or lost, or made rote supplications for safety or forgiveness, or asked for special favors to suit the devices and desires of their hearts. Others were more apt to think back and assess the results of an event, like a party or a meeting, or an effort they had made to gain someone's attention. A few others now had time to relive the risky actions they had committed, which for one of them had resulted in traumatic injury. Of course there was no reason for anyone to see their individual actions fitting into one overall story. No one was aware of a "larger picture" that a historian or a storyteller might use to describe the times.

But there was one common aspect to all these evening meditations. Whether rich or poor, old or young, alone or not, in each circumstance the people would agree these were the best of times, here at the pinnacle of civilization. This was how life would go on, essentially the same, for themselves and their children after them. Things would soon be different in the South, of course, after the slaves were set free on the big plantations, but the South would eventually adjust to the new order, and the progress, matching conditions in the North. Contentious as it was, this political matter was still safely distant, something to be settled by the army, while in Pontiac the fashions would continue to change, new machines and medicines would be invented, and the city would continue to expand. The world around us would always be recognizable, *quod verum est.*[87]

This was the underlying presumption, even in a very dynamic world such as Pontiac in the year 1861. One day will lead to the next, and one year to the next, until everyone's detailed memories of events

---

87   Quod verum est: literally, "what is true"; idiomatic "yes, for sure."

will eventually dissolve into a dim, perfunctory history. So this evening, with the story still fresh, it may be worthwhile to recount what was going on in a number of the homes. After all, the day just ended had brought a variety of outcomes for the characters involved.

Cleantha McConnell, for one, was glad to have some restful moments to think about her party, which by all indications had been a resounding success. After the last guests left the house, she and her husband returned to the parlor where they had Eliza light the wicks of the two argand lamps on the mantel; and they bid her shut the hallway door on her way out. Cleantha and Willard were now alone in their chairs to recount the day's events, talk about their guests and their family, and comment on what news they had learned. Cleantha mulled over the conversations she had with each of her close friends, and she remembered happily the sight of everyone listening to all the speakers on her porch. The boys did a good job with their orations, especially that rascal Lewis Drake. Everyone appeared to be enjoying themselves, and even poor old Horace Thurber was perfectly gracious making his return from mourning. Eliza and Mary and Jackson fulfilled all duties competently, so yes, there was every reason to be satisfied with the whole affair.

The Gorham silver had been fairly admired, as it should. But also— the Haughwout china serving plate, placed in the dining room for the dainties. Three of Cleantha's friends had appreciated the plate enough to ask when and where she had acquired it—not surprising, since articles had been appearing in "Peterson's" and other papers about the President's wife and her recent travel to Haughwout's in New York to replace most of the china at the White House. *If it's good enough for Mary Todd Lincoln, then it's good enough for me*, was Cleantha's offhand remark more than once. The sudden prestige of the Haughwout name on her own china piece may not have been expected but there it was—yet another understated coup for good taste, casually set out among all the sundry items on Cleantha's table. *Oh, I'm so glad you noticed!* A minor indulgence like that was always so very gratifying.

Beyond all the merriment, however, was the lingering heartache about her son Joseph leaving for the army—not just for three months as Cleantha expected, but for a full three years. The military campaign should not last for that much time, so why did the army require such a long commitment? And would Joseph ever finish his college studies at Union? Cleantha was still troubled by this unexpected development as she sat pondering over a vision of Joseph waving goodbye as he boarded the train with Colonel Richardson to go join the regiment. For his part, Willard did not seem to be as concerned about it. He offered some comforting words about how everything should turn out all right, and he tried distracting Cleantha with a compliment on her tact of leaving the fireplaces exposed without the decorative fireboards. The boards would be installed later on in the summer, but for today it was a fine choice to have the well-polished andirons on display. And by the way, Willard wanted to know, what was the medical emergency that called away Abiram? But Cleantha had no information either on what that was all about. Perhaps Eliza might know what had happened.

Outside the house and across the street, David Jackson was also relaxing after the party, seated alone at the wooden table in the carriage park field. The other drivers had all left, so the park was once again a vacant field, quiet, with no horses, no carriages. In a few minutes he would have to walk over to the McConnells' side yard to help put away all the tables and gather up any dishes or other service items, but first, what he needed to do was to sit and think about some weightier issues on his mind. He would soon be making important decisions about his own private ambitions, in fact his very livelihood, and here was a good moment to fix his mind. It was dusk, the air was beginning to cool, and just above the eastern horizon the first star was becoming visible—Jackson pondered whether it was the planet Venus or the star Arcturus.

In his old life one the aunties used to know all the names of the stars and constellations, but that was too long ago for him to remember now, except for the sound of her voice.

The plan was coming down to this: Jackson would leave his job at the McConnell's and take on work at McCallum's sheep tannery. This meant working indoors in the heat of a workshop, and more onerous labor but it would pay more, and it was the only path towards getting his own home and starting a family with Martha Parker. He wouldn't have to stay at the tannery forever, and meantimes he could go on learning more and more words for reading. And there was a larger possibility, too, that all his plans might be thrown off anyway, if other chances came his way like joining the army or working for a balloon professor. So the first step was this: tomorrow he would go the meeting in town with Mayor Thatcher and Professor Bannister at Palmer's wagon shop, to see if he might be hired to become an aeronaut. Even if nothing came of it, he had to try. Jackson knew if he went to see Bannister then word would get back to McConnell sooner or later, but so be it. There was no law against it. It was the mayor of the city, of all people, who had asked him to go. Tomorrow he was going to do it.

Sallie Parke French had returned to the herb garden to find that it was indeed abandoned, offering the chance for solitude and reflection for a time before dark. She had enjoyed herself at the party, and the time spent with Emily Darrow, and especially with the college boys in the drawing room. Perhaps she shouldn't have divulged so much to that out-of-town visitor about Hervey and Marcus and Cornelia—she knew she had a tendency to prattle on about people she admired. But there it was, and Sallie was not one to regret talking openly with people, or teasing the younger folk, or speaking her mind about how to pursue commercial success. What's more, she felt no qualms about joining Marcus Kelsey today for lunch as his properly invited guest. Every day, every social event, ought to be an adventure of some sort.

Except that today, in contrast, she had also felt beleaguered by the same old annoying dilemma about how to stay separate from her husband Benjamin French. As if her situation weren't already spurious enough, living as a dependent upon Uncle Willard. This had to be socially discomfiting for him to be supporting a misfit niece, despite his loathing for Benjamin which was no secret. And now here was her brother Hervey, as sincere and caring as ever, extending his best wishes for a proper resolution. Maybe the time had come to move on to a new life, though not necessarily with Ben in Washington, where she knew nobody, but out west, where she could join with her brothers Frank, Ira and Lyman at the silver mines. Yes, the West! *That* seemed far more appealing. But how to get there? She could go to Washington first, as a pretense, and at some point arrange for a visit to see her family in Nevada.

And so Sallie paced the garden, deep in thought as Jackson was at his table across the street, and contemplating a change in direction, come what may.

Elsewhere in town there were people who were using this hour to do some correspondence, sitting alone at desks or tables in their bedchambers and taking the time to prepare their paper, their steel pens and their capped ink jars, and their thoughts. There was still sufficient daylight coming through windows, although it was starting to fade in the dusk; in any case there were candles in single holders always available in the rooms, unlit but standing ready at hand when their additional light would be needed.

Hervey Coke Parke was one of these writers. He was a guest at the home of his friend Charles Palmer, and was now quartered comfortably in the Palmers' spare bedroom, which had afforded him some welcome privacy at last. He was crafting a letter to send to Elkanah Comstock, thanking him for the meeting earlier today and following up on the points of discussion about legitimate vendors of medicinal products in Pontiac and Detroit. Another point of the letter was to convey his keen interest in any investment opportunities in Pontiac for starting a business in drug manufacture. This was something Hervey had been hinting at during the meeting, but judging from Elkanah's reaction apparently nothing and no one had sprung to mind in this regard.

Hervey stroked his beard and looked over his note. No, this wasn't working. It was just too difficult to focus on drafting a courtesy letter just now, after all that he had witnessed this afternoon with Marcus Kelsey's wounding, and the aftermath of his violent encounter with Ben French. Thank God, matters seemed to have settled safely enough, so far. Dr. McConnell had arranged for Marcus to stay at the Hodges for a day or two during his initial recovery before removing home, which must be a prudent measure. Nonetheless Hervey was surprised, and dejected, honestly, to see the same sort of ruffian behavior in Pontiac as he had witnessed among the miners in Keweenaw. Admittedly, he was not in a frame of mind to write this or any other letters, not tonight, just for the sake of reporting cheerfully on the McConnells' reception . . . or his worries about Sallie and her marriage, or about Marcus and his wound and his failing health. What good was there in elaborating such private matters in a letter to his wife, or his brothers, or to anyone, really?

Pen in hand, Hervey still felt as though he ought to craft something for Elkanah. The wicker chair creaked as he shifted his posture and dipped his steel pen into the inkwell. Of course he could write. He needed to express more desire to start the project. The visit with his sister to the McConnells' herb garden, earlier that afternoon, had been an inspiration for him, stirring an old interest in medicinal herbs and whether their properties might be scientifically reproduced. Should he express as much in this letter to Elkanah? He stopped, and held up the pen. And at last he decided, that no, it was too much. A short, courteous thank-you note was only appropriate. Besides, he mused with a wry grin, he should dash this off quickly, since his feet still hurt from walking around all day in those new Balmorals. Marcus would understand.

Another writer was Myron Howell, the editor of the Gazette. He enjoyed his work at the paper and could be counted on to produce a treatise of witty remarks about the McConnells' event, but at the moment he was occupied not with work but with some personal correspondence. Anyway it was too late to run any more articles for the Gazette's weekly issue coming out tomorrow, Friday, so he may as well put off drafting his report until tomorrow. For now, then, Myron sat alone in his boardinghouse room, dispatching a quick note to some friends in Vermont—the Mott family, who lived in Alburgh, a town in the far north of the state. Myron was sending his letter to Mr. and Mrs. Mott, the parents of Judd Mott, who was Myron's enduring friend since they had been classmates at the University of Michigan, class of '58. Judd was currently traveling about Europe and was probably in Switzerland now, or Italy; his parents would be more in a position to pass along any news to Judd, presumably.

Not that there was much personal news to pass on: that Myron was thinking of asking his brother Charles to help run the paper; that his mother was still ailing; that he had learned today that two of the local boys, Joseph McConnell and Danny Thurber, were members of Delta Phi, the same fraternity that Judd had joined at the university; and that the 2nd Michigan infantry regiment would soon be leaving for Washington. Enough news, then. Now for something of a digression: Myron added some lines with his opinion about the Homestead Act, which would surely be enacted in Washington now that all the southern legislators had walked out with the onset of the war.[88] As soon as the Act was passed, Myron felt, the federal Land Office would have to expand its workforce to process all the thousands of applications for land grants that would surely come pouring in. With that in mind, perhaps Myron could submit an application for employment at the Land Office for a clerkship—why not? And the Gazette should be able to carry on without him, direct management being turned over to his brother Charles. For that matter, Myron's work in Washington should also enable him to act as the Gazette's own war correspondent, wiring his dispatches home and keeping everyone well advised of any military actions. There—*that should do it for tonight*, Myron felt, and he signed off to the Mott's with his customary respect and affection. Pushing his chair away from the table he sat looking at a calendar that he kept propped up on a small stand, the palms of his hands brought together in front of his chin.

Over on Parke Street at the home of the Holley family the evening was normal and quiet. Tranquility had prevailed despite some underlying tension, especially when Carrie Holley was brought home by her Uncle Erastus Thatcher, His Honor the Mayor. Carrie's mother Marion Holley was just sitting down to dinner with her relatives and her employee tenant Fanny, but the presence of company would not have restrained her from reprimanding her daughter severely—Carrie had furtively dropped in on the McConnells' reception, uninvited, and in the process she had compelled her mother to reschedule her photography appointment at John Bray's studio. A scene was imminent; however, three factors combined to mollify Marion's resentment. For one thing, her husband John was still not home from his sales call at a farm in Waterford, and Marion was reticent to speak forcefully on family matters in his absence. Another thing: as long as her brother Erastus

---

88 Homestead Act: the government would grant free land in the western territories, in lot sizes up to 160 acres, to anyone who wished to settle there. Having paid a nominal fee, a settler would only have to reside for at least five years and show bona fide development of the land in terms of crops or livestock. The Act had been held up in Congress for several years due to the question of whether to allow slavery on the settlements.

was in the room it would do no good to chastise Carrie for anything he would only contradict later in steadfast support of his favorite niece. And last but not least, there was the appearance and comportment of Carrie herself, in her borrowed gown, which made an unexpected impact on Marion. She realized suddenly how grown up her daughter had become, truly lovely by anyone's judgment, poised, serene, and no doubt capable of ignoring any criticisms her mother might have in mind to render. The girl was seventeen, and fully mature now, a young woman ready to embark on her own life.

Marion remained alone now in the dining room, paperwork spread before her on the table, with plenty of light all around coming from the many candles she had adamantly kept lit—the city's gas line had yet to be installed on Parke Street but Marion wasn't about to sacrifice her eyesight waiting for it. For a while she sat quietly, gazing at the curtains drawn over the windows, thinking back on what she had said to Carrie at dinner, and what she had not said. She tried to imagine what Carrie would do this summer and what dreams she must have. So, then, nothing to be done about it. Marion dismissed all other thoughts to focus on the work before her. It was not bookkeeping pertaining to her dressmaking shop; it was not household money matters; it was not personal correspondence. What Marion needed to do this evening was to clear her mind and prepare a Sunday school lesson for her class of 10-to-12-year-olds at the Congregational Church. She lowered her chin to gaze downwards, her eyes fixed on her dinner plate and shifting towards the center of the table, and pursed her lips as she trained her thoughts on the Trinity lesson, and the need for obtaining the Anglican hymnbook. The only sound in the room was the tapping of her finger on the table.

Outdoors the nighttime darkness had descended over the town almost completely, save for a streak of lighter grayness that lingered low on the western horizon. The gaslights were lit all along Saginaw and the main side streets, providing a soft glow sufficient for moving about safely, although few people were about at such a late hour on a Thursday evening. There was still some subdued activity going on inside the Arcade and, nearby up Saginaw, at the Ogle House saloon, but on the whole the streets were quiet. The millwheels had stopped rotating. The crossroad traffic at Saginaw and Huron had diminished to almost nothing, and this evening there was nothing scheduled at the Court House, no meetings, no public debates. The army camp at the Fairgrounds was completely bedded down for the night and guards posted.

Quieter outside, now. Quieter inside, in the room at the Hodges House where Marcus Kelsey had been bedded down for the night, his first night of recovery from the gunshot wound. In fact the only sound in the room came from Marcus, breathing steadily in a sound sleep, doped up as he was from the opium-laced tincture administered to him by Dr. McConnell while dressing the leg wound. The doctor had little difficulty extracting the small, 22-caliber bullet out of the thigh muscle, so there was nothing left to do but rest safely in a comfortable place where there were bandages and medicines at hand, and watch closely for any signs of gangrene.

Marcus's wife Mary had arrived some time ago and was keeping her vigil at bedside, awake though closed-eyed. She still hadn't heard the whole story of the incident at the railroad lane, so here she was, nodding off in the room's armchair and still trying to picture her husband grappling with an armed criminal. For his part Marcus seemed to have been very much encouraged to see Mary, and he had listened patiently to all her admonishments about staying put at home, in Pontiac, as soon as he could be brought back to the house. They hadn't yet spoken openly about whether or not Mary might be pregnant, and just now was certainly not the time or place, but Marcus sensed the extra measure of fear in her remonstrance. And as for Cornelia . . . ah well,

Cornelia would never show up in the room, of course, while Mary was there. There was no call for the Holy Ghost to attend a peaceful setting like this, now that the danger had passed.

The peacefulness of the evening more generally would not be lost on younger folks in the town, the grown children who were not yet sleepy for bed but dreamy enough to sense the romance of the day just lived. Certainly all those who had attended the McConnell reception had much to reflect on, whether happily or regretfully. Younger folks, the zestful folks, characters like Julia Comstock.

Julia was especially restless this evening, lying in bed in her room at the Goodale's home on Perry Street, her mind touring through her memories of friends' faces and their clever remarks. Her sister Emma lay next to her but had definitely fallen asleep, so Julia blew out her candle and fell back on her pillow, hands behind her head, and let her thoughts drift over the scene in the McConnell family room. And what was the harm in guessing all the attractions between the boys and the girls, the hidden longings, the signals given? What pairings might be in the works here?

Danny Thurber and Carrie Holley, of course. That was made clear today, and will have to be investigated further. Lewis Drake and Fannie Mathews: that's an easy one. Joe McConnell and Malvina Taylor: she prefers a strong, handsome military man, and both their families have a lot of money. Charlie Draper and Sarah Thurber? He's so shy, but so is she, which could make them a good match. Jimmy Goodsell and Ella Draper: they're always fun together. And me, Julia, with . . . George Mathews. No, not likely. A girl should dream, should she not? He did look at me. He knows how good I am at managing things.

If Julia had thought longer on these pairings, and not as playfully, she might also have imagined how the subjects themselves were faring at this same moment. After all, the romantic air of a quiet evening may be felt as strongly by two people who are still apart, not yet together.

Danny and Carrie, as it turns out, were also still awake, Danny at his home on Garland Street and Carrie across town in her home on Parke Street. Danny could look eastward through his window and see the moon, almost full but not quite, while Carrie looked westward through her window and had a clear view of the line of buildings rising  on the other side of the Clinton River. They could both see an array of small lights in the darkness between them, coming from windows along Saginaw on the top floors of the Hodges House and other tall buildings. The lights seemed to exaggerate the height of the skyline, as if the city center might straddle the top of a hill, like some old medieval citadel. It was only a whimsical illusion, a frivolous idea, just something Carrie had mentioned at the Bell Party last winter. But these were the sorts of things that came to mind at nightfall, for both of them, when nothing else about the day was left to worry about. Carrie thought about all the times she had managed to break Danny's guarded reserve into a burst of genuine laughter, his smile lighting up his eyes just for her. And Danny thought about the Holley's coming to his home and seated around the dining room table, with his father and Mr. Thatcher, and his sister Sarah, too, which would help Carrie feel more at ease. At some point he would take Carrie into the parlor to show her the blue-and-white delft tiles bordering the hearth, and one tile in particular that he liked, which depicted an 18th century man holding a telescope for his lady to peer through the eyepiece. She might enjoy the whimsical nature of the artwork, and how it blended with the idea of looking ahead.

And one more person was in town that evening, preparing for a night's rest after a full day. Hardly the romantic type but enamored nonetheless by the town itself and most everyone in it, he felt engaging and well met. It was the Visitor, now back in his room in the Hodges House. He didn't know that Marcus Kelsey had just been installed in another room three doors down, attended by Abiram McConnell and by Kelsey's wife, and a young Irish teamster, and a Hodges concierge who ensured that plenty of linens and basins were on hand. Indeed the Visitor was still unaware that anything in the way of a harrowing incident had taken place near the railroad station. Apparently few people had heard the shots fired anyway, or if they did they paid little attention. In these times there were gunshots going off so often in celebration of the war.

The Visitor closed his notebook and set it down on the side table, and removed his candle to the small bedside nightstand. He pulled away the blankets and then sat on the side of the bed, pausing to gaze at the candle and conjure a final assessment of how the day had gone. Yes, it would be an exciting experience to move here and take up residence in Pontiac. It still offered the spirit of a frontier town. Despite the criticisms leveled by the newspaperman, the character of the town seemed generally pleasant, and the Visitor still wanted to have a part in the great "inland movement" of settlers coming into the state. And Detroit would always be only an hour and a half away on the D&M, allowing handy access to a major source of materials, resources and transports. Or to stay in touch with investors like Hervey Parke, should Detroit end up being the site for his new drugs business. These were encouraging ideas, and they led the Visitor to make one last realization that he found amusing: that today, perhaps for the first time, he was being viewed with as much scrutiny by people like Hervey and Elkanah, as he himself was scrutinizing Pontiac. A reasonable assumption. And with that, a yawn, and a glance at his pocket watch that lay open-faced by the candle on the table. It was high time to crawl down under covers for the night.

Thursday, May 23, 1861 was closing down throughout Pontiac—people yawning, snuffing candles, thinking about tomorrow's tasks and errands, reflecting upon today's mistakes and successes. Tomorrow would be here soon enough, desired or loathed, just as vibrant or humdrum as the day just passed. Whether it mattered to anyone or not, and probably not, they had lived through another day sharing one common tenet, that their era was a notable one, and that modern times had reached a pinnacle in terms of conveniences and quality of life. Thank goodness they were alive today and not in a primitive past era. There was every reason to believe that their fine community would always thrive, despite the usual foibles and frictions among civilized people. And the war would keep things exciting and purposeful, for as long as it lasts, a year at least.

So far the spring season has progressed fair and fresh. In good times like these you could see the town come to life once again. The year may be young, the trees leafy once again and the evening air warm and comfortable. It's an age-old feeling that everyone has, as if we have all the time in the world, on into summer, on into the autumn. Time enough to pursue a dream, this year or next, it doesn't matter. There will always be time ahead for pursuing dreams.

Spirit of *Modern* Times

APPENDICES

APPENDICES

i. FICTIONS AND RECORDS

ALL OF the characters were real people, with the exception of the "Visitor" who is fictional, as is his trip to Pontiac to investigate a commercial real estate investment on Saginaw Street.

Depictions of the historical characters are based on genealogical records, on published chronicles about the town and the county, and on contemporaneous newspaper articles. The characters' personalities, opinions and the words they speak are presumptive, offered here only as a means to peer into a community that vanished long ago, leaving behind only a few daguerreotype images and other published hints about what their personal experiences may have been.

The story has a number of events and relationships that are fictional, or undocumented based on the author's research to date. These include:

The reception held at the McConnell residence in honor of their son's enlistment in the army;

The usage of an east side yard at the McConnell house as a venue for the reception, and the existence of an herb garden in the rear yard;

Hervey Coke Parke's visit to Pontiac during the same week as the reception;

The relationship between Sallie Parke French and Marquis Kelsey;

Ben French's arrival in Pontiac on the day of the reception, and the resulting altercation with Marquis Kelsey and authorities near the train station;

David Jackson's interest and pursuit of balloon aeronautics;

David Jackson is included in the roster of people living at the Mc-Connell house in the official 1860 census; however, in the story his allocation to a room that has been partitioned within the stable building is not documented.

The actual fate of individual characters is beyond the scope of the story, although it may be easily tracked down. Knowing the full life story of a character is useful for a fictional depiction in this narrative, of course, though it will also distract from a reader's appreciation of what it would be like to spend time with that person then and there. Suffice it to say, a variety of destinies lay in store: one character will go on to achieve considerable fame and fortune in commerce; another will disappear suddenly when just on the cusp of a successful investment. A number of pairings will lead to marriages as expected, although a few of them will soon face hardship and calamity. One character will find success in military service; another will be shot and killed in battle. Some characters will live on for many more years while the town continues to grow and thrive. Others will not be as settled or fortunate.

ii. MCCONNELL HOUSE

THE MCCONNELL house still stands today, as of the spring of 2023, some 180 years after it was built. Willard McConnell had the house built in 1843 on property then owned by his father-in-law Captain Hervey Parke. By the time of this story in 1861 the house was 18 years old and all five of the McConnell children had been raised there.

Thirty years later the house was sold in the 1890's to Edward M. Murphy, a prominent manufacturer of buggies and early automobiles. At some point during the 1870-1900 time period, either the McConnell's or the Murphy's changed the structure of the house by adding a 3rd floor ballroom and a grandiose two-story colonnaded front porch entrance.

After the First World War the house was sold to The American Legion who have

owned and maintained the building to this day as Cook-Nelson Post #20. In the summer of 2021 the commander of the Post was most kind in arranging for the author a brief tour of the interior of the house on all three floors. A few pictures from this tour are provided below and on the following pages:

The author standing at the front entrance.

View of the west side of the house, showing the rear wing and the southeast bay window.

Its former grandeur has largely faded, of course, and its first occupants are far dispersed and all but forgotten. But the building remains, with many of the walls and rooms and windows as originally laid out. After so many years it still offers an invitation to look upon an old home and imagine the lives and the family stories, the daily routines, and the parties, and a chance to step through the door on a breezy, sunny afternoon

East side of the McConnell House, looking north from the rear yard.
The colonnaded side porch is visible in the center right of the photo.
In the story the outdoor reception takes place in the east side yard,
extending out from this porch. The kitchen is on the first floor of the
rear wing, its windows covered by the ivy, visible below the modern
fire escape stairs. The bay windows of the dining room have been
boarded over. In 1861 the house did not yet accommodate a full-
sized third floor, only an attic.

Family Room looking north
towards front of house.

Fireplace in Family Room

Main hall looking south towards rear of house. Front door
is behind the camera angle. The door at back left leads to the
Dining Room. Opposite this door, hidden behind the stairs, is the
door leading to the rear portion of the Family Room which, in the
story, is the venue for the young people's separate party.

Main Hall looking north towards the front entrance. Door at left leads to front portion of the Family Room. Door at right leads to the Parlor where the McConnell's greeted their guests.

Fireplace in Parlor

iii. MODERN MAP OVERLAY

HOWN ON the next page is an excerpt of the historical map of Pontiac used in the story, with an overlay of selected items from a modern-day map of the same area. Most prominent is the addition of the "Woodward loop" roadway, running one-way counter-clockwise, which has replaced Parke Street on the east side of town, School Street on the north end, and Garland Street on the west. The segment of the Clinton River in the downtown area, along with the Mill Pond, is now covered up. The Phoenix Center complex blocks off a stretch of South Saginaw Street, and the entire section where the Hodges Hotel once stood is now an expansive parking lot, which also covers the grounds where the Thurber House once stood on Garland Street. The old Court House, the old public school, and the Holley residence are all long gone. Only the McConnell House still exists on Auburn Avenue.

Other modern-day items on the map:

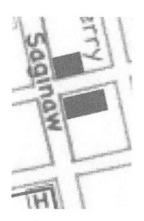

Two iconic skyscrapers in downtown Pontiac, at the intersection
of Saginaw and Lawrence:
The Treasury (8 stories);
Oakland Towne Center (15 stories).

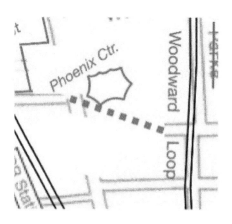

The tunnel running underneath the Phoenix Center, connecting
Orchard Lake Road with Auburn Avenue.

Map of Pontiac, Michigan
showing present-day "Woodward Loop" road and Phoenix Center
superimposed on historical map.

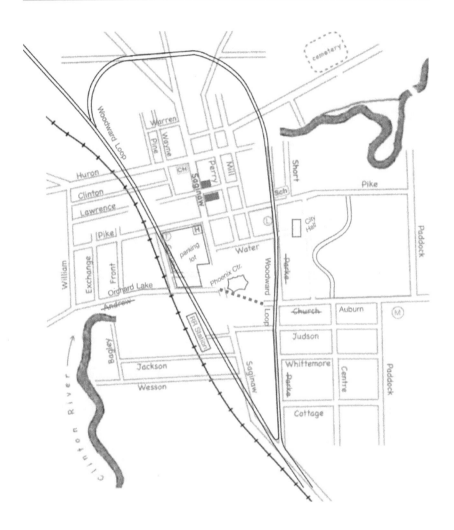

iv. THE MILL POND

THE MILL Pond was an enduring feature of the Pontiac land-scape until it was rechanneled and buried by the 1960's along with the stretch of the Clinton River that ran through the center of the city. This "pond" was really a segment of the river where the flowing water was allowed to accumulate in a wider area before narrowing back to its normal, faster course to pass under the water wheels operated by mills along Mill Street on the city's east side.

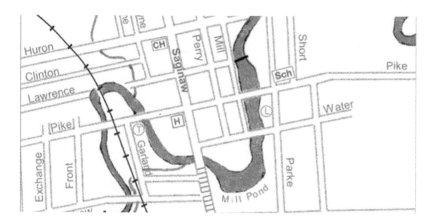

In examining the pond's size that lies in between Saginaw and Parke Streets, the author estimates the area to be approximately 200 yards long by 70 yards wide.

In order to present a visual rendition of a pond of this size, a modern-day photograph appears on the next page which may be considered for comparison. The picture shows "The Pond" in New York City's Central Park, where a portion of the pond resembles the dimensions of Pontiac's old Mill Pond.

Photo taken by the author in 2023

Eastern half of "The Pond" in New York City's Central Park. The stone bridge at the far end is approximately 200 yards away. The pond's width from left to right is approximately 70 yards.

In Pontiac in 1861 the view of the Mill Pond from the bridge on Saginaw Street would have shown a body of water about this size.

V. THE 22ⁿᵈ MICHIGAN VOLUNTEER INFANTRY

ONE YEAR after this story takes place, in the summer of 1862 Oakland County along with neighboring counties will raise a regiment of infantry for the Union's war effort, locally organized and trained at the fairgrounds of the City of Pontiac.

This will happen towards the end of the first year of the Civil War. By then the country had already experienced the battles at Bull Run, the Seven Days campaign near Richmond, and at Shiloh in Tennessee. It was clear to everyone that the war was not going to end anytime soon, and that the battles were horrendously bloody, the casualty lists long and grim. In fact there was a very real chance that the North could lose the war, as Confederate armies were invading northward into Maryland and Kentucky.

The 22ⁿᵈ will be commanded by Moses Wisner, the former governor of Michigan. The regimental surgeon will be Dr. Abiram McConnell, the brother of Willard McConnell. Company D of the regiment will be commanded by Lieut. Almeron Mathews, possibly a relative of

George Mathews. In Company G's ranks will stand Corporal Lewis Drake.

On September 4, 1862, the 22nd regiment will assemble and march out of the fairgrounds with a total muster just under 1,000 men, to parade down Saginaw Street en route to the Pontiac train station. The occasion will be grandly celebrated and attended by thousands of family members, friends, and well-wishers. At noontime a picnic will be provided for the entire unit, followed by re-assembly of the ranks to hear speeches and observe a ceremony for the "presenting of the colors," the official the regimental flag.

The flag will be formally presented to the regiment by the Pontiac Young Ladies' Soldiers' Aid Society. As reported in newspaper accounts, the young women of the Society will stand in a half circle while two of their officers, Julia Comstock and Emma Adams, present the flag to Colonel Wisner. Among the Society's members standing behind them will be Carrie Holley, Fannie Pittman, Sarah Thurber, Malvina Taylor, Ella Draper, Fannie Mathews (probably keeping an eye on Corporal Drake as he stood with Company G), Molly Bacon, and many others.

By 4:00 PM the regiment will complete its march down Saginaw and load onto the train cars waiting at the station, and an hour later will arrive in Detroit for more ceremony and a picnic dinner. That same evening they will load onto a boat at the Detroit River and be transported overnight to Cleveland, and from there they will ride by train to Cincinnati. The regiment will ultimately become part of the Union Army of the Cumberland, operating in Kentucky and Tennessee, and brought into terrible combat at the battle of Chickamauga in September, 1863.

During the desperate fighting at Chickamauga the 22nd Michigan was forced to surrender and its battle flag was lost to the enemy. In the Civil War era the loss of a flag in battle would always weigh heavily in the memories of the surviving veterans, a symbol of lives lost and the wounds sustained by the regiment.

Thirty years later . . .

The 22nd's flag, frayed and bloodstained, was discovered in an army warehouse in Washington and returned to the veteran's association in Pontiac.

Below is an excerpt from an article in the Pontiac Gazette, in the August 31, 1894 issue, page 6, reporting on the solemn ceremony observed when the battle flag was formally returned to the veterans.

The movers in this very appropriate testimonial were a band of young ladies an organization under the name of Young Ladies' Soldiers' Aid Society. The members of that patriotic little band by death and life's changes have become decimated and scattered. A few are here at the present feast of rejoicing. By good fortune the two most prominent in the presentation of the silken colors to the regiment, Sept. 4, 1862, the details of which presentation are given below, were with the remnant of the regiment at the reunion of Aug. 30, 1894: Mrs. D. S. Howard, Julia Comstock, President, and Mrs. Wells Utley, Emma Adams, Treasurer, who delivered the unstained flag to the regiment through Col. Moses Wisner.

vi. O Z Y M A N D I A S

POEM BY Percy Bysshe Shelley, 1818

I met a traveler from an antique land,
Who said—"Two vast and trunkless legs of stone
Stand in the desert. . . . Near them, on the sand,
Half sunk a shattered visage lies, whose frown,
And wrinkled lip, and sneer of cold command,
Tell that its sculptor well those passions read
Which yet survive, stamped on these lifeless things,
The hand that mocked them, and the heart that fed;
And on the pedestal, these words appear:
My name is Ozymandias, King of Kings;
Look on my works, ye Mighty, and despair!
Nothing beside remains. Round the decay
Of that colossal wreck, boundless and bare
The lone and level sands stretch far away."

Notes: "Ozymandias" was a Greek name for the Egyptian pharaoh Ramesses II. When the British Museum in London in 1817 acquired a head-and-torso fragment of a statue of the pharaoh, which dated from the 13th century BC, Shelley was inspired to write this sonnet.

vii. COMSTOCK FAMILY TREE

IN THE story there are only three Comstock characters; however, in Michigan at the time the Comstock clan was a very large group.

On the next page a family tree is presented, which in its entirety presents a complex graphic. The three characters who participate in the story are circled.

Note that there are two "Elkanah's"—Julia's grandfather the Reverend Comstock who was very well known as the first Baptist minister in Michigan; and Julia's uncle Elkanah Bee Comstock, a banker in Pontiac and director of the school board. Julia's father Solon Buck Comstock died in 1852, nine years before the story, and her mother never remarried. It is unclear whether Julia and her two sisters were raised by their mother or by foster parents, Mr. & Mrs. Goodale.

In the graphic, deceased persons as of 1861 are ghosted.

Notes:

Elkanah Bee Comstock's first wife Lucretia (1810-1842) bore 3 children, the first two being sons Edwin (b. 1836) and Erwin (b. 1839), and a daughter Lucretia who died in infancy in 1842 a few days after her mother had died, apparently both lost as a result of the childbirth. These three children are omitted from the family tree graphic.

Elkanah married Eliza, his 2nd wife, two years after Lucretia died. In addition to their two surviving sons Albert and Charles, the couple also adopted a daughter, Jennie (not shown).

After Solon died in 1852 his wife Elizabeth never remarried. Apparently their 3 daughters were raised by the Goodale family, husband "F.B." and wife "E.S."

Julia Comstock had two aunts in Wisconsin who were married successively to the same man, Amasa Andrews: the first being Aunt Sarah who married in 1829 and died a year later; the second being Aunt Mary who married in 1831 and died in 1889. Amasa died in 1853.

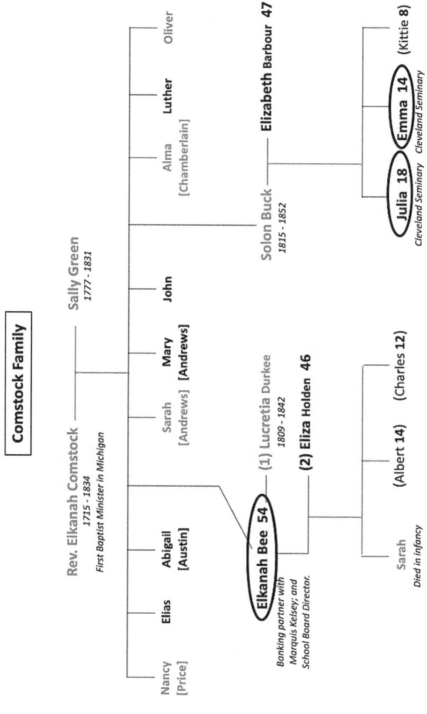

Comstock Family

Rev. Elkanah Comstock — Sally Green
1715 - 1834   1777 - 1831
First Baptist Minister in Michigan

Nancy   Elias   Abigail   Sarah   Mary   John   Alma   Luther   Oliver
[Price]   [Austin]   [Andrews] [Andrews]   [Chamberlain]

Elkanah Bee 54 —— (1) Lucretia Durkee   Solon Buck —— Elizabeth Barbour 47
                     1809 - 1842   1815 - 1852
Banking partner with (2) Eliza Holden 46
Marquis Kelsey; and
School Board Director.

Sarah   (Albert 14)   (Charles 12)   Julia 18   Emma 14   (Kittie 8)
Died in infancy   Cleveland Seminary   Cleveland Seminary

viii. CHARACTERS' LIKENESSES: ARTIST'S SKETCHES

MANY YEARS ago an unknown conservator in Pontiac, Michigan, assembled a remarkable collection of photographs of local residents, and perhaps more importantly, organized *and labeled* the pictures to identify each face for posterity. This valuable historical resource has been carefully maintained by the Oakland County Pioneer and Historical Society in Pontiac.

It is one thing to write about the people who lived in the town a century and a half ago, based on research of published data in contemporary records and chronicles; it is quite another to see their faces, as if you were being finally introduced to someone in person after hearing so much about them. Now they are no longer mere recorded data. They have become characters.

But another question then follows: how best to turn around and introduce these characters to a modern reader? An image taken in a photographer's studio in 1861 might not render the whole picture. The technology of that era made for a studio session that was tedious and definitely not an occasion to strike and hold an animated expression, let alone a smile. It was more akin to posing for an oil portrait by an artist. The main objective was to avoid blurring the image.

In a story that is written as historical fiction, the old images are accurate but inevitably still lacking a certain animation. For this usage, by themselves, they are not enough. The objective here is the opposite, to avoid suspending the character.

For this reason the characters in the story have been illustrated not with actual daguerreotype and ambrotype images, but with the presentation of *hand-drawn sketches* of the characters, inspired by the images. The illustrator who drew the sketches worked with the author, using the images but adhering to these guidelines:

-- that the sketches would *enliven* the characters, based on the storyline;

-- that the sketches would adapt, where necessary, the appearance of a character to adapt the character's age to *how old they were* on the date of the story.

On the following pages is a review of all of the sketches created by Madelyn Lehde that are placed throughout the book. Each sketch is presented next to its corresponding historical image. Note again—accuracy in recreating the original image is not the priority; rather, the purpose is to render the characters as per the two guidelines shown above. With this objective in mind the reader may well agree it is art well rendered.

Adams, Emma

Bacon, Levi

Baldwin, Augustus

Comstock, Julia

Draper, Charles

Parke Family Archives

French, Sallie Parke

Green, Rev. Augustus

Holley, Carrie

Holley, Marion

Howell, Myron E. N.

Jackson, David

Mathews, George

McConnell, Cleantha

McConnell, Willard

McConnell, Joseph

Parke Family Archives

Parke, Hervey Coke

Pittman, Fannie

No image
yet found

Taylor, Malvina

Thatcher, Erastus

Thurber, Daniel

Courtesy, Lee M Withey

Thurber, Horace

ix. JULIA COMSTOCK
AND FRIENDS

Molly
Bacon

Libbie
Hixson

Emma
Comstock

Fannie
Mathews

Fannie
Pittman

Emma
Adams

Julia
Comstock

Carrie
Holley

Sarah
Thurber

Ella
Draper

This image from the OCPHS archives was taken in Pontiac on August 18th, 1860, several months before the story takes place. Someone wrote the label "Julia E. Comstock & Friends." The occasion for the photo is not known—note: Julia's eighteenth birthday is not until October 24. The girls in this photo, on the day it was taken, were 15 to 17 years old.

ACKNOWLEDGEMENTS

THE CREATION of this story was inspired by research, both historical and genealogical, meant to recognize real human experiences
behind all the facts and data. A wide variety of sources and people
were consulted for perspectives and bits of information that contributed towards developing the personality and circumstances for each
historical character.

First and foremost the author wishes to give special thanks to the
Oakland County Pioneer and Historical Society in for their guidance
and kind support of the research for this project. The Society maintains
an invaluable collection of historical reference materials, maps, and
original photographs, all of which were made accessible to the author
during visits to their Pine Grove History Center in Pontiac, Michigan.
Two of the Society's directors, Barbara Frye and Dave Decker, were
especially generous with their time and friendly assistance.

A second resource that also proved exceedingly useful was the on-
line access to 19th century newspaper articles from various historical
Michigan publications, particularly the ""Pontiac Gazette" and "Pontiac Jacksonian newspapers." Internet users may access scanned copies
of hundreds of articles via the website "Digital Michigan Newspapers"
maintained by the Clarke Historical Library at Central Michigan
University in Mount Pleasant, Michigan. As a database of newspa-

per texts, the website also enables the user to filter and sort content subject matter in articles and advertisements that appear anywhere in the entire repository. It is a handy tool not only to help substantiate references and ideas, but it can also lead to stumbling across some fascinating serendipitous items along the way.

The author also extends sincere thanks to family and friends for their patience and helpful suggestions during the long process of refining this composition into a coherent work. Proofreading someone else's text can be a true test of friendship and tact; for this, the author is especially grateful to Ramon Meyer, a neighbor and most worthy literary critic, steadfast in his encouragement as this work progressed.

ILLUSTRATION CREDITS AND PERMISSIONS

All sketches of characters are the artistry of Madelyn Lehde.

Unless otherwise noted, all photographic images embedded in the text are courtesy of Oakland County Pioneer and Historical Society (OCPHS).

Unless otherwise noted, all newspaper articles or excerpts thereof, or advertisements, embedded in the text are courtesy of Clarke Historical Library of Central Michigan University.

Images of the Horace Thurber family are courtesy of Lee M. Withey.

Images of the Hervey Parke family have been provided by the Parke family archives. The author is grateful to his sister Polly Parke Gately for her efforts in maintaining the archives and for her thoughtful contributions toward the research for this project.

Additional informational sources:

Pontiac business directories published during the 1860's; copies archived at the Oakland County Pioneer and Historical Society:
- Hawes's Business Directory 1860
- Loomis & Talbott's Directory 1860-61;

Published books on Pontiac history:
- "Pontiac" by Ronald Gay (Arcadia Publishing, 2010)
- "The Saginaw Trail" by Leslie Pielack (The History Press, 2018);

Cleveland History Center of the Western Reserve Historical Society, maintaining archives of the Cleveland Female Seminary;

Monroe County Historical Museum, Monroe, Michigan, maintaining archives of the Monroe Young Ladies Seminary and Collegiate Institute;

Milton Keynes UK
Ingram Content Group UK Ltd.
UKHW050742040324
438876UK00008B/198